PLAY, REWIND

PLAY, REWIND

JOHN VURRO

TORTOISE BOOKS
CHICAGO

FIRST EDITION, April, 2025

Published in the United States by Tortoise Books

www.tortoisebooks.com

ISBN-13: 978-1948954990

For my family.

"Mothers of America/ let your kids go to the movies!"
— Frank O'Hara

CHAPTER 1

Mom's checking out, again.

She chucks rolled-up socks over her shoulder and they ricochet off her bedpost, sailing right, a cottony foul ball. Strewn along the carpet are sweaters with sparkly beads and moissanite pins. There are her business cards from Chemical Bank and seafoam-colored curlers—objects that were important enough to stow away in her dresser, but now, post-dementia, are a muddle of useless bric-a-brac.

I say, "What are you doing?"

She repeats the question, attenuating the syllables, elongating the vowels. Mom's way of delaying her response, or whatever you'd call it now. Within seconds, she stops decoding my riddle and sidearms another sock-ball. It hits the door with a soft thud. I scoop it up and squeeze. Three short pulses. Three long pulses. Three short pulses: S.O.S.

Mom says, "Get dressed," and lobs a pair of panties, pink and impossibly large, ceilingward. They sway in a parachute motion until they touch down onto her mattress. She used to call them bloomers. Now, she can't recognize them. Sadly, I can.

"You want to miss the plane to Idlewild?"

It takes me a second. "You mean Kennedy? We're not going to JFK, Mom."

Mom says, "Course you'd book LaGuardia."

She tosses a flesh toned bra, its straps twisting herky-jerky until they sling a blade of the ceiling-fan. A nightshirt streaks across the room like a specter.

"Why'd I pack so much?"

I say, "Cause that's your dresser."

"Yeah, sure."

She's only sixty-five, but looks a decade or so older. Her scalp is startlingly pale. Her skin is sallow. Wiry hairs sprout from her chin. In a movie, she's the character you'd flee from without glancing back. In real life, she's my mother. In real life, there is no escape.

She says, "Did you hail a cab?"

"We don't need a taxi, Mom."

"Taxi. Cab. Taxicab." She skims her palms along the empty drawer, the pressed-wood making a shushy sound.

Look. Here's Wes at nine-years old being tugged around by parents who are oblivious to the havoc they're causing. In my younger and more blunderable years, I'd spend weekends with my father trapped inside the local OTB on Cross Bay Boulevard. If he hit, we'd eat at Liberty Diner. He usually crapped out. So we'd split a slice at Gino's. Sitting at the skinny table, I'd nibble on my skinny pizza while he spoke the dialect of parlays and trifectas. Then we'd skulk into the house like thieves and pretend that we spent our day riding Tilt-a-Whirls at Coney Island. But Mom knew his sleight-of-hand. They'd fight for hours, days.

Look. Here's Wes at twenty-six wishing he was nine again.

On cue, Mom says, "How long have we been here?"

I say, "Decades."

Through the parted curtains I see the first snippet of the morning sky, pinkish and sad, contrasting with the darker frame of the El that runs above Liberty Avenue in Going Nowhere, Queens. A camera shot of shadows and light. It's six-thirty. In three hours, I have to unlock Video Planet. Since four, I've been trying to convince my mother that we're not relaxing in a hotel or gambling in a casino. That we're home, a lonely place, if only for one of us. "Let's have coffee."

"It's all-inclusive?"

I say, "Only costs me sanity."

She stares into the mirror fastened to the vanity and repeats S-A-N-I-T-Y, long and sing-songy, all the while watching her reflection. Sometimes she mistakes herself for a former co-worker. Her dead sister Joan. She offers herself chamomile tea and chocolate eclairs. When her reflection refuses her hospitality, she berates herself. Our nurse Gloria has asked me to unscrew the mirror, but if I leave things the way they are, maybe Mom will remember, and then just maybe, this isn't happening. I say to her reflection, "So milk. two sugars, right?" Again, she asks me if it's all-inclusive. "Hope so. I spent all my dollars at the club."

Mom says, "I used to dance." There's a mental image I could've been spared. "In a disco. With your father." She glances around the room. "Where is he?"

He flew to Florida and left us to our own devices. I was eleven.

I can't handle another one of her crying jags. I say, "Never mind."

I hold out my hand. She watches me, a confused look on her face. Either she doesn't recognize me or she's worried about the slight stretch forward, the gentle clasping of my palm. Oh, the things we take for granted. As I walk toward her, I kick a sweater underneath the bed, clearing a path. I take her wrist, which feels thinner than a week ago, and rescue her hand from the clutches of the drawer. I lead her from the room with the same brisk purpose that you'd lead a toddler through the grocery store. She steps heel-to-toe, off-balance and fragile. I'm walking too fast. I should slow down, like she must've done for me when I was the toddler, our ages, in some ways, reversed. But time is tricky. Four years ago she managed a bank. Now she can't manage to pull her socks on. The tragedy of it all tilts operatic.

Mom says, "Is this the lobby?"

"Take a guess."

"I've never been here before."

I say, "Right."

The kitchen walls and laminate tiles are yellow as dried pus. The cabinets are shellacked the color of a molting canary. Mom equates yellow with intelligence: pencils, schoolbuses. But it's as though we're living in a jar of expired mustard. I lead her to the small table, then twist her towards me and give her a nudge. She flops into the kitchen chair, a sloppy, arm-waving collapse.

She recovers and says, "Hey, that was rough."

I want to apologize, but instead I say, "Oopsies."

I shuffle over to the coffeepot. I pour the only joy I'll have today into a mug, then pour the rest into my Thermos. Here's a secret: she can't drink coffee. The caffeine makes her agitated. I fill her mug with tapwater, feeling guilty about the trickery. I swerve around the eggs she tossed onto the floor a few hours ago and place the mug onto the table.

She says, "Sanka tastes like cat spray," and pushes the mug into the napkin holder, jammed with bills and insurance forms.

Growing up, it was a steady diet of microwavable pot-pies, canned soup, or a hot dog floating in a pot of greasy water, bloated as a drowned body. The only exception was on Sundays when Mom cooked a pot of sauce. Mom didn't count this as cooking—she called it part of our heritage. She is Irish-German. It's my father who is Italian. We had the leftovers on Wednesdays, which meant she tossed the saved pasta from Sunday into a frying pan. The rigatoni was mush. The sauce tasted metallic. Then three years ago, she swore off cooking. I thought she was bluffing until I witnessed her inability to pour olive oil into a frying pan. I should've asked her what was wrong. Instead, we ignored the obvious until the obvious refused to be ignored.

At this point, what's a shot of caffeine? "Try mine, then."

I sip and then place the mug in front of her. If she's quietly drinking, I can tidy up for Gloria. She's our nurse, not our maid. Mom pushes that mug until it clinks into the other one. "Too strong."

"Here. How about this one." I place her "coffee" back in front of her. I'm Bill Murray in *Groundhog Day*. The world forgets but he remembers. To prove me right, Mom sniffs the mug, then slides it away.

A coffee is a coffee is a coffee.

"Well," I say, "I have to clean up."

"You're a dirty birdy. A dirty turdy. A birdy turdy."

"Relax. You'll pop your last brain cell."

"Up your nose with a rubber hose," she says, an insult she smacked me for saying to her when I was ten. Now that she's confused, there's only her leftovers of ridicule. Her essence, her being. Trying to reacclimate myself, I recover my mug and sip some coffee, milky and sugary and wonderful.

She points toward the floor. "That's some mess right there."

I say, "Yup." I place the mug on the table, then unfurl some paper towels and scrub at the yellow stain in our yellow room, a yolk inside a yolk. I'm not sure how it happened. I was asleep until I heard movement coming from the other end of the house. By the time I hurried into the kitchen, the eggs were cracked on the floor.

She says, "You need W-a-t-e-r. Wet stuff. Aqua Velva."

"I know."

She says, "Who taught you to clean?"

"Milli Vanilli."

"What are you saying?"

She lifts the mug of water and puts it down. Up down, up down, each time with a slight staccato, as though she's Mickey in Steamboat Willie. It's crazy-making.

 I say, "Please. Go to bed."

"I just got here."

I drop the paper towels and sit on the tile floor. Her nightgown has slid off her shoulder, revealing the darker estuaries of veins branching along her chest. Her body is shriveled, depleted. Then there's her brain, rooking her at every turn. She asks for coffee. She asks for room service. She says, "You have a familiar face." I tell her I'm her son. She says, "Not that familiar."

Play, Rewind.

If this were a movie, Mom would take this moment to snap out of her confusion and confess her guilt for being meaner than she should've been, both when she was healthy, and sick. The John Williams music swells, poignant, and redemptive. The camera lens widens. Happily Ever After.

In real life, Mom skims her finger along the handle of what used to be her favorite mug, what's now the mug

I give her out of habit. It's green with *Best Mom Ever* written in white script. Years ago, we had a fight and I claimed she was "The worst mom from Medea on down." The next day, she bought the mug to razz me. Now, she scratches at the *Best* with her fingernail. I listen to the glassy scraping and my chest flutters with panic, as though once the letters disappear, the history of the mug, our lives together, will disappear as well. Suddenly, it's important that she hears this—what, apology? Yes. I say, "I'm sorry. If I was mean. Before. Or ever. Okay?"

She picks up the coffee, clasping the mug with both hands. She nods, though it seems more to herself, then continues scratching.

I stand, then flick the paper towels into the garbage. Can't she forgive this one thing? "I said I'll take it back."

"I'm not finished," she says.

"Well, drink up, then."

She places the mug onto the table and leans forward, gathering momentum as she tries to stand. "You're a dickhole. I'm playing cards."

I say, "Mom, just stay there," but she elbows the mug and it tips onto its side.

Mom snaps her fingers. "Waiter! A towel."

I glance around the kitchen, as though it would morph into something easier to understand. When the room refuses to adjust to my chosen reality, I say, "Mom, I am not a waiter. We are not in a casino. We're not taxiing to Idlewild. JFK. Newark. Not even shitty LaGuardia. We are home. I am your lame son and you're my demented mother." I tap my ears. "Do you hear me?"

Wait. I hear dripping. It's my waterlogged heart. No. It's her faux coffee cascading onto the floor. She sets the mug upright. *Best Mom Ever*. She nods, impressed, then says, "Where'd she scurry off to?"

I say, "Who?"

"The best mom ever." She glances underneath the table. "She lives here?"

The front door opens. Gloria calls hello in her perky timbre.

I picture her wearing her sensible coat, the blue one with the tie in the middle. Her hair is combed. Her teeth are brushed. Her pants are pressed. She's together, neat, with a mind she possesses. As hurt and angry as I am, I lean close, our noses almost touching, as though proximity will nudge understanding. Mom smells like the citrusy shampoo that Gloria slathers her hair with, playing counterpoint to the piss that wafts from her diaper, soggy and bursting to be changed.

Gloria calls my name.

Before she enters the kitchen, I have enough time to say, "No, the best mom just hopped a taxi to Idlewild."

CHAPTER 2

It's just another Tuesday at Video Planet.

Mice are rotting inside the walls, their slick innards poisoned from the emerald cubes the exterminator called bait. For weeks, they've scurried into the stacks of cases. Scooted underneath the racks. Scampered along the aisles. Last night, a mouse peeped at me from behind the bell of the toilet, the little perv.

Now, they're bloated and oozy and dead.

I stick my keys into my pocket and jam the front door open with my heel, hoping to de-fumigate the store before I start my shift.

A box-truck zips past the strip-mall, belching smoggy exhaust. A 747 hurtles towards JFK, spewing noxious jet fuel. There's that smoldering rubber smell from the recycling plant at the end of the lot greeted by the reedy field littered with stripped autos and, occasionally, a stripped body. The sidewalk is strewn with cigarette butts. A condom is pasted against the concrete, a sad deflated balloon. I hold my hands into a boxy frame, a camera lens, imagining an establishing shot, but my day has been too sloppy for that sort of thing.

This morning, before Gloria washed her hands, I fled the house. Outside, I waited for the Cutlass to warm awake and replayed my missteps. I wanted to go inside and apologize, but Mom's videotape brain had already dubbed over our kitchen debacle. Pulling onto Cross Bay

Boulevard, I promised myself that next time (there's always a next time) I'd be a better son.

Play, Rewind.

I check the sidewalk to see if I should sweep and I notice a bag with something flat inside tilted against my storefront. Sometimes renters ditch their lates to avoid the two-dollar charge. I keep my foot against the door and drag the bag towards me. It's a home movie, not one of ours, but it breaks clerk protocol to leave the videotape there. Also, if Dom sees this tape (or any tape) outside, he'll yell at me. I tuck the abandoned movie underneath my arm, too tired to guess why someone would do such a thing.

It still stinks inside of the store so I hold the door open for a bit longer and imagine guys driving to college. Guys meeting their girlfriends for breakfast. Guys visiting their healthy mothers. At least I have movies. Things seem fine enough, I guess, until I hear this beeping sound.

Then I remember the alarm.

I pivot into the store. I shuck off my knapsack for extra speed, tuck the bag with the video under my arm and hustle down the aisle, formed by metal racks. On the other side of the racks are plastic shelves bolted against the gray walls. The metallic HVAC conduits are slung low from the ceiling. The carpet is bumpy and balding, making me trip as I weave around the life-size Terminator cutout and swing open the waist-high door back to the counter. I charge around to the countertop and stop in front of the keypad fastened onto the wall. I press the code, *2345*, to shut off the alarm. The beeping refuses to stop. I place the bag with the videotape onto the counter and punch the code again.

The beeping stops. The phone rings.

It's one of those rotary phones. Dom refuses to buy a cordless. Salmon-colored, except for the line of smiley-faced *Be Kind, Rewind* stickers I stuck along the handle while watching *Blue Velvet*.

I press my ear against the headset. I want to pull a Dennis Hopper and say, "Where's my bourbon, shithead?" Instead it's: "Hello?"

"Yes." It's a woman. She says, "This is Forcefield Security. Is this Dominick?"

"No, I'm Wesley. I work here."

"Okay. The alarm timed-out so I'll need the password."

I press my wrist against my forehead. Soon Dom will materialize to collect yesterday's meager earnings. If he sees the police in front of the store, he'll never stop abusing me. So I say, "Moist one," and hang up before I can hear her reaction.

I reach over the register and flip the switch. The lights blink and cast a dwindling yellow hue as Video Planet crawls back to life.

When I started this job, I only worked three days a week. I've always loved watching movies. The directors, actors, and sets. The stories. The special effects, but I was just a dummy from Queens, son of a bank-teller and a gambler, so I thought making movies was what other people did. That was until I found an old catalog for Manhattan School of Film on one of the benches of the "A" train. On the cover, a guy around my age stared into the viewfinder of a camera. Underneath the picture read *Film Your Dreams*. As I stared at the guy, I envisioned myself as a screenwriter, or a director. I was surprised that this school wasn't in California; it was less than an hour away. It's silly, but staring at the cover, I felt that if he could do it then I could, too.

The next day, I went to the library and pulled a tattered book that summarized the five hundred greatest movies of all time. I photocopied the index. Each week, I'd watch three movies a day, taking notes on blocking, mise-en-scene, set design. Paydays, I stashed some tuition money into my old E.T. lunchbox. I had saved so much that I could barely fasten the latch.

Then Mom got sick. At first she'd misplace her keys, forget milk or her precious Gingersnaps at the Food Town. Soon after, it was how to dial the phone, unlock a door. Cook. Her general practitioner suggested a neurologist. I was taking her for CT scans to see if she had a stroke. An EEG scan to make sure she wasn't having seizures. Force feeding her Donepezil and Klonopin prescriptions. Spiking her chamomile tea with stool softeners. I raided my lunchbox to pay for hospital parking (forty dollars a day), lunches, and medications. During Mom's stay at the hospital I'd buy the nurses and doctors bagels, as though I could bribe them into giving her a better outcome. How could I go to college or find an apartment? Mom needed my help. I fought the state for her disability. She has a savings account that bleeds $1500 a month on bills. $985 busted on the mortgage. $300 goes to Gloria, and the rest of the money is spent on Mom's meds. My job covers basic stuff like food, electricity, and my cellphone. I need a better job, but my work experience ends as the lone employee of Video Planet.

So now, when I pretend I'm planning to go to college, I watch *Wonder Boys*. When I dream of backpacking through Europe, I watch *Night on Earth*. When I want to fight against insurmountable odds, I watch *Rocky*. I swear things will change, but the only thing that does is the date on the rental stamp, which I now twist to today: *3-3-00*.

Play, Rewind.

Even after opening the front door, the store smells terrible. I tuck my nose into my sweater and walk around the counter. I lift my backpack off the floor, revealing a dead mouse, gray with a white underside. He's surrounded by a wet halo of poisoned blood. I imagine the mouse's family dressed in mini-immigrant clothes, like Fievel Mousekewitz in *An American Tail*. I know Dom will be mad, but it's so depressing that I don't have the energy to scoop him up. I walk around the counter. I say, "Happy, happy, happy." Still unhappy, I toss my bag onto Dom's favorite chair.

Next to the register stands a crooked pillar of videotapes. I twist the column towards me. *Varsity Blues*. *Green Mile*. The disappointment that was called *Episode I*. I stop at *Eyes Wide Shut*. I've watched that movie five times. Twice because it was Kubrick, then three more times for the orgy scene. I run my finger along the crinkly label of the plastic box. The halogen lights buzz above me, the only light source in the store. The two bay windows are sealed shut. The sunlight is obscured by the dusty racks. If a customer feels ambitious enough to check the display, his efforts are rewarded with a few blockbusters from a few years ago, their covers faded with age and indirect sunlight. The rush doesn't start until after twelve, so I have time before I attack the column of movies.

Then I remember the videotape.

I shake the bag and the tape slides onto the counter. I was right. It's a home movie. The label is torn off. I push the tabs on the sides of the video and pull down the cover. The ribbon is shiny with secrets. I stand the video upright on the counter, then crumple the bag.

Something crinkles. There is a slip of paper. I expect an address, a phone number, a name.

A note reads: *COPY DON'T WATCH. BE BACK SOON.*

Great. The law requires that I watch the first fifteen minutes of all home movies to check for illegal activity, such as drug use or child pornography. That makes for a kaboodle of footage that no one wants to see. I once watched a woman dressed as a clown tie the shoelaces of her flipper-sized shoes to the base of her boyfriend's penis. Then they blew kazoos while having sex. It's not as fun as it sounds.

Going by the amount of ribbon on the tapeheads, there's six hours of footage here. If it's wacky, I'd rather preview it alone.

I press Play, waiting for cults, aliens, clown sex. It's a long establishing shot of a beach. I'm a little confused. What's the big deal about watching this? Who cares?

I wait for something to happen. The camera holds its gaze on the ocean. The water is crystalline blue, shifting darker as the ocean sinks deeper. I hear kettle drums. The camera pans the length of the beach. In the distance are jagged mountains. The lens points toward the sand, capturing a shadow outline with muscular shoulders, only the slightest knobs of fat on his waist. A man's voice says, "We made it. Paradise," and I'm startled by the break in silence. The camera pans to an empty hammock tied onto palm trees. The lens swerves down to his feet. Waves lap his toes. He says, "So warm." Foam shaped like spiderwebs float past him. I focus on the repetition of the water. In a theatrical movie, this shot would cut into a scene, filled with characters and conflict, cause and effect, narrative elements demanding the viewer's attention. This footage is serene, enticing, with zero expectations. The ocean solicits nothing. There are no consequences. Only landscape. After only a few minutes of watching this footage, I feel eerily calm. I'm not convincing Mom I'm her son. I'm not yelling at her because she's wandering the house naked. Even the reek of dead mice wafts to the background. I stay this way until there's a rush of cold air and see him. Hurricane Dominick.

I jab the Stop button and I'm hit with a crushing sadness, as though it was the last day of my vacation. I'm not sure how five minutes of watching someone else's video has caused this, but Dom is here now and it only escalates my existential dread.

He strides towards me, fists clenched at his sides. He's wearing a black polo and matching slacks. His fake knee tilts him left-to-right, as though he's a wind-up toy. His thinning hair is slicked with so much gel that I see the comb lines. He swishes the match he gnaws on into the side of his mouth. This day already feels impossible so there's a fleeting moment where I wish he'd choke on his matchstick. No, that's harsh. I like Dom. He's overbearing and volatile and mildly psychotic, but at least he doesn't pester me about TPS reports.

He says, "What the hell is that?"

I say, "A mouse."

Dom straightens the cross tangled in his chest hair. He spent yesterday feeding the horses at OTB. I worked ten hours. I inhale, hinting at the stench, but he'd never admit that his store reeks of rodents. He says, "Why didn't you pick him up?"

"I was too busy telling security your password." Dom nudges Fievel with his shoe, which I find mildly disrespectful. "Next time I'm not saying it. Let the cops figure it out."

"That you? A rat?"

"That's a mouse, Dom."

"Yeah, well. Even a mouse ain't a rat."

Video Planet is packed with bootleg videos. He used to have the bootlegs delivered to the store in garbage bags, but after Royal Video was raided by the police, Dom has gotten skittish. So Wednesdays he drives to what he calls an "unexposed location" and picks up the bootlegs. I feel bad about renting fake movies, but our sales have plummeted. If we didn't work this way, I'd be out of a job. It's simple math. A legit movie costs forty dollars. Independent movies cost seventy. Foreign films are over a hundred. Bootlegs cost ten each. On average, there's at least fifteen new releases each month. If you buy four legit movies at forty dollars each and you charge two dollars a rental, a single movie has to be rented twenty times before it turns a profit. Also, even the biggest new release will only stay popular for around two weeks before being replaced with the next hot rental. In other words, rentals are perpetually losing their market value. Sure, movies like *Jurassic Park* or *Titanic* are exceptions, but 99% of newly released movies are part of this rental cycle. Side note: you can't bootleg Disney. Micky sticks on special tab blockers and sprinkles pixie dust over the tapes.

I say, "I meant about the alarm going off."

He says, "You're just backstroking."

"That's backpedaling."

I want to tease him, but Dom has this amazing ability to insult whoever he wants, and then crumble if you retaliate. When I started working here, I thought he was keeping me off-kilter. Then I realized he's a whackjob.

We listen to the hum of the lights. I say, "I'm sorry," and I'm surprised that I mean it. He's crazy, but besides Gloria, he's my only friend. And I pay Gloria.

He says, "Them suckers at Royal got raided." He nods slowly, as though giving me a trade secret. I know this already. After Royal's demise, Dom had shown me a Polaroid he snapped the day he watched the store get cleaned out. Royal's windows were boarded with particle board, orange police citations stuck on its doors. He tacked the picture onto the bathroom wall, above the toilet. I don't know what he's so happy about. We could be next. I say, "You told me this already."

"Anyway, Royal spillover. More money for you."

Here's where I should mention my mother, but I'll end up telling him about this morning and I'd rather forget it. I point to the column of movies that he left for me to put away. "It's just a lot. That's all."

"Nah. You're a pro."

Pro or not, whenever I come home late from Video Planet, Gloria's greeting me at the door, her coat zipped, lime-colored hat on, ready to go. I don't think she'd agree to longer hours. I can't believe the time she puts in already. I imagine her squeezing me for a final goodbye, her soft pat on the back. Then there's the struggle of finding another nurse, a nurse I trust and who likes Mom. With my luck I'll hire Annie Wilkes. I need Video Planet. I need Gloria. Besides, she's the only sane person I know. She deserves more than what I pay her. Actually, this is one of those rare moments when I realize that I deserve to be paid more too. I'm afraid to ask him, but if I was paid more, I'd pay Gloria more. She's worth the risk. I say, "I need a raise."

"What did you say?"

"You just told me I'll make more money."

"Right. More people, more money."

I shake my head. "C'mon Dom. That doesn't make sense. We can be busier, but I'm paid hourly."

Dom says, "Your point?"

"It's the same money. I've never asked. Please, man."

He says, "Okay. How about a dollar?" I cross my arms. "Two." I tell him no. He says, "Okay, Gordon Gekko." He wobbles his head, haggling with himself. "Fuck it, five. Boom. What's that, fifteen an hour?" I hop onto my toes with excitement until Dom swishes his match from side-to-side, a subtle shift in his eyes, and suddenly his offer feels very *Devil's Advocate*. I'll be paying for the pay I'm getting. Still, we all have our weaknesses, mine being Gloria and Video Planet. And the money, always the money. Greed is good. I say, "Alright."

"I should've done it sooner." He pats my shoulder. "Mom okay?"

Dom's mother Angela died from lung cancer. Before I started working here, I'd rent videos and see her seated behind the counter burning through episodes of *Upstairs, Downstairs*. She'd lean close to the television, the *psft* of her oxygen tank barely audible over the show. Other times, they'd sit next to each other, eating pastrami sandwiches, playing pinochle. She'd ask me to buy her cigarettes, just to tease her son. Until my mother's brain started to spiral, I thought Angela was how parents leave their children. That we'd have that waning time together. That there would be an arc, a freytag triangle to it all. But I was wrong. Each ending is its own. Now, I'm a bit jealous of what's being stolen from me. I shrug. "The same."

"At least she's not worse."

"Yeah." She's not better either.

Dom slaps my shoulder. "Gotta get the movies," he says winking, which means he's walking two stores over to sip coffee in Tubby's Diner for three hours. He walks around Fievel and behind the counter. He taps the sale button and the register opens with a ping. He wriggles the twenties from the till.

I don't care that he's lazy or loud or even that he's a sociopath. What annoys me is his indifference toward movies. He once told me that he'd sell handguns to nuns if he could earn enough to retire.

He says, "I left you change," and disappears into the back room. The metal door slams, echoing through Video Planet.

I walk around the counter and flop onto Angela's old chair, its gray fabric threadbare. The seat still wreaks of her sneaked cigarettes.

Now that I have a quiet moment, I keep thinking about the home movie. The guy who filmed the footage was probably the one who'd left the video. But if you care enough about the tape to leave a note, why would you leave it in front of a closed store? Maybe it was left there on purpose for me? No, the video obviously belongs to someone. The owner wants a copy. The only way to figure it out is to watch more of the footage. I hit Play. The camera flashes.

For some reason, I'm surprised to see the same beach. The guy says, "Lemme see if I can manage this one-handed." His voice sounds young. Not a kid, but well, my age. The camera shakes. When it stops it points towards his feet again, crossed, and resting on the hammock ropes. "Mission accomplished." The lens points towards the palm trees. The fronds are pale green, darker towards the top.

My cell phone buzzes, and I jump like a teenager. I dig into my pocket and flip the cover, waiting for answers. I get, "Wesley, it's Gloria."

I press the cellphone harder to my face as a montage of scenes in my homespun catastrophe film I call *The Worst Possible Thing* flashes on the screen: Mom tumbled headlong down the basement steps. Mom spilled out of the shower. Less slapstick ways of death, like 'The Cancer,' as Mom called it. I spend my hours waiting for the next disaster and then I'm surprised when the disaster happens.

I take a deep breath. "Is she okay?"

"Camilla's fine. Wes, there was someone standing in the driveway."

I focus on the words, trying to understand. I say, "A guy? Like a delivery?"

"They had a hood on. Anyway, I can't tell the way you kids look." She pauses. "I opened the door and I asked them what they wanted."

Before taking care of my mother, Gloria was a full-time nurse at Jamaica Hospital's ER. She doesn't rattle easily, not that she seems rattled. It was probably someone looking for directions. A neighbor wanting sugar, like it's 1950.

"Did they say anything?"

She says, "They waved and walked down the block. Maybe they know you?"

I don't know anyone who would want to visit me. "Maybe it was an old coworker of Mom's? In the area or something?"

Gloria says, "Yeah. I just wanted to let you know."

I say, "Did you call the police?"

She laughs. "No, it's not that serious. I couldn't anyway. The cordless wasn't on the base. Then Camilla said the television broke, but she was using the phone as the remote. I sound ridiculous. Forget I even called. We're fine, really."

It was weird. A friend would stick around. Unless they saw Gloria instead of Mom answer the door and thought they had the wrong house? I want Gloria to feel safe. Not that she seems afraid. Again, unpayable debts.

I say, "I'm on my way."

She tells me not to bother, but I flip my phone closed and walk around the counter, determined to help, or maybe it is penance for this morning. I circle around Fivel and lock the door. I leave a sign. In ten minutes I'll unlock it again.

Play, Rewind.

CHAPTER 3

I park the Cutlass on the corner and walk the block, greeted by a blinding sun playing counterpoint to an icepick breeze. Most of the houses are attached, the red-paneled left side split with the green-shingled right. In one of the front yards, I pass Mary encased in her concrete bell, her hands outstretched as though she can't decide whether to embrace you or smack you in the face. My house is the only Colonial on our block. It has a narrow, pitched roof, each of the three levels separated by boxy windows. The yellow siding is faded, like margarine left in the fridge too long. I stare at the cracked cement steps. The rusted outline of the address instead of the plates. This house is unremarkable in every way. Just an ailing house on an ailing block, housing an ailing woman. Who would want to steal from this tragedy?

I stand on the stoop and watch the neighborhood. The person who Gloria saw acted strange, but it had to be one of Mom's old coworkers. A mistaken address. My phone buzzes. I reach into my pocket and flip it. It's Gloria. "Hello?"

"Hi. Where are you?"

I say, "I'm outside." A maroon van passes, its side panel tagged in electric-blue spray paint. "Everything okay?"

"Yes. I was making sure you didn't leave work. I don't want you to get in trouble." She muffles the phone and says something to Mom.

"I'm here now."

"Okay. I want to talk to you. I was going to wait, but you're here."

I wish people would just say what they needed to say, instead of saying that they needed to say something. Bad news always gets a preface. The dishwasher is busted. Mom grew a talking goiter. She wants less hours. She is quitting. Gloria isn't the type to just pick up and leave, but if my father can do it then I guess anyone can. Please let it only be a talking goiter. I wait for the news.

Gloria tells my mother not to touch the bowl. "Mom is making a mess. Come into her room." Before I answer, she hangs up.

I unlock the door and step inside the hall. I wait for my eyes to adjust to the darkness of the hallway. Once they're there, I cut left into the living room and my insides do that swirly thing when I don't see Mom seated on the couch, her elbows resting on her knees, smoking a Chesterfield King. The room is silent, empty: the coffee table that belonged to my grandmother. The pole-lamp with its paper shade that Mom bought at a garage sale with my father. The red couch with its plastic-covered cushions, swag carried out of a box-truck in Corona. The fake palm with its wicker base that she bought at a flea-market. As a kid I was forbidden to eat on the couch, or walk across the gold-colored rug wearing sneakers. Now, she has forgotten that she once loved that couch, or this lamp. She doesn't understand how to dust the palm fronds with a dishrag. The room has transformed into a museum with the relics of a disappearing person on display. I peek through the shades. A pair of sneakers swing from the phone-lines.

For some reason, I have a memory, or maybe a wish, where my father lassoed his sneakers there. I was four? Later, I discovered that people roped their sneakers onto the lines as a sign the house sold drugs. Mom is silent about my father's history, but I'm pretty sure he wasn't a dealer. Again, I'm not sure it even happened.

This happened: Rockaway Beach, where me and my father skewered translucent jellyfish with sticks and flicked them at my snoozing mother. I was six. The Halloween we cruised the neighborhood in his Regal and pitched hard-boiled eggs at fellow bombers. I was eight. I remember fights. My father's shirts, twirling on the ceiling-fan. That Easter morning he reappeared, drunk. He had bought an iguana. He chased me around the living room yelling, "I pissed myself," as my mother beat his back with a ladle. Three days later he left us. I was eleven. The sneakers swing on the wires. They're a pair of Converse, one red, one black. They're probably not his. I wish my memories of him went a bit further, that he was here.

I walk into the kitchen. I smell cooked bacon. Mugs are upside-down in the drainboard. Pots placed neatly, one on each of the burners. The kitchen being used for something other than brewing coffee feels stranger than the living room's emptiness. That's not magic, though, it's Gloria. She distributes my mother's medications, dresses her, guides her into the bathroom. She finds my mother's toothbrush. When my mother wants to "buy" something in the house, Gloria finds her wallet filled with Monopoly money. Gloria spends her days finding things.

I found Gloria after searching for my mother on a Saturday morning. Over the last few weeks she had become more confused. She'd wear her shirts inside-out. She'd wake at midnight, thinking she was late for work. I'd try to convince her of the time, then navigate her into bed, then set my alarm for six-thirty. She usually slept past ten, so usually I'd have plenty of time to make breakfast and then wake her. But that morning, I woke up and found the front door open. From the stoop, I saw one of her red slippers resting against our neighbor's cyclone fence. Confused, I picked it up and followed her path. A few blocks away, I found her other slipper. I was mad. I hadn't scratched my balls yet and now I was chasing her in my flannels through the neighborhood. But the longer I searched, the more scared I got. What if she'd been hit by a car? I wandered the streets like this until I came to Blessed Heart Catholic School. Across the courtyard was a yellow-bricked church with orange spires. The school was surrounded by a metal-post fence. Two maple trees were in the center of the yard. A prayer garden ran along the wall of the school, filled with daffodils and tulips.

I spotted Mom standing in front of the school doors, arms crossed, rocking slowly. She was wearing her flowered pajamas. Her hair was a frizzy helmet. Maybe she was sleepwalking? I stood next to her, hoping she'd snap out of it. I touched her shoulder and said, "Mom? Here, let me help you."

I placed the slippers on the ground. In the sunlight, the dirt on her feet sparkled. I dusted her toes and slid the slippers on. "Let's go." She glanced at her wrist. The yard smelled like baking concrete. Maybe she had heatstroke?

"Please. I want to call Dr. Adler."

She glanced at me. Her face looked slack, as though her emotions had evaporated. If she sat across from me on the subway, I'd change cars.

She said, "I have to get my son."

Traffic beeped. A train rattled past on the El. She couldn't sleepwalk through all of this light and noise. She watched the door.

"Look at me. I'm Wes. You never sent me to Catholic school. And it's Saturday. In late June. Summer vacation."

"Fine. You're big Wesley. I'm waiting for little Wesley."

"What?" She had never talked like this. Did she mean that she's seeing my older face, but thinking of me as a child? Or did she believe that a little Wesley was going to pop through those doors? Before I could ask what she meant, the corner of her lip shook until the twitching traveled up to her left eye, and it started to twitch as well. It scared me. I said, "Something is wrong with you, Mom." She didn't move, or even speak. We watched the school until I finally had an idea. I said, "Mom, little John forgot his lunch."

She said, "What will he eat? I packed him tuna."

I said, "Let's go get it, okay?"

I clasped her wrist and guided her home. Once there, Mom was so exhausted that she went into her bedroom and fell asleep.

After that I knew something had to change. She couldn't flee the house, but a nursing home wasn't an option. The only other thing to do was to find a visiting nurse. Mom's insurance only covered three visits every six months. I had to find someone we could afford. I had heard horror stories. But for once, I was lucky. I skimmed the classifieds and picked Gloria.

I instantly liked her. She had a kind face that radiated strength. She reminded me of 90s-era Sally Field, one of Mom's favorite actresses. Gloria said that after thirty years of working in the ER at Jamaica Hospital, she'd retired. Only to realize that she hated "loafing around" watching talk shows, so she quit retirement to work as a homecare nurse. I checked her references. Mom liked her, especially after she gave her fruit salad. Gloria suggested a neurologist. There were tests. A diagnosis, medications. Gloria has been with us ever since.

Now I walk down the hall and knock. "I'm here." I open Mom's door.

The bedroom is just as depressing as it was this morning. The floral wallpaper is yellowed from cigarette smoke. The rug has faded to the color of thickening pea soup. Gloria placed the clothes into the dresser. The jewelry is on the nightstand.

Gloria is sitting on a folding chair in front of Mom, who is slumped on the edge of her bed, watching *Rear Window*, again, on mute. Beside Gloria is a moveable tray, like the ones in hospitals. Mom's pink robe hangs off her shoulders, its belt stretched across the mattress. She used to jack the heat up to eighty-three. So I'd gone to Macy's and bought her the thickest terrycloth robe I could find.

I lean against the dresser. I'm afraid of what Gloria needs to tell me, so I say, "Nobody's around. I really think it was a misunderstanding."

"You're right. Maybe I'm just getting old." She watches me. Here's where I should tell her she's not old. But I'm too busy thinking of my answer instead of answering and she says, "Sorry you left work."

"I don't mind seeing you." I catch myself. "I mean helping."

Gloria says, "I know what you mean, honey."

She doesn't. What I meant was how she causes this glowing warmth inside of me. She is the nicest person I've ever met. This one time, when Mom was better than she is now, I was making her try to solve a jigsaw puzzle with me. I thought all Mom needed was a brain exercise to help keep her memory and thinking active. We were framing the border of the puzzle, an orange kitten sitting inside of a bucket, when Mom said, "Look at this crap," and swiped the pieces across the room. I was so upset that I yelled, "You ruined our puzzle!" and left Mom sitting at the table. A bit later, Gloria knocked on my bedroom door. She said, "Wes, you have to be calm. She can't help it," and handed me the puzzle box, filled with all of the pieces. "Why don't we try together?" With Gloria's help, we finished the puzzle. If she didn't do that, I would've sulked for days. Gloria treats me with respect. She values my opinions. I'm a twenty-six year old guy who yearns for approval. Dignity. That's what she gives me. What she gives my mother.

I say, "How is she?"

Gloria points the nail file at Mom. "Bad day."

She has no idea about the JFK ordeal. It's best to hide as many of those episodes from Gloria as possible. She has enough to worry about when she's here. Besides, I'm terrified that she'll suggest a home. Gloria hasn't mentioned it yet, but when Mom dumps her oatmeal onto the floor or searches the rooms for her money, Gloria's face looks like she's ready to bail. I promised Mom I'd never stick her in one of "those places," as Norman Bates called them. But in a way it doesn't even matter because we can't afford a place. Sure, there's her social security and Medicaid, but that will only land Mom in a jail with no bars, and nurses who are nothing like Gloria. So I lie, "Tomorrow will be better," and it hangs there, ringing with absurdity.

Mom says, "Shh. I'm watching these people."

I say, "You've seen this before."

Mom says, "Yeah, sure."

I wait for Gloria to tell me what she wanted to say only a minute ago. She picks up Mom's hand and examines her fingers. She's wearing a purple shirt and jeans. Her hair tucked behind her ears, revealing amethyst studs. I say, "Isn't your birthday in February?" I point. "Your earrings are the stone."

"You guessed it."

Trying to impress her I add, "You're an Aquarius. The kindest of the zodiacs." I almost tell her I'm a Scorpio, but I decide against it. We're a secretive bunch, so my muteness aligns with the stars. "Mom's stone is a Sapphire. She's born on September eighteenth. Libra, I think."

Gloria says, "It's Virgo. The most difficult to get along with."

Is that a hint about what she wants? I say, "They're just practical, that's all."

"That too."

She places Mom's palms flat on the wheeled tray. There's an emery board, nail clippers. Red nail polish. A small bowl of water. Mom scratches her face when she's agitated. Before Gloria, Dr. Adler gave me mittens that I secured to her wrists with Velcro straps. She wore them until I came into her room and a glove was sticking out of her mouth. She must've had the clarity to undo the straps with her teeth, but then she forgot how to spit it out. After I yanked the mitten out of her mouth, she said, "Glad that's over." She would've died if her old self saw her new self. I'm speaking about her in the past tense, again. She's here, though obviously parts of her are missing. It's hard to reconcile. I say, "Anyway, that's her sign."

She files Mom's nails as Mom stares up at the screen, oblivious. Gloria has delicate fingers that seem to glow. She doesn't wear a wedding ring. She might be single. My face prickles, hot and embarrassed. "What are you staring at, honey?"

I flinch. I say, "Just thinking."

Gloria starts filing Mom's nails, scratching them in sets of three. "About?"

"Work. That's all." Mom tries to pull her hand away, but Gloria brings it toward her. "Don't you have to talk to me?"

She dips Mom's fingers into the water bowl. "Wait for Mom to be settled."

She seems settled to me, but honestly, I don't want to know. Mom stares at Jimmy Stewart wheeling himself around his apartment, gripping his camera lens, unraveling tightly wound plots. She always loved this movie. It's wacky, living inside someone else's story. You watch the actors move through the scenes. Jimmy Stewart has been trapped in his wheelchair since 1954. Then there's neorealism, but the landscape, with its dioramas of characters held in steady focus for lengthy shots, always felt hyper-aware by feigning the camera's unobtrusiveness. That's cinema, not a movie. Sure, I love those films, but they feel as real as *Armageddon*. Maybe I'm just tired of the cause-and-effect of marriages, car chases, fight scenes, love scenes, all meaningful scenes building toward a crescendo, a purpose. In the movies, mothers are cured. In the movies, girls say yes. That video footage I watched this morning unfolds in real-time. It's calming, but it is also continuous, plotless. It's strange to feel this way-- preferring a non-narrative filmic experience. Movies are my life. For a brief moment, I'm convinced that all of those plot points and narrative causality may have done more harm than good. Mom says, "Can he see us?" and points to the screen, watching Jimmy Stewert watch his neighbors, both of them, again for the first time. Thinking about all this makes me depressed.

Mom sucks her teeth, says, "That's how you dress for work?"

I glance down at my wrinkled sweatshirt with holes in its sleeves, and laugh. But it hurts too. Gloria asks me how work is going. I say, "Play, Rewind."

"Routine is good." She points the emery board at Mom. "Helps when you lose control over other things." Mom shushes us and Gloria winks at me.

Mom says, "Lady. Would you let your kid go to work like that?"

Gloria says, "Sure."

I can't remember if Gloria has kids. It's probably better. If I don't know, I can pretend that I'm the one she cares the most about. I say, "Mom I'll change."

"Don't. I like this show."

Jimmy Stewert stares into the viewfinder of his camera at the courtyard. I turn and Mom thrusts her hand at me. "You dirty cocksuckers get it in the end."

Gloria says, "Enough now."

She lifts the tray of food off her nightstand and places it onto the little table. "Here, eat." She lifts the plastic cover and it's tomato soup, so red it seems fake. A basil leaf floats in the center, a garnished ship in a flavored ocean. There's also a bacon sandwich on toast. A cup of tea, tepid so Mom won't burn herself.

"I'll check the yard. But I really think there's nothing to worry about."

"I know." Gloria stands. "Just watch her a second. I have to do something."

"What?" I say.

"I have to use the bathroom." Gloria nudges the dish. "Maybe she'll eat for you." Gloria shifts past me and pulls the door closed.

I feel the bed, the dresser, creeping closer. I'd rather eat broken glass than witness her deterioration. Sometimes, I dream that she snaps out of her stupor. She finally understands how hard I've worked at crappy Video Planet to pay for Gloria. How well I've taken care of her. And she begs me for forgiveness. Other times, like now, when she's cursing and mean, I want to strap her into a wheelchair and pitch her off of the bay bridge. It's complicated.

Play, Rewind.

I blow on the spoon, a habit, though the broth is cold, and hold it towards her. I say, "Whoosh, here comes the airplane."

Mom licks her lips. She's hungry. She understands that the spoon is in front of her, but she can't put the want to eat and the motion of eating together. Sometimes she understands. Today, she doesn't. Oh, the things we take for granted. "Here like this." I open my mouth wide, put the spoon into my mouth and wink. I take the spoon out of my mouth and twirl it like a wand. I spoon more soup. "C'mon. Eat."

She says, "Think I don't know food?"

I'll distract her and try again. "Mom, what's the best part of dementia?" She sticks her finger in the soup. "You can hide your own Easter eggs." No reaction.

"Maybe you'll like the joke when you hear it for the first time, tonight. Have soup."

"I hate lettuce."

"That's basil."

"Basilico?" I tell her yes and I imagine her brain clicking over to Italian or some other language that she doesn't know but has decided to understand. She says, in the Queen's English, "I hate green."

I drop the spoon onto the tray. "Eat the sandwich, then."

"I don't need any insurance."

I think she means reassurance. I tell her at least she has insurance. Growing up, we had zilch. Instead of doctors, I got supermarket-brand ibuprofen and hot-water bottles. She'd strap garlic to my feet to relieve fevers. Brewed coffee grains for pink-eye. Tea bags for canker sores. Piss on warts, which is harder than you'd think. In the last two years, she has been examined by more doctors than I've seen my entire life.

I say, "Please, eat."

She slides the bowl and a soup blot hits the tray. "You. Fetch a napkin."

I say, "Not this again."

She pokes the basil and it disappears. When she moves her finger out of the bowl the basil pops up again and she laughs. Mom says, "It's a lily pad."

I say, "No, Mom. It's basilico."

"What are you saying?" She snorts. "Gibberish."

I want to show Gloria that I can take care of Mom too. That despite it all we're doing okay, even if there's a lot I'm hiding from her. I say, "Try the sandwich." She picks up half and bites. It's a win until Mom goes squirrely and lumps the food into the pocket of her mouth. "Like this." I open wide and close, smacking my lips.

Mom pops the soggy ball out with her tongue and the food drops onto the tray. She whispers, "Poison."

"That's great." I glance at the television. Raymond Burr is burying something in his flowerbed. Secrets soon to be unraveled.

I say, "If you don't eat, you're getting a tube."

She sniffs the sandwich. "A tube of what?"

"Food. They pump it from an IV bag."

She must've believed me, because she pops the mush into her mouth again. I say, "Good. Chew."

She chews, smacking her lips. Either imitating or teasing or just being gross. She gulps and then opens her mouth, proving it's gone. I think of featherless hatchlings, frail and helpless.

"I have to hurry," she says. "Aunt Joan's waiting."

"Not Wonkyland again."

"No. Manhattan."

"Eat first, please." I am hoping she'll forget this conversation.

She says, "My. Sister. Is. Waiting. For. Me."

Her sister Joan died of polio when she was eleven. My mom was thirteen. They lived in an apartment on 50th street between 10th and 11th Avenue. Hell's Kitchen. When Mom was okay, I'd catch her grazing her fingers along her sister's picture. In the photo, Joan's standing in front of their apartment door, a quiet look on her face. Aunt Joan is eight years old. She's wearing a wool jacket with large buttons and saddle shoes. Her hair is curled around her face in that Shirley Temple way. Behind her is the brickface of what must've been their apartment building. She's holding a bunch of dandelions, their limping heads slung over her clenched hand. Joan was young, but you could tell by the softness of her face that if she had a chance to grow up she would've been caring, in that Gloria kind of way. If Mom caught me looking at her dead sister's picture, she'd spend the rest of the day telling me stories about how they shared a bed in their railroad apartment. How they'd buy eels from the fishmonger. My mother was afraid of the snake-like fish squirming in the bag, so Joan carried it. How they dressed as angels for their school play. They wore white dresses with wings that their mother, Grandma Rose, had sewn. There's a lapse in Mom's history. I know up until her sister died, and then the history we shared. I know virtually nothing about her marriage to my father. I'm more interested in that than a woman I've never met, one of the heaviest anchors in my mother's slow and steady drowning. Maybe I'm jealous. I'm in so few of her memories.

I say, "You don't know what you're talking about."

She gulps. "Don't tell me what I know."

"What do you know?"

She repeats my question, long and sing-songy. Her hallucinations are crazy making. It's easy: this is real; this is loony. But she seems so convinced. What if she is seeing her sister? Neurons or synapses, or whatever, firing in her brain, summoning loved ones like ghosts into the present, or rather the past, more vivid than this room. That day at Blessed Heart, I still thought it was a spiteful game. It wasn't until I saw the MRI and EKG results, physical proof of her illness, that I truly believed. Now, she hums to herself, atonal and sporadic.

I should let it go, but I say, "Who's waiting for you? Joan?"

"My sister?" She sucks her teeth. "No. Course not. She's at the other place. With the gates and flowers. Everyone's there?"

Okay. Mom's confused, tired, medicated. But I'll ask. "You mean heaven?"

She snorts. "Are you crazy? Central Park! She wanted to ride the carousel."

"Christ. Go buy a ticket, then."

Her face brightens as her peach-pit of misery glows a fiery, spiteful red. "None for you, fucking boner. You can sit. Watch us twirly and whirly."

"I don't care," I say. "Have fun."

"Have fun what?"

"Forget it."

When I was younger she'd come home late sometimes. I'd ask her where she went and she'd tell me the zoo, the circus, the aquarium. I'd be upset that she went to those places alone. Then she'd laugh and admit that she was working at the bank. It's silly, but it feels as though they're going to the carousel without me. Gloria opens the door, snipping the memory short. She says, "How is she?"

"She didn't eat."

Gloria rolls her eyes.

I touch Mom's hand, knobby and cold, trying to leave an impression, a warmth, an easing of her confusion. She pulls away. And that's as close as we get. Upset by the literal sleight-of-hand, I rush from the room, refusing to glance at Mom, Gloria, my reflection in the vanity mirror, the one that I still haven't unfastened. The hallway feels cooler, safer. I linger near the door as Gloria tells her that if she doesn't eat the soup she's shutting the movie. Mom asks what movie? Unlike me, Gloria laughs. I feel relieved that I'm away from her until I remember that in some ways she's closer to Joan now. So I have to keep moving further, farther away. Father. My chest twitches. I move down the hall. Soon I'll be nested deep inside Video Planet. Fly away, birdy.

I step outside and glance down the block.

A guy wearing a red leather jacket is walking his German Shepard, hobbling from a skewed hip. Pigeons sit on the power line, their beaks tucked into their charcoal-colored feathers. Below them, the sneakers twirl in the wind. The tinny voice of the subway booth announcer echoes from the platform speakers. The Manhattan-bound train is delayed. I take the front steps in two hops and walk down the pathway that separates our house and the neighbors'.

The yard is scattered with years of leftover junk. A wiffle bat, a deflated basketball, milk crates. A folding chair, knocked onto its side, its legs splayed. Just for fun, I pick up the wiffle bat, the sole object in the yard that qualifies as a weapon. I say "Don't make me use this" in my best Dirty Harry voice. Gloria probably saw kids taking a shortcut through the yards. I used to do it all the time. It's nothing. Still in Dirty Harry mode, I hold the bat like a shotgun and jog down the steps leading to the basement. I take out my keys, unlock the knob and swing open the door.

The basement has wood paneling on the walls and stick-tiles the color of vomit after a holiday. There are bins filled with my father's records, other things that we deemed valuable enough to hoard, yet worthless enough to keep in the basement.

I press my back against the wall and imagine I'm in a movie. There's someone lurking in the house, an assassin. That's it. The assassin creeps through the shadows, gloved hands reaching forward, forcing Mom towards the window. Wait. I just narrated the climax of *Rear Window*. Regardless, I have to protect her. I jump out and say, "Got you, motherfucker!"

Gloria screams and teeters backwards. I drop the bat like it's on fire. She says, "What were you doing?"

"I'm sorry. Sorry. I was just playing around. The yard's empty. The person must've had the wrong house. What are you doing?"

She whispers, "I thought it was better to find you. I didn't want Mom to worry." As though she'd understand us. She stares at a knot in the paneling with the same look she had when she told me that Mom needed diapers. "Camilla's getting worse."

I knew it was serious. I say, "Don't quit. Dom gave me a raise. Please. I'll pay you more."

"It's not about the money, sweetie."

"Medication? She's pretty gassed up as it is. I will, if you think it's best."

"It's okay. I'm not quitting. I mean a home."

My legs go noodley. I say, "But this is her home."

"Of course it is. But it's not safe anymore."

I imagine carpets being ripped up. Rugs being rolled and folded. Rubber edge-guards glued onto furniture. Plastic protectors being sexually wriggled into sockets. Grab-bars being fastened to shower-stalls. Booster rings secured onto toilet seats. Forks being replaced by sporks wrapped in cellophane. Favorite mugs being swapped for sippy cups. Her box-spring being traded in for a hospital bed fully loaded with arm rails and straps and hydraulics. Tip her forward. Tilt her back. A life of Tilt-a-Whirls. I'll fix, buy, replace, until the house, our home, is encased inside a geriatrically safe, elderly approved plastic bubble. I'll do whatever it takes for her to stay with me. She's all I have.

I take a deep breath. Before I outline my plan, Gloria says, "It'll take more than that."

"Like what?"

"Things a son shouldn't have to see."

If I was filming a movie, the scene would be captured with an over-the-shoulder shot, the lens focusing on her face. Timid light. Soft music. Intimate. A shot that's close enough to see the green flecks in her eyes, yet away enough to convey how Gloria's farewell is the muted climax of the Worst Possible Thing. Watching her, I realize that everyone I love, one way or another, leaves me.

I slide my palm along the paneling. My mental camera pans left, blurs (insert augmented chord) and the lens focuses on the ocean. I wait for birds to flutter between us. When nothing happens, I say, "Mom's just having a bad day."

She nudges the bat with her shoe. "Gonna zonk me with that?"

I say, "Only if you zonk me first."

"Oh, C'mere." She hugs me. Not the stiff, slaps-on-the-back kind. She tells me it'll be okay. I hear it so rarely that I wish I could press Pause. Like that favorite scene in your favorite movie, when you freeze it, just before the sad parts.

CHAPTER 4

Dom passes me his sidearm.

It's a Raven automatic, silver with a pearl grip. Six rounds. .25 ACP. It's an older pistol, but I've watched him bore-brushing the barrel, polishing the frame with a luster cloth, spreading the gun parts across the counter as though building a model airplane. The pistol is illegal, but Dom gives a flying one about authority.

On the drive back to Video Planet, I'd weighed my promise to Mom versus Gloria's suggestion for a nursing home. I tried to be unbiased. Like Judge Judy, minus the berating. I listed all of the reasons why Mom should stay: One, I'm taking care of her. Two, there's my inability to afford a nice place. Three, Mom should live in her house as long as possible. Four, I promised her. Here are Gloria's reasons she should go: Onc, she'll be safer and have constant medical care. That's it for her list. I'm up on points. Also, injuries happen in nursing homes. I read a story about a man who lay dead in his cot for three days before the nurses realized what had happened. I'm not a medical professional but I'd know if Mom died. Then another reason crept into my psyche. If Mom went into a nursing home I'd never see Gloria again. No more Gloria patting me on the back. No more Gloria asking me how my day went. All of it, along with Mom, gone. This can't be what she wants. Maybe Gloria had a bad morning and Mom's mood made it worse?

Gloria knows better than anyone that there's a flow to Mom's confusion. She must've suggested a home out of frustration. Today will be better, and then Gloria will forget that she even mentioned the home. Then I'll still see Mom and Gloria everyday.

Play, Rewind.

When I'd finally made it back to Video Planet, Dom had been sitting behind the counter, smoking a cigarette. I wanted him to leave. Tubby's had coffee. OTB had races running. After ten minutes, I got antsy and blurted about the person Gloria saw. I emphasized the lack of big deal it was because I really wanted to talk about Gloria and the nursing home. Dom is the last person I'd ask for advice, but I needed to say it, if only for myself. Before I reached the real source of anxiety, though, he said, "You know what you need?" and flashed his sidearm. I realized what I needed was a quiet, soothing beach. Dom's sidearm would be the opposite of that.

Now I roll onto my toes and check the store. It's just me, Dom, and his gun. I expected him to carry a .38 wheel-gun like the one Gene Hackman carries in *The French Connection*. This gun is petite, toyish. Or maybe I'm jaded. I've seen so many in the movies that the real thing is a letdown.

He runs his finger along the barrel. "I named her Vicki."

"Great," I say. "But I don't need it. It was just a delivery or something."

"A gun is like a belt. Every man needs one."

He knows I never wear belts. Here's something else he knows: I hate guns. Two years ago, he'd dragged me into the basement, an unfinished concrete tunnel that runs the length of the store. He had set up a cardboard cutout of Sylvester Stallone, an old display the distributor had sent him for *Rambo 2*. Red headband, M-60, that stroke-ish expression of anger on Sly's face. Dom adjusted the cutout. He raised his gun and yelled, "Grab your ankles, motherfucker!" then blasted holes through Stallone's cardboard frame. Without saying a word, Dom reloaded and lobbed the pistol at me. "Your turn, Bronson." My ears were ringing from the noise; I waited for shooting advice so I wouldn't cap myself in the testicles. He said nothing. So I tried to channel Jean Reno in *The Professional*. I closed my eyes and squeezed the trigger, which is harder than it looks in movies. The bullet ricocheted off the ground. Asbestos-laced dust swirled around my feet. Instead of Reno, I was Fredo in *The Godfather*, fumbling and stupid. Disgusted by my sharpshooting abilities, Dom snatched the pistol back and emptied the clip, screaming about rubbing Troutman off next. After Rambo hunting, he disappeared for three days. Maybe he felt guilty about pulling his heat in front of his lone employee. Maybe he thought I'd quit. At the time, I'd thought that watching movies was worth his insanity. I was hoarding experience for my film. Now, I'm a guest star in the Dom Show. I try to stay out of as many episodes as possible.

Here's a joke with no punchline: a customer walks into the store.

She's wearing a flamingo-colored flannel shirt tucked into her jeans. Her blond hair is spun in tight curls. She's an updated version of Heather Graham in *License to Drive*. She wanders into Foreign, which is a surprise since most people in this neighborhood shoot right for either Action or Comedy. She chooses a box and reads the description. I think about my favorite foreign movies: *Russian Ark, Bicycle Thieves, Breathless, Life is Beautiful, The 400 Blows, Wild Strawberries, Run Lola Run,*

L'Avventura. If I suggest a movie, I'll be breaking my 'No Recommendation' rule, but I'll take a chance.

Dom is scratching behind his ear, head tilted, like a Doberman. Dom recommends hits like *Double Team* or *Cutthroat Island.* Again, he hates movies. He sniffs at his finger, then with the same finger pokes my arm. "I gotta grab covers."

I say, "No problem," happy to see him go.

Dom places the gun on top of the VCR as though it's the remote control. He says, "Think about my offer," then hobbles towards the backroom.

The last thing I want is for her to see Dom's gun.

Before I can hide it, she walks across the aisle, her purple bag stuck in the crook of her arm. She peeks over the rack and smiles. I do this wavy-noddy 'Hello.' Embarrassed, I glance down at a note Dom left on the counter. The words *I NEED MONEY* are written in boxy script.

When I look up, she is there, sliding the movie across the counter. *The Music of Chance.* My stomach twitches, the movie's title ringing a little too close. I smile, but it's tight-faced, like the ones you see in fiber commercials. She says, "980, please."

"Here to serve." I wriggle her card out of the file.

Tina Hart. She owes a two-dollar fee. She says, "Can I pay when I return it?" She leans close and a strand of hair falls across her face, a blond windshield wiper. A close-up shot, intimate, blocking the rest of the frame, connecting with her solitary audience, meaning me. She's only doing this to slip past the fee. If it didn't happen so much, I'd be annoyed. She whispers, "Our secret?"

It's sleazy for a video clerk to check out female customers, but things have been so hard lately, I could really use a win here, even if it's just a conversation with someone who isn't sick or crazy or desperate to leave. I say, "What do you need it for?" The words hang there and I realize how gross and desperate I sound.

She says, "It's for a stupid film history class."

Class, meaning college. I feel a twinge of jealousy. In my MFS catalog, some of the classes are about movies directed by Truffaut, Bergman, Kazin. Hitchcock. If the professor is younger, maybe it's a class about Tarantino, Lynch, Jarmusch. This was one of the best movies I'd seen in awhile. It could never work between us. I switch out the box for the movie. I say, "Don't worry about the fee."

She says, "I'll pay next time," and snatches it and marches down the aisle.

No she won't. They never do. I say, "Be kind, rewind."

She leaves. The halogen lights buzz, as though a giant fly is swirling above me. The phone rings. I'm afraid it's Gloria, wanting to push more, or quit on the spot. I wait for it to stop. When it doesn't, I grab the receiver.

"How's it going?"

It's a girl, her voice perky, excited. Something I haven't heard in a long time. I say, "Okay, can I help you?"

"Do I sound that bad?"

I laugh. "No. I mean this is Video Planet. I'm asking if you want a movie."

"Not especially." There's a long pause. "You know who this is?"

I concentrate, trying to place the customer. She reminds me of the kid who lives across the street who rents Wrestlemania videos for her father. I say, "Janice?"

"Aw, is that your girlfriend?"

"I don't have a girlfriend."

"Figures."

Now I'm offended. "Why? I could have, like, six girlfriends."

She sings, "Are you lonely tonight? Is your heart filled with pain? Tell me...are you lonely tonighhhttt," her voice straining to hit the bass-ey, Elvis register.

"It's lonesome." I hang up, then pick up fast. She's gone.

It's just some bored kid cutting school. She asked if I had a girlfriend. Maybe Tina had a change of Hart? Probably not. Anyway, I'm oblivious to the ins and outs of dating. When I was sixteen, I went on my first date. Suzie Florintino. We saw that horrible race movie *Days of Thunder*, starring Tom Cruise. She demanded that we sit in the last row, which confused me since we were alone in the theater. We sat through the whole movie, Suzie with her arms crossed, and me munching on popcorn spewing wisdom like, "They're drag racing in broad daylight, where are the police?" When the movie ended, she wanted to walk home alone. I insisted that we walk together. I prepared myself for that all-important kiss. Swallowing hard to rid my mouth of saliva. Pretending to itch my shoulder with my chin so I could sniff my breath: buttery, but not hitting grossout levels. She stopped at her corner, pivoted, and said, "This is fine," but something in the way she said it made me want to recreate my favorite kissing scene: Han Solo edging Princess Leia into the quiet corner of the Millennium Falcon. But before I could tilt my head and whisper, "I'm nice men" (a line I had rehearsed to hit that perfect mixture of suave and arrogant), she shoved me and said, "Little late, you fucking prude. Go join a convent."

I stood there dumbfounded.

As she hustled down the block, she reached behind her back and shot me the middle finger.

I called after her, "Isn't that for nuns?"

It's ridiculous, but that experience ruined my interactions with women. I'd be fine if we just watched movies, but what if, say Tina Hart, wanted to go to a bar? Then there's sex. The intricacies of penis size and hopeful erections and premature ejaculations. I'd love to do the hippity-dippity, but spotting your mom as she wanders the house topless really shoots buckshot through your libido.

Now, I wait for the phone to ring. It doesn't.

But I hear tapping. Maybe it's the radiator? I hear it again. It isn't tapping. Someone is knocking, out back. What if it's that guy Gloria saw? What if that girl calling was to see if I was alone? The tapping turns into pounding. The gun still rests on top of the VCR: silver, pearly protection. But I don't want to shoot myself in the testicles, so I leave it and shift towards the back room.

Large holes pockmark the walls from Dom's various fits. There are posters, mutilated VCRs, and plastic video cases. Empty Crown Royal bottles. The door is gray with deep gashes, as though it was clawed at by a werewolf.

There's another bang. I say hello, and from outside, Dom yells my name. I slide the 2x4 free and open the door.

The alley has a row of dumpsters, behind them a field of reeds. A few of the cattails have bags caught on their cigar-shaped heads, the plastic puffing with each gust of wind. He says, "You almost hit me." He watches the alley.

I say, "Why didn't you just go in the front?"

"This store's mine. I'll dive through the fucking ceiling I want to." He digs into his pocket, pulls his money roll, counts off three hundred dollars. "Want this?" I stare at the money. I want, I want. "Take a walk through the store. It's still empty, call my cell."

"What happened?"

"Mistakes were made." He hands me the money plus another hundred. I stick the cash into my pocket. "Something goes awry, ring my cell. Grab Vicki."

Did he really use 'awry?' Also, I'm calling him if something is wrong, and if everything's fine? Trying to pin down his directions, I say, "Who am I looking for?"

He says, "Anyone who ain't Pope John Paul, Paul McCartney or John Paul Jones, ring me."

"Well that narrows it down."

"Does, don't it?" A mouse squeezes underneath the door of the takeout place next door. Dom pokes my gut. "Skedawdle." He hobbles behind the dumpsters.

I didn't think anyone else had come in, but I walk through the store, clenching the money as though it'll evaporate. What traits do the Pauls have in common? One prays to God, one thinks he's God, and the one is as reserved as God (well, compared to the other members of Zep). They have nothing in common. I reach the counter and listen for movement. I hear the mechanical breathing of the ducts. The buzz of the lights. The swoosh of cars along the Boulevard. The store is empty.

I pick up the receiver to let Dom know that All's Quiet on the Western Front just as this guy walks out of the Disney section.

Now I'm nervous.

I have a theory that you can tell if a guy's connected by paying attention to their rentals. If someone wearing a red tracksuit tosses *Mean Streets* onto the counter, you have nothing to worry about. If that same guy tosses *Cinderella*, watch your balls. Which is to say I think the mafioso tend to rent Disney. Still, just because some guy is wearing athletic wear and rents *Peter Pan* doesn't make him a gangster. Also, everyone in this neighborhood thinks they're connected in a roundabout way. You can't always tell who is legit versus who is made of rubber. Therein lies the danger.

The might-be-gangster is wearing a maroon shirt and black pants. He has large black-rimmed glasses, enlarging his bulgy eyes. He's a hybrid of Joe Pesci and Marty Feldman. He peeks behind the counter, as though Dom might be hiding on the floor. His earlobes crop a beard of black hairs, reminding me of anemones clinging onto reefs. He says, "This," and tosses *Pocahontas* onto the counter. His voice is high-pitched, like Judge Doom in the final scene of *Who Framed Roger Rabbit?* It's weird that Dom is ducking these guys. He usually brags about the wiseguys he pals around with as if they were famous actors.

They're not, though.

I remember my father making stops with me. He'd tell me to lie down in the backseat of his parked Sierra while he entered their club, its door unmarked, its windows boarded so you couldn't see the inner workings of their thievery. Most times he'd hurry out of the club holding football tickets. Other times he'd stay in there for hours. I'd pick at the cracked leather and imagine scenarios where he was dragged into a dusty backroom that reeked of stale beer. He was getting stabbed in the gut with an icepick, or hacksawed into bits, or garroted. I imagined any number of explicit *Faces of Death* scenarios as I lay there, scared and cold or sweating, depending on the weather. When he had finally exited onto the street, alive and squinting from the rush of daylight, he'd hop into the car and glance over his shoulder to make sure I hadn't been kidnapped. He never apologized. Anyway, I was just happy that he was alive. My hatred of these guys is the cowardly kind.

I say, "Number?"

He doesn't answer. I fetch the movie and place it onto the counter. I ring two dollars. He's focusing on the back room. He has no intention of paying for the rental, so I cancel the sale. He says, "He's around?"

"Who?"

"Marlon Brando, kid. Who do you think?"

Wow. The *Godfather*/*On the Waterfront* reference makes me think maybe he's a nobody after all. Maybe Dom is so wonky that he has me all twisted, too. I say, "He was here before," which doesn't really answer the question. He's not in the store. But he said 'Around' which includes the vicinity. So technically, I'm not lying. My answer is more of a fib, which I figure is a lesser, diet version of a lie. A word my mother used, as in, "Stop your fucking fibbing." She was weird with words. She'd say "dear" for "expensive." She'd say "parlor" for "living room." The toilet was the "turlet," and "boil" was "berr-il" and "oil" was "er-il," though that's her antiquated Manhattan accent, as though I was living inside *Angels with Dirty Faces*.

I almost slip and say: He's berril-ing, er-il in the turlet. Instead, it's: "He went to get movies."

"My movies?"

I'm unsure what he means. This morning, Dom mentioned that he was going to get movies. Now, Dom's hiding in the alley and this guy is asking about him. Dom must owe him money. Of course he does. Once I had a horde of angry Girl Scouts searching for Dom because he welched on a Tagalongs payment. I stand there, not sure what to do. He slides his rental off the counter. He says, "Anyway, it stinks here."

I shimmy a wad of cards from the 'Out' file and place them onto the counter. I scrawl a check on the corner of the card. I'll just act busy until he leaves. "We have issues with rodents," I say, as though they shoplift.

Ignoring me, he points at the column of movies on the counter. "Like those movies." He points at the dusty racks. "Those too. Mine."

Should I thank him for the movies? That would come off wise. I picture the camera shot. An extreme closeup of his eyebrows, the hair falling slightly over the rims of his glasses. I say, "I'll tell Dom."

"Right. Just say Vic came by. He'll understand."

I nod.

"Good, then." He steps to the side to leave, but stops and points. "What's that gun, illegal?"

"It's not mine." Again, not answering the question.

He holds out his hand, his gold bracelet sliding into his palm. "Wouldn't want you to hurt yourself."

I stare at his fingers, arthritic and lumpy. Handing him the gun is the stupidest thing I can do, but I still pass Vicki to Vic.

He sticks the gun in his pocket and moves down the aisle. He says, "Tell him," and swings open the door. He walks towards Tubby's Diner like a character moving off set. It's only when he vanishes that it sinks in that I handed him Dom's favorite possession. I can't help thinking that in some way Dom probably deserves it.

I rush into the alley and jump behind the dumpster, wanting to ask what's going on. But Dom is gone. His keys are there. I grab them and walk back into the store. I half expect him to be standing at the counter. He isn't, so I sit in his chair.

I can't worry about Dom's bootleg problems. Trying to distract myself, I take the video out of my bag, turn on the television, and hit Play. The camera flashes on. The lens points towards the palm trees. The fronds are pale green. I wait for a plot twist or the big reveal, a climax. But it's just a vacation. Staring at the footage, I can almost smell the salty ocean. Tropical, not the garbage smell of Rockaway. I watch until I feel calm. I have an old dubbing machine. I'll make the copy at home. Why would someone leave a note not to watch a video like this? It's just a beach so beautiful that watching it is like when Dorothy wakes up into a Technicolor Oz. I shimmy the cards back into the file.

The phone rings. I snatch it fast, hoping it's Dom. I say, "Hello, Video."

"Why'd you hang up?" It's her again.

A halogen light flickers and dies. "Just busy."

"Must be rough. Being busy." She yawns. "Did you like *Episode 1*? Meesa thinks it blew. Just some galactic senate arguing. Like watching C-SPAN."

"Yeah, it was shitty." I watch cars navigate the lot, hoping to see Dom. I don't. She sighs. Three minutes on the phone talking to me and she's already bored. Sounds about right. Still, if I get her talking, maybe I'll recognize her voice. "What's your name?"

"Three guesses. Wait. Do you ever wonder why it's always three?

"I've never thought about it."

"You should. Okay, here's a hint." I stick my finger in my free ear to really listen, concentrate. "My name isn't Rumpelstiltskin." I hear a candy wrapper. She chews, smacking her lips. "OH. I saw this porno once. It was called *Rumpelforeskin*."

"Jesus Christ."

"Two more. That counted."

"How can that count?"

"It's a name, ain't it?"

I don't argue. I'm afraid she'll hang up. She turns on the television. I hear booing. Jerry Springer, unless it's Maury. If I ask, it'll count as a guess. Her voice sounds familiar. I say, "Did you drop off a video here this morning?"

"I'm not a member."

"It was a home movie," I say, suddenly annoyed that I asked her about the video. If it belongs to her, I'll have to tell her the VCR ate it. So I say, "Nevermind."

She mutes the television. "Okay. C'mon, just say some names."

I tap the counter with my thumb. I can't think of a single one. With my luck it's Mrs. Green, the receptionist from Dr. Adler's office. She's like seventy. Her dentures click when she talks. She mutes the television. I say the only name of the only girl in high school that talked to me: "Lola?"

"I'll call back." I ask when. She laughs and hangs up.

I *69 her, but she'd *67'd and blocked her number.

I rewind our conversation. I think of her laugh, her fast-paced, nervous talk. It sounded just like her, but why would she call me now, after all these years? It's just a prank call. Unless it's Lola. A flutter of happiness fills my chest, but no hope. The last few years with Mom has taught me that hope is dangerous.

I say, "It's just a prank. That's all. A prank."

Another light buzzes, then dies. Half of the store is erased. I'm trapped inside the dull innards of Video Planet. I wait for a sign, a beacon, a ring in the darkness.

CHAPTER 5

Mom shuffles towards me, her slippers scuffing along the polished wood of the hallway, her hands tucked behind her back, elbows flaring out.

During the holidays, we'd take the subway to Rockefeller Centre. I remember staring at the glowing tree while the wind whipped my mother's hair, then long and black. To keep warm, we passed a bag of chestnuts we bought from a pushcart. We didn't have the money to rent skates, but she told me that as a girl she loved skating in Central Park. That she could perform a toe loop, an Axel, a Salchow. I had no idea what those tricks were, but that's how I wanted my mother to be: graceful, happy.

This is the memory I'm stuck in when my mother's hands come around in front of her and she's holding her pocketbook. It's one of those sack-like bags with gold buttons stamped along the sides. A bra, caught on the silver loop of the zipper, spills over from the side like a nude-colored rope-ladder. A set of utensils, wrapped in cellophane, peeks out from her half-opened zipper. She drops the pocketbook with a thud and drags the pocketbook by its straps, the studs scratching along the floor.

Mom is wearing her pink robe. Her hair is pinned with a red clip, but the other side poofs out, frizzy and reckless. She only remembered half her head.

She walks into the kitchen, says, "We're going to A.C. today."

I say, "In a bit. I'm hungry," hoping she'll reset. It's 11 PM. I have to make sure Mom falls asleep before I can sit in my room. Usually, this part of Mom's routine is the last checkmark in our movie I call "Together." I'm kind of a night person anyway, so waiting for her to fall asleep isn't really a problem. But tonight I feel this smoldering anticipation to watch the vacation footage, its blissful calm.

Dom never returned to Video Planet. As the hours passed, I felt as though I'd made a mistake about Vic. Maybe Vic had merchandise that Dom promised to buy, but Dom never picked it up. Even the gun could be explained. Maybe Vic was afraid I'd hurt myself? Anyway, it's not my problem. I'm just a video clerk making fifteen bucks an hour.

Besides, I've got Mom to worry about. Before Gloria left tonight, we stood in the hallway as she explained why keeping Mom home was dangerous. How as her dementia progresses, she'll be unable to handle even the simplest of tasks. Walking to the bathroom. Steadying herself to get dressed. Eating. I didn't want to argue with her, so as a distraction, I gave Gloria half of the payola that Dom had passed me in the alley. She told me it wasn't necessary and then plucked it from my hand. Nobody's that nice. Watching Mom now, it's hard to agree with Gloria. Mom doesn't have those problems. Sure, she's confused, but she's not an invalid. If I put her in a home, I'd lose our quiet moments like this. When she's here, with me. Besides, if you forget about the hair or the bag or A.C., she's just a mom wanting to cook for her son. It's almost a regular day. I say, "Sit. Let's just talk."

"Hungry? I'll cook. It's a long ride."

Mom's food prep is insane, but I'll act in this scene. I place my bag on the table. I feel for the tape, making sure it's nestled safe inside.

I say, "Okay, then."

Mom abandons her pocketbook on the linoleum floor next to me and shuffles towards the refrigerator. I hear the rubber kiss as she opens the door. She stares inside the fridge, the light pale across her paler face, as though the shelves are empty, but the fridge is filled with food that Gloria had cooked while I was at Video Planet.

Mom takes a plate of fried chicken cutlets and places it on the counter.

The last thing I want is to hustle to the ER for a burn. "Mom, I'll just eat it cold."

"No. Eat right." The anger in her voice is so familiar that I smile. Still, Gloria has warned me about letting her wander the rooms at night. When she's tired, she becomes even more disoriented. Gloria called it sundowning. But what if she needs the action? Rev those misfiring brain-cells. Spark a memory or two. Besides, she seems happier in the kitchen than being stuck in her musty bedroom.

I say, "If you say so."

She slides the coffee pot off the burner and drops it into the sink. She turns on the faucet. Water splashes off of the coffee bell and sprays onto the counter. Instead of shutting the faucet, she scoots over and rips the plastic fastened to the dish. She pinches the side of the cutlet and holds it up, as though examining an ancient relic.

I say, "What are you doing?"

"I'm cooking." She tosses the cutlet onto the coffee burner and flips the switch. To almost know what you're doing seems worse than being oblivious. I don't think it'll start a fire so I leave it alone. She shuffles to the table and sits. "I love the Taj." She runs her hands along her robe lapels. "Think I'm dressed nice?"

I say, "Perfect."

"Wear something nice."

I tell her I'll change.

"You never do."

When I turned twenty-one, we celebrated by staying overnight in Atlantic City. She rented a suite that had two bedrooms and a kitchen. The windows overlooked the Atlantic, flat and cement colored, a November ocean. The first night, she wore white pants and a flower-printed top. She wanted me to dress up, but all I'd brought were the jeans I always wore and a pair of sweats for bed. She gave me two hundred dollars, which I squandered while playing a slot with a mermaid theme. Mom won six hundred dollars and gave me two hundred more, which I lost playing a slot with a wizard theme. Now, she glances around the room. "Where's my money?"

"It's in your wallet." I pick up her bag, tug the bra free and unzip it. I dig through the nonsense she packed and give her the yellow, red, and blue bills.

She says, "I can still count, you know."

I whisper, "Will miracles never cease."

For a while, at the beginning of her decline, she was obsessed with money. If we went to the supermarket, she'd accuse the pimply faced cashier of short-changing her. She didn't understand the price of groceries, the simple math of making change of her twenty-dollar bill, so it had to be theft. After all, she had worked at a bank where a robbery was a legitimate possibility. Add that to her gambling husband, who'd pawn anything from my baseball cards to her jewelry, and it's easy to understand her paranoia. After Gloria started helping us, I stopped taking Mom to stores. She still complained about her money, so I stuffed Monopoly dollars into her purse, hoping to relieve her fear. She still hasn't realized the switcheroo. The trust issue bothers me, but she's haggling over play money so I can't feel that bad about it. She touches the funny money, then shoves it into her bag.

"That man would take my money."

She means my father. "It's okay."

"He sold my ring, you know."

Great, the ring again. I say, "I'll get it back." I smell the chicken. I'm surprised it actually heated up on the coffee burner that way. "Just let me eat first."

Mom says, "Eat. We have a long drive." She shuffles towards the coffee machine and drops the cutlet onto the counter. "Dish." She turns the water off and then on again. Three times. Then she pulls a paper plate off the stack next to the microwave and sticks it into the sink. She grabs the sponge and scrubs, the flabby U of her underarm swishing with each push.

I say, "Mom, give me the chicken."

"Who's chicken?"

"No Mom, the food?"

"That's right." She takes the plate from the sink and drops the cutlet onto it. Mom holds the edges of the plate and it folds, wet and taco-like. She places it in front of me. I'm so patient, smart. Now I have to eat this soggy crap. She waits, proud that she's feeding her son. I tear off a corner. The top feels hot, the bottom, cold and wet. I chew as little as possible. I'm getting hot-dog PTSD. I swallow and nod, hoping she's satisfied. She says, "You nibble like a mouse."

I picture Fievel and gag. I try to slide the paper plate away, but it's stuck to the table. When Mom glances at the fridge, I spit the cutlet out and stash the chicken onto my lap.

I say, "That was good, thanks."

"What's good?" She picks the plate off the table. "Did we move?" I tell her no. "Well I feel like I don't live here."

I pick at the corner of the table. I say, "We're at the hotel."

"Does it have a kitchen?"

"Yup. We got a suite. My treat."

She shuffles toward me, her hand sliding along the table, steadying herself. Once she reaches her destination, she tips into me for a hug. She smells of urine and sweat and I'm a bit skeeved until she says, "You're so nice," and my chest does that swing-chain hiccup thing, and maybe it's the weight of the day, but I go full-on sob.

Here's when I decide that I'm never dumping her in a home. Gloria is a nurse, but I'm her son. I know what she needs. She digs her chin into my forehead and sways. I lean into her, clingy, regressing. Look: here I am at four-years old, crying over a halo of strawberry ice cream splattered onto the pavement. Look: here I am at ten after a savage game of stickball, hobbling home with barked knees. Look: here I am at twelve with a busted RC car, its spiked wheel, a jewel in my palm. As she holds onto me, I realize that if I could stay inside this moment, all our faults could be forgiven. But, of course, that's when she pulls away.

Play, Rewind.

I wipe my face. I say, "How about a tour?"

She pulls the clip out of her hair. "Of what?"

I slide off my chair, careful not to bump her over. I say, "Our hotel room."

"We're in a hotel?"

"Yup." I hold her hand, cracked and dry, feeling even smaller than this morning. When we walk into the living room, a frail breath catches in her throat. I feel guilty that I'm lying to her, but she seems so happy, sincere. Sure, she's hallucinating, but if real means wasted time at Video Planet, sick mom, and nursing homes, then give me faux casinos and recorded vacations any day. It's all pretend. It's all a projected image.

Mom drops back onto the cushion of the couch, the plastic crumpling. I sit next to her.

She says, "Can we afford this room?"

I nudge her with my elbow. "If not, we're washing a lot of paper plates."

"What?"

"Nothing."

If this was before, she'd have her crystal ashtray placed on her thigh, though she'd let the ash burn into a long gray finger before flicking. She'd ask me how work was, and I'd say okay, even if it wasn't, and she'd nod. I'd ask her the same question and she'd volley the same, uninterested reaction. It's sad to think that the days will keep rolling, always the same. And they do, I guess, until they don't. The good news is, if you end up like my mom, at least you won't remember all the time you squandered watching quiz shows.

No. I picture her memories like a mixtape.

Do you remember making those? The Saturdays you'd spend sitting cross-legged by the radio, feet tingly, fighting the urge to piss or grab a soda in case the song that you needed to record, plays. After a few hours, your waiting pays off. But after a month of listening while stomping toadstools, or blasting through your headphones while reading comics, the greatness of the song fades. Sooner than later, you discover a newer, better song, so you press Play, Record over the old tape, not bothering to rewind. Then time passes and you're cleaning your room and all these mixtapes are scattered along your dresser—unlabeled of course. You pop one into the radio, hit Play, and Poison's "Nothing But a Good Time" starts, but then the guitar solo is blotted by the thumping drums of RUN DMC's "Walk This Way," but that song melds into Nirvana's "Smells Like Teen Spirit." The songs are an uninterrupted string of music, all demanding attention. Other times, the second song ends and the first song reemerges to the forefront. Anyway, that dubbed-over mess is my mother's brain.

Mom coughs, wheezy and strained, her face shifting to the color of raw beef. I do this leany thing and pat her back. Tapping ribs works better, but she's braless and I'm not grazing a boob. She straightens, her face still bright red. I ask if she's okay.

She says, "Yeah. Sperm's stuck in my throat."

"Mom, it's called phlegm. Snot. Even a lugee. But not what you said."

"I didn't say anything."

A car passes our house, its headlights shifting across the floor. Mom tilts her head toward the ceiling as though gazing at a spirit. The worst part of Mom's illness is her silence. I watch her profile, her frizzy hair, the collar of her robe bunched into her neck. The slats of the blinds cut the streetlights into knife blades that slice the carpet. I steady my mental lens, a sustained wide-shot of the window, the wall, the room. Mom, a still life, consumed by her stillness.

I decide to prod her a bit. "How was dinner?"

Another car passes. "Same old stuff."

"Like what? Cornflakes or lobster ravioli?"

She leans forward, the plastic crinkling. She squints in concentration and says, "You know that guy who lives here? Green eyes. Handsome, but couldn't keep a job?"

She means my father. I say, "Yes, why?"

"I think I miss him."

I say, "Not me though."

"God. Never getting rid of you."

I know she's confused, or maybe joking around, so I can't get all that mad. Trying to let the feeling pass, I run my hand along the cushion; the plastic feels cold. One night she sat at the kitchen table and rehashed how he went to work and never came back. A week later he sent her a letter that said, "Thanks for the memories." No return address. I understand there were addictions. People separate. Still, I have an impossible time even throwing out old toys, so I can't imagine how a person, my father, could trash his entire family.

"This is the hotel lobby?"

"Sure is." I almost tell her about Dom's troubles. Mom never liked him. I think he reminds her of my father. So I say, "This girl called today. We talked." Mom hugs herself, rocking slowly, her lips puckered. Of course she glazes over as I reach for a connection. Annoyed, I say, "Okay, well." I touch her arm. "Bedtime Mom."

She flinches, says, "Where were you horsedick? With the boys?"

I say, "Please don't rev up. Let's just go to bed. I'm tired."

"I bet. Come in late, then hit me?"

She has never mentioned abuse before. Not about my father, anyway. Did he abuse her? I only remember yelling. "What are you talking about?"

"You know what you did, you bastard. You! Married man!"

Great. She thinks I'm my father. I tell her to calm down, but she claws the armrest and hauls herself off of the couch, her body listing forward, stiff and lumpy. I pop up and grab her arm, steadying her. She punches me in the chest, a hollow thud. She's too frail for it to hurt, but I step back, surprised.

"Get off me, stealing louse!"

I say, "It's me, Wes."

"No. You're the fucking mess! You. You, you, you, you."

She shuffles into the kitchen and down the hallway, her slippers snapping against her heels. I follow her, a few steps behind, as she pulls away in a long dolly shot. She passes her bedroom. I tell her to stop.

She says, "Stay away from me!"

She rushes into the bathroom and slams the door. I get to it in time to hear the ping of the lock. All the doorknobs in the house have twists where you can jimmy the lock open with a knife. Except the bathroom.

I say, "Open the door. Mom. It's your son."

Mom says, "Yeah, sure." The rusted hinges of the medicine cabinet creak open. I hear bottles spilling. The shower door opens. "Save it for your floozies!" The toilet seat slams. The cabinets open and bang shut. Bottles spill from the vanity. The toilet flushes. The faucet turns on. The shower. She's doing everything and nothing.

I say, "Open the door. Please."

She says, "Open. The. Door," long and sing-songy.

I say, "Right. The one you're behind. The bathroom door."

I wait. Nothing. And this is why you don't let her wander. I was being selfish, hoarding a quiet moment. Is it wrong to just want some normalcy, even if I'm pretending? Now she's going to burn herself, or slash her arm. Or slash her arm and then burn herself. The glass door slides. Then again, then again.

She says, "Foggy in here."

Steam. Hot water. Great. "Open up."

Mom says, "I'm indisposed."

Where'd she pull that word from? I say, "That's fine."

The door is hollow. Flimsy. Smashable. But I'm afraid that if I break it down, she'll have another Dad flashback, get scared and slip.

The toilet seat slams into the tank. The toilet paper roll bangs as it unfurls. Then all I hear is the sound of the shower. "Mom?" I press my ear against the door, as though that ever works. It's quiet for a few minutes until I hear the *sh-loosh* of shaving foam. My razor is in there.

I yell, "Stop! I'll save you."

I jog into the kitchen and shimmy open the junk-drawer. I dig through batteries, nails, matchbooks, and rubber-bands. It's taking too long. I dump the drawer. The contents scatter across the tile. I sweep my hands through the mess, shoving things out of the way until I find a screwdriver. I rush down the hallway.

I knock, then say, "I'm opening the door."

The knob is one of those fancy ones with a floral pattern. I finagle the flathead into the screw on the doorplate. I twist. The cabinet slams shut. I twist. A body part knocks against the glass. I'm twisting, twisting, twisting. The screw gets longer, longer, longer. But how big is this fucking screw?

I drop the flathead and pinch the screwhead with my fingers and twist until my forearm cramps. The screw pings to the floor. I shift to the other one.

The steam—balmy, tropical—pushes from under-neath the door. Can you suffocate from steam? If anybody could, it'd be her.

Mom says, "Where's the soap?"

I twist until I pull the second screw out. I pull the doorknob off. I poke my finger through the hole. The other doorknob drops on the tile. I push. The door is still locked. The half-inch bolt is still set in the frame. I say, "Please just open."

It doesn't.

I totally muffed my break-in, but I can see what she's doing.

I peek through the hole. Steam curls and billows inside the room. The bathroom is small. It's a walk-in stall on the left, sink and toilet on the right. No bathtub. Flowered wallpaper that meets wainscoting, which is painted the same bismuth pink. White-and-black octagonal flooring. I see everything but her.

The glass door slides.

"Mom?"

She moans, a long winding sound.

I slap the door. "I can't see. Are you okay? Mom. Mom, answer me!"

The water thrums against the stall. Steam. Maybe she fell?

And then: "Did I ever tell you you're my heeerroo."

She's going to slip. Crack her head on the toilet. And die. Kaput, null, void. D-i-e. And her last words will be Bette Fucking Midler. I hate that song.

I step back, revving up, and ram the door. I ricochet into the wall. I charge again. "Everything I wanted to beeeee!" I ram again. My shoulder feels tingly, already bruising. "La-ta-ti-da-ti-da-mmhmm." She forgot the words.

I start laughing, desperate, hysterical. The kind of laugh your body does when it loses the oomph for crying. I'll just call Gloria. Admit failure. No, I can't. This locked-bathroom mishap will be her argument for dumping Mom in a home. She'd be right. It's the perfect reason.

That's why she'll never find out.

The glass door slides. I'm getting ready to ram the door, but my legs go rubbery and I slide down the wall. My chin falls into my chest, heavy. She's still in danger, but I feel as though I'm watching a movie. The edges of the door seem fake, hollow. Then again, I'm hollow too.

I sit there until I feel heat drifting into my face.

As though the director crosscut to another scene, Mom is standing in the doorway. Steam curls around her. She's naked. Her pale skin is shiny. An orange hand-towel sits on her head. Yeah, tonight could've gone better.

I heave myself off the floor. "How'd you get out of the bathroom?"

She shrugs. "I wasn't in the bathroom."

At least she's okay. I say, "Right."

We wait. I'm not expecting her to realize that she locked herself in the bathroom. I'm simply waiting for her to step aside. She stands there, a tableau, naked and clueless. I say, "Excuse me." I squeeze past her and gather her soaked robe off the floor and drape it over her shoulders. I clutch her wrist and slip her arms through the sleeve. I'm not wrestling with her nightshirt. She'll sleep like this tonight.

She says, "This room has a shower, yeah?"

"The door even locks, Mom." I hold her hand, shriveled and frail and damp, feeling even smaller than an hour ago, and lead her into her room.

We walk to the dresser's side of her bed. Mom says, "I'm lying down?"

"That's the plan." I stand there, listening to her breathing. As she inhales there's that familiar click, from all those years of smoking. She's still here. She's okay. I say, "You remember how to get in?"

"Think I don't know beds?"

I say, "Show me, then."

She places her hands flat against her thighs and timbers backwards, in that trust exercise way, and only her waist hits the mattress. Her legs are pin straight, feet together, heels digging into the carpet. She slides, slowly, steadily, the blankets crumpling around her. I really don't want to touch body parts a son shouldn't be touching. (As if seeing her naked is fine.) I search for a flailing arm, an easy shoulder, to grab. She plops onto the floor. She says, "I can't sleep like this."

"No shit, Mom. Come on."

"Stop cursing, cockknocker." Her arms are straight over her head. I grab her hands and heave. She's leaden weight. She falls, banging into the mattress.

I let go of her hands. I say, "Can't you try?"

She wriggles her hand underneath her breast and gives the curve of her belly a flicky-fingered scratch. "Try what?"

"The Macarena." I point. "Getting into bed."

She snorts. "That's not my bed."

I press my wrist against my forehead. Yelling will make this escalate. Besides, this isn't her fault. She doesn't understand. I say, "Please, give me your hands."

"Will I get them back?"

"Yes." I grab her wrists, lean forward and then tilt back and heave. I say, "Mom stand." My thighs shake. My forearms burn. Her body starts to lift. "Keep going, keep at it," I say, rooting for myself.

I slide my arms into her robe for a better grip. I feel the folds of bare skin. Her breasts press against my stomach. Her breath smells like shampoo. I try to ignore her physicality. I squat and lift until her hips are higher than the mattress, then flop her into the bed as though she were a sack of concrete dust.

She is lying across the bed, but her feet are hanging off the side of the mattress. I say, "Don't move." I grip her calves and slide her legs onto the mattress, her body shifting in a fluid, almost cartoonish motion, until she is vertical, head below the headboard. I close her robe and knot the belt three times. Winded, I lean against the dresser.

Mom is laying on her back as she stares at the ceiling. She says, "Comfy."

I wipe sweat off my forehead. "It's comfy, alright."

I watch her watch the ceiling. I feel this shaky, overwhelmed feeling, a kind of grief for what is happening to her, our situation, all these lingering, horrible choices that I'm being pressured into making. I've failed her in ways that I can't even verbalize. In ways that, in her condition, she wouldn't understand.

She says, "Nice room."

The bathroom fiasco has already been erased. It seems impossible, but it's true.

Play, Rewind.

I say, "Only the best for you."

"That's my boy. My good boy."

Look: here's the good boy who can't let her go. I say, barely audible, "I'm trying to be, Mom. I'm really trying."

"Try what?"

"Nothing, Mom."

"Good. Cause I think I'm tired."

Maybe tonight was just a hard lesson, letting me know what happens when I break her routine. If I keep to Mom's schedule, there's no chance of this happening again. Gloria even said it, right? Routine is good. I was being greedy. Stuck in our past life. This will never happen again. Tomorrow if Gloria asks why she's not dressed, I'll tell her that Mom must've undressed while I was sleeping. Either way, she'll argue for placing Mom into a home again. I hate the word 'home.' This is her home, whether she knows it or not.

I say, "Want to hear a joke?" A train clacks past on the El. "What's the best part of dementia?"

She grabs the sides of her blanket and folds it over her, burrito-like.

"Give up? You can hide your own Easter eggs."

Mom says, "That's terrible. Make fun of sick people." She sucks her teeth. "God, I hope that never happens to me."

CHAPTER 6

I place my knapsack onto the shag carpet and sit on the edge of my bed, the springs creaking. The rush of adrenaline has drained, so now I'm exhausted. In the next room, I hear my mother snoring, as though she's a quiet elderly woman who would never lock herself in a bathroom.

I stare at a knot in the paneling that's shaped like a parrot. A loose bundle of clothes leads to the wicker hamper, its cymbal-shaped cover half open, choking with towels. Between work and Mom, there's no time to clean.

There's a lot to be upset about tonight, but one moment sticks out more than the rest. I stab around between the mattress and box-spring for the 8x6 photo. The edges are curved. Along the top, the celluloid's peeled.

In the picture my father is wearing a jean jacket and bell-bottom pants. He's hunched towards me so that his handlebar mustache grazes my cheek. I'm holding a plastic bat, its barrel large and red. A layer of dead leaves carpets the grass. I don't know my age. My mother probably took the photo. I'm not smiling. I search for a hidden rage in his face. He seems happy enough. For a second I endure my mother's illness. I see evidence of the world but there is no memory or even understanding attached to it; I'm only conjuring a blank space.

When I was younger I'd go to friends' houses. It was always the same: me and Joey Silva, Vince Parker, or Lou Defano would hustle towards the stairs to play a slew of Tecmo Bowl, but were stopped short by their fathers, who'd beckon us into the room. Their fathers, bricklayers, plumbers, truck drivers, sagged in their recliners, the leather reeking of stale smoke playing counterpoint to fresh beer. If the fathers weren't too drunk, they'd heave themselves up for forced games of two-hand touch. If they were drunk, the fathers would grill us about girls, their eyes greedy and desperate. I'd stand there in the living-room, counting the lumps in the flowered wallpaper as my friend answered quickly, yet respectfully enough, for us to flee. After my third visit or so, my friends had told their fathers about my family situation. Lou's dad offered to teach me how to ride a bike. Vince's father herded us into the bathroom for a shaving lesson. I was twelve. I didn't have facial hair. I didn't want another father. If I'd aligned myself with these men, I'd have been betraying my own.

I realized that my friends hated their fathers, too. They'd talk about how their fathers punched them off of kitchen chairs for a tone of voice, or how they were dragged down the stairs by their ankles while trying to escape their beating. Vince even let me run my hand along his crew cut so I could feel the small dent in his skull left by his father's high-school ring. He said, "Everyone should learn to take a punch." I caught the judgment in his voice. If being abused by a parent made you tougher, then it was assumed that having an absent father meant that I was weaker. So I said "But does your dad have to teach you?" Vince stared at me, his eyes watery. Even if he hated his father, he still had to defend him. He charged. We were rolling around the floor fighting until his dad busted in. He ripped Vince off of me, a smile on his face, proud his son was winning. He made us apologize, then he sat on the bed and held out his palms. "Wrists straight. With your sissy punches, you'd fight all week until my son won." Vince never invited me to his house again.

I stare at the photo. I'm uncovering a past confessed to me through a jigsaw of hallucinations. Did I know her at all? Or maybe if she had confessed to me about his violence, she'd have to answer for her own paralysis? I shimmy the picture in the center of the bed platform. Once again, my father vanishes. I feel this revving in my chest, my heart refusing to make a pit stop.

I know what to do. I unzip my bag and take the tape.

I kneel in front of the television and open the cabinet doors. Inside are my movies. My private collection (as though they're rare bottles of wine): the *Star Wars* trilogy, all of Kubrick's movies, *The Godfather*, *The Deer Hunter*, *Poltergeist*, John Carpenter's *The Thing* and *Big Trouble in Little China*, *Bicycle Thieves*, *Wild Strawberries*, *Vertigo*, *Elevator to the Gallows*. I've experienced these movies so many times the tapeheads squeak; I talk the lines with the actors as though I'm on screen, or better, we're talking to each other. I've memorized their barely perceptible facial tics and audible inflections. They're closer than family.

But not tonight.

A dubbing machine resembles a VCR but it has two decks, one for the video, one for the copy. I stick the tape into the player and the machine beeps to life. I grab a blank tape next to my cabinet, peel the plastic, and stick the video into the slot of the machine. I hit Rewind, count to ten and let the tape play.

The camera is pointing into a pool formed by craggy rock. On the other side of the barrier is the ocean. The pool is about nine feet across. The water shimmers pale except where it's shadowed by the rock. He says, "This is amazing." At first, I think he's talking to me, but a woman's voice says, "Wonderful." The wind whips across the microphone, then she says, "I can't believe we're doing this, Greg." I wait for him to turn the lens on her, but he pans slightly along the rocks. The ocean is darker, rougher, the peaks cresting on the swells. A wave crashes, spraying water into the pool. She says, "We're the only couple here." I lean so close that my nose fizzes from the charge of the screen. "Show me, Greg." The lens follows a large white bird, its neck ropey and white. The camera drops to eye level. I see her. She's sitting on the edge of the rocks, staring into the pool. Her hair is blond, darker towards the center. Her back is thin and muscular. She's wearing a pink bikini. He says, "Sarah, jump in." She shakes her head no but doesn't turn around. I say, "Sarah," the words soft and sibilant, as though mumbling a quiet prayer.

He says, "You want to head back?"

I slap my leg. "Why would you do that, Greg?"

She runs her hand through her hair, her arm muscles flexing. I imagine her as someone who jogs through Central Park, keeping track of the miles she's put on each pair of sneakers. I imagine she's watching me watching her from the pool. I'm there as much as they are there.

Greg says, "Hey babe, what are you thinking?"

I wait for her to say my name.

She says, "This," then rolls forward and dives into the water.

He places the camera on the rock, leaving the power on—thank you for that—and stumbles to the edge. He's wearing a pink tank and purple swimsuit. Vacation clothes. He takes off his shirt and drops it on the rock. He has black hair, a slight taper in his torso, as though he bikes or runs, but just enough to maintain his weight. When he jumps, the water sprays the lens. The camera films the other side of the rocks. A boat passes. Splashing, laughing, then quiet. The camera goes black. Their battery died. I'm winded like I was the one swimming. I eject the tape, slip it out of the dubbing machine, place it on the carpet. The tape feels precious, a gift. Watching this tape has made me the happiest I've been in the last forty-eight hours.

Hearing Sarah talk reminds me of that phone call today, which reminds me of Lola. During our senior year in high school, we shared a few classes: Math, English, Art. Lola's last name is Sclafani and mine is Viola, so our desks were in alphabetical proximity. Meaning, I'd cheat off her in Math. During English, I'd watch her scrawl curling vines along the trestle of her wrist. After Art, we'd hike to Leo's Pizza for their lunch specials, two grandma Sicilians and a fountain drink for three bucks. I'd give her one of my slices. She never had enough money to buy her own. We'd split a fruit punch. Her brown lipstick left a kiss on the straw. Other times, we'd take our lunch to the park. We'd sit on the rotted border of the bocce court. She'd draw fish in the sand. We'd talk about movies, or Lola would tell me about applying to graphic design programs, but mostly we sat in silence, our legs touching, as we listened to the "A" train clack towards Manhattan, less than an hour but a lifetime away. Just two borough kids hoping to make it work in some way.

Here's a list: she chewed with her mouth open. She read comic books; *Swamp Thing*, *Tank Girl*, and *Batman* were her favorite. She had curly brown hair. Her laugh would start high then drop a minor third. She was proud of being a lefty. She'd stick unicorn stickers on her binders. She was all about painting and drawing.

Each day before lunch, I promised myself I'd ask her to hang out on the weekend. I decided that I'd ask her after our graduation ceremony. But she disappeared the last week of school. During our ceremony I searched the bleachers as if she'd appear. I wished our school had left an empty chair onstage in case she had changed her mind. A few days later, I looked up her address, an apartment across from the same Catholic school where later I'd find my mother. Lola had lived less than ten blocks away from my house and I'd never asked her to hang out. It really bothered me. I wanted to ring her bell, but I was afraid of rejection. Sometimes when Video Planet was extra slow, I'd lean against the counter, thinking about graduation and our time together with a deep longing. The truest friend I had. Of course there was always this desperate hope that she'd call.

And now, she possibly did call. It sounded so much like her. Lola's fast talk, her nervous laugh. Who else could it be?

I lift my phone off my empty milk crate and place it on my bed. It's one of those clear phones with the blue neon light that runs along the bottom. I switch it on and the glow ebbs along my covers, a pattern of waves. Wading pools fluttering with fish. Tomorrow if she calls, I'm going to be confident, funny. More like Greg. Maybe Mike Myers in *Austin Powers*: Yeeeeaahhh baby. Nope, too corny. Nicholson, from *As Good as it Gets*: You make me want to be a better man. No, she'll think I'm a bastard. Cruise in *Jerry Maguire*: You complete me. Too strong? Daniel Day Lewis in *Last of the Mohicans*: Stay alive, I will find you. Too urgent. Gina Gershon in

Bound: Know the difference between you and me? Me neither. Nope, too cool.

Here's something I do know: if she calls back, I'm asking her to meet me.

That's what she wants, obviously. I trace the light with my finger. Lola sitting on those craggy rocks, gazing into the pool. She said she'd call. She's going to call.

I realize I'm praying this aloud. She's going to call. Call. Just call. Please.

CHAPTER 7

For the first time ever, I'm late opening Video Planet.

I swerve the Cutlass around a garbage truck, the balding tires chirping higher than the scraping brake-pads, yet lower than the screeching belts. Last night icy rain pelted the ground, so the streets are slick and shiny, as though a film crew had sprayed water on the concrete to catch more reflective light. I speed down Liberty Avenue until the Pinto in front of me jams on its brakes. Our bumpers stop inches away from their metallic smooch. I'm stuck at a red light.

This morning, I'd set my alarm extra early. I knew it was going to be a struggle to finesse Mom into morning appropriate clothing, even if it was simply peeling off her robe for a dry nightgown. The one from last night was still damp from the water on the bathroom floor. I tried to solve how she had the sense to lock the bathroom door, get undressed, and turn on the shower. Mom's abilities spark on and off are like a misfiring engine, stubborn and unpredictable. Maybe it was some kind of muscle memory? Shadow routines that still cling to repetitive tasks? I'm not a neurologist. I'm only her son. So as her son, I rummaged through her dresser and fetched her another nightie. I found one with the same boring pattern of splotchy roses. I opened her hamper and scooped the dirty clothes, then ditched yesterday's gown into the hamper, as though I were Anthony Perkins hiding his mother's crimes. Usually, I let her sleep until Gloria arrived, but I had to dress her. I opened the blinds, letting the light in. I shook her leg, "Mom. Rise and shine." Not a twitch. I poked her shoulder. She was lying on top of her blankets, her arms at her sides. I thought: This is how she'll look in her casket. For a second I did think she was dead, but then her mouth dropped open, slowly as though on hinges.

I said, "Mom, time to get up."

She glanced around the room, her face pale and froggish. "I'm late?"

"Sorry," I said, "I just got up too."

I folded the lapels of her robe and heaved her up. Mom sat on the edge of her bed. I closed my eyes, slipped off her robe. I turned towards the window, made sure the nightgown faced the collar forward, then shut my eyes and slipped it over her head. By some small mercy, she remembered how to slide her arms through the sleeves. She said, "Hungry? I'll make breakfast."

I say, "No, just lay down a bit."

Without arguing, she plopped down onto her side. I waited until she started snoring and I closed the blinds and snuck out of the room.

Back in my bedroom, I was lulled by the VCR, its shiny silver face, and its hieroglyphic button pad. I didn't have time for new footage, so I hit Rewind and watched the same old bits for what felt like ten minutes, but when I looked again, the time was ten minutes past when Video Planet needed to open. I scooped the clothes from yesterday, dressed, and hustled into the Cutlass. The only grace of being late was that Gloria didn't have time to confront me about placing Mom in a home. Last night I thought I'd rekindle enough past to help her be in the present. Snap out of it. But I failed. I always fail.

I miss her.

A horn beeps and I'm still on Liberty Avenue. I speed along and cut the corner and pull into the spot in front of the store. At least, I think it's the store. The sidewalk is swept. Even the lights of the display windows are blinking and alive. I'm trapped inside *The Truman Show*. Does someone care enough to watch me stumble through my days? I search the storefront for a concealed camera and then shut the Cutlass.

Instead of the stench of decaying mice, Video Planet smells like lemon-scented bleach. The video boxes are dusted. The ancient plastic covers have been replaced. The boxes on the racks are facing outwards for easy viewing. I joined a few years after Video Planet opened, so it was always grubby Video Planet. This is how the store's first day must've looked. Clean, filled with promise. Until today, cleaning the store was an impossible dream. Dom refused to splurge on supplies. I was forced to use sour-smelling mops. Brooms with their corn bristles angled and short and black. Windex cut with water. Yet here's Video Planet: scrubbed and swept, primed and eager for customers. Yes. I'm in a movie.

As I walk toward him, Dom leans against the counter, watching me. I wait for him to dismantle me about how I never perked Video Planet up so nice, or for being late, or for both. I say, "Were you visited by three ghosts?"

He points towards the wall, mumbles, "Nope. Just one."

From behind the rack, I hear a squeaky, "Watch it."

It's Vic. Whatever happened yesterday must've been sorted out. They're together. As I walk past Vic, he pats me on the back, gently, paternally. He's happy to see me. I walk around the counter and place my knapsack underneath the chair. I take videos off the column near the register. I say, "The store looks great."

Dom says, "Yeah. Only cost me blood, B.O., and ball sweat."

Vic says, "Relax, huh?" He's wearing a red sweatshirt and slacks. His hair is combed to the side, the part as wide as my pinky. Using his thumb, he pushes his boxy glasses against his forehead. He could be Charlie Scorsese, performing a bit part for one of his son's movies. Though with Charlie there's a softness, a concealed smile. Vic looks as jovial as a rhino-bear wrestling with a weeklong bout of constipation. Sadly, it's the look we all have after spending too much time around Dom. Vic says, "We been open an hour. You okay?"

The word *We* blinks, red and strange. Stranger still, he asked me how I was doing. Nobody ever asks me that, especially here. I say, "Thanks. I'm ready to work."

Dom says, "If you're saying it. Guess I gotta believe it." He's wearing a jean-shirt with the first three buttons undone, revealing the gold cross entangled in his chest hair. A pair of red sweatpants. His face sags. He looks washed-out, stressed. Maybe Dom actually paid Vic and now they're simply hanging out? Maybe Vic gave Dom his gun back? Maybe he's returning *Pocahontas*?

I switch out the box for *Big Night*.

Vic points an arthritic finger at Dom. He shakes his head. Vic tells him to do it. Dom says nope. Vic says, "Then I'll say it. You're in charge, kid. Of Dom too."

Dom holds up his hands. "'Till things straighten out."

I say, "Sorry...you mean that I'm the manager?"

Vic says, "Yup. I can read people, kid. You got an easy way. Got to be..." (He juts his chin at Dom.) "...dealing with Mr. Fun everyday."

Dom says, "Hey, I'm fun!"

"How about it?" Vic says.

If I'm the manager and something goes wrong, then I'll have to answer both Vic and Dom, who even if I am in charge, will never stop berating me. Plus I'll be dragged into whatever nonsense is going on. I say, "It's a lot of responsibility." Great. A fib. "With my mom and all."

I start to drift toward the counter door, but Dom grabs my wrist and mumbles, "Help me out."

This is another dimension. Dom just admitted he needs me. I exhale, then say, "What do I have to do?"

"Your job." Vic reaches into his pocket. "End of the night, take your pay, then put the rest in here. Do a good job, I'll give you a raise." He places the envelope on the counter. It's wrinkled, folded in half. The corner has a coffee stain. He gives it a pat as though it's a trophy. Vic must be in charge now if Dom isn't even counting his closing totals. He shifts down the aisle. "Favor. *Cinderella* comes in, put it on the side. I'll get coffee. For the two of us, anyway." He walks out the front door, probably to Tubby's.

Dom waits until he's clear out of sight to give him the finger. "Die of crotch-rot you fucking hump!" I just wanted to watch the footage until that girl, possibly Lola, called me. Now I'm babysitting Dom, who says, "Move your car! Blocking my customers."

"They're my customers now. What's happening?"

He drops into his mother's chair, his knee clicking. Settled, he runs his finger alongside the seat, as though he is trying to conjure her back to this temporal plain. It never happens. At least, not the way you want. I wait. He says, "The Royal thing."

I think of the clipping above the toilet. How he was crowing. And now I get it. "So you're the one who called the cops."

He picks lint off the seat, flicks it.

I go on. "And Vic owns it?"

"Just a piece. I didn't know."

"And now he's taking over this place."

"Just a slice." Dom watches me with the face you make when you realize that your car has been stolen but are still clutching to the fleeting hope that the guy will cut the corner and give it back. "Until I pay him down."

"How much do you have to pay for his store being raided?"

"Yeah," Dom sighs. "I should probably get him to clarify that."

I pinch the bridge of my nose. He's giving me what I call a Mom Headache. I plan my exit strategy. I can apply to Food Town, even Blockbuster, which would feel like I was slumming hard. It's an okay plan, but finding a new job could take me weeks. Mom's bills will be late. I would still need money for the medications that Mom's insurance doesn't cover. Even if I pretend I'm sincere about sticking Mom into a home, Gloria can't work for free. I'm trapped here.

"So, what, he's like, connected or whatever?" I can't believe it.

"Ehhhh." He gives a shrug that could mean many things.

"So am I in danger?"

"Let's put it this way. I'm not, like, *worried* worried."

"Then why let him do this?"

"If nothing else, he knows I got bootlegs. He can call a raid on my store." He tilts forward, exhaling, holding his knees, until he stands.

This is the type of cockeyed situation only Dom could find himself in. I tell myself I have nothing to worry about. I didn't call the cops.

Dom says, "It's a misunderstanding. Life knocks you down, get back on the donkey."

"Don't you mean horse?"

"You ride what you like. I'll ride what I like."

He laughs. I don't.

Dom says, "Be back."

"Where are you going?"

"Hey, you're the manager. Manage."

He walks past the shelves and into the back room. The door slams. I'm alone.

I glance around. There's nothing for me to do. The store is clean. The column of returns has disappeared. Video Planet has finally reached its full potential. It only took Vic to pressure (or whatever) Dom to do it. When Dom comes back, I'll tell him he can't leave. If I'm left to manage, then I'm going to manage.

Before I can truly relax, this guy swings open the door and walks the aisle. He's wearing a peacoat and sweatpants. The brim of his Yankees' cap is pushed to the side. As he gets closer I see it's Rich, this real pain in the ass who hasn't been here since Royal shut down. Now he's back. Lucky me.

Rich raises his arms like he wants to hug me. "There he is!" He wheels his arms as he shuffles back and forth. He shimmies to the counter. One-part cha-cha to two-parts "Where the hell did I put my keys?" He does his snappy-pointy thing. "Whaddaya know?"

"Not much."

"Least you know that, right?" He smiles and his front teeth are missing. "Got *Platoon*?"

I pull the movie. I slide it across the counter.

"Gotta see my doctor about the SSI disability from 'Nam." He straightens. "Gonna replay this mother till zonkers rings my bell like I'm stuck in that tiger cage."

"If that's your plan, why not rent them all? *Hamburger Hill*, *Full Metal Jacket*, *Apocalypse Now*, *The Deer Hunter*. Really blast off?"

"Sold." He sticks his tongue through that gummy space. "You're alright."

I grab the movies and stack them on the counter. "Trying to be."

He says, "There is no try. Do or do not." He holds out his hand as though trying to levitate my X-wing from a murky bog. He says, in a familiar alien cadence: "Yoda, that is!"

"I could tell."

He slaps his thigh. "Talking cock-eyed reminds me of my brother Bob."

"Big *Star Wars* fan?"

Rich says, "Nah, he got hit in the head with a pipe wrench and went dyslexic."

I don't catch his comparison. "That's unfortunate."

"Ah, a hump, he is!" He hands me the money.

I ring him up, waiting to hear a comment about Royal's cheaper prices. Finally I say: "Good luck with your freakout."

"Hey, thanks for that," he says, then cha-chas down the lane and out the door.

I wait for Dom to appear. A customer. Vic.

After I've waited long enough, I take the movie out of my bag. I feel guilty, like I'm doing something perverted. But what? This isn't really spying or peeping.

The video was left here for me to copy. I place my hand close to the television screen and the static fuzz billows against my palm. I have this awful thought that Greg will pop in and tell me he wants his tape back. I hope not.

The mystery of the tape heightens its value. I curl my toes into the sandy beach, with no desire to swim to the end. I hit Play, Rewind, so I can watch the beginning again. Next time I need a vacation, I'll watch it again. Then again. And again. Again. Again. Again. Again. Again. Again. Again. Again. Again. Again. Again.

CHAPTER 8

There's a videotape placed on my front stoop.

The tape is standing upright, teetering on the edge of the cracked concrete. At first I think it's my beloved copy, a possessed item that materializes when I least expect it. Deciding to check that I'm not living in an episode of *The Twilight Zone*, I twist my backpack in front of me and feel for the footage. It's still there, of course. I watch the halo of streetlights, the parked cars. A cold breeze shakes the phone lines, the gust still clinging to its winter's chill.

I sling my backpack onto my shoulder and grab the tape off the step. It's *Memento*, a movie that I've never brought home. Maybe someone found the tape and knows I work at Video Planet? I press the button and open the flaps. The tape looks fine. Out of habit, I stick my finger in one of the reels to wind the tape taut and feel something inside. I flip the tape over. There is a piece of paper, folded into a tiny cube taped into place. It's a note written in red ink. *Check the yard.* The words are bookmarked by a pair of tiny hearts, though it feels like the opposite of love. Dom wouldn't bother with games. Vic doesn't care about me. There's only one other person: the person that Gloria saw yesterday morning. I want to go inside and lock the door, but I can't ignore this note. What if they grab Gloria when she leaves? I watch the row of parked cars. Nothing. The paper smells like a cherry Tootsie Pop. Would a killer eat candy? No, but kids would.

The living room light switches on and I flinch, startled. Gloria must've seen me out front. She's in there getting her sensible jacket. This feeling of dread twitches inside my chest. Now that she's pressuring me to put Mom into a home, encountering Gloria feels just as hazardous as checking the yard. She kept telling me to "be realistic," but I'm tired of this reality. I want to fly away from Dom's bootlegs and Vic's blitzkrieg of Video Planet. I want to avoid Gloria and her nursing homes. I want tropical islands, honey-tanned couples. I want a healthy mother.

A cold wind blows past, twirling the pair of sneakers hanging from the phone lines. It's best to check.

I step away from the stoop. The way back is a long concrete path, the size of a sidewalk, between us and our neighbors.

I'm so tired of this X-Files bullshit. The yard will be empty, and I'll feel like an idiot. I wait, searching for movement, but the only source of light is from our windows and our neighbors', and it isn't much. (My neighbor always watches television in the dark, and Gloria turns off the lights she's not using.) Now it feels like the alley in *Fright Night*, or the stairs in *The Exorcist*. Every horror movie I've ever seen is screaming at me: GO INTO THE YARD AND IT'S YOUR ASS.

Still, I follow slasher logic and walk back there. I'm swallowed by darkness. My neighbor's television blasts the news. As I walk past, I see the crown of his balding head. I reach the edge of the house. I stop. The line of bushes cast shadows across the yard. Wind rustles the shrubbery. I step into the middle of the yard.

A train clacks past.

"Look, I've had a bad day! So. If you're going to decorate your sneakers with my molars and fingernails, do it already."

I hear a muffled laugh. It is a bunch of kids, I'm sure of it.

I raise the tape like it's a broadsword. "Show yourself."

On cue, someone steps out from between the bushes. They're wearing jeans and a hooded sweatshirt and a pair of maroon-colored Doc Martens. "Are you surprised?" the voice says.

She sounds like the one who called me on the phone. Then again, I'm scared. Maybe that's wishful thinking. "I'm calling the police. Surprise them."

"Do you like that movie? It's one of my favorites."

I edge toward the pathway and say, "Okay."

"Nice house. I live in an apartment. Barely enough room for me and Mother."

Does that mean she's taking care of her mother? I think of last night. The quiet drudgery of an ailing loved one. "Glad you like it, but you're trespassing."

"You know me." She gives me a thumbs up.

"Then take off your hood."

"Come here."

"You're kidding, right? You just snuck out of my foliage!"

She turns toward the shrubbery. "I guess it is weird, right? Still, we talked already!"

We did talk. Her voice confirms it, but still, she's the one skulking around my backyard. I say, "Take off your hood. Or I'm not moving."

"Meet me halfway?" She holds up her hand. "Wait. This reminds me of a joke. Why didn't the skeleton cross the road?" She steps towards me. "He didn't have the balls!"

The joke is so stupid, I laugh. I should call the police, but I can't. I think it's her laugh that I'm softening to. It's familiar. "If you're who I think you are, today has truly been a strange day."

She steps toward me. "Strange is good."

I say, "Sometimes," which is true.

"Okay, then. Strange will come to you."

She walks across the yard, her arms crossed, a steady pace, but not a hazardous rush. It's self-aware, cautious, as though she's traversing a forest. She stops when we're inches apart and takes off her hood. "Surprise!" Before I can say her name, she hugs me. I squirm, but she squeezes. She smells like Chapstick and fries.

I struggle free. It really *is* Lola, though a punkier version. Instead of the curly black hair she wore in high school, her head is buzzed. She has a line of hoop earrings rising around the curve of her left ear, a silver stud underneath her lip. Her cheeks are knobby points jutting from her thin face. She's Ripley in *Alien 3*. We watch each other, a fuzzy static between us. I've spent a long time thinking about why we never saw each other again, and now she's here hiding in my yard. I have so many questions, but my head is a blank video cassette.

I say, "Hey, I guessed right."

"I was nervous."

I touch her hand to convince myself that she's really here. What the romantic comedies call a "first touch," only this isn't the first time. In high school we'd hold hands, bump shoulders, share straws. Hell, she even chewed the piece of blueberry gum I was chewing after I told her it was my last piece. But that was eight years ago.

She grabs my hand and squeezes as though no time had passed; her fingers are cold, yet this familiar warmth fills my chest. She says, "I'm sorry for that."

"How long have you been out here?"

A train clacks past on the El. "About twelve 'A's." She smiles. "I was going to ring the bell, but that lady moved past the window. So I decided to leave you the tape instead of giving it to you. Sorry if that's weird."

"Why didn't you go to Video Planet? Evidently you know I work there."

"Good plan. But I did this."

In high school, one of my favorite things about Lola was how she talked. Her sentences were a series of pauses and rushes, her vowels elongated, her verb endings snipped. Her words built velocity. Listening to her talk helps me believe that she's here more than seeing her does, or even touching her hand. How long will she stay? I need to go inside, but I'm afraid this will end up like our graduation. I hear a tapping. Gloria is watching us from my mother's window. I wave. "Come in for a second."

Lola says, "She looked scary."

"No, she's really nice. A nurse. She takes care of my mom."

"I don't trust nurses. Even nice ones. I'll wait."

I glance at the dead grass slanting toward the garage. I say, "Here."

She nods.

"Okay. Coming right back. Don't flee." I jog back up front and go around the house. The door is open, an arrow of yellow light shooting down the steps, and I get this cheesy feeling, as though the light is a happy future being unlocked for me.

When I get inside, Gloria is waiting in the living room, her arms crossed. She's already wearing her jacket, her pocketbook resting on her shoulder. She looks annoyed, or maybe she's just tired. She says, "Who was that?"

"It's an old friend. From school."

"If she's a friend, why didn't she ring the doorbell?"

It's a good question. She's always been a bit wonky. Harmless, but wonky. I can't explain a two-year friendship in two minutes. So she snuck into the yard to surprise me. It's silly, a bit unnerving, if you don't know her, but it's only Lola. "She wants to take a walk. Catch up."

"I really need to go home, Wesley." Behind her, my mother laughs. Then, silence.

"I know. Please, like, twenty minutes!"

She unzips her coat. "Ten."

I rush to the door.

"Wait."

I turn.

"Your mother had a very bad day. She refused to eat. I thought maybe she'd drink a malted, just for calories. She threw the glass."

"Did it break?"

"That's not the point." She fiddles with her jacket zipper. "She kept talking about Atlantic City. Searching her bag for the fake money."

I nod, feigning surprise. "I'm sorry."

"And what happened to the bathroom door? The knob is loose."

That's right. I'd meant to double-check it, but then became so absorbed with the video that I'd forgotten. "It fell off."

"Knobs don't fall off."

"Ours do."

"Unless you screw them off."

I was right. Gloria is more hazardous than the yard. "I'll fix it. I promise."

"Did she lock herself in?" Her questions feel very Columbo-like. She feigns ignorance and waits for me to crack.

I shift towards the door. She knows, she definitely knows. I say, "Of course not," trying to keep my voice steady, soft. I realize this is the first time I've ever lied to her and it feels awful.

She nods, unconvinced, but I think she wants to leave more than she wants to flip me into a confession. "Ten minutes. Please."

I nod.

"Tomorrow we have to talk more. If your Mom locked herself in the bathroom, that's really dangerous."

"I know! I mean, she didn't lock herself in. I mean...I know. About talking." Before she completely flips me, I open the door and hustle down the steps.

I stop midway back to the yard. I cup my hands and sniff my breath, then slick my hair back with my palms. I wish I would've showered. Whatever, we're just walking. I'll get her number, address. I'll make plans. PLANS! Yes, I'm really doing this. I step into the yard.

"Hey. Back. Sorry I took so long." The wind rustles the bushes. "Lola?"

Of course she's gone. Run, Lola, Run.

I lean against the fence and stare up at the sky, as if I'll see a star, as if the heavens shine down on people like me.

CHAPTER 9

The streetlight from outside shines into Mom's bedroom, casting white bars along her comforter. I look out the window, checking the yard. There's no guarantee that Lola will reappear, but why would she hide in my yard, only to not re-reappear?

Once I'd realized that she had vanished, I'd ran out to the sidewalk, hoping I'd spot her. She was gone. Then when I opened the fence to go inside, Gloria stepped onto the stoop. I told her that Lola had to leave and that I'd see her tomorrow. She walked down the steps and patted my shoulder in a way that said, "I doubt it," although that could've been my frustration with Lola's re-disappearance. We stood there until Gloria asked me about a nursing home. I said, "I'll tell you soon." She said, "How soon?" as though we had missed our opportunity. But I need time. It takes me an hour to choose what movie I want to watch.

Anyway, when I didn't answer, she hurried past me. She shut the gate and said, "See you tomorrow," but it felt like she was telling me her tomorrows weren't infinite.

Now, I'm with Mom.

She's sleeping on her back, her arms placed at her sides. She looks quiet, peaceful. Her head is slightly raised from the double pillows, propping her up. When she's asleep it's easy to forget how much trouble she is when she's awake.

Before Mom got sick, I dreamed of having my script bought by a major production company. After the record-breaking deal was done, I'd rush into our house, waving the contract until I found her in the kitchen, cooking anything but lentils. Whooping and hollering, I'd pick her up and spin her around the room like we were in a Frank Capra movie. I'd tell her in a slightly arrogant tone how the producers had recognized my genius and agreed to my terms. Of course she'd be impressed, but also proud. She'd even feel lucky to have me for a son, which is all I've ever wanted from her. And best of all, I'd tell her we'd never have to worry about money any more.

But in real life, the problem is money, again and again.

Even with insurance, I'd never make enough money to cover the remaining balance of a nursing home. Then there's her medicines, her medi-van taxis to Dr. Adler. OT, PT, speech therapy, blood-pressure, stool samples. Any deviation in her breathing or heart-rate or hearing or eyesight will mean more tests, which means more money. The nurse, or whoever, will say, "Of course your mom is safe. Here's the bill." If you're unable to pay, you obviously don't love her.

Mom opens her eyes, sees me and smiles, then falls back asleep. Okay. I'll admit the truth: I'm worried Mom will have a moment of clarity and realize that I've dumped her into a home. It has happened before.

After Gloria helped me find Dr. Adler, we had to do an EEG test to check if seizures were the cause of her confusion. It wasn't a scan, where they flop you onto a plank and run you through the machine. No, Mom had to wear a cloth cap covered in electrodes which measured her brainwaves. The cap was a cross between the helmet Egon fits onto Louis Tully so he can see the Keymaster's hellhound form in *Ghostbusters*, and the bras Lewis and Wyatt stick onto their heads in *Weird Science*. The doctor said I could take her home; in order to get an accurate reading, she just needed to wear the cap for three days straight. But after three hours, she tossed it onto our carpet and said, "My hair is dry now."

The next morning, they refitted the cap.

Two hours later, she pulled it off.

I brought her back to Dr. Adler, who decided to admit Mom into Columbia-Presbyterian for the duration of the test. Mom pulled the cap off twice, each time extending her stay. After she tried to leave her room to play the slots, the nurses stuck her in isolation. The isolation room had green walls and white tiled floors that smelled like lemon-scented wax. There was a television on a rotating arm that stretched over her bed, a clock radio, and a flesh-colored phone. The room had two doors, both medically heavy, with glass inlays and white frames. The first door opened into a small vestibule with cabinets, a sink and a coat rack, and a padded chair. The next door led into the bathroom. Her window faced the George Washington Bridge. The cliffs of New Jersey. It was early fall, so the trees were shifting in color. At night the lights along the bridge's towers burned white and cold.

The nurses had tethered Mom's wrists with cuffs made from Velcro that had straps around the railings, restraining her hands to the bed in a prisoner-like way.

I wasn't the only one there. Mom also had Gail, a nurse-aid who sat in the vestibule. Gail changed Mom's hospital gown and made sure Mom didn't rip off her cap when she was taken out of her restraints to go to the bathroom. Gail would hum songs, which might've been hymns, but mostly she fiddled with her phone. In the morning, I'd buy her coffee (milk and six sugars) and a donut (chocolate with sprinkles). Partly, I hoped my breakfast offering would make Gail soften towards my mother, who cursed constantly, but mostly I wanted her to like me. Sometimes while my mother slept, I'd creep into the vestibule and tell Gail about growing up in Queens, hoping she'd tell me about growing up in the Bahamas.

The doctors made their rounds at six in the morning, when I wasn't there. They'd explain to her their initial assessments, possible medications. It was ridiculous. I started sleeping on the green cushioned-chair next to her bed so I could be there when they arrived. Mom refused to 'enjoy herself,' which meant no television. We sat in her room for hours, doing nothing.

The only change in our routine was her meals. On our fourth day, I wheeled the tray in front of her. I taped the tan lid that covered the plate. I knew how this would go. Still, I said, "What do you think it is?"

"Eggplant rollatini." She bit her lip. "No, spaghetti carbonara. No, pork chop pizzaiola. Anything but fish. Like a cheesy barf in my throat. That fucking fish."

I opened the lid. It was a slab of fish filet soaked in buttery sauce.

"What is it?" She tried to sit up, but her cuffs held her back and she flopped down onto the pillows. "Fish? I can smell it."

"I think it's fish, Mom."

"Those fish fuckers."

But that very morning, I'd read her the options from the menu-paper, checking the boxes with a tiny pencil, and guess what? She had picked the fish. And she had picked fish the day before. Both times I'd tried to convince her to get something else. And she'd told me (repeatedly) that "Fish is brain food," which is what she always used to say when she'd cook flounder and I'd be picking out the hook-like bones that had speared my cheeks.

I said, "Looks okay." But I was glad the fish wasn't my dinner. I promised myself that tomorrow I'd check chicken, or steak—anything but the fish.

"You eat it, then." She smacked the rail, the metal ringing. "Untie me."

I ripped open the spork's wrapper with my teeth. "I'll feed you. Look, there's rice!"

She tugged her arm. "I said untie me."

"Carrots. You like carrots! Coffee." I picked up the roll. "What about this?"

She said, "What about pussy?"

I flinched, surprised. "Mom. Don't talk like that."

"Let me go."

I told her that I couldn't.

She said, "You can." She stared at the bridge. "You think I'm a miserable mother. So now I'm paying for it."

"You're sick."

"I'm tied to a bed. And what's that smell?"

"It's fish."

"Again with that fucking fish?"

"I know, right?"

"What do you know?"

I knew it was hard to see her like that. Though I also felt relieved. Being chained to a hospital bed meant she couldn't wander the house, or fiddle with the stove, or slice her pillows to feathery ribbons with a pair of safety scissors. And there were deeper consolations. She couldn't pinch or slap me. And if she started yelling, I could leave the room. For once, I had control, or at least a more peaceful existence. But I also knew that I didn't want her chained to a hospital bed while she slowly lost her mind, either. Mom twisted her wrist, as though she could wriggle her hand free. In the movie-version of that moment, I told her that I loved her. That she wasn't alone. But it just didn't happen that way. Instead I placed the lid back onto the plate and promised to walk to El Presidente Diner and buy her whatever she wanted.

She nodded, then watched the traffic flow across the bridge, two single beams of red and white. "Why am I here?"

"They're testing to see your brain."

She snorted. "Of course I have a brain. Let's go."

"We can't leave."

"You can leave. Men always leave. Husbands. Sons."

I told her that wasn't true. Well, half of it wasn't true.

"It's true. You give and give. Cook and clean and shop and iron. Work a job or two. Raise kids that you're too tired to even get to know. And what do you get back? Liars, cheaters, gamblers. In the morning he greets you with a smack. And at night, he stumbles into the bed in a woozy swoon and mounts you."

"Mom. Stop it."

"Why? My husband never does, does he?"

"You're going to be sedated."

She shrugged. "Why not? I haven't dated in years."

"No. Se-dated. We're in a hos-pi-tal."

"Yeah sure."

I told her it was the truth.

She raised her hand, but it snapped back against the railing, so she pointed with her chin toward the window. "A hospital. I'd rather jump off the Brooklyn Bridge. Than spend my life in a hospital."

I tore the roll in two and placed it on the tray. "That's the George Washington Bridge."

"Same shit to me."

"It's actually completely different."

"Push me right off." She slaps the bed. "Promise."

"Sure, Mom. I'll get Gail to help. We'll wheel your bed right off the bridge. Like a log-flume."

She turned to face me. The white cloth of her cap had loosened, shielding one of her eyes. "Promise. That I won't end up in a hospital. Those crappy homes."

"We're leaving in a day or so. They're just checking stuff."

"You really believe that? Then promise you won't put me in a home."

I didn't believe it was just a test. She didn't remember ripping off the cap, or even ordering fish. She was an old woman, my mother, tied to a bed. She looked shriveled, tired, helpless in a way I had never seen. It scared me. So I said, "Okay. I promise," and lifted the lid off of the plate.

She smiled. I thought it was about our agreement. She said, "Oh, is that fish? Can we share?"

Now her illness is bigger than my promise. All illnesses are bigger than our promises. I promised myself that I'd go to film school, that I'd direct and write screenplays. I promised Mom that I'd take care of her. That she'd never see the inside of a home. Do promises become lies when you're unable to keep them?

If she could still decide, she'd want to stay in her home. Wouldn't we all want to be sick at home? But there's something else, bigger and scarier than all of this: I don't want to live here alone. I grew up first afraid of, and then dependent on her—the only constant, the only parent in my life. I don't want her taken away from me. It's not like I'm neglecting her or she's being mistreated. She has a nurse. I'm constantly checking on her. I fight with her insurance. I call her doctor. Pay our bills. I've even given up film school for her. I'm a good son. We don't deserve this.

I glance out of Mom's bedroom window, hoping Lola has reappeared. She hasn't. I whisper, "Can't you just be okay?"

I listen to her sleeping, a clicking sound with each breath. I'm thankful for each click. Maybe that's enough. I move out of the room and shut the door.

I think I'll celebrate a helping of loneliness with a side of failure.

In the kitchen, I open the freezer and grab a tub of chocolate-chip ice cream for dinner. I grab a spoon and walk into my bedroom. I unzip my bag and pop the tape into the machine. Time for something new. I sit cross-legged in front of the television, then hit Play.

The screen flashes and the lens focuses on a long wooden walkway. On either side of the walk is the ocean, teal and flat. At the end is a wooden hut. Pitched, straw roof, white satin curtains. Tiki torches. Potted palms. Greg says, "Guess the massage ended early." He stops and pans left. I see the beach, but this time there are no mountains, only sand. He's in a different location. As he walks toward the gazebo, his sandals snap against his heels.

I peel the plastic film from the ice cream tub and scrape off the beard of ice. I stab in the spoon until I have a sizable chunk. As Greg gets closer, I notice a white ladder that hangs off the side of the hut. Greg walks into the hut and Sarah turns around. "Hey. It's Spielberg."

Greg says, "I taught him everything he knows."

People that know nothing about directing films always say Spielberg. I fucking hate that. Be original and pick someone else. I lick ice cream off the spoon, then say, "I doubt that, Greggy-boy." My words coming out muffled and cold.

He says, "So what's what?"

"The waiter brought us daiquiris. Yours melted."

The lens pans down, and a strawberry is sunken into the middle of pinkish goop. He says, "Bummer." I jab the spoon into the tub. In the next room, Mom yells something. I scoop another spoonful. I say, "Worse things can happen, Greg."

Sarah says, "Bet I can cheer you up!"

She leans forward and unhooks her yellow top and flicks it at the camera. I roll onto my knees, spoon hanging from my mouth. I say, "Itchee-wah-wah!"

The camera angles off to the side. I hear fabric against skin. Greg taking off his shorts. Greg says, "I need a wider lens," and they both laugh.

Then the screen goes black. Of course.

I stuff my face with ice cream and wait. I feel this tremble of panic until I remember that I can rewind it and play it over and over. There is still too much unwatched film in the tape reel for this to be the end. "It's fine. We're fine." I lean forward to hit Rewind, but before I do, the screen flashes back to life.

They're still in the hut. Greg is lying on the chair next to Sarah. He says, "Don't worry, there's going to be a director's cut." She slaps him and laughs.

Does he mean me? No, he's just joking. So I say, "There isn't one."

I hear a tick behind me. I turn and the blue light of my phone is blinking. I crawl over and pick it up. "Hello?"

I hear chewing, then: "Hey, sorry for vanishing."

I sit on the edge of the bed, the springs creaking.

She says: "I got nervous, then remembered I had to feed Mother."

I picture my mother in isolation, strapped to the bed. I say, "Is she okay?"

"She's a cranky-pants. That's all."

On the phone, a subway car passes. I look out my window and the "A" train is pulling into the station. "Are you outside on the El?"

"No, I'm out front." She laughs. "Can Wes come play?"

I just checked Mom. She's fine. We'll sit on my stoop and talk. But that's a long distance from her bedroom. I might not hear her if she wanders. I imagine Mom in the kitchen grilling cutlets on the coffee burner, or trapped in the bathroom, or making toast with a chainsaw. Gloria is all over me. If anything goes even slightly wrong, I won't have a good reason to delay putting Mom in a home. But I'm not telling her no. "Come in for a bit?"

"Yeah?" She bites into something, chews. She sings, "I *will* do that," in her best Meatloaf and hangs up.

This time I'm happy.

CHAPTER 10

You don't realize how chaotic your room is until it needs to be clean. I have less than three minutes to perk the place up. I take in the wood paneling, the shag carpet. The saggy middle of my mattress, as though I dribbled a bowling ball on it for six hours. My room is the opposite of a tropical hut on stilts. There's nothing I can do about that, so I fix my blanket flat onto my bed. I scoop up sock balls and toss them into the far corner. I take a deep breath and inhale the sexual ambience of my dirty carpet. That hamster smell of dirty clothes. I swipe the Windex across the top of my dresser. I hold the bottle above my head and machine gun the trigger, then lift the hamper lid and toss the bottle inside. I don't have a clean shirt so I pull lint balls off my sweater until the doorbell rings.

I assess my half-assed cleaning job and I'm instantly worried. She'll take one look at my pathetic room in my pathetic house and run. But she's here now. She's really here. I leave my bedroom. "Please sleep," I mutter as I rush past Mom's door. "I've earned it."

In the living-room I feel giddy, like when I saw *Empire Strikes Back* for the first time. I take a deep breath and open the door.

Lola says, "Ta-da!"

"Here you are."

She looks down at her feet, as though convincing herself that she is in fact actually standing on my stoop. She's wearing a black skirt that falls to her ankles, a purple sweater, its sleeves hanging over her hands. Her face is barked from the cold. As we stand there, her eyes seem to shimmer, which I hope means that she's glad she found me. I am. This tingly, fizz pushes from my chest, to my face. I wait for her to vanish like a camera trick. She steps into the house. There's no turning back.

I say, "You changed."

"For the better." She looks down. "Oh, my clothes. Yeah."

"You look nice."

"Thanks. Canal Jeans. Brand new secondhand."

I cross my arms, trying to conceal my sweater. "C'mon in. I mean, more in."

She laughs. "I know what you mean."

I follow her into the living room. "This is my house," I say, feeling silly.

"It's my first time here."

I'm not sure if she's asking or telling me. "Well I was going to invite you to hang out. After graduation." What I don't tell her is how I sat on my stoop like a loser waiting, as if she'd magically appear. Then again, that is exactly what she did. It only took about a decade. "Anyway, here it is."

She points toward the couch. "I love sitting on plastic. Like you're trapped inside of a Twinkie wrapper."

I think she's poking fun until she runs her hand across the cushion, the plastic crinkling, and I remember seeing her sketchpad filled with drawings of brand characters. The icons were saturated in grungy disdain. Tony the Tiger holding an elephant tusk. Cap'n

Crunch hauling up a net full of dolphins. But she'd drawn the Twinkie cowboy on the inside of her math notebook, minus the social spin. I decide that she is actually impressed.

"And it keeps things clean," she adds.

"Yeah. I guess it's okay."

"Except in July, when your legs get sweaty and there's that ripping noise when you stand."

She waits for me to say something, but I'm nervous and it's causing a blank space, as though instead of me living here my whole life, I'm a realtor leading her through the rooms, stalling out on my quick sale.

Thankfully, the awkward moment passes when she says, "Kitchen's there?"

I nod, in my realtor way, relieved I can keep this going. "Sure is."

"Let's take a looky, then."

I follow her. I wince. The walls appear yellower than usual. The curtains hang limp and smoke-stained. It's depressing. It occurs to me that I could've perked the room up. At some point, I could've bought new curtains, or stick tiles, or even an appliance. Since Mom got sick, I've wanted to keep the house the way she likes it, in case she had a moment of clarity, but a coat of paint probably wouldn't have hurt anything. Then again, I never had a reason to fix it. Until now.

I say, "Are you hungry?"

"A little." She swings open the fridge, the door knocking into the wall, and grabs a plate of chicken. "Mind?"

I think of that scene in *Jaws*, when Hooper pulled Brody's plate of food in front of him, sharpening the knife and fork against each other before digging in. Minus the wine. I shrug. "Yeah. If you're hungry."

"I'm starving."

She peels the cellophane and grabs a chicken leg, bites and holds it with her teeth while she cinches the plastic back around the dish, which she sticks back into the fridge. Nudging the door shut, she rips off a piece of meat and chews.

She says, "This is balls-kicking."

"Yeah, Gloria's a great cook."

"You know what this needs? Juicy Juice."

In high school, she'd always carry Juicy Juice in her bag with her. If she was bored, she'd fix the straw upright and crush the box until a geyser of juice shot out and then catch the stream in her mouth. She called it her Dirty Squirty Trick. "Still drink that, yeah?"

"Never stopped." She sticks the drumstick into the side of her mouth, as though it was a cigar. She says, "What else?"

Again the white space takes over. I'm trying to think of something interesting to say. I'm not so great at conversation, especially this kind. I'm not used to people listening. Dom talks until you surrender and let him keep talking. Mom is always confused, and even when she was fine, I can't say she ever really listened. Anything that couldn't be answered with an "Okay," or a head nod would turn real quick into, "I have a headache, please shut up already." If this was a movie, I'd say something slick yet cool in a Harrison Ford, Kurt Russell, or even Christian Slater (*Pump Up the Volume* Slater) way. Instead, I'm staring at her like I'm Sloth from *The Goonies*. "R-O-C-K-Y R-O-A-D???"

She misreads my look of desperate urgency as annoyance. "Sorry to be weird. I haven't eaten. Blood sugar tanks, but my nerves skyrocket."

"It's okay."

She pulls the chicken leg from her mouth, the meat stripped off. "This reminds me of my aunt's chicken. Sometimes she'd bring it to me in the hospital. This lemony chicken with parsley and garlic. So good." I wait for her to say the type of hospital. I'd ask, but she might not want to talk about it. She shrugs and her face softens. "Can't get that anymore."

Before I ask why, she pokes me in the stomach. "What else?"

"Here? I don't know."

"I think you do know. So." She lobs the drumstick into the garbage. She shoots her arms into the air, "Three pointer, baby! Bet you didn't know I like basketball." I can't remember, so I shrug. "Before I knew you, I'd take the subway to the Garden and watch St. John's games. It was like ten bucks. A row to yourself. Popcorn. Soda. Sometimes I'd sneak in a Happy Meal. Yup. I'm all about dunking balls."

Watching her, I remember that she was always this, what, erratic? In high school she flipped the weird switch when she was nervous. I remember her twitchy movements and her machinegun chattering, her squeaky laugh. I wish she'd notice how happy I am to see her. I rip off a paper towel for her to wipe her hands. I turn. She's gone. "Lola?" I walk out of the kitchen and down the hallway.

She's in front of my mother's door. She points. I whisper, "No, keep walking." She mouths "What?" then peeks inside Mom's room. I say, "Shut the door!" A panicked fluttering fills my chest. I step in front of her and pull it closed like Bluebeard. I press my ear against the door and listen. She's still asleep. "Next one."

"I thought it was your room."

"I know. It's just." I stop, unsure what to say next. At first I thought it was that I was afraid of my mother seeing Lola. Her cursing, her unpredictable behavior. But I realize I'm afraid of what Lola might think of Mom. I need to keep them mutually exclusive, at least for now. I say, "I'm sorry. Mom wakes up and it's impossible to talk."

She shrugs. "I get it."

She walks into my room and takes off her boots. She rubs her feet together, making a scratchy sound. Her toenails are painted different colors, green, blue, purple, red, but there isn't a pattern to it, making it look frantic.

"So. How are you living?"

Here's where I should lie. Before I can think of one, "Barely," pops out.

She sings, "Have you thought about the army?"

I laugh. "No."

She says, "I guess it doesn't suit you. The military. You're a sad quiet type."

I don't have the oomph to defend my personality, which means she's right.

She goes on. "I like that. The last thing the world needs is testosterone. Hasn't Lilith Fair taught us anything?" She pats the bed. "So this is where the magic happens."

I've worn the same boxers for three days. I say, "I think so?"

"The famous say it on *MTV Cribs* all the time. Same joke. Like, don't they watch the show? Anyway, are you okay? You sound worried."

I say, "Of course not," though, of course I'm worried. I'm worried that she'll think seeing me was a mistake. That I'm just saying the wrong things. I think about the tape, Greg's confidence. But then Mom yells out, "Where's the slots?" and I shudder awake, or whatever.

Lola says, "That your mom?"

"A version of her. Stay here."

I walk down the hall. We should've stayed outside. I lean towards the door. I don't hear anything. I wait there until I'm convinced that she must've fallen back asleep. As I walk towards my room, I hear static, a click. A familiar sound. I rush into the room and Lola is sitting in front of the television.

On the screen Sarah is climbing down the ladder, lowering herself into the water, as Greg films from the walkway. I feel as though Lola has caught me watching clown porn. I take a deep breath and walk over toward the television, feeling floaty. I can't explain my detached feeling. I say, "I'll shut it," trying to sound calm, as though I'm not exposing my obsession with the footage to everyone, especially Lola, to see.

Lola says, "What is this?"

"I'm making copies of it for work."

"Phew. I thought she was your ex-girlfriend."

"No!" Oddly, it does feel as if Sarah is an ex. Wait. If Lola's relieved, then maybe she's interested in me.

She grabs the container of ice cream. "Can't compete with that. All suntanny and stuff." She sticks her finger into the tub, swirls, then sucks her finger. "Just us mortals, here." Sarah winks at the camera, as though she's seeing us from the water.

I hear, "Now what?" I think it's Lola, but I realize it's Sarah.

I say, "It's vacation footage. Work, that's all." I move to turn it off.

She says, "Wait. I haven't been on a trip in forever. It's nice! I don't mind." She scoops ice cream, licks her finger. "It's soothing."

"Yeah." I'm happy to have someone else cosign my attachment to Greg's home movie, or at least, make me feel less weird about it.

She scoops more ice cream. "It goes from your eyes to your heart to your body in this weird way."

Still clutching the ladder, Sarah submerges, her blond hair ebbing away from her, as though its flaxen-colored seaweed, as she treads just below the surface. Greg holds the shot. We listen to the water lapping against the pilings. Sarah pushes off the ladder. Still submerged, she sticks her arm out of the water and waves, then her hand disappears.

"It's beautiful," Lola whispers.

"It is." I'm feeling the same intimacy we had in high school. Not an icky, gropey intimacy. It's sincere, our friendship clicking back into place.

Lola taps her thumb against the container, "I got it."

"You do?"

"Yup." Lola scoops more ice cream, holds out her finger for me, then sticks it into her mouth. "In the hospital, we had these classes. I took painting. I'd paint daisies set into a green vase and stare at the picture until the petals started moving." She picks at the loose fibers of the carpet, still caught in the lull of the painting.

"You mean, like meditation?" I'm hoping her explanation helps me understand my own sense of drifting, my own obsession with the footage.

"No, I was in a field of flowers." She bumps me just as Sarah surfaces, and then backstrokes a few feet away from the ladder. Beneath her are black rocks, or coral. Fish dart past her, silvery and shy. "It just felt nice for that moment. To be somewhere else, if only in a painting."

"What happened?"

"Nothing, I'd stop staring at the flower and move on."

"No, I mean...graduation."

"Oh, that 'What happened.' Graduation? A week before graduation, I was crossing Liberty Avenue and was hit by a car." She claps. "SLAMMO."

I flinch, as though I'm seeing the accident. Suddenly, I feel awful that all this time I thought she'd just ditched our graduation, when she was actually hurt. I should've asked one of our teachers. I should've looked up her phone number and called to check if she was okay. I did nothing but feel bad for myself. I tell her I'm sorry.

She says, "I was in a coma. Then I needed rehab. So I went upstate to live with my aunt."

That was eight years ago. I want to ask her what kind of rehab it was without seeming like I'm interrogating her. So I wait.

She scoops more ice cream. "When I got out of the hospital, I didn't really. Well I couldn't live with my Mom."

"Why not?"

"You know how moms can be."

I nod. "Sure do."

"So I moved in with my aunt. She was really nice. She had this apartment with this little yard. There was this swath of woods with a stream. It was all chirpy and loamy. So I bought paint and canvases. I set up there, painting the landscape. I even taught my aunt to paint. She was really good."

I realize she's talking about her in the past tense. "Then what?"

She scoops more ice cream but wipes it along the container, her lips pinched, sad, but thoughtful, as she mulls over the best way to frame the story. Lola says, "She got sick. Fucking cancer. I told her to stop smoking those skinny cigars. But nope. I couldn't leave her. So I cooked and bought her groceries. She couldn't do too much. I didn't have a license, but I drove her to the clinic anyway. Medical emergency, man. We'd sit for hours, staring out the window. Reading newspapers and magazines. It was really sad. At night, though, we'd watch movies. She liked the classics."

"Like what?"

She pokes my arm. "I knew you were gonna ask. Like, *Streetcar Named Desire*, *Marnie*, *Roman Holiday*. Oh. She really loved Cary Grant. *The Bishop's Wife*, *Arsenic and Old Lace*. *North by Northwest*. The good ones.

"My mom loves Cary Grant too. *Suspicion* is her favorite."

"She liked that one." She takes a jagged breath. "They did chemo, radiation. Poking and prodding. It left for a bit, like it was hiding in a closet, only to pounce onto her again, bigger and uglier and meaner."

Sarah flips around and kicks her heels, the water splashing.

Lola goes on. "After. Well, after the funeral. She left me some money. Her insurance. Jerry the landlord guy said he'd sign over the lease."

Greg pans the camera across the beach, empty and beautiful.

"I couldn't stay there, though." She shrugs. "How can I paint in the yard where my aunt used to sit? Her green lawn chair, lonely and empty, except for some crumbly leaves on its seat. No thanks."

Sarah says the water is really warm.

"But coming back didn't work out either," Lola says. "Everything changed. Pins was gone. Hair Mania was gone. Odd Job, Liberty Diner, Meows and Paws, Super Sneaker, Captain Lobster. Arthouse Drawing supplies. Gone. All gone. And what the fuck happened to Gino's Pizza?"

"It burnt down. A year after graduation."

"It torched itself from grief after I left."

Greg pans out toward the water. Sarah waves for him to join her.

Lola says, "So I left upstate and was in my new apartment. I was extra slushy. Thinking about her hospital, my hospital. I felt like I needed to find one person I liked. I mean, I knew people at the hospital, but once they left they wanted that part of their lives gone. Which makes sense. I have a small family, mostly dead or strangers. I really didn't know what to do. But just when I thought I was going to pop from grief, I thought about movies. Then I thought about how you loved movies. So all these movie feelings mushed together." She touches my nose. "And I thought I'd give you a try. That if you were around here, I'd know that I still belonged here. In Queens. That I'm okay. But I lost a lot of time."

"Yeah. We only think about time when we waste it."

Lola says, "That's deep."

"I have my moments."

"Sure do, bubbaloo."

As she watches me, the screen casts an ocean-colored light across Lola's face, as though we're sitting on the sand, staring at the sea. Of course she understands the footage. Its quiet. Its solace. It's a refuge from our lost chances, our failed hopes and vanishing wishes.

I say, "You knew I worked at Video Planet?"

"Well, I called six different stores. I knew you wouldn't sell out to Blockbuster. Narrowed it down a bit. I mean, I had other reasons. I figured if I came back here, I could take art classes at the Y or the library. Workshops. Classes in the city, maybe. That's what I meant about the flowers. Anyway, I still paint."

"At least you do what you love. I work at Video Planet or help my mom."

"Not the worst job."

"No. But I'm slowly realizing that I can't make films rotting in a video store."

"Then why don't you make films?"

"Well I don't have the education, for one."

"You don't need an education to make movies."

"Well, you learn shots, lenses. Editing. Film history."

"Learn that onsite. Be punk!" She shoots up her hand and makes the devil horns. "You just need the will, man!"

"I don't have a camera." I feel as though I'm only making excuses. Then again I find a lot of comfort in excuses. Excuses are open-ended. They keep alive the thin hopes and slim chances to still do it.

"I have one. It was my uncle's. Well, it's a camcorder. He would film girls. Had like nine restraining orders. When he left for jail I stole it. Guess I was doing him a favor." She laughs. "Crazy Uncle Steve."

"That's just a camcorder. Not a movie camera."

"Tell that to the fellas at Blair Witch."

"You're making it sound so easy."

"Look. I know what you're saying about film school. Wanting to do it perfect. But I also know that painting makes me a painter." She points toward the television. "I mean, this guy filmed it. How about Warhol movies?" Lola turns. We watch Sarah swim out until we can barely see the high swing of her arms as she backstrokes further out to sea. She points at the screen. "That's art, right? Besides, it's not the product. Like some sellout way, man. It's the doing. And even if it goes nowhere, so what? Spend time doing what makes you feel, and you feel better."

I never thought of it that way. I thought so much about the technical side of it that I forgot the emotion. Maybe doing it is enough.

"Here," she says. "Maybe this will help." She leans forward and kisses me. Her lips are cold and taste like chocolate chips. She's here, kissing me in my awful ugly room, here, convincing me to make movies, of all things. She pulls back and her face shifts blue from the TV screen.

I feel this rush of emotion, a warm, unpredictable joy. Something I haven't felt in a long time. But here, in this messy room...

"Sorry," she says.

"No, it's okay."

"I just thought I..."

"No, it's...I mean, it's not exactly tropical waters here."

She smiles. Nods at the room. "Well. I guess our movie's a little different."

We turn. The ocean is there. The lens pans, and in the distance, there are a pair of birds, long necked and black. "See. This one's soothing. Evokes emotion. That's a movie." She winks. "But you could film me eating a Happy Meal. Or your stupid boss."

She's right. I don't have the luxury of a tropical island. But I'll film my house, or the subway train clacking toward the city, or the Lelands swaying in the yard, where Lola found me.

Wait. I smile. It's so obvious.

Or my mother. I can film my mother.

CHAPTER 11

So here I am, the director, le auteur, the recorder of memory.

I'm excited about starting a movie, if only a small one. Sure, I'll practice directing, lighting, and setting up shots. But more than anything, I want to capture my mother's decline in a sympathetic way. Naturalistic. Her shaky voice. Her particular gestures. Yes. I'll film her and ask questions that will, hopefully, build a scaffold of images. Maybe it will trigger some inner peace, like when I watch the vacation footage. Also, there's a chance that by playing the footage back to her, it'll help her hold onto the past that hasn't already dissolved. Bring other, unmentioned moments, forward. Maybe she'll even reveal why my father left us. What part of Florida he decided on to hang his racing form. Did she really never hear from him again? If she gives me nothing, that's okay too. I want her audience (even if it's only me) to understand her struggle. But most of all, I want to capture her on film, when one day, well, the worst possible thing happens.

That's not now. Now, I'll record it all.

This morning, Friday, I set my alarm for 4 AM. I showered, shaved. Ran a wash so I'd have clean clothes (and boxers). Lola said she'd be over by eight. Lately, Mom sleeps into the afternoon, so I'll have time to talk to Lola. I walk through the house and note out the best angles, where the natural light hits. I ask myself: what is worthy of being in the composition? The ugliest place—the kitchen—also happens to be the best for other reasons. The window is behind the table and gives the room a happy feeling. Also, Mom thinks better when she's eating. She can't scoop food up with forks, but with cookies or toast she manages well.

I pull the yellow curtains wide and open the window, hoping the chilly March air will keep her a bit focused. I scoop the stack of bills off the table and toss them into a shopping bag. I wash the dishes, wipe down the counter (though Gloria always leaves it spotless). I sweep. I wipe down the front of the fridge.

I box my hands and pan from the sink to the table to the wall. If I sit Mom in the middle of the table, her back to the window, the sunlight will fall nicely over her shoulder. I see her sitting at the table, hunched over a bowl of oatmeal in a very *Potato Eaters* kind of way. Framing the shot like that is a bit depressing, but necessary.

I pick up the phone and call Gloria.

It rings three times. "Wes? Everything okay?"

I lean against the wall, a tingly feeling in my stomach. "Yes."

"Okay. Do you need me to get something?"

I concentrate on keeping my voice even, yet stuffy somehow. "I'm not going in to work. I was up all night coughing. I'm going to stay home."

She laughs. "That's fine. I bought stuff for lentil soup."

"No, I'm giving you a day off."

"Wesley, how are you going to rest if you're watching Camilla? Wouldn't you rather have me there? I won't bother you. What if your mom catches it?"

Shit. I didn't think this far ahead. "I'm not sick-sick." I do this dry-cough thing. "Just a tad buggy. I'm fine."

Gloria breathes into the phone. She's annoyed about last night, or that I haven't mentioned the home. She says, "Look. I'm sorry about...well, you know. I understand why you were happy to see her. I had a long day."

Her apology makes me feel sad and horrible that I even argued with her. "I'm sorry too." I wait, then, "What will you do?"

"I'll probably watch a movie."

I fall into video-clerk mode. "Check out *Erin Brockovich*. People are saying good things." I've never recommended a movie to her. Strange. I don't even remember her asking for suggestions. I bet she's a Sally Field fan. I should've recommended *Places in the Heart, Forrest Gump,* or *Steel Magnolias*. Maybe she doesn't trust my taste in film? No. She probably feels weird that I'd give her freebies, which I totally would.

"Are you sure? I can give her meds, at least. Check her vitals?"

Her meds are nestled in a yellow dispenser, separated by times and dosages. I say, "It's pretty straightforward." I wait for her to ask about Lola. I don't want to tell her, but I want her to ask. Maybe she's jealous? She's making lentils, which she knows I hate. Is that her passive-aggressive meal? But she did apologize, and if I made her mad again she might have the oomph to start in on the nursing home again, so begrudgingly, I let the Lola conversation go and say, "I'll be fine."

"Okay. Call if you need me."

I try to sniffle. "Take tomorrow too. If I feel better I'll call you tonight." She tells me that it's okay and I try to detect a hint of something in her voice. I can't, so I hang up and call Dom's cell. "Sick. Thanks." That's good enough for his crazy ass. He'll curse me regardless of my excuse, but this is my first sick day in three years.

Besides, I am the manager.

Back in my room, I kneel in front of the television. Lola knocked over the tub so the rug smells like souring ice cream. I'm not sure where we stopped. I hit Play. The lens focuses on a giant conch shell. The top of the shell is cream-colored and has that typical spiny spiral. The flared lip of the shell is pink, vaginal. I'm glad Lola didn't see this part. I laugh, embarrassed.

His hand comes into the shot as he picks up the conch. "Sarah will love that." In the distance, there's a log, beer bottles, the remnants of a campfire. A halo of footprints circles the log. I imagine Lola twirling, carefree and happy, in front of the fire with Greg and Sarah as I film. We're friends, as though we lived on the same block or pushed through high school together.

I've heard of people who find books left on park benches or in libraries when they need them most. Maybe it's the same way with this videotape for me? It harnessed my psychic longing and breached the darkness. A gift, a jewel—from God? the universe? or just Greg to me. After Lola's story about her aunt, the hospital, how she'd searched for the city she'd left during high school, and how she realized it had disappeared until she found me, I thought then maybe, just possibly, the footage had brought us back together. Why else would she have the same reaction to it as I did? She wasn't weirded out by my obsession. She didn't run screaming from the house. She understands. Before I can dissect this theory further, Mom calls my name. I leave my room and open her door.

She's teetering against the foot of her bed, trying to slip her leg through the sleeves of the robe. She tugs the robe, trying to bring it to her waist. She's wearing her purple nightgown, Gloria's favorite. She's only wearing one slipper. She says, "I think I gained weight." She folds the ends of the robe around her waist.

I say, "You're wearing your robe."

"Mr. Riddles in a Rhyme."

I ask her if she wants help.

She scratches her hair with both hands. The robe falls to her feet, a huddle of folded pink on the carpet. I will make a note to record the heap of terrycloth later. "Arm two hurts."

She's right-handed. That's probably arm one. "Your left?"

"I left what?"

Her arms seem well enough to slip on her robe-pants. "I made breakfast," trying to distract her. "Hungry?"

She says, "We have to wait. For my sister Joan."

For the slightest second, I wish I'd gone to work after all. She's never bonkers this early. Mom tugs on her sleeve. When it snaps back at her she flinches. This was a bad idea. Mom is being crazy. Gloria is probably mad. Then there's the money I'm missing. It's easier to stay in the routine of being miserable than it is to escape the misery briefly, only to be tossed back into it. I feel ridiculous with my camera shots and shooting locations, as though this would be easy. We plan, Mom laughs.

I say, "I'll get your breakfast."

"Joan is on her way." She looks around the room. "And where is your father?"

I pick up her slipper. "I have no idea. And your sister Joan is dead." I lift her ankle, her skin feels cold.

"You're saying she's dead?"

"Yes."

Her face collapses and she's sobbing now. She shakes her head. "Oh, my sister." Snot runs from her nose. Her lip quivers. "How did I miss the funeral?"

Now I'm a monster. I flatten her nightgown. I'm not sure how to straighten this out. Hopefully she'll forget this conversation. "She's okay," I say. "Bad joke."

I hear more than feel the slap. "Fibber."

"You're right. I'm sorry." Maybe I deserved it.

She watches her hand, confused that it's an extension of her. Her face is flushed from crying. I pull my sleeve over my hand and wipe her face, an apology.

"You're always a disappointment," she says.

I nod—every mistake, letdown, and failure spiraling inside of me like a dust storm. My cheek doesn't sting. She doesn't have the strength to open a bag of potato chips. It's the 'always' that hurts.

Mom says, "We're waiting. Disappointment."

"Good luck waiting, then." I leave and shut the door. I can't have her by herself standing in the middle of her room mourning her dead sister, but I have to be away from her. I stand in front of her door, listening, while also trying to let her insult go.

Mom yells, "What's that sound? Joan, is that you?"

Wait. It's a sliding sound. When I open her door, she's holding a picture of her sister. I say, "I'm sorry."

She wipes her face. "Thank you."

Tapping. Banging. I close Mom's door and walk into my room.

Lola is trying to climb in through the window. Of course she is. There's a large camcorder at the foot of my bed. If I hadn't known her for so long, I'd be nervous about her window entry. She also thought hiding in my yard was the best way to rekindle our friendship. This is just a typical day for Lola.

Her face is planted into the carpet, her boots stuck in the window frame. She's wearing a jean jacket; a hood drapes over her left ear. She braces her forehead into the rug to talk. "I'm stuck," she says, as if there's any doubt. She shimmies, but doesn't move. "You really need to vacuum. Balls and B.O. Woof. Help, please."

"What are you doing?"

"Ta-da!" she says.

I slip my hands into her armpits and slide her out of the window.

She pops up. "Surprise."

Technically it's called breaking and entering, but I say, "You sure did." Lola touches my cheek, which I thought was fine. I lie, "I had an accident."

"Get. Life. Alert." I wait for her to laugh. She's serious.

"This Christmas." I step back. She takes off her coat, unzips her hoodie and tosses them onto the floor. She's wearing black jeans and a Radiohead t-shirt, from *The Bends*. She smiles and I think of Thom Yorke's shaky pitched singing on "Bulletproof ... " I wish I was, too. "Look. Mom's having a bad morning."

She runs her hand along her shaved head, making a scratchy sound. "Is it the window thing? I'll use the door. I just wanted to surprise you."

"No. It's fine." I say, "I just don't think filming is such a good idea."

"What would Warhol say?" She picks up the camera. "I woke my super to get into storage. He kept saying, 'Chu 'ave dee key. Chu 'ave dee key.' And guess what?" She rolls her tongue, drum-like, then says, "I had the key."

"It's not about the camera or the window, really."

She wraps her arms around my waist. "Maybe it's not the end of the world."

I look at her and she kisses me. Her lips taste like grape Juicy Juice. She kicks off her shoes; the left one sails into my door, the right somersaults before resting on the floor. We flop onto the bed. She rolls on top of me and I'm glad I had the foresight to do laundry. In the movie version, this would be right after the big car chase, but right before Lola gets kidnapped, which would push the movie into its final act. We kiss until something crashes in my mother's bedroom. Lola rolls off me. She stands. "I'll handle this, don't worry."

Handle? She's never even met her before! "Lola, come back!"

I roll off the bed and charge toward the door but trip on a bump in the carpet. I stumble forward and sidecheck the wall, slowing me a bit from getting to them. As I move down the hall, I imagine seeing Mom pestering Lola about her suite being ready, or Mom tossing her remote control at Lola because she's hungry or confused. There are worse scenarios: Lola seeing the condition of my mother, the care needed, and then fleeing the bedroom, horrified that I would've even considered her being part of this film, or my life. Certain that she has made a horrible mistake about finding me. I hustle into Mom's bedroom.

I'm wrong. Instead of yelling, or tossing or fleeing, they're sitting on the edge of Mom's bed. Mom holding Lola's hand, smiling, and Lola, her face flushed, is whispering how happy she is to see her, too.

I lean against the wall, trying to process the scene, then wishing I'd had the sense to bring my camera with me. I say, "Is everything okay?"

Lola gives a nod. "Sure, we're just in the middle of our greetings." She winks, which I refuse to even guess at the meaning.

Mom says, "Wesley, don't be a horsefucker. Make coffee."

Lola says, "I never heard that one before."

"She loves saying it. To me."

Mom says, "Where have you been?"

Lola shrugs, "Around. You know."

I say, "This is—"

Mom says, "Don't you tell me." She rests her head on Lola's shoulder. Mom smiles. "Think I don't know my own sister?"

I wait for Lola to explain that she's my friend, but she rests her head against Mom's head. "Sissy. It's been too long." She gives me the thumbs up.

Mom says, "Don't worry. You're here now."

"Mom, you're just confused. This is—"

Lola says, "Look, if it isn't my nephew! My, how you've grown?"

I watch, deciding whether I should still stop this, more for Lola than Mom. She hasn't seen me in years and now she's being mistaken for my mother's dead sister Joan. How do I even attempt to stop this insanity? But Lola seems okay. She hasn't fled for the bathroom. She hasn't side-eyed me with that "Please rescue me" face. She wasn't even skeeved when Mom kissed her cheek. Still, it seems way too much.

I say, "Lola, can I talk to you for a second?"

Mom says, "Who the hell is Lola?"

"I mean...I mean Joan, Mom."

Lola makes a kissy-face, says, "Respect your elders. It's Auntie Joan to you."

"Are you sure?"

"Really it's fine," Lola says. She reminds me of," and then her face flushes, softens, as though she's in her yard, alone, painting the clusters of birches, the huddles of mossy rocks, their darkened curves peeking out from the creek, as her aunt's lawn chair holds nothing but the weight of crumbly leaves. "Well...you know." Lola wipes her face.

Mom says, "Don't worry. We're together now. Like when we'd hide under the covers with Dad's flashlight? We'd read from *The Wizard of Oz*. Remember?"

I really should've filmed this.

Lola says, "Sure, I remember," her voice quiet, achy.

Mom says, "You have a good memory. You know, sometimes I forget stuff."

Lola bites her lip, nods.

Mom touches Lola's shoulder. "My sister."

I say, "Are you sure this isn't weird? Being..." I point to Mom. "You know?"

"Nopesies. It's nice to be someone else," Lola says. "For a bit."

I think of Greg and Denise. "Yeah, for a bit."

Mom says, "A bit of what?"

I watch them sitting on the bed. I say, "Exactly."

CHAPTER 12

It takes a while for Mom to tell "Aunt Joan" the gossip about a bevy of people who died fifteen-plus years ago. Mom is unpredictable, so I stay close in case Lola needs a break from being Joan. As they talk in a timecut-crazy-way, I get a burning urgency to film. Lola reads the quiet desperation on my face. She suggests we go into the kitchen to "Gab it up," like they used to in the "olden times," like we're Vikings boasting about our sea-fairings and bountiful pillages.

As we walk into the kitchen Lola says, "She's so nice."

I say, "Thanks," waiting for her to laugh, or say something snarky. She doesn't.

I never had many girlfriends. I think after a while they grew tired of my mopey ways, so they moved on to happier guys. Then Mom got sick. For years, I'd rehearsed answers to my imaginary girlfriend's questions about Mom: Yes she has a nurse. No she isn't violent. Of course I'd rather spend time with you. Lola's easy way with Mom is a complete surprise. Maybe it's because she's stayed in a hospital, and has an empathy that most people lack. Maybe, like she said, Mom reminds Lola of her aunt. Or just maybe she's doing this for me.

Anyway, I'm not sure about the psychological impact of keeping this charade going, but Mom is talkative, nicer, and more alert than I've seen her since she was diagnosed. Who am I to deny her those things?

Also, this is the only way to film her.

When we finally make it to the kitchen, the sunlight has shifted. I have to shut the curtains to keep out the blinding glare. I place Mom in the seat at the far end of the table, with her back facing the window. Lola sits at the head, which allows me to film them freely, while providing me with over-the-shoulder shots, if needed.

Crazy Uncle Steve's camera is a Hi-8, Sony DCR-TRV900. It's from 1998. It has an ion battery with around eight hours of life, a digital zoom, and a side LCD panel. I can film them without one eye in the viewfinder. The best feature, though, is its steadicam. I can move without making the viewer woozy. I think of Danny riding his Big Wheel in *The Shining*, or Henry Hill leading Karen through the basement of the Copa Club in *Goodfellas*. Long unwavering shots. Fancy stuff. There was a tape inside the camera. I already peaked at the footage that I'll be taping over; it was taken inside a nestle of bushes in what looked like the Great Lawn in Central Park. Stevie Boy was filming two women. They were sprawled on pink towels wearing matching blue bikini tops and jean shorts. One was face-up, the other was face-down. They must had heard Uncle Steve saying, "She has cheeks like a gazelle," in his really bad David Attenborough accent, because they shot up fast and called him a fucking pervert. He yelled, "I've been made!" and then the camera twisted away from the bushes as he fled the scene. The final moments Uncle Steve captured on film were a pair of cops walking toward him, ordering him to shut that thing off. Lola wasn't kidding about her uncle. Scuzzy bastard.

Now I press Power, then Record. Mom is so engrossed with her sister that she doesn't notice. With her piercings and shaved head, Lola looks nothing like Aunt Joan, who died before she even reached Lola's age of twenty-five. I don't think the lack of resemblance even matters, though. Mom mistakes me for a waiter or a croupier all the time. Maybe it's Lola's aura of happiness, or her fun-loving way? Whatever the reason, Mom is completely convinced she's sitting across from Aunt Joan.

Mom edges closer to Lola and clasps her hand. She circles her thumb inside Lola's palm and asks where she got her 'Shorty-cut.' Lola tells her about a shop called Peaches on Liberty Avenue. Mom asks about her 'Love life.'

Lola says, "It's getting there."

I say, "Mom, talk about something else."

Mom giggles. "He's mopey. When he was little I'd call him Charlie Brown."

Lola snorts. "You should've seen him last night. Mr. Sensitive!" They laugh.

Mom says, "You know who he really reminds me of?"

God this is humiliating. I tell her to forget it, which is too ironic to be ironic.

She says, "His father."

I zoom in and Mom glances at me, a secretive look on her face. She whispers to Lola. "You know all about it, Joan."

I stop the camcorder. "Mom, can I talk to Joan?"

Lola slides off her chair and walks over to me. "This about Mr. Sensitive? I'm sorry. I mean you *are* sensitive, but—"

"No. Get her to talk about my father."

"Like...what?"

"Anything you can." Mom sniffs the bowl of oatmeal, then pushes it away. I should've fed her before I started filming. "She's hungry now."

"Right." Lola opens the fridge and grabs a carton of orange juice, then the box of crumb cake on the counter. She takes the *Best Mom Ever* mug from the drain and pours her juice. She must've done this for her aunt. The weight of the moment would've upset me, but Lola doesn't seem to mind. Mom tells her not to go through all the trouble. Lola tells her she's worth every bit of trouble. She seems happy, even excited to be helping. I thank her. "Just some cake. No biggie."

She asks me if I'm ready. For a fleeting second I'm afraid. Once I turn the camera back on, I'm fully committed. I make a pact with myself to refuse to delete scenes just because they're hurtful. I'll portray her as unwaveringly as the lens allows. It's worth it. I want to learn more about my father. "I think so."

"Okay. Keep shooting."

I stand in front of the table. Lola sits on the right, closest to the cabinets, and Mom is sitting in the center, her chair touching the kitchen wall. Beams of dusty sunlight stream through the curtains above her. I hit Record and say, "Ready."

Lola points to the bowl. "Can I have cake, too?" She rips a corner wedge and bites. Mom picks a crumb off her cake and sniffs it. Lola says, "So Sissy, how'd you meet your husband?"

"You know all about that."

I wave my hand, signaling for her to push. Lola says, "I like that story."

"Why am I in this kitchen?" She glances around the room. It was stupid to think she was going to go into this long-winded narrative flashback as though she's Paul

Edgecomb from *The Green Mile*. I hit Stop. "She's dazed again"

"Give it a minute," Lola says, and tells Mom to drink some juice. I wait for her to curse. Mom takes a sip, says: "Tart."

Lola nods. "Minute Maid is like that. You know who has the best OJ? McDonald's."

Mom takes another sip and places the glass down, no spills this time. I'm a bit jealous that Lola got her to eat so easily. Not even Gloria can make her eat that fast. I realize she's doing it for Joan.

Lola says, "So how'd you meet your husband?"

I'm still recording when Mom says, "Well, we moved to City Line. So I was walking Aunt Kitty's chicken, Pecker. We used to keep chickens in the yard, but Pecker liked to walk the block. So we'd tie a string around her neck. Uh, loosely. Don't want to choke my Pecker. So my husband saw me. He wasn't my husband then. I didn't know him. He asked if I liked animals. I told him only farm animals. So the next day he rode down the block on a white horse. We rode through Forest Park."

I've waited my whole life for some family history and it's chicken-fried garbled nonsense. I lower the camera. "Mom, you're making that up."

"What?"

"The horses and the stable."

Mom says, "Stable? My husband's friend owned a stable once."

Lola says, "The one off the Belt Parkway, right? She's telling the truth."

I say, "Okay. She met my father at seventeen. Almost fifty years ago. So you're saying my father rode a steed across the Belt Parkway, through Canarsie and

East New York to get to City Line? And even then, if they trotted north toward Forest Park, that means they're galloping along Cross Bay Boulevard. Then after tra-la-laing through the park, they'd end up somewhere in Woodhaven. Then…what, they rode through Ozone Park to get Patsy Cline here back home? That's, like, thirty miles!"

Lola says, "Well I believe it."

Mom says, "Me too."

I stop the camera. "This was a waste of time."

Lola says, "You're giving up?"

Mom adds: "Charlie Brown."

"Can you stop saying that, Mom?"

Mom sours her face. "I didn't say anything." She takes a bite of cake. Crumbs spurt from her mouth when she says, "He always liked horses. That's why he bet on them so much."

I hit Record. "Remember that big hurricane? The one in the eighties?" Lola tells her it was Gloria. "When the eye was passing over, my husband drove to Aqueduct." She slides the cake into the middle of the table. "He hoped they'd open for a race in between. Isn't that crazy, Joan?"

Lola whispers, "It is."

I remember when that happened. Water had flooded into the basement from a cracked window. I was getting towels from the dryer when we heard the door close above us. My mother rushed outside as his car peeled away. When Mom came back into the basement, I asked, "Stores open during a hurricane?" She snatched a towel and said, "Shut up and dry."

Now Mom stares at the cake, possibly remembering. I film it, a long still shot. Outside a subway passes. She glances at me and I watch her through the camera as she watches the camera watching her. For a second, I'm relieved that there's a slight disconnect between the moment and the memory. That I am only the viewfinder. I thumb the Stop button, feeling guilty for making her upset. No. I'm making a film. I have to keep going.

She says, "I'm tired. Sorry, Joan. I want to go to bed."

I lower the camera to help her, but Lola hops up, "I'll do it. Keep going."

I raise the camera and Lola comes around the table. She supports Mom's arm and lifts her gently. I follow behind as they move down the hallway, a mottled shot of shadow and light. Lola walks her to the bed. Mom tells her the other side. Lola leads her around, and Mom steps on the box I put there after the bathroom mishap before finally flopping onto the blanket. Lola covers her with the dust-ruffle and watches her as though she's looking at her sister, although maybe she's just seeing her aunt.

Mom grabs her hand. She says, "Long time." I'm not sure if Mom means she should stay a long time, or that it's been a while since she last saw Joan. Even if it's the latter, we'll just roll with it. She's happy, and I've learned more about her in an hour than I've known in my whole life. All I needed to do was summon Joan from the dead.

Mom says, "I'm so glad to see you."

Lola says, "Me too, Sis. Me too."

A gust of wind that smells like wet cement lifts the curtains from the sill. The fabric snaps between Lola and my mother, between her sister and her younger self. They smile, as though passing an inside joke between them, one that has hurtled through decades to reach its punchline. I catch it all on tape. This can't be real.

CHAPTER 13

Lola strides into my room, her hands pressed to her sides, her chin slightly raised, a look of refined judgment. Her 'Joan Walk.' I'm not sure why she has adopted this way of moving around in front of my mother. There's an uppity properness to it all, as though Joan roamed the hallways of an English abbey instead of a tenement walkup in 1950s Hell's Kitchen. But Lola's in character, so I'm not going to critique her. When Pacino played Tony Montana in *Scarface* he stayed in character for the entire shoot. Off camera, he refused to answer to his real name. Method acting. I imagine Lola pulling a Pacino. I should be happy she's so invested in our project, though it's slightly weird, now that Mom is nestled in bed in the next room.

I say, "Thanks, Aunt Joan. But Mom can't hear you."

Her shoulders relax. "Oh good. It was getting wonky." She kicks off her shoes, the left sailing into the closet, the right into my TV stand. "Did you learn anything?"

"Other than that she owned a duck? No."

"You learned a little about your dad. That's something."

"This doesn't freak you out? That she thinks you're a dead relative?"

"I've been worse things."

I laugh, but she just stares at me. "Sorry. It just sounded funny."

"Look, I missed so much time with my mom. Just staring out the hospital window at a swath of birch trees. Just thinking about what she was doing." She sits in front of the television. "I called her. Mostly she didn't answer. It's hard to reach people." I imagine her staring at her phone, trying to get the nerve to call her mother. The ringing and ringing. "Anyway, I like your mom."

I sit on the mattress and the springs creak. She slides into me, our arms touching, her skin hot. I place the camera on my lap. "Mom's happy, at least."

"Not easy. Being happy."

"It isn't." We listen to a train clack across the El.

"I want to be happy. Every day I told the birches how I wished I was better and happy. I told my doctor that."

In the movie version of this moment, I kiss her. The camera pulls into a parting shot, maybe fading to black, if the movie is mostly a tragedy. Maybe lifting toward the sky, if the movie is mostly a comedy: Happy Ever After. But this isn't a movie and I'm afraid that if I tell her how much I care, the universe will pounce, so I bump her shoulder like we're in high school again. In the next room my mother yells something, then silence. Lola says, "I'll check."

"She does that."

"Okay, then." She grabs the camera, stands. The red light flicks on, a close-up shot. She says, "Guten Abend. Sprechen Sie mit mir, Herr Doktor."

I flinch, being on the wrong side of the lens, or maybe it's her perfect German.

She says, "Well, c'mon."

As she waits for me to say something, I feel the lens's mute stare. I tug her t-shirt over her belly, covering her purple-stoned navel ring, trying to distract her. "I'm boring."

"C'mon. Before your mom gets up. A quickie. Talk."

"Talking isn't so easy."

Lola bites her lip, mulling her next move. "An interview then."

I forgot who, but I saw this interview once where a director said that you'll never truly know yourself until you're flirting with the camera's eye. Maybe that's what I need? A little self-discovery. "Fine. What'cha want to know?"

She looks into the viewfinder. "I'll ask questions. Important ones. This is the interview part of your film, Herr Doctor." I tell her that I'm not Murnau and she shushes me. "Okay. Director, please state your name."

I fidget on the mattress. "Wesley."

"Are you Prince? Or Cher? Last name too, please."

"Wesley Viola. I'm twenty-six. I live in Queens, New York."

"That's great. Beat me to the age, place stuff. What else?"

I shrug. "I'm a Scorpio."

"Mr. Mysterious." I tell her to stop. "Distracted, sorry. Why are you filming your mother?"

Of course she goes for the jugular question. "I'm not sure."

She stops the camera. "Answer right. Or I'll ask, like, kinky stuff."

No one wants that. "Fine. But I'm filming you next."

"Fine. But no talk about the hospital."

"Why?"

"Cause it's boring! Wake up. Breakfast, meds, bed. Boring, boring, boring!"

I think there's some ditches to fill, but I'll worry about her plot holes when it's my turn to film. "Okay, then."

Lola presses Record. The lens zooms in for a sharper view. She steps back. "I'll start easier. What is your favorite memory of your mother?"

"When I learned how to ride a bike. My dad had left about a year earlier. I don't know if she bought the bike as a distraction, or to help me get around. Or maybe I wanted a bike. Anyway, the bike was orange on steroids. Banana seat. Red streamers on the handlebars. It had this metal cover along the back wheel. She tried to perk it up by putting cards between the spokes, so that when you pedaled it made that snapping sound. Like I was in some 1950s movie. This was the late eighties, when it was all BMX bikes. Mags, pegs. 360-degree twisting handlebars. Everyone watching the movie *Rad*. My bike was hideous. But I loved it. It is one of the nicest things she ever bought for me." I wait for the train to pass. "So she took me to this weedy lot. She gripped the bar of the seat as I pedaled. The bike listed left and right. She smoked like three packs a day, so she exhaled these wheezy breaths as she ran to keep me upright. I was afraid she'd collapse." What I edit out of the story is how Mom smacked me in the head every time I quit pedaling.

"Keep going."

"Okay. And the lot was infested with broken glass, bottlecaps. All these weedy cracks, the big ones with dandelions poking through. I'd hit a bump and lose control. She held on, though, helping me along. We went five days straight. Until I finally took off. I remember her clapping." I feel this tightness in my chest. "Anyway, until I figured it out, she never let go."

"What happened to the bike?"

"Someone robbed it."

"That's so Queens. Of course. My Wes can't have anything nice."

"Yeah." I feel relaxed, calmer. I haven't thought about that in years and it just popped out. What is it about a camera that makes us want to talk? I watch the lens, glad my memory was recorded, that it's now a part of my mother's history, a part of us. I say, "What else?"

"Earliest memory?"

"Sitting underneath the kitchen table as my father called in bets to OTB while my mom washed dishes. I remember the smell of pork chops."

Lola says, "That's sensory memory. Heavy shit. Like this one lunch in the hospital. They gave everybody tuna and a boiled egg. The whole hallway smelled like Chicken of the Sea. I closed my eyes and prayed to Jesus to miracle me a Happy Meal. Just a nip of a burger. Half a nug. A couple of fries. Oh, God. So anyway, I ate it cause Saint Ronny wasn't redeeming my hospitalized ass. We all did. Now whenever I smell tuna or eggs I want a Happy Meal."

Ditches to fill. Before I can ask her why she couldn't have it delivered, Lola shifts her head away from the camera. "Right. No hospital."

She gets back in to it. "Sorry. I have to ask. Worst memory?"

"When I was nine I went to CCD. Religious instruction."

"Hope this isn't a Father Feely O'Touchy confessional?"

I shake my head. "You want the answer, right?"

"Bitte, Herr Doktor."

I say, "So my mother would drop me off ten minutes early so she could run to the Foodtown. It was just me and these two other kids, Lou Defano and Richy

Pelegrino. Lou decided that he 'Didn't like my face,' and so every time Mom dropped me off they'd drag me behind the statue of the Virgin Mother and toss me a beating. I didn't tell the teachers. They would've beaten me up more for finking on them. I kept getting beat up until this one time I shoved Richy to get away, but they caught me. Really worked me over." I take a shallow breath. I'm really upset. "So I come home all bruised up. I told my mother, who of course told my father. He was pissed. Not about the fight. That I never fought back. The next week he drove me. We got out of the car. He made me point them out. I thought he was going to talk to the teacher. Even scare the two kids. He shoved my shoulder and said, 'If you don't beat them up I'm going to smack you around when we get home. Understand? I'm watching.'" I pick at my thigh.

"Your dad beat you up?"

"No. Lou was leaning against the wall and I attacked them. Punching, kicking. I think I even bit him. A teacher had to pull me off of him. Lou was curled on the floor, moaning and crying. He had a bloody nose. Watching him, I felt bad, like there was part of me on the floor. Anyway, they ended up kicking me out of CCD."

"What's so bad about that? Those horse fuckers deserved it."

I listen to a train's brakes as it squeals into the station. "None of that's why it's bad." Mom yells something, then silence. "So when it was done, the teacher grabbed my arm, yelling at me. And I looked over at my dad, hoping for help. But he just had his head poked between the bars. This smile on his face." I think of years later when I found my mother in the schoolyard, and I realize this is one of the reasons I was so upset that day. Her standing there, so fragile and helpless…it was exactly how I felt watching my father. I realized how small I'd been, how I'd just needed someone to intervene. Instead he dropped me into an adolescent *Fight Club*. "I'd just beat this kid up. I was getting in trouble. And he was so amped up about it! It just disgusted me. I guess he was doing what he thought was right. But then there's all the stuff he did to my mother. Gambling. All of their fights. I always waited up with Mom when he stayed out. I always helped clean up the broken dishes. Yet after that bad beating by them, I told her what happened in secret. Made her promise she wouldn't tell him, but...she took his side."

Lola stops the camera. "I don't think it's about sides, Wes."

"Felt like it."

"She probably thought he'd help you. I'm sure that if she knew he was going to bring you there to fight, she would have said something."

"You don't know my mother."

"No. I do."

She sits on the bed and pinches the blanket into a large fold. She doesn't know my mother at all. This diet version of my mother, this imposter who narrates fairytales to faux Joan isn't the woman who raised me. I have other worst memories to tell: The time Mom poured water into my Nintendo's microchipped guts after I blamed her for Dad leaving. That time she whacked me with a ladle in front of my friends when I mumbled that the chicken soup smelled like armpit broth. Smaller grievances, though more embarrassing, like how she'd rub her licked palms across my cheeks to clean my face before I'd march into P.S. 63. But I've chosen a story about my father, the gambler, the drinker, the easy bad guy. I don't want to spook Lola by telling her about Mom's worst moments. Lola likes Mom and I like Lola, so I agree that Lola knows Mom, or at least this version of her. "So, anyway...that was the worst."

"Thank you for your honesty. Last one. Why are you filming your mom?"

Because her memory fades with each passing day, and soon she won't remember me, and I know nothing about her, and maybe after recording her for days, if I play her back the tape, something will click, and her memories will rewind and play with a clearer vision, and she'll be okay, and then my tape will feel peaceful, a reprieve, like Greg and Sarah wading across tidepools, and I'll be transported to a truer version of her, myself. But I just say, "I dunno."

Lola shuts the camera. "Okay. Enough for now." She holds the camcorder out. "Unless you want to film me?"

As much as I want to know more about the hospital, her aunt, I feel sick from my interview. My hands are shaking, so I slide them under my thighs. "Later. I'm kind of depleted, if that's alright?"

"This'll cheer you up."

She walks over to the television and flips it on. She presses Play.

The vacation footage rolls. I fall into the pillow and scoot towards the wall. She slides in next to me and wraps my arm around her. She grabs my hand, presses it into her chest. Sarah walks along the shoreline. The sky is purplish-pink. Maybe a sunrise, maybe a sunset, but it's the color that brings an ache to your chest, the color so perfect, you realize that we're all fragile and temporary. Her sarong ripples as a breeze gusts across the edge of the water. Lola's ears are small, delicate. I follow the curve and it reminds me of the conch shell Greg found. Sarah turns toward the lens. I hear: "Today was a good day," and at first I think it's Sarah, but it's Lola.

She asks me what makes me happy. I say just low enough so the world can't hear, won't conspire and ruin it: "You do."

CHAPTER 14

After the third day of calling out, I'm pulled back into Video Planet.

I would've called out another day, but Dom kept leaving messages for me, my phone buzzing on the nightstand above my head. First, "Feeling better?" then "You're a shitty manager!" then "Mom okay?" then "Suck it!" I could've told Dom I was still sick, but I need the money. We can't film with Gloria there. Besides, sick pay isn't a perk for humble retail workers, even managers.

I left Lola sleeping in my bed, her legs swaddled in my blankets, faded to a seagreen, our private beach. I'd waited for her to vanish, like in high school, or an unexplained jump cut, but as I was leaving, she'd opened an eye and whispered, "Be kind, rewind," and I knew she'd be waiting for me after work. That we'd keep filming.

It is terrifying when you decide, really decide, how you want things to go. For years, I felt as though something was wrong with me. I should've wanted a full-time job, a career. My parents represented the work extremes and the choice was clear: either I was going to live like my mother, who had working six-day, fifty-hour weeks only to return home tired from a job she hated, or I was going to live like my father, unemployed and betting on blind luck while wrecking a family in the process. So instead, I had chosen not to choose. But filming, or even watching the footage, has shown me a third option: movies. Movies are what I've always wanted in this life, and if I die without a pension but I've made one decent film, then spending the rest of my final days scurrying around the dusty boiler of a basement apartment will have been worth it. Lola's right. You just need the fuck 'em to do it.

When I left my bedroom, Gloria was standing in front of Mom's room carrying a basket of clothes, which I should've washed but had forgotten about because of filming and then sleeping next to Lola. Gloria had watched me with a concerned look, as though I was a five-year old fidgeting with scissors. I explained to her that Lola was going to hang around in my room—in other words, out of the way. Then I said, "Mom likes her a lot."

"Have a good day" was all Gloria said.

Her cold reaction surprised me. I wanted her to be happy for me. Maybe she was annoyed that Lola was alone in the house with her, but it wasn't really a problem. Lola was nervous about Gloria, so I knew she would either stay in my room, or leave and visit us later when I got back from Video Planet. I decided it was better to leave Gloria alone. There was no point in pushing the issue. Both Lola and Gloria were here to stay, so they'd have to get along. Eventually.

For the first time in its history, Video Planet has opened early.

Forty-five minutes early. I get out of the Cutlass and take a long look around. The traffic is there. The 747s flying towards JFK are there. Even the heavy chemical, ocean-scented wind is there, dirty and familiar. I'm in the right place, but the place feels wrong. The sidewalk is swept. The window is squeaky clean. The front door is held open by a wedge, which the store has never had, meaning Dom bought one.

Weirdest of all, Dean Martin is crooning "Ain't That a Kick in the Head." I'm not sure how that's possible. Video Planet doesn't have a stereo, or speakers. I've always wanted music in the store, to perk things up, but Dom never wanted to spend the money. Deano asks in his boozy swoon, "How lucky can one man be?" If this was a movie, I just sold my soul for a glass of beer.

In my best Nicholson, I say, "Thanks, Lloyd," and step inside.

All of the videos have their covers facing outwards. Off to the side is a bin with discounted stock for sale. Tacked along the walls are posters: *Raiders of the Lost Ark*, *Jurassic Park*, *Star Wars*, *Jaws*. Their crisp lines and matte finishes make the wall look otherworldly. The store no longer feels drab, depressing. It feels like a place where people will want to rent movies. Seeing it, I should be happy. This is the push I've always wanted for Video Planet. But it all seems fake, like props on a set.

Dom rises from his seat behind the counter, throws up his hands like the Jets won the Super Bowl, and says, "Well, looky who's in our humble establishment!"

"Who gave us a sound system?"

Dom leans against the files. He's wearing a pink polo shirt, but it's wrinkled and faded like he wrestled it out of a storage bin. "Gilda the Good Witch."

"It's Glinda."

As I walk to the counter I hear, "Watch it," and notice Vic is there, behind the counter, half-hidden by the video rack. I kind of expected him to be here.

What I didn't expect, though, is the popcorn machine.

It's one of those old-fashioned kinds, placed at the end of the counter, just before the door. Fire-engine red. Gold bands stenciled along the sides. *Popcorn* written in gold script. I hear the popping kernels, smell the butter. It's real, and I suddenly remember how my mother used to ask me to bring home a movie—*Pretty Woman, Sleepless in Seattle, The First Wives Club*—and before she came home from work, she'd stop at Crossbay Cinema and buy a bucket of popcorn. I don't know how she ate it without getting sick, but she always finished the tub. Now seeing the machine, fused with that snapshot memory of Mom's life, her real life, I feel this gauzy ache that makes me want to bawl. "Popcorn, huh?"

Vic picks up a candy-striped container and waves me closer. "Here, kid." He's wearing a green turtleneck and brown slacks and a black fedora tilted left, Sinatra-style. I wait for him to break into "Stormy Weather," though he's probably a "'My Way," kind of a guy. He opens the door, tinting his glasses yellow, and scoops the box towards the corner of the machine into a popcorn drift, then closes the glass. He holds the box out to me. "If you feel up to it, that is."

Dom says, "Three bucks, Sick Boy."

"That's a bit steep."

Dom says, "You really think I made the price?"

Vic pokes me in the chest with the box to take it. "Sure, it's a bit much, but what's better than popcorn and a movie? Besides, it's still cheaper than a theater."

"That's true." I take the box. I want to eat it and razz Dom, but I place it on the counter to maintain the ruse of my sick days. "Later." Dom winks, as though I've taken his side. I wait for him to ask me how I'm feeling, if my mother is okay, but he runs his thumb along the cards, making a shuffling sound. I say, "How's things?"

Dom says, "Take a guess, Pollyanna."

Vic pinches a kernel from the box and flicks it in his mouth. "Don't mind Mr. Happy over there. He's just pissed about the DVDs."

"We don't have DVDs."

Vic pushes his glasses up the bridge of his nose. "On the way, Kiddo. Getting a slew from Canal Street, friend prices."

Dom fidgets with the cross tangled in his chest hair, his tell of being upset. I don't blame him. Canal Street translates to bootlegs. Whatever DVDs are rented or sold, the cash is going into Vic's pocket. Also, Vic could be planning to wait until the DVDs are in stock, then call his own police raid as payback for Royal. I feel bad for Dom, but he invited this on himself. The real problem, for me anyway, is that if this plays out less than perfectly, or if (God forbid) Video Planet gets shut down in a raid, I can't pay for Gloria. That means a nursing home for Mom. It's that simple.

I say, "I don't know, Vic. People here are kind of antiquated."

Vic shrugs. "We're selling DVDs. They want lamps? Go down the block."

"No. Like, stuck in their ways."

Dom slaps the table. "See, told you. He's smart, the manager."

Vic tosses his hat on the counter. "Can't believe youse two. Here I am, trying to make this shithole better. Before I helped, the place stunk of rats."

Dom says, "Mice, Vic."

"Don't you correct me. DVDs are the future." All I can think is the future's one-part-stolen-to-two-parts-fake, but this is Dom's fight. "Question." Vic puts his hat on, tilts the brim into place. "Who's the boss here?"

Dom plops into his chair. "Tony Danza."

"Watch it, Dominick," Vic says, his voice squeaky.

I mouth Dom to "Stop it." He mouths what I think is "Blow me."

Dom has dark circles underneath his eyes. He looks washed-out, his face sunken and thin. He doesn't reek of cologne. He's all pits. He's losing his store one rental at a time. This is going to get ugly.

I say, "I think Dom's just saying."

Dom says, "Oh do tell, whatever does your lackey mean?"

Vic says, "He means you should shut up."

Dom says, "Well, I can stop anytime."

Vic says, "Then start." He pushes his glasses along the bridge of his nose. "Lemme ask you, kid. When's the last time you got a raise? Besides mine."

Dom says, "About a week ago."

Vic nods. "Impressive. Before that."

I should lie here, but his question makes me realize how I've been treated all these years. Suddenly, I blame Dom for my family situation. He knows how I've been taking care of my mother. That I have a nurse. That a raise would've helped. Even the guy who is blackmailing Dom knows he should've given me a raise. Still, Vic has the potential to have us raided. So I give a noncommittal shrug.

Vic says, "Exactly." He waits for Dom to make a snide comment. When he doesn't he says, "When's the last time you called off sick?"

"I can't remember," which is the truth.

Dom says, "July 5th 1998."

Vic looks at his watch, "It's 2000."

Dom says, "Thanks, Jules Verne."

I say, "Actually, that was H.G. Wells."

Dom says, "Sure, take his side." He rolls forward, his hands gripping his thighs, and stands. His right leg dips forward, his bum knee giving out, and he stumbles into the counter. He places both palms flat on it, legs slightly spread, like he's being arrested. Watching him, I realize how little I want to be watching these two guys argue their claims to Video Planet. I imagine shooting my film, making my speech at the Oscars, spending the rest of my life lying next to Lola, our legs intertwined, studying the spiral of her buzzed hair. Just me and Lola. Us.

Vic picks up the box of popcorn. "Lucky I'm here helping you out." He squeezes and popcorn flows over the top.

If Dom has any sense of self-preservation, he'll use it now. But it's Dom, so he says, "Hey, all I'm saying is that he needs to work." He glances around the empty store. "If he can't work on his scheduled days, then he should..." (Dom bites his lip.) "...be fired. There. I said it."

I feel this nervous ache, imagining a life without Video Planet. No, I'm safe. He doesn't know anything about ordering movies, making copies, or buying cases. Who the distributors are for the legit foreign and independent films. He has locked the store a total of six times since I've started, and that's counting the three days I missed this week. I say, "You want me to fire me after all these years? Even though I was sick?"

Dom says, "Yupski."

Before I can react, Vic grabs my arm. "You ain't ordering him around, Dominick. He's your manager. Fact, I don't know how the kid's working here. Must be a saint. Abused by your fat stupid mean ass."

Dom says, "Hey, I ain't fat!"

Vic pushes the box of popcorn towards me as though it were a tissue. I take a kernel and toss it into my mouth and focus on the taste. The song changes to Neil Diamond's "I Am... I Said." Vic asks, "Why did you stay, kid?"

No one has ever asked me that question. I've always hoped it would be Mom. I wanted it to be Gloria. Last night, I was positive it'd be Lola with her camera. But it's Vic. I answer honestly: "I took this job because I love movies. I thought it'd help me go to college to study film." I wait for him to roll his eyes. He doesn't. I toss more popcorn into my mouth, a tribute to Mom. I feel as though I've confessed a dark secret. "But she got sick. I'm working to pay the bills. I'm all the family she has." He bites his lip, his eyes soft with concern. "Her name is Camilla. She has dementia." I finish my tragedy just as Neil Diamond sings, "I am lost and I can't even say why."

Vic tosses his hat onto the counter. "I had a mother once." Dom laughs, but Vic stabs a look at him that could kill a brick. "She took a heart attack coming home from Bingo with her sister, my Aunt Carol. Mom dropped dead right on the curb."

I say, "I'm sorry."

He smiles. "That's alright, kid. Long time now."

Dom says, "I got a dead mother too, you know."

Vic says, "That's nice. So you know the kid's mom's sick? Still you ride him like a racehorse at Aqueduct?"

Dom knows that there's no excuse for his behavior when it comes to ill parents, especially mothers. I take more popcorn. His forehead wrinkles as he drifts away from us until he's half hiding behind the shelf. He says, "He leaves when he has to, right? Tell him the truth."

Vic says, "New truth. He's getting another raise. You owe him at least a year of sick days."

Dom argues that Video Planet isn't union.

Vic tells him that I've paid my dues over three times twenty, then reaches into his pocket. He pulls out a roll of money, three sizes larger than the one Dom flashed in the alley. He yanks the rubber-band and flicks his wrist. The roll flops open. He licks his thumb and counts off a hundred and sixty dollars. He hands it to me. "Take four days. On me."

Dom slaps the counter, unable to control his anger. "He just had three days! I can't work twelve hour days, five days straight!"

I stick the money in my pocket. "I do."

Vic pats me on the arm. "See. You're a shitty boss, Dominick! Bleeding this kid of his time, underpaying him. Mom sick at home. When I had my store, I treated my workers right." He bites his lip and mumbles that he misses his store, more to himself, and I immediately feel horrible for him. I've been working for Vic for less than three days and he has already been a better boss than Dom. He perked up the store. I've gotten a promotion and a goddamn raise. He doesn't yell or argue with me. Even if Dom didn't know who's store it was, someone owned it. I get that Dom was trying to save the store, himself. Still I think it's not fair, as though I'm some kid on the playground, as though parents aren't allowed to get sick, or stores to get raided, or girlfriends to be stuck in hospitals only to be released in enough time to watch their aunt die. God, there should be rules against it, though, there should be.

Dom says, "I can't be alone in here."

Vic says, "Yeah, why not?"

Dom says, "What if I have to take a crap?"

I say, "Lock the front door like I do." I smile at Vic and he rolls his eyes at me, and it feels warm, even paternal, as though we're in on the long running joke that is Dom. I laugh, glad Dom is getting teased.

Vic says, "See, this kid knows what I'm saying."

Dom hobbles past Vic and around the counter, then stops in front of me and places a hand on his heart. In a nasally voice—a stab at Vic—he says "I've been a Grade-A Certified Douche. I'm sorry."

In six years, he's never apologized, so it sounds like he's speaking a foreign language, even if he is being as insincere as possible. I say, "Yeah, thanks."

Vic says, "Good. I don't want any beef between youse."

Walking past me, Dom bumps my shoulder. As he moves towards the door, he knocks boxes off the racks and onto the floor. Vic yells to pick them up, his voice cracking. Dom says, "Let my Teflon employee heap them up before he goes. Taking a smoke." Something he hasn't done since his mother died. Dom swings open the door and leaves. He watches traffic, pats some guy on the back as he passes the store, as though it's a normal day at Video Planet. He walks toward Tubby's. I wouldn't be surprised if he vanishes for good.

Vic says, "Always like this?" I nod. "Don't let it get to you kid. You're dealing with a lot. Last thing you need is to get upset by that donkey. Anyway, at least you got movies, right?"

I say, "Yeah. It's the only thing that keeps me going, sometimes," and my honesty surprises me. Embarrassed, I turn to pick up the boxes.

Vic says, "Ah, leave them."

And because things just aren't insane enough, the door swings open and Rich strides down the aisle. He's wearing a leather jacket, jeans and no shirt. He stops mid-aisle. "Hey Vic, how's things?"

Vic waves.

"Where's the new movies?" I point to the wall. "No, the newest of the new movies." He knocks on the glass of the popcorn machine, as though he's a kid scaring the fish in an aquarium. Vic sucks his teeth and Rich eases away from it.

I say, "Those are the newest ones we have."

"Nah. Like, I was buying some laxatives and this guy under the El was selling all these movies. Like, stuff in theaters!"

"Those are copies," I say, feeling a bit ridiculous.

"Too bad. I bought, like, ten of them."

Vic walks around the counter. "You bought ten?"

Rich unzips his jacket and his stomach peeks out. "Nah. Like twenty."

"How much did that set you back?"

Rich shrugs. "Like three for twelve bucks."

I see where this is going. "Yeah, the quality is horrible. The movies cut off."

"Mine were bellissimo!" Rich kisses his fingers and opens his hand. He scoots up his sleeve and glances at his wrist. "Going back. See if they got that *Mission to Mars*." He walks down the aisle, then turns. "You'd do some business with them."

Vic watches the popcorn machine, yellow dots cascading down his glasses. I know what he's thinking.

I say "The customers are real sticklers. They complain about everything. We get movies like that and they'd want their money back." I wish for once that Dom would return to the store so he could help me persuade Vic not to do it. Of course, he doesn't.

Vic sits in Dom's chair. "What am I gonna do with this guy?"

I'm hoping that he's pleading to the cosmos. The last thing I want to do is give advice to Vic about Dom. And now I'm the manager of this disaster. I try to distract him by holding up the box of popcorn. "It's good!" Even though he lacquered it in butter and my mouth feels greasy. "Want a box?"

He says, "Later. Let's watch a movie, kid. Ever see *Toy Story*?"

CHAPTER 15

I pull the Cutlas into my driveway and shut the car. A spear of starlings dart between the phone lines, then dip between the line of my neighbor's hedges before a van speeds down the block and they startle again into flight.

I don't feel this way very often, but I have to say I'm glad to be home. After *Toy Story*, Vic let me leave. I'd wanted to wait for Dom to explain to him about Rich and the bootlegs. Getting bootleg films that are out for rent is far less of a hazard than selling DVDs of movies out in theaters, as far as the police are concerned. Also, if a customer bought a faulty DVD, they might call and fink on the store well before Vic does. Plus, Dom's completely out of his mind with paranoia on a good day. Working alongside him when he's actually got something to be paranoid about will be a miserable slog. The least I could do was give him a heads-up.

But Vic gave me another popcorn for the road and sent me on my way. He obviously thinks I'm on his side. And I gotta admit, the money was a nice surprise. But for all his popcorn and sad-mom stories, Vic is bleeding Dom. They both feel that I'm their employee. Fine. I'll keep quiet, do what they both tell me to do. In the meantime, I'll take notes in that skeevy writer way.

It's still early, only four o'clock, so I have time to film. I'll let Gloria leave, which might win points since she didn't seem to want to work today.

I grab the popcorn box and shut the car door. I inhale the March air, laced with the faintest spring smell of possibility. Whether I'm thanking Demeter or Jesus, it feels good. It might all just work out. I climb the steps and unlock the door.

Inside I hear yelling. At first, it sounds like my mother, but as I walk into my kitchen, I see Lola standing on her tippy-toes, her arm straight above her head, and Gloria, who is about a foot shorter than Lola, hopping and swatting as she tries to yank a bag of McDonald's out of Lola's hand.

Gloria says, "Give it to me."

Lola shakes the bag, revealing a curve of grease along the bottom. "Buy your own!"

Gloria hops again, keeping up the half-assed game of keepaway.

Lola spins and says, "That's a McMiss!"

I say hello, but they continue to hop and spin, hop and spin. It feels like Dom vs Vic Part Deux. "What is going on?"

Lola darts behind me. "She's a McDonald's stealer!"

Gloria adjusts the sleeves of her purple sweater. Winded, she says, "She wants to give your mother fast food!"

Lola peeks inside the bag as if Gloria had stolen its contents. "I know she's sick. I bought her a Happy Meal! Just a taste. I promise."

Gloria says, "Yes, of grease and sugar." She gives me a look, a hybrid of both *She's crazy* and *I warned you*. I'd agree with Gloria, but it's not like Lola's getting Mom to mainline heroin. At this point, what does it matter?

Gloria finally realizes I've hidden a treat of my own behind my back. "And what is that?"

"Nothing. I mean, popcorn."

Gloria exhales. "I hope not for your mother?"

I shrug.

"C'mon Wesley, you know she can't have that."

"Maybe it'll make her remember. Or something."

"Popcorn isn't going to do it, Wes."

Lola peeks out from behind my shoulder. "I bought you fries, lady! But forget that now." She darts back, reminding me of the startled birds on the lawn. I hear the bag crinkle. She's chewing fries in my ear, lips smacking. "What's the big deal?"

"The sugar will spike her blood. She'll become agitated. And popcorn will make her sick." When I don't answer, she says, "You know this, Wes."

I take a neutral step toward the wall, staying between Lola and Gloria. "Lola, let me talk to Gloria, okay?"

She pops another fry, the golden end poking out of her mouth. "Why can't I hear? I mean, I'm your girlfriend at this point, right?"

The word 'girlfriend' hangs like a Christmas bulb, lit in neon. I want to kiss her, but it would only amp up Gloria, who is acting like the healthy version of my mother, annoyed with the girl I've brought home.

I say, "Please. Let me talk to her for a minute."

Lola does this snorty-huffy sound and paces down the hall.

My bedroom door slams shut.

Now that it's quiet, I notice that there's a pot simmering on the burner. It's stew, one of the few things my mother eats without a fuss. The table is pulled away from the wall. Bills are scattered on the floor. I imagine

Gloria chasing Lola around the table like a *Tom & Jerry* cartoon.

As we stand there, I reinhabit the role of the troubled son, hoping that'll appease Gloria. In a low sorrowful voice—the one you use when you're at a funeral for the friend of a friend, where you need sadness but lack the gusto—I say, "I know."

Gloria actually shushes me. "No, you don't. She has a serious problem."

I edge closer and whisper, "She's just a little wonky."

"She's a hazard! This afternoon I walked into Camilla's room and Lola was sitting next to her, using your mother's tray as a drawing table. I asked her to leave so I could feed your mother. When I brought the dishes to wash them in the kitchen sink, I found her slurping my stew with the ladle. She could have just gotten a bowl! It's unsanitary. I told her to wait until it's fully cooked. She left the house and returned with McDonald's, and all these art supplies. Which is fine. But she bought the food for your mother."

She hasn't mentioned Joan, at least. So I'm actually a little relieved. I think about explaining to Gloria how Lola always grabs food for others. Or maybe she wants to draw with Mom, or use it for our film. But I can't imagine Gloria approving of my explanations. So: "I'll talk to her, and I'll clean up, too."

She pinches the top of the ladle-handle Lola left in the pot and tosses it into the sink. It feels a bit much. She stares at the yellow wall. "I realize how I sound. I'm glad your life is not only your mother and your job."

"Thanks."

"But if you have her here, you have to make extra sure your Mom is okay."

"Lola would never do anything to hurt her."

"That's not what I'm saying, Wes. Your mother gets agitated, and if she eats the wrong thing, it affects her behavior. Burgers. Popcorn. I want her to be safe. What's best for both of you."

"That's what I want as well."

She nods. "Of course. But if something bad happened. If she fell, or choked. I wouldn't want you to live with that guilt. Just think about it."

I absorb the softness in her voice, her sympathy. I remember how I unscrewed the bathroom doorknob, and I make myself push the moment to its logical extreme, seeing the worst possible thing: Mom sprawled on the bathroom floor, soaked and bleeding. That was a big mistake, but I'm smart enough to never let it happen again. I know what I'm doing. Gloria fixes her shirt, her nervous habit.

I say, "I have more days off. I'll look for jobs with insurance." A fib, but I have a habit of lying to keep people happy with me, even when I'm mad at them.

"Good. We'll find the right place for your mother."

That backfired. "Well, it'll take a while, you know?"

"So does finding a home, honey."

I watch the pot on the stove, unable to look at her.

Gloria says, "I know it's hard. Talk to me."

I can't tell Gloria about the Joan thing. About how I haven't seen Mom this happy, or even this talkative, in years. How can I dump Mom into a home and steal her final joy? Since I've been filming her, she's definitely better. Even if she stays the same, filming my mother has given her back her life, or at least the part when she seemed the happiest. But instead of all that, I say, "This is a good place for her."

"Your mother is confused. And Lola isn't helping. I'm not saying you can't have fun. But Lola's impulsive. Unpredictable."

"I've known her since high school."

"How come I've never seen her? She's never called."

Even more things I can't explain. "She was in an accident. She lived with her aunt, and when her aunt got sick, she spent time caring for her. See? She's responsible."

She says, "Like giving a sick woman fast food? I can tell what's up with your friend, honey. I've worked in an ER."

I push the chair against the table. "What does that mean?"

She places the lid onto the pot. "If I had to guess, I'd say drugs."

"Ohh, drugs!" Like it's the bogey man. "What kind of drugs?"

"You know...drugs."

"That's insane. If she was messed up, I'd know. She's weird, especially when she's nervous. She was in an accident."

Gloria nods, slowly, knowingly. I can't change her diagnosis.

I clear my throat and say, "If she was on drugs, I'd never leave her around Mom," which feels so true that I'm surprised by the words. "She's fine."

"Then she used them heavily in the past."

Wrong again, Gloria, she's always been this way. I think back to high school. She never seemed messed up. She never talked to me about drinking or drugs. In fact I remember conversations where she tried to convince me that we should get straight-edge tattoos. Besides,

I've seen addicts roll into Video Planet, their knobby faces, their sweating, their corn-chip stink. Lola's a painter, an artist. She lost her aunt. And she's hampering Gloria's routine. That's all this is about.

I say, "Can't I be happy?"

Gloria taps her leg. "I'm telling you to be!"

"Fine. Then maybe you're just jealous."

Gloria laughs. "Now I'd say *you're* on drugs."

She meant it as a joke, but I feel this jolt. I watch the legs of the table, the faucet. "Fine. We're all on drugs. You can go, if you want."

"Be careful. I might start to like all these days off."

Her face is flushed. She's upset. So much for the tough ER nurse, I think, though that's not really fair. Watching her shift her weight side-to-side as she stares at the pot, time she had spent for us, I feel horrible about arguing with her. I want to tell her that at times I feel closer to her than I do to Mom. When I was driving home, I imagined us spending holidays together, being a family.

Before I get a chance, she walks past. If this was a movie, I'd touch her arm, tell her I'm just tired, or had a hard day, or sad, or...well, anything. But she just continues into the living room. I hear the rustle of her jacket.

She says, "If you need me just call." Her way of apologizing.

There's a stillness, a chance to follow the movie moment, but it passes. The door shuts, the storm-door hits the frame with a metallic clank. I picture her fleeing down the block, her purse pinned beneath her arm, cursing the decisions she's made. The pot of stew, the perp that caused the brouhaha, sits on the shut burner, its lid on, sauce splattered down the face of the oven. I should chase after her and beg for forgiveness, or at least apologize. I don't, and hate myself for it.

Once my legs feel like they're part of me again, I walk down the hallway. I open Mom's door. She's sleeping. The blankets are crumpled in a way that suggests Lola was there, too. When they were kids, my mother and aunt shared a bed. For Mom, she's twelve again, hiding under the sheets with a flashlight and reading *The Wizard of Oz*. How can I say anything to Lola about arguing with Gloria? I need Gloria. But Mom needs Lola. I need Lola too. I watch her, trying to decide who Mom needs most, then I shut the door.

My bedroom smells like fries. Lola is sitting on the floor, her back against my bed. She's watching the vacation footage. Greg is filming the ocean. This time the water is greenish and flat. There's a line of clouds, cranial and perfect.

Lola says, "I felt upset so I put this on. That's okay?"

Yes Lola, it's fine. I say, "I have to start recording anyway," though I have no intention of returning this tape.

"Cool. Figured." She picks up the cheeseburger, leans over the wrapper, and bites, careful that crumbs don't drop onto the dirty carpet. Behind her thigh is the notorious Happy Meal. She fishes her fries from the bag and spills them onto the wrapper with a snap of the wrist, as though she's a chef flipping shrimp with a teppanyaki flourish. She nudges them towards me.

I take one because fast-food fixes everything. "Thanks." I pop it into my mouth and chew. Next to us sits the sea. I hear the surf; an ocean bird cries.

Lola fixes the fries until they're parallel to each other a centimeter apart. Either she has OCD or she's embarrassed by what happened with Gloria and is focusing on the alignment of her fries instead of talking about it. I take a fry from the line and she replaces it. I tell her it's good. When she doesn't answer, I sit across from her. "I'm sorry about what happened before."

"We can't eat stew tainted with Lola germs."

"You mean Lol-coli?"

She tilts her chin into her chest, fighting hard not to smile.

"Or Lol-monella? Clostri-lola perfringens?"

"Hey, that one blows your ass out!"

"Sure does."

"I knew this guy and his name was Sal Minella. It's spelled differently. Still. Parents, hello?"

"I saw a Family Feud with the Lester family. The dad's name was Moe."

"In the hospital, there was this orderly named Pete Ennis. It had P. Ennis on his nameplate."

I tell her she wins.

She tilts back and onions are pasted onto her knee. "Shit. My food."

"You still have the Happy Meal."

"That's for my sister. No. I mean your mom." She sticks a fry in her mouth. "Sorry. I get confused. It's hard to realize that you're you. I mean which version for a particular moment. Like that poem we learned in high school: "'Prepare a face to meet the faces that you will meet?'" She shrugs. "I'm a painter, not a poet."

I think of Gloria's warning. I'll prove she's overreacting. "How long were you in the hospital?"

She picks up the flattened cheeseburger. She sniffs the bun, then takes a bite. "Six months." She spins the empty fry box, sighs. "I had a concussion. I had rehab and stayed with my aunt. Then she got sick and I took care of her. I told you this."

"I know." Last time, she said coma, not concussion. Are they the same? People use them interchangeably. Her arms don't have any scars. If it was that horrible, wouldn't there be some evidence of her accident? I watch Lola as though she'll reveal more. She's already upset, so I don't want to push too much. I'm not even sure if I'm proving Gloria right or Lola wrong? If she was using drugs, I'd know. Right? She itches her chin with her thumb. I feel awful asking, but just to make sure, for Mom and a clear head about all this, I say, as casually as possible, "So...you're not on drugs?"

Her face changes. "Jesus Christ. Well, I took two Advil today. I always take Tums before McDonald's. Uh, Metamucil for regularity. Whoops, T-M-I. And I'm on Xanax, but like who ain't, right?" Her eyes bore into me. "Lemme guess, Gloria is making you ask?"

I imagine Lola leaving my room, vanishing again for another bevvy of years. Leaving me worse off than I was before. A fizzing panic hits me. "I'm sorry. It was just a question."

"It's fine. The whole fry thing. But like the bumper sticker says, I'm just high on life, baby!"

"Sorry. Seriously. Forget I asked."

"It's all right." She deflates. "You know, if you were around my aunt, I'd probably ask you the same thing."

"You would?"

"Probably. Oh wait." She rocks forward. "I have a surprise." She twists and pulls a piece of folded yellow construction paper from my blanket. "For you."

I take the paper and unfold it.

It's a pencil sketch of my mother. Her face is contained in a six-inch box. The drawing starts just above her eyebrows, a series of dark frown lines, then cuts off just before her scalp starts. The only hints at hair are a few scraggly curls falling across her forehead. The bottom of the box ends with the dark shadows below her lower lip meeting the curved shadows of her chin. Her eyes are larger, her lids heavier. Her face is wrinkled, deepened by crosshatched shadows. The sketch is gritty, honest. There's a hint of confusion, yet sadness, in her stare, which punches through the drawing. Mom is watching us, watching everything. A fully realized version of Dr. Eckleburg. I think of our troubles, her illness. I place the drawing on the carpet.

Lola says, "It's kind of a Chuck Close rip-off. But do you like it?"

"I don't know what to say," which is true. I love it and it terrifies me. "You're really talented."

"Pfft. It's not that good." She twists herself for a straight-on look at the picture. "I'll admit it's the first time I've really wanted to draw, since my aunt."

I touch her leg.

"I was thinking of making a series. Anyway, it's yours." Lola twists back around to watch the screen as a slight breeze rustles the microphone.

I say, "I wish we were there."

"Me too. But I don't think we're those kinds of people."

She is right, but for some reason her saying it aloud causes me to feel this crushing weight from my toes to my balls to the crown of my head. "We're young. There's time," I say, but I couldn't feel any older, or any more rushed.

"I have an idea." She crawls to the television and cranks the volume. She stands and turns off the light. The room is green, clashing against the neon-blue of my phone. "Let's pretend we're already those people." She takes off her t-shirt. She's wearing a purple bra. She slips off her skirt, revealing yellow underwear. She tosses her clothes at me.

Wait. I think I know where this is going.

I was seriously overweight in high school. I had curly hair and sported a double-chin. I thought the best way to combat my hideous face was to grow a goatee. With my slightly upturned nose and small nostrils I resembled a pig. Whenever I felt particularly overcome with self-loathing, I'd stand in front of the bathroom mirror and in a snorty voice say, "I'm Pigboy! You're never rid of me!"

This is what I think of when Lola says, "Now you."

"I'm wearing Ninja Turtles boxers."

She turns the volume up and lays on her back. She runs her palms along the shaggy carpet, pinching the fibers between her fingers. "We're at the beach."

Wait. I don't think I know where this is going.

"C'mon, the water feels great!" Her face is lit blue. Greg's feet splash as he walks into the ocean. Lola touches my socks. She's smiling, relaxed. We are seated along the shore, the water lapping her body. It's funny how you can think you're living your own private illusion until someone else believes it. Then you have to wonder if it's an illusion at all.

I slip off my jeans and toss them onto the bed-cum-beach-chair. I tug off my sweater and flip it behind me. "I forgot suntan lotion."

"That's okay. I forgot towels." She whispers, "Forgot our key. Forgot lunch." She turns her face, resting her cheek on the carpet. I lie next to her. "Forgot everything but you."

When the train passes on the El, it sounds like the waves. We roll towards each other. I run my finger along her arm. Her skin prickles. I don't care about drug addictions or rehabs. She's here. We're not feigning a life, we're here. She stretches, her hands knocking into the bed's platform, though it could be the hull of a lifeboat.

A seagull cries. I roll onto my back. Water splashes. She sings, her voice low and raspy, "Under a blanket of blue, wrapped underneath the stars." She grabs my hand, running her thumb along my finger. Wind, surf. Lola slides my hand to her heart. Lola shifts to Joan, Lola shifts to Sarah, Lola shifts to versions of Lola. Prepare a face. I squeeze her hand. She's here. Lola squeezes. I'm here. A videotape, a set, a stage, a beach. Emotions transcribed into film, transcribed into images, transcribed back into emotions. We believe it. We do. We're floating. Reeds tickle my back. Under a blanket of blue. It's all blue. The ocean, the sea. We're adrift.

We wade farther, farther.

CHAPTER 16

Mom's left eye is blinky, an incessant flapping that just won't go away. We're sitting on the couch, waiting for Lola, who is singing in the shower, an off-pitch version of "I Wish it Would Rain Down." In between verses she hums Clapton's fills.

This morning I woke up early and started to copy the Mom footage onto a blank VHS. Lola was sound asleep on the floor, wrapped in a blanket. Last night, the footage rolled. The waves, the surf: at times it was disorienting, which I guess is the point, our hideaway, our vast tropical sea, not exactly being Sarah and Greg, but not exactly being ourselves either. Lying next to her, I realized that I hadn't been that close to anyone my whole life. I didn't have time to analyze what had happened. I was happy. I am happy, and that's all that matters.

Also, I had to focus on filming. I watched the Mom footage and wrote down on a legal pad the shots I still wanted: one in her bedroom, one in the basement. Flipping through her photo albums. As long as Mom talks to Joan, I can film her memories before they disappear.

But Mom woke up early. I made her cereal, which she refused to eat, then I brought her into the living room. I slid open the blinds to give her a quick shot of serotonin, then opened the window to let some freshly polluted air into our house. That's when her eyes went blinky. Maybe it's a nervous twitch? Unless it's a tic from the higher dosage of donepezil. Unless it's a seizure. Unless it's olanzapine. Unless it's another case of Bell's palsy. Unless it's the Sanka. Decaf, so I thought she'd be alright. Unless it's dust that touched down on the surface of her cornea. Mom tells you nothing, so by default it might be everything.

I place the camera next to her on the couch. "Mom, are you okay?" She blinks three times. I go into the kitchen and run paper towels under the faucet. I bring them to the living room. I place the wet ball against her eye. It must've been dust, because her body relaxes in a way that shows it feels soothing.

I toss it onto the coffee table, say, "Better?"

Her eye twitches, three, pause, three, as though it had to catch up.

I hear: "Better what?"

But Mom's lips didn't move. Holy shit, Mom's telepathic. I watch her face. Say: "Better?" Something smacks my ass. I jump up and twist around.

Lola says, "Spanking time."

"Jesus fuck. That was you."

"Sure was." Her face is shiny with water, as though she swam out of the video and walked into the room. She's wearing my gray sweatpants, the elastic rolled shipwreck-style so it cinches her waist. She's barefoot. There's an infinity symbol tattooed on her left big toe, a stenciled-looking daisy tattoo on the right one.

"Didn't I give you a towel?"

"I drip-dry, baby." Mom is staring at the ceiling. "What's wrong with her eye?" She slides her palm along her sweatpants, then feels Mom's forehead. "She's cool."

"She didn't eat her breakfast." As though meal consumption would explain facial twitches. Maybe I should call Gloria? But Gloria hates Lola. And after last night, I'm sure she hates me, too. If I tell her Mom's blinking, she'll hate that, too. I imagine her with her penlight and blood-pressure cuff. Talking about proper care. Every pothole Mom hits is a reason to park her ass into a hospital. I'm tired of Gloria swooping in and saving my failures. I can do this. "Maybe she needs a nap."

"She slept all night. What should we do?"

"I don't know." I watch her, hoping for the tiniest of miracles. Obviously, Mom didn't plan on her eye being twitchy, but it feels intentional. I decide to film, and here's my mother, once again sabotaging my plans with a literal blink of an eye. I want her to be okay, but I kind of want to film more. Illnesses on film sets happen. Harrison Ford's fever during the shooting of *Raiders*. Poor Shelly Duvall's illness during *The Shining*. I can't say this to Lola. Maybe the living room is a kind of trigger. It led to the horrible bathroom incident.

I say, "Let's move her."

Mom garbles a string of sounds that might pass for words.

Lola kneels. "What, sis?"

Mom clears her throat. She says, "The garden."

Lola nods. "It's kind of warm. Should we?"

Can we? Gloria never takes her out. It's mid-March. The sun is peeking through the blinds. Birds are chirping. I hear the jingle of a dog leash. There's those sanatoriums in the Alps where afflicted people flee to lessen their maladies. I'll bundle her up in her robe and that hideous peacock-colored overcoat she wears on holidays. She'll be warm. She's sick and that's what she wants. Besides, my film needs outside shots. "We just have to be careful."

I open the hallway closet and dig out the shoebox filled with hats and gloves. I grab her pink scarf and beanie, a blue mitten and a green one, both lefties. Mom loved to buy winter jackets. In this closet alone, I count ten before I stop. There are jackets the color of orchids, plums, and dandelions, sensible grays, dressy blacks. Jackets made of leather, suede, polyester hybrids, some still with tags. Others are wrapped in cellophane, dry-cleaned and ready for the morning commute she'll never take again. I run my finger along each of the hangers, feeling her unkept plans to wear them, like the hats Doc Archibald bought for his wife in *Field of Dreams*. Soon, Mom's coats will end up either tossed in a dumpster or donated to the Salvation Army. I think of the time Mom spent in A&S, Macy's, or Sears, sliding coats along the rack, twisting in front of mirrors, deciding if she liked them, only for the jackets to be encased in this musty closet. I know we're not our stuff, but our stuff is us, kind of. I can't keep these jackets, but I don't want to give them away, either. I stare into the closet negotiating with myself on a plan I can live with until Lola calls my name.

I unhook one of Mom's overcoats. It still reeks of cigarettes and hairspray.

When I get back to the living room, Mom and Lola—now Joan—are laughing, as though they were playing a practical joke. Stupid jealousy overtakes me. I tried for twenty-minutes to get Mom to talk, and Lola did it within seconds. "Ready?"

Lola turns. "She's still doing that eye thingy."

I say, "Let's just go with it," in what sounds like a director's tone. I clasp Mom's hands and haul her upright, all dead weight. Once she's standing, I slip her left mitten on, then the right one. She says, "Flippers," a joke from when I was a kid, though she's serious. I drape the overcoat onto her shoulders like she is John Gotti, then slip on her hat, covering her eyebrows.

Mom says, "How do I look?"

"Dapper."

Mom shucks her teeth. "I need a woman's opinion."

Lola says, "You look warm."

Mom says, "Good. Let's go see the beach."

"The beach?" Lola says, confused.

"She thinks we're in Atlantic City."

Lola pokes my stomach. "Oh yeah, betting it all on number nine."

Mom snorts. "That's roulette. Blackjack is my game."

I debate with myself about what would be easier: to say she won, or to tell her we're not playing yet. I say, "Come on. The deck. The beach."

She watches me as though I'm lying, which is half true. "I don't want that."

Lola says, "C'mon, Sis. It'll be fun."

Mom watches Lola, working out who she is, or maybe her response. "Okay."

I say, "Just give me a second." I pick up the camera and walk down the hall. I slide open the closet and hit Record. I push myself into the jackets and then slowly pan along the closet bar, trying to get as many jackets in the shot as possible, feeling silly, urgent. Still filming, I step back and slide the closet door closed, then touch the gold-colored knob, as though it were a seashell. I hit Stop and then walk into the living room. I tuck the camera under my arm. "Ready?"

Lola says, "Let's do it."

We each grab an arm. Mom teeters, but we steady her. I say, "The side door."

We shuffle her into the kitchen. I open the door to the stairway that leads to the side door. The stairs are a big risk. The hallway is too narrow for us to be lined up marching-band-style. I tell Lola to stand in front of us in case Mom tumbles.

"Got it. So she's the cream in between."

"Right."

I poke Mom's back, a bulk of outerwear. As we line up single-file for our descent, I remember a game I called Bumps from childhood. I'd sit on the landing, extend my legs, and rock forward until I slid down the steps. This is the XSports version. If Mom takes a header down the stairs, she'll definitely land in a home, though whether it's a nursing or a funeral home is anyone's guess. For a second, I hesitate, but we're here now. We have no choice.

I clench her arm tighter and tell her to place her hands on Lola's shoulders. Mom says, "Her what?" I lift her arms and do it for her.

Mom says, "What's this, a congo line?"

"Take a step, Mom."

Lola sings, "Oh, you put one foot in front of the other. And soon you'll be walking across the floor." I give her a look. "Sorry. My favorite Christmas show."

It might be Mom's favorite too, because we take the five steps like this until Lola opens the door. The sunlight feels hot and blinding.

Mom covers her face. "Turn off that flashlight!"

"Give us a second."

We wait, Lola standing outside, wearing my old puff jacket and a Mets hat, its brim tilted backwards, and Mom standing on the landing, bulky and confused, while I lean against the wall, a step higher, wearing my old peacoat, which for some reason smells like cat piss. We must look ridiculous.

Mom says she needs to sit.

I say, "Remember there's a step outside."

"A step. Outside," she says, as though I'm speaking Pig Latin.

Lola says, "I've got her." She twists and grabs her hands. Mom half-steps, half flops down and leans back against the house.

We're outside. I say, "You did it."

Mom says, "I didn't do anything!" And Lola laughs.

This time of day, the sun hits the yard fully. I smell the pavement of the baking patio, the tracks of the El; even the dirt wafts with a cityish loaminess. I open the folding chair, its rusted hinges stiff and creaking. I press on the seat, checking that it'll hold Mom's weight. Satisfied, I place it next to the rusted barbeque.

The yard isn't much of a set, but with my two neighbors' cyclone fences and their clotheslines and car tires, and with the zigzag of power lines above us, there's a dirty realism, a *Rear Window* feel. As for staging, if I sit her on the patio, I'll use the backdrop of the house. It's not a tropical beach, or even a casino, but it'll have to do.

Lola says, "We're coming around the mountain."

She walks Mom to me, carefully, as though she's walking over a patch of ice. I brace my hip against the back of the chair and say, "Sit, Mom." She drops into the seat. The chair legs skid from the force. "Keep still or you'll tip."

Mom says, "Tip who?"

"Just stay there." I grab two milk-crates and place them upright.

Lola says, "Thank you, kind sir," in a mock-English accent and sits.

We've traveled fifteen feet in fifteen minutes, and I'm exhausted from the stress. "Let's take a minute."

I sit and my shoulders sag as this dull ache pulses inside my forehead. Mom slides her feet against the patio, finding the scuffing sound amusing. It's upsetting, so I focus on the sway of the bushes, the sparrows sitting on the neighbor's clothesline, happy and chirping. It's hot, one of those days when you know that spring has finally elbowed its way into the month. Watching her, I wonder how many more springs Mom will enjoy, or even understand. Seasons seem limitless until they're not. But today, we're fine. Maybe that's what matters.

Lola points towards the trees. "That was where we rekindled our love. I got scared. Like I had the wrong house. Good thing I had snacks."

I imagine her hiding underneath my neighbor's patio furniture, stealing bites from a McDonald's apple pie. She spins the purple stud in her nostril as she stares at Mom, enjoying every minute that she's in her aura. I say, "You weren't sure?"

She bites her fingernail. "Got lucky on the second try."

"Where was the first house?"

"It wasn't here." Lola pats Mom on her thigh. "I think her blinking stopped."

"I hope so," I say. "And I'm glad you found me."

She sings, "At last, my love has come along," in her swoony timbre.

Mom says, "I danced to that song. I had that nice dress and a quail."

Lola says, "She means veil. Her wedding."

I open the side panel and hit Record. Mom turns toward Lola and rubs her cheek. Lola closes her eyes, a relaxed look on her face, like when you scratch underneath a cat's chin. Mom starts humming some amalgamation of three different songs, none of them "At Last." Lola asks what song it is and I shrug.

Mom says, "We should drink. It's all comped."

Apparently, we're back at the casino. I pull back the lens, capturing her hunched, jacketed-and-robed frame. In the sun, I see the estuaries of veins flowing along her forehead. How wrinkles crumble around her chin as she gnaws on her lip. She's an animated version of Lola's drawing. Except the portrait showed an alertness in Mom's eyes. Now, that's been blotted out. I want to take her back inside the house, but the thought of trekking the flight of stairs seems impossible. Besides, the yard is helping her eye. I've committed to this project. Spielberg pulled off *Jaws* despite hemorrhaging funding and struggling to rig up three mechanical sharks (all named Bruce); Coppola did *Apocalypse Now* despite jungles, Hurricane Olga, heart attacks, and fat Brando. I've only gotta deal with Mom. I raise the camera and hit Record.

On cue, she says,"Where's the waiter?"

"He just went inside."

She tries to stand but flops into the chair, the metal legs creaking. "You! Cameraman! Make sure you're getting all the tables."

So now we're at a wedding. "How many people were at your wedding?"

Lola says, "I bet it was a big one."

I say, "My dad has a brother. Mom only had her sister, and she couldn't come."

"She's right here," Mom says. "I'm looking for my husband," as though he'll stroll into the yard, bowtie askew, drink in hand, sweaty-faced and leering.

Lola says, "Where was your wedding?"

Mom pats the side of her head, fixing her hairdo. "Rooftop wedding." Lola shrugs and I tell her that it's a citified version of a barn wedding on the roof of your apartment building. Like the montage scene from *Raging Bull.*

Mom says, "Oh, but remember all that trouble?" Mom straightens in her chair. She's trying hard to remember. I hold the camera steady, capturing her portrait, behind her the stale yellow of the aluminum siding. A gust of wind blows the strands of hair sticking across her face. "It was a big mess."

"How?"

She glances over her shoulder. "Where is that waiter?"

Lola says, "We ordered already. They're getting it."

Mom nods in agreement, but doesn't seem to understand what she was told.

Lola says, "What was all the trouble?"

"The big mess?"

I say, "Yes."

"Bit nosey for a cameraman."

Lola touches Mom's arm and mumbles something. They laugh. Mom says, "The day before the wedding my father made me take him to my husband's house. He wasn't my husband yet. You know." She closes her eyes. "Dad told his father that he didn't like his son. That my daddy saw him playing the horses. My husband hurled a tomato at the car. Big mess."

My stomach churns. I want to ask her why he waited to complain until right before her wedding day, but I don't want to confuse her. Lola clenches her hand and Mom shudders, possibly for the present, but most likely for the past.

She says, "So this and that happened. Badda-beep, badda-boop. Mom hid my dress. She was afraid Dad was going to slice it up. He stayed out all night. I was afraid he got killed. I couldn't believe he'd miss my wedding. I even made Mom drive to Friend's Bar. I went inside in my gown, asking the owner." She sucks her teeth. "His name? Dom?"

Lola says, "You stopped looking?"

"I had to! I went back to the church and Dad was sitting in the last pew. He clenched my elbow and rushed me down the aisle. He dropped me off at the altar, then he looped around the pews and went home!"

I say, "What about your mother?"

Mom watches the line of trees. "Mom went to the party. Not Dad."

My grandfather, her father, died when I was five. I remember him shifting on his rocking chair. I'd filch the quarters that shook loose from his pocket as he dozed in front of the TV. My parents' marriage was doomed from the start. Mom had to fight so hard from the first day. Of course it failed miserably. I run my thumb along the Stop button. She's clearly upset, and I feel like a flea sucking that last pint of her blood. Still, I push, "The parents never saw each other?"

Mom says, "They lived together." A wind gusts across the yard. Mom watches the branches shake.

"No, your parents and your husband's parents."

Mom squints, concentrating. She says, "My father went to my husband's father's funeral."

Lola says, "That's some icy shit, right there."

"So you went on your honeymoon?"

"We just got married. Tomorrow we're moving."

Lola says, "Where?"

"You know. Next to Jack Kerouac and the cows."

What if she's riffing off a soap opera she watched last weekend? The wedding seemed real enough. Then you get this blurry cockeyed nonsense. "Are you sure about this, Mom?"

Mom says, "I used to talk to his mom. I can't remember her name."

Lola sings, "Hey Jack Kerouac, I think about your mother."

"10,000 Maniacs, really?"

Lola laughs. "It just popped into my head."

I point the camera at my feet and hit Stop. "All right, that's enough." Lola asks why, sincerely confused. I say, "She's talking about writers and dairy farms!"

Lola says, "She means the milk factory. He lived behind it. Well, first he lived above a bakery in Ozone Park. Not far from where you live. Then they moved because he was shacked up with his mom, like a loser!"

I glare at her until she remembers my living situation.

"Anyway, uhhh...that house is by the expressway. Right Sis?"

I say, "How do you know this?"

She says, "Everybody knows this. It's Jack Fucking Kerouac."

Mom picks fuzz off her coat. "Let's play the slots."

I say, "Forget it," afraid to hear more. "It's cold."

"Two minutes. *On the Road* is like my favorite book ever. The only people for me are the mad ones."

Again I give her a look.

"Well, I...uhh..." She slaps her thigh. "Wow. If she knew him, what a gas!"

"She didn't. She would've mentioned it to me. Let's face it. Every guy at the age of eighteen hits a Jack Kerouac phase. I would read it on the couch while she watched television. She never said anything." I hold out my hand to lead her inside. Mom watches it, confused by the motor planning. "That's enough for today."

Lola says, "But I want to hear what she says!"

"That's funny."

"What do you mean by that?"

"Well," I go on. "You're sitting here listening to tall tales, and you've told me nothing about yourself."

"That's not true."

"Uh, yes it is! I'm just saying, all the time you've spent here, I should know more." I flick my wrist and point. "Daddy-O."

"I'm helping you! I'm being here for you! The mysterious crazy dream girl who shows up out of nowhere and takes the guy's problems away. Isn't that what guys want? You're telling me that's not good enough?"

"That's not what I'm saying!"

Lola says, "Then what are you saying? I told you why I came back. Everything. What else do you want?" She pulls the strings on her hood and it cradles her face, only her nose peeking out.

I'm taking my frustration for Mom out on her, but that doesn't mean I'm wrong. She told me why she's here, why she wanted to find me, but she hasn't answered, or even let me ask her any more questions about it. Gloria's warning creeps into view again, but I refuse to believe that nonsense. I feel like an idiot. I can't ask her now. All I can say is: "I just want to know more about you."

Lola pulls her hood open and watches me. "I'm here, right? Isn't that enough? Who cares about the hospital. We're together now. I'm even helping you with your Mom."

Does she mean it's a hassle? She has never complained. She has never asked to do anything else, besides filming. The word "even" is doing a lot of work, blinking hot and resentful. A sparrow lands on the dirt, hops twice and flutters away. Lola can fly away too, if she wants. "Do you hate it? Helping, I mean."

"With Sis? Of course not." She takes her hood off. "I just love Kerouac, okay?"

"I'm sorry." I point toward Mom, who picks her ear, then sniffs her finger, then sticks the finger into her mouth. "This is just a lot. And I can't decipher between all of this cockeyed bullshit."

"Film it all, then. Let your movie figure it out."

That's the most sensible thing I've heard all morning. I flip on the camera and say, "Where are you moving with your husband?"

Her eye is twitching again. At first a small misfire, then a blinking flutter. Just when I'm about to give up, she says, "Sis, want to hear a secret? He never moved to Florida. He lives where we started."

I say, "Who? Jack Kerouac?"

Mom says, "Hired help, fetch me a drink!"

"Who, your father?"

"The other father."

To Lola I say, "Is she saying what I think she's saying?"

"Jesus, I think so."

It can't be my father. She's confused. Mom slides her hands underneath her thighs. My lips, face go numb. Trying to distract myself, I zoom closer, focusing on her reveal as the reality of what she's saying hits, until her reveal is a plot point in a script, a dramatic arc in a film, a release of information that's easier to process than family secrets. Mom watches the sky, her eyes still misfiring. I don't believe it. She's talking wonky. My father can't live in Queens. He would've contacted me. Right? Hell, he could've strolled into Video Planet and I wouldn't have known.

Mom coughs that phlegmy hack, and says, "He circled back." She nods, letting her secret sink it. A train passes on the El, the wheels sparking, leaving that burnt track smell.

She pulls on her sleeve. "Let's play blackjack."

I say, "Did you see him?"

Lola says, "Give her a minute. If you yell, she'll get more confused."

"I need to know," I say.

I realize that I'm lying. I'd rather wallow in ignorance than hear that my father never left Queens, he only left me. Things are pretty sad around here, but at least it's a familiar sadness. The camera feels heavy as my head becomes spacey and distant. If I wasn't filming this debacle, I'd stop. The film propels me. Against my fear, doubt and better judgment, I keep recording. I say, "See who?"

Mom reaches into her robe pocket and pulls out a purple Monopoly bill. "Lucky day." She smiles, "Let's play the slots."

"Later. Where did your husband move to?"

She glances around the yard. "He's at the track."

Lola says, "I have an idea. No, he's at the house. With the cows."

Mom says, "He moved to a farm?"

I say, "No. With Jack Kerouac's mom."

Lola whispers her name. "Gabrielle."

Mom's face shrivels as she sucks in a sob. "He shacked up with Gabby? How could he move in with her? I know she's lonely. But we're friends!"

Lola rubs her shoulder. "This is going off the rails, Wes."

She's right. Mom looks tired, confused. She needs to eat lunch. The joys of a diaper change. If she hadn't just revealed that she's known for thirteen years that my father never moved to Florida, I'd almost feel bad. But how could she hide this? Mom closes her eyes, lifts her head towards the sun. We're either at the beach, the casino, or the wedding. She's too confused to believe anything she says, let alone to tell the truth. I laugh, feeling foolish for getting absorbed in her demented fables. But then she says, "Leave him alone, Wes. Please. He wants nothing from us," in that same tone she'd use sometimes during my childhood when he'd decided to send me a random card with five dollars in it, and I'd beg her to write a letter back. That's what she'd say: "Wants nothing from us," which always felt like a thousand pins sticking into my cushy heart, and that's how I know now that she's telling the truth. Mom says, "I promised him."

Lola mumbles, "Holy shit."

"I don't believe you," I say, the lie so obvious that every sparrow sitting on the clothesline is laughing at me. I place the camera on Lola's lap and stumble towards the side door. Lola calls after me. I make it out of eyesight and lurch forward, stomach churning. My entire body refuses to accept this reality. Lola calls from the yard, asks me if I'm okay.

No Lola, I'm not. I tell her to keep my mother there. She says something, but I just hear ringing in my ears. It's better than hearing the truth. Want to hear a joke?

What's worse than being dumped by your father? Being lied to by your mother.

CHAPTER 17

My world feels made out of paper.

I open the side door and the house feels colder than it did a few minutes ago. I slide the bolt. I move through the kitchen and into Mom's room. I think of movies with complicated relationships, trying to find a context for my emotions. There's *Parents*, where the kid thinks his Mom and Dad, played by Randy Quaid (totally underrated actor) and Mary Beth Hurt, are cannibals. *Home Alone*? No, the parents rush back for their son. I surrender my comparisons. Mom emptied her dresser a few days ago, so I know there's nothing hidden. I open her closet. I kneel, push aside shoes, sneakers, and a wicker box stuffed with hats. At least I didn't find a vibrator.

I sit on the edge of the bed as though the missing secret will materialize. The movies make finding clues seem easy. The encrypted documents are displayed on the desk blotter. The murderer left a recorded phone message. It's a matchbook from the secret mafia hideout. In real life, it's just not that way.

Lola is knocking on the outside door.

Maybe Mom uses the same hiding places as I do? I squat onto the carpet and jam my hands between the mattress and box spring, then drag my hands along as I crawl to her side of the bed. Over here, I feel something and I yank it free.

It's the second manilla envelope this week. She might've just stuck it there when she was confused, but I don't think she has the strength to lift the mattress. I'm scared to open it, but I tip the envelope, as though I'd find another videotape.

Instead, a stack of papers spills out.

I see the deed to the house, in my mother's name. Her 401(k) papers and insurance forms. Her social security card. Things I needed when she first got sick but could never find. She even saved her signed job offer from thirty years ago. I tap the papers against the carpet, lining up the pages, and place them into a stack on the right. I take another page. It's her birth certificate. There's my birth certificate. The title for the Cutlass. Lola bangs on the door. I need to search Mom's papers, find something, anything, to know if she's telling the truth or if this is just a crazy story. I keep sorting. I find my first report card, all check pluses. Her first report card, all A's. A picture of a young woman holding a duck. Joan's death certificate. Her mother's prayer card. Her father's prayer card. Morbid shit.

I stare down at the fan of papers and bills. I say, "Come on, give me something else." I move an old electric bill, revealing a yellow square of paper. I unfold it.

At first, I don't understand what I'm looking at. Then I realize it's an apartment lease. 134th Street. That's the block of Jack's house by the milk factory. On the bottom of the page is my father's signature, written in tiny script. My mother's signature is on the line next to it. They've been separated for over a decade, yet here their names are, together. Did she co-sign his apartment? The date is crossed out. I stare at the secret lease. She must've known she was sick and hid this stuff until she could destroy the evidence, but her illness ran faster than she did and she lost her chance. It's a crazy hypothesis, but why else would she hide such important papers? If Mom signed his rental, she must've been talking to him. She knew where he was this whole time. I imagine them sneaking off to dinners without me while she pretended that she had to work late. She was having an affair with her husband.

Maybe I'm overreacting. Maybe she signed his lease as a peace offering. No, as a way of knowing he was still around.

I stare at the blacked-out date. I fall back onto the carpet and stare at the popcorn ceiling until it spins. I can throw out the lease and pretend it doesn't exist. He's never bothered to reach me. He's never wanted to. I have so many larger problems: Mom's illness, Video Planet, my film, Gloria and her nursing home campaign. Maybe the best thing to do is let it go? I hold up the paper above me, staring at mother's loopy script and my father's tiny scrawl, pushed so hard against the paper that you can see the indentation on the other side, tense and desperate and angry. I can't ignore this. Maybe I can crawl under the bed and die.

The bell rings like a machine gun.

I sit up and stick the paper into my back pocket. I stuff the rest of the papers into Mom's sacred envelope and stick it all under the mattress again.

I walk down the hall and peek out the window, expecting to see Lola. Nope. It's Dom. The last person I want to deal with. I pull back fast.

He says, "Peekaboo."

I open the door, waiting for him to step inside.

He leans against the staircase railing, crosses his arms. He's wearing gray sweats and a Mets' t-shirt. Number 17, Keith Hernandez. He must've bought it back in '86 when he was eighty-six pounds lighter. The orange and blue letters are faded. The material is stretched to encase his girth. I step outside and shut the door. A cool breeze cuts against us. He says, "How's it going, sicko?"

Exactly how you think. "Okay, I guess."

"Goody gumdrops."

I point to his shirt. "I thought you were a Yankees fan."

He pulls the bottom of his shirt for a peek, as though he was abducted, probed and then dressed by aliens. "Everybody loves the '86 Mets." He lets his t-shirt fall back. "I'm not the traitor in this conversation." He means, in his demented brain, siding with Vic.

I need to ask Mom about the lease, record her answers and decipher looney from the truth and then figure out what to do next. The longer I entertain Dom's insanity, the less likely Mom will be coherent enough today to answer my questions. A station wagon speeds down the block. I sigh: "You asked me to stay. I stayed. You wanted me to help. I'm helping. If Vic gives me days off, or a raise, there's nothing either of us can do about it. So just stop it."

He says, "Stop what, Judas?"

"What did you expect he'd do? You narc'd his store."

"It's a misunderstanding."

"Right. You 'accidentally' dialed the police."

He strangles the railing. Rust flakes sprinkle the concrete. He's not listening. Without turning around, he dusts his palms. "Things are getting messy," he says, by which I think he means that he can't handle actually working at his own store.

"I'll come back, okay? Tomorrow. The next day."

Dom wipes his forehead, leaving a rusty streak. "He's selling bootleg movies."

"We're renting them. So why not sell some stock?"

"No, you savant. Movies from the theaters."

I look away. "Yeah, I thought that might be happening." I can see it all play out: the tapes will be blurry or mute like they always are, people will demand their money back, and Vic will make Dom pay the customer with whatever cash Dom has left, completely bleeding Dom. I squirm with guilt for not telling him earlier.

"Video Planet was my mother's dream. And to have that fucker selling them. Right in front of the store." He exhales and it's a vat of whiskey. He pokes me in the chest. "This is all your fault. I'm losing my underwear."

Typical Dom, blame everyone else. "What if we moved them where it's not so easy to see them. Like into the Adult room?"

"Sure. Granny'll mistake *Forrest Hump* for *Forrest Gump*. Good move."

This is exhausting. "I'll help, but I have stuff going on with my mom."

I wait for him to ask *What kind of stuff?* But Dom doesn't have room for other people's problems, especially today. He pats my shoulder as if to let me know that he's said everything that he needed to say. "I better get back before Vic starts selling bootleg whiskey."

He smiles, I don't. "Yeah, you better go."

Dom nods. "Look, I know I can be a bit testy, but Video Planet needs you. I need you." Before I tell him—however weird it'll be to say—that I need him too, and I'll do everything I can to help, his face prickles red and he says, "Fine. Don't say it back."

"I was going to say it!"

"You only love me for my body."

I say, "Guilty," and we smile, the smile you give a dying man, or a video store.

"Tomorrow, then."

I nod, but I'm not going anywhere until I figure out the lease.

He teeters down the stairs, holding his leg with the fake knee. He grunts with each step and swings the gate and hobbles towards the El before he finally turns the corner and disappears.

CHAPTER 18

Ten minutes after Dom, there's a knock, and Lola enters my bedroom.

I'm sitting on the floor picking fibers from the carpet. She sits on the corner of the bed; her knee grazes my shoulder, and it takes everything not to collapse into her lap and bawl like a four-year-old.

Lola says, "Took a long time to get her in, Wes. Could've used your help. I made her take two feet on one step. I was calling for you."

I shrug, and she curls her finger around a swath of my hair. It's soothing. She's right. I should've helped her bring my mother into the house. But I needed to be alone. I say, "Sorry."

"I get it. Your Mom's okay. She's in the kitchen wolfing donuts."

I shift to the side and slide my hand into my back pocket and hand Lola the lease.

"What the fuck is this?"

I lean back, surprised. "Read it."

She reads the paper, her lips moving. "Is that your parents' signatures?" She flips to the back of the paper and reads the legalese. "She was telling the truth." She holds the lease out. When I refuse to take it, she places it on the carpet.

From the kitchen, Mom asks for another donut.

Lola says, "Sure, Sis! The box is on the table!"

"What table?"

"The one you're sitting at!"

"Oh, that table."

Lola shrugs at Mom's absurdity. I say, "I hope she chokes."

"No you don't." She grabs my hand. "He probably moved. That lease was probably signed years ago."

Gamblers burrow into a place until they shrivel and die. Their credit is abysmal. They win and lay with the neighborhood bookies. And this address: the OTB is on Liberty. There's Aqueduct, and Belmont. And a bus to Atlantic City. It's a degenerate paradise.

It's not about if he's still there. I want to know why she lied. I want to know the whole story, for myself, for my film. I say, "He's there. I need to ask her."

"Okay. I'll do what I can to help. But like, if they talked to each other all this time, and your mom got sick...wouldn't he check on her?"

"Or maybe Mom told him not to check up on her. She knew she was slipping enough to hide the lease. Maybe she thought if he showed up, and she was confused, it would just be me and him. Maybe Mom didn't want that. Or maybe my father made her promise never to tell me."

"Then maybe we should let it go."

"I can't."

"I know it's not easy. When I was in the hospital my mom never visited me. Didn't even call. And it sucks. But you have to just let it go. I mean, your mom is here. I'm here. You're making a movie!"

"Yeah a disaster film."

"Oh yeah," she says. "Bad timing, but I was thumbing through the *Village Voice* and there's this ad.

A summer program that Manhattan Film School is doing."

At this moment, standing seems impossible. "What money do I have to spend on tuition?"

"You don't have to enroll! It's a contest. You submit your movie, and the winner goes there for the summer. But the deadline is next month. I'll help you."

"I can't think about school right now." I sit for a second, thinking: What do I need right now? I need to know the truth.

"This movie will keep you alive."

I shrug. "That's a bit cheesy, no?"

"The real stuff always is. Do you have pictures of your Dad?"

I give her the one I pulled from the mattress. I watch him watching me. It's ridiculous. I almost understand why she would have hidden the truth when I was younger—it would be impossible for me to know he lived close but didn't want to see his boy—but at a certain age, Mom should've come clean. And why did I keep falling for that flaky story? One day he packed his belongings into his busted valise (my mother's phrase) and hauled his raggedy ass to Florida, and then we never heard from him again...why did I believe that?

When he first left, I spent weeks in my room, crying, begging her to find him. At first I was ignored, then smacked for 'acting like a baby,' and then finally I was forbidden to say his name, like he was the Candyman. And all the while, my mother was sneaking off to meet him. Did they talk about me? Did our separation ever bother him enough for him to sneak a seat on the splintering bleachers during one of my Little League games? Did he ever hide behind a pin oak to steal peeks of me playing handball in Tudor Park? I hope so.

And if he did materialize—and he must've—did I fail to notice him because I had accepted my mother's excuses so blindly? It's too much for me. Overwhelmed, I pass Lola the photo.

She says, "Well, we know where he lives, right?"

"I doubt he's still there."

I wonder what Greg and Sarah would do in my situation. Whatever other choices they've made, I bet they know where their parents live. Their parents must've given them something that mine lacked. They have the confidence that only comes from years of emotional stability. Even to have the oomph to plan a vacation must come from someplace I'm lacking. I understand that everyone is different. I know that crazy couples can plan vacations, too. But I'm also guessing that their parents must've taken them seriously and valued their ambitions and consoled them when they failed, instead of berating and slapping them and then leaving them to figure out the important stuff for themselves. I remember once my mom told me that "You have children, and then you hope they figure it out." I'm not being naïve; I do understand that success comes from the gutter too. But it must be easier when your parents respect, and dare I say, love you. Or at the very least, when they decide to be around. It feels like Lola and I are Sarah and Greg's opposites, the other side of a diptych, watching a rosy existence through shit-colored glasses. I'd give my life to spend a minute on that beach.

She picks up the lease. "What if Joan asks? We can catch it on video."

"She told us all she knows. If she even knows what she's telling us."

"She seemed pretty sure about it."

"Lola, Mom thought she was at her frigging rooftop wedding!"

Mom yells from the kitchen: "Who ate all of the donuts?"

Lola says, "Check on her. I need a minute."

"I can't."

"Peas and carrots? Trust me. It'll cheer you up."

I ask how, and she tells me it's a surprise. There's a look of mischief in her eyes, as though she just asked me to play a round of Ring-and-Run. "Your Lo-lo's got it."

It takes everything in me to stand.

She shoos me out of the room and says, "No peeking," then slaps my ass and shuts the door.

In the kitchen, Mom sits at the table, her back against the wall. She holds the donut box upside-down, peeking in from the corner as though a donut is hiding behind a tiny couch. She tosses the box onto the table. The faucet is running for no reason. It's hard to look at her lying face. I shut the faucet. I pick up the camera, lean against the counter. I open the side-panel, pretending to be busy while Lola does fuck knows what.

Mom says, "I want a donut!"

Still staring at the static of the panel, I say, "You ate them already."

Her lips are powdered with sugar. Crumbs litter her robe lapels. She looks like a kid, a deceitful one. "I need a snack!"

"In a bit."

"You bit what?" She nods towards the box. "The donuts? Yeah, *you* ate them! Liar!"

The urge to strangle her is so visceral I can practically feel the loose skin of her throat in my sweaty hands. It's terrifying, so I concentrate on my feet, helpless and immobile. I curl my toes, then say, "Nope. I have eyewitness testimony to the contrary."

"Whoever smelt it, dealt it."

I have no oomph for this, but I have to ask her while there is even a lintball of memory about what she told me outside. I hit Record and point the lens at the curtains and pan down, a slow establishing shot. Mom watches me, her hair frizzy, her jacket still draped onto her shoulders. Lola stuck a dandelion above her ear, reminding me of *King Lear* and high-school English. Who is it that can tell me who I am...

Mom says, "Donuts, please!"

I zoom in. "Okay, Nuncle."

"Who? Uncle Carmine? He lives on West Fifty-Seventh."

"He's not here."

Mom clutches her chest, relieved. She says, "Oh, thank god. He never shuts up! Eats your food. Never leaves. Then he does, right after he leaves piss in your terlet. Uncle Carmine never flushed. What do you think his hangup was?"

I'm never going to find out about my father.

My bedroom door swings open. Lola sings in a high-pitched voice, "OOOOHHHH you take the good, you take the bad, you take them both and there you haaaavvvveeee—" Lola jumps into the kitchen from the hallway. When she lands, she spreads her legs and tosses her arms into the air, magician-like. She's wearing white jeans and a neon sweatshirt, its neck cut wide so it hangs off her shoulder. She scissors upright. "It's so *Facts of Life*, right?" She shakes yellow wristbands. "They lost their glow, but hey, that's vintage. If I was on that show, who would I be?"

I don't have a clue why this will help me find more info about my dad, so I shrug.

"C'mon, try!"

"Jo, I guess."

She kisses my cheek. "My favorite. Blair's an uppity bitch. Natalie's totally dopey. I'm not cute enough to pull off a Tootie. But Jo." She jabs. "Tough girl." She whispers, "It'll make Joan seem more real."

It occurs to me I never told her the whole chronology, how Joan died in the early fifties. They didn't even have neon wristbands. But it'll break her heart if I tell her this, so I just say, "Good thinking."

"Totally," Lola says, in eighties surf talk. She sits down next to Mom and squeezes her hand. "Hey Sis."

Mom kisses her fingers. To me she says: "You ate the donut I was saving her." She puffs her cheeks for the camera. "Porko."

"Right," I say, and record her as though she'll just start talking. With all of her lies, did I even know her? There is the Mom who worked at the bank, complained about bills and a husband who ditched her. Then there's the Mom who was signing leases, who knew he lived less than a mile away. Watching her, I peruse my memories, trying to pluck an odd moment, a slipup where she inadvertently gave me a signal that he was around. I try to decide which version of Mom is real.

She touches Lola's bracelet.

I say, "Okay Joan. Let's get started."

"I just realized that if you slice the '-an' off 'Joan,' it's 'Jo.'"

I give her a thumb's up. She takes a deep breath, easing into character. She picks lint off her robe. Mom's face blocks the frame. She slumps over, her chin touching her chest. She closes her eyes, exhausted from sitting in the yard. She mumbles a string of words, hitting different pitches as though humming a nursery rhyme like a child. I feel guilty for pushing her so hard. I pivot around and open the pantry. I take out a roll of

Oreos, her favorite, and put them on the table. The sugar will perk her up until I'm done filming, and I'll get the answers that I need.

Mom snatches the cookies. "I'm not sharing."

Lola laughs. "That's okay!"

Fixated on the Oreos, Mom tries to tear the wrapper, but her hands shake. Lola reaches for the package and Mom pulls them away. "I'll just open them, okay?" She places the roll on the table.

Lola rips it open with her mouth.

Mom laughs and says, "You can have one." She points at me. "But not him."

Lola hands her the roll. Mom shakes one loose from the wrapper and gives it to Lola. "Sis." She wiggles another Oreo free, then places the tube on her lap and winks, razzing me.

Mom bites a cookie. "Now I'm happy." She smiles at the camera and her teeth are streaked with chocolate.

Lola pops the Oreo in her mouth, something I'd never do after Mom touched them with her fingers, which I guess makes Lola a nicer sister than I am a son.

Mom goes on: "Now I need a squirt of moojuice."

Lola says, "Wow, that sounded gross."

"Yes it did."

I stop the camera and get the milk from the fridge, then move to the drainboard and fetch *Best Mom Ever*. Lola twists open the milk, smells the container, then pours Mom a mugfull. Lola swigs from the container and places it on the table. She burps, then says, "So, Sis. Remember you and your husband had that big fight?"

"The blowout? Wait. Where's those cookies?"

Lola places the Oreos back on the table. Mom shakes another one loose. Sticks it into the pocket of her mouth and it just sits there.

I think she forgot how to eat. "Drink milk," I say.

"I'll have strong boners." She is lispy from the cookie melting in her mouth.

"You mean bones, Mom."

She rolls her eyes, then picks up the mug and drinks. "Same thing."

Lola says, "They sure are," and reaches for another cookie, but Mom places the roll onto her lap. "So about the blowout."

Mom chews—praise Yahweh for small mercies—and says, "Oh, it was a bad one."

I say, "Right. We're talking about the fight with your husband."

She turns around and waits as though he'll appear. Then she says, "Ice cream!"

Gloria's right: once she starts with sugar, it never ends. "We ran out."

"Porko." She puffs her cheeks, then she says, "My husband drove an ice cream truck."

Here we go. Camilla in Blunderland. "An ice cream truck?"

"Yeah. for those people."

Lola says, "What happened again?"

"He was collecting bets for those people. Him and his friend. Gill or Phil. He skimmed off the top. I'd come home from work and find jewelry missing. My leather coat. I had to borrow money from our mother after our electric got shut off." She sighs, pinches the wrapper. "He'd wander home all scumbari. Then finally this guy knocked. Looking for my husband. Robbing bets. I told him he wasn't here."

"What did you do?" I zoom the lens in, watching her. "About the guy."

She rocks slowly. "Those people? He searched the house. He said he was taxing us. He took the TV in the bedroom. Then he said he'd be back tomorrow. He said my husband needed to atone." I imagine my mother standing in our kitchen, worrying about what else he'd take from her. She must've been terrified. "My husband owed eighteen thousand dollars. He made me remortgage the house."

I lean against the counter, shaking with anger that she had to live that way.

She spins the roll of cookies, trying hard to remember. "So he drove an ice-cream truck."

If I carpet-bomb her with questions, she'll get confused, so I stick close to her story. "Why not a regular job? Better pay."

Feeling bad for her sister, Lola gives her a cookie. She drops it into the milk. I capture the cookie lapping the mug. "He worked for free." She pokes the cookie to submerge it and when it pops up, she flinches, surprised.

Lola says, "You mean they owned the truck?"

"The one full of ice cream."

I say, "So that was the blowout? He left?"

Mom says, "He wanted to sell the house. I said no. So he left." She sniffs the mug, then slides it to the center of the table. She closes her eyes. I zoom the camera and hold the shot. She opens them and glances around the room, lost. "I'm tired."

I say, "What was the name of the guy who came into the house?"

Mom gasps. "You know about that? A real blowout."

Lola says, "What was his name?"

"Henry?"

I tell Lola: "That's her father's name. I mean, this is all pretty flimsy. Besides the lease."

Mom picks at the crumbs on the table. She's confused, and I'm tired of asking. Still, just to be positive, I say, "What was his name again?"

"Who?"

"The guy that stole the television."

"He's here!" She tries to stand. "Hide my ring." Lola tells her it's okay. "He'll take it. And the television! And my bracelet! And the fan! And the toolbox! And the toaster! And the silverware! He'll take everything, just like last time."

I imagine some guy pacing through my house, picking items as though he won a gameshow. "Mom, it's okay. He's not here."

Mom says, "Hide. Our. Stuff." She tries to slide off the chair, but Lola grabs her shoulder, steadying her. "It's that man's fault! Gamble or leave! You can't have both! Help me! Sis, stick the clock under the bed."

Lola hugs her. At first, Mom struggles, but Lola whispers something in her ear, and my mother's body relaxes. Lola says, "We're talking about old times. I swear, Sis. You're okay." Mom closes her eyes and falls asleep on Lola's shoulder, as Lola hums the *Facts of Life* theme song.

As sick as she is, my mother was terrified. She's telling the truth. Someone did this to her. My father did this to her. I want to apologize for the choices she had to make and yell about the choices she has made. I want all of it and none of it.

Still, I can't stop myself from filming.

CHAPTER 19

I open my bedroom door to a painting of Mom's face lying on my carpet.

It's a rendering of Lola's drawing. I stand it upright. Instead of canvas it's actually a sheet of oak-tag. Mom's face is in acrylic; sharp lines of yellow and orange highlight her cheekbones; her hair is gray, white and purple. Her eyes bother me. Lola painted her eyes green, instead of brown, and they're haloed in red. Another red band is streaked across her forehead. It's not a flattering portrait, but it speaks to her inner turmoil, the hardships of her life.

I place the painting on the floor again, trying to angle it so it's exactly how I found it: not quite parallel to the wall, Mom's eyes watching the popcorn ceiling. I flip open the camera panel, hit Record, and hold a long shot of her, panning the camera left to right, until her eyes are following the lens.

I say, "Why didn't you tell me where my father lived?" The lens zooms closer, but she's mute. "What happened to you?"

Her eyes watch the camera, unwavering, un-blinking.

I hit Stop and sit next to the portrait. Maybe my parents never met in secret. He was an addict, and the lease was one last condition to keep him away from us. Or maybe the lease was an incentive? She wanted to keep him close enough for him to decide to quit gambling and come back to his family. Everything from my mother is confusing, but if I had to try to parse out a timeline: they moved from their old apartment to the house we're living in now. Then my father owed money to the bookies, so much he wanted to sell the house to cover it. Mom said no way, but then agreed to sign a lease for that old apartment next to the Kerouacs so he wouldn't be homeless. Did Mom put him right back in their first apartment, as a reminder of happier times? Or she is confused, and she signed a lease that happened to be the same block as Jack's mom, and she's just rolling that tidbit of history into her own history? Either way is both plausible and absolutely crazy. The important thing is that he chose gambling, so she never told me the truth. Maybe she was protecting me? If guys were taxing our house, she knew it was dangerous for me to be with Dad, walking around the neighborhood. If that was the scenario, then it makes sense that she was still seeing him. She could gauge his behavior, see if he was straight before she allowed him to see me. I stare at the painting, hoping she'll be able to let me know somehow which of my convoluted guesses is right. All I get is silence. I lay next to Mom, both of us staring at the cirrus clouds of dust caught on the ceiling.

In Mom's room Lola sings the Bangles version of "Hazy Shade of Winter." Before Lola closed her bedroom door, she asked Mom if she wanted a story or a song before her nap. Mom always picks the last choice given to her. Lola told her to pick three songs from the eighties. Mom chose "Peggy Sue," "That'll be the Day" and "Splish Splash." Lola said those songs are pre-eighties. Mom picked "Be-Bop-a-Lula"and "Rockin' Robin." Mom doesn't know 1989 from 1889. I don't know if Mom kept requesting songs, but Lola is singing "Tainted Love," so I'm guessing she didn't.

Mom tells Joan she has a lovely voice. Lola thanks her, tells her to try the fish, and breaks into "Heart of Glass." Then she says "Click" as though she's a jukebox, and switches over to Aretha Franklin's "Freeway of Love." Mom asks for swoony and Lola says, "Click," and sings, "Give me time, to recognize my crimes..."

I steamroll on my carpet to the phone and dial Gloria. She answers on the second ring. "Wes? Everything okay?"

"Mom's fine. But Dom is sick and asked me to come in to the store."

She sucks her teeth "Aren't you sick too?"

"That's right." I do this coughy thing. "I got better." I sing: "Riiii-cola!"

"I'm cooking lentil soup. I'll bring it."

Can't wait for lentils. Lola is singing "Our Lips are Sealed." I say, "Sounds good." Lola finishes and Mom claps and Lola tells her there are no autographs.

Gloria says "Don't let her watch TV so loud!"

"I'll lower it. So like four?" Lola breaks into the B-52's "Roam."

"Uhhh...what is she watching?"

"MTV, I think." Lola breaks into Billy Ocean's "When the Going Gets Tough, the Tough Get Going." Hearing her version, I realize how much I like that song. I curl my finger around the phone cord. What am I even doing?

She says, "That's not Lola, is it?"

I'm afraid that if I tell her she won't come here. "She went home."

"She went home." A flat tone. Disbelief? Hard to say. "You know," she goes on, "your mom is a lot more relaxed without her." Of course, she's talking about herself.

"Okay."

"Be there in an hour."

"Okay." I wait. Lola breaks into, "Nothing's Gonna Stop Us Now."

Gloria says, "I didn't mean what I said."

We've broken up. Time for our make-up scene.

I imagine her pacing her living room, filled with sensible, yet moderately priced furniture, hoping I'll take her back. I will. I will, I will, I will. "It's fine, Gloria. I'm sorry too. You do a lot for us."

Lola rips into her encore, belting out, "That's What Friends are For," at the top of her range. Mom actually yells, "Bellissimo."

Gloria laughs. "Don't apologize. Keep the noise to a minimum."

As if it were that easy. "I will. Thanks, I really appreciate it." A normal human would hang up the phone, but I stay on and wait for the click like some needy, desperate teenager.

Gloria goes on: "I was stopping by anyway. I have a friend named Julia. She's a social worker at Jamaica Hospital. I told her about your situation and she brought me some pamphlets..."

Every nerve, tendon, organ and capillary in my body screams for me to get off the phone. I'm Drew Barrymore in *Scream*, talking beyond sense and reason.

Still Gloria talks, implacable: "There's a place in Staten Island called ShadyPines Glen. The grounds are beautiful. Cherry blossoms—"

"It sounds expensive," I say, as if I'd actually bring her there.

There's a pause. "It can be. My friend can help you with that."

"How?"

"There's different ways. First, they take her social security and disability benefits. Then they work from there."

"What does that mean?"

She sighs. "The best thing to do is look at the pamphlet and talk to her. I can come with you. Or better, she can stop by and meet your mom."

Boy, was I just bamboozled! So much for big make-up scenes. "I...uhhh. Okay, I'll see you in a bit."

"Okay, see you soon." She disconnects.

I slam the receiver onto the cradle. Not that it matters.

I shift over and lean Mom's portrait against the bed so she's facing me. I say, "Okay Mom. Let's say you go to ShadyPines Glen." I wait for her to argue. She doesn't. "I will give them your benefits, insurance. Say it's more than that. How can I possibly pay for your care, pay for the house, *and* pay the everyday bills? I'm a video flunky in a video store that's flunking." This is where she'll tell me how I'm lazy and work at Video Planet because I don't have to sweat too much. She's never given me even decent advice before she was sick, and she's not going start now.

I tilt my forehead into the mattress, the springs creaking. I try to come to a decision. I'm a blank space. I lift my head. Mom is still there. But for how long? I kiss her forehead, which is jagged and smells of acrylics. I say, "Please just help me. Just this once."

Painting Mom keeps her vow of silence. In the next room Lola finished with a request, "What a Difference a Day Makes."

I stand and go into Mom's bedroom.

Lola is up on Mom's dresser, using a green curler for a microphone, head hunched against the ceiling. Mom lays on her bed, her back propped with pillows. Front row. Lola winks at me and sings, "Burning up for Your Love." She swings her hips around. "Bend over backwards boy would you be pleased," running her palms along her sides as Mom claps.

I say, "Okay, Madonna. Let's give Mom a break."

Lola hops off the dresser and dances towards me, tilting forward. She collapses into me and whispers, "Thanks for letting me sing to her," as though I had a choice. She hurries out of the room, waving as though walking off stage for another costume change.

Mom says, "My sister." I shut the door and sit on the bed. "She had pizza."

"You mean pizzazz."

She picks at the lint off her blanket, watching me. "You look like that man I know!" She peeks under her quilt. "Wherever he is."

Maybe closer than we think. I still don't understand why she talked about him disappearing all through my childhood if she didn't know where he lived. I imagine her standing in front of my father's apartment, showing him various class photos, my portrait gradually getting older, as she tried to convince him to stop gambling, to be part of us. That had to be horrible for her. If *The Worst Possible Thing* has taught me anything, it's that her life has been a perfect struggle. I've spent so much of our expiring time together fighting with her and blaming her for being a single parent. But she had regrets. She had missed opportunities, embarrassments, and failures. Now it's all a jumbled mess of stories, which might be hallucinations or straight lies. I'd wanted to document the final years. Now, I'm only more confused. I'll never learn from her what really happened.

But I can get the truth from him. I'll make him tell me what Mom hid. He'll tell me what I want to know.

Mom smacks her lips. She's thirsty. I should've brought her water. I say, "Rest. Gloria is coming in a bit."

She shrugs. "I don't know any Gloria."

"Well, she's nice."

I move next to her and kiss her head. It's nicer when it's the real Mom. I pull away and watch her left eye twitch. Hopefully it'll stop before Gloria arrives. I better hide Lola. I better hide the cookies. I doubt they have Oreos in ShadyPines Glen. I imagine melba toast, prunes, skim milk, and oodles of bananas. Gloria bragging about cherry blossoms, trips. I'm forbidden to take her outside. Mom leans back, her pillow curling around her ears like soundproof headphones. As long as she's mobile and her meds stay the same, I'm keeping her here. I can't put her in a home, especially now, knowing the sacrifices she has made for me.

Mom closes her eyes, quiet, content, at least for now.

I say, "I'm sorry for everything." I watch her sleep for a bit, then shut her door.

Back in my room, Lola is seated on the carpet; her painting of my mother is propped on the side of the bed, facing the television. To stop the top edge from curling, she's taped the top corners of Mom's portrait to the mattress. Lola's still dressed in her eighties gear. I want to be closer to Lola, inside. I don't mean sex, friction, tumbling for an effect. I want to inhabit someone besides me. Greg, Sarah. Again, osmosis.

I sit and Lola bumps my shoulder like we're seniors again. She stretches, her sweatshirt collar sliding down. "How do you like my painting?"

"It's great. Thank you," I say, though I'm not sure how I really feel about it.

She runs her finger along Mom's cheek. "It's some of the best work I've done. I've reached a higher plateau with it, you know? I want to do as many portraits as I can. Something about chronicling this is just..." Giddy, she flaps her hands. "Being here feeds my artist."

Is that the only reason she's here? I take a deep breath, taken aback. No. We're together, always. Right? "Me too, I guess."

"So what is the plan?"

"I think we should scope out the house."

"What about your Mom?"

"Gloria's coming in like twenty-minutes. Sorry."

"Nope. Don't worry about it. I'll hide behind the trees. Tell her she owes me a Happy Meal."

"Okay." I'm relieved that I didn't have to ask her to leave. "If you hide, I'll buy you one later. I'll supersize."

"They don't supersize kid-size, but I love you for that." She scoots back. "Are you sure you want to go looking? I mean, we just found out."

"Yes." I want to confront him. I want to see where he lives. His car. I want to see his tired, old gambling face. I want him to see me. But most of all, I want to tell him about all the years my mother wasted waiting for him. "We'll go there. I have the lease."

"You have a lease."

I stand. "It has signatures. It's our only lead."

She pulls her sweatshirt onto her shoulder. She says, "Okay." She stands, grabs her jacket, balled on the bed. "Meet you in the yard." She picks up Mom and places her on the bed, then throws a blanket over the painting.

I give her a look, like: What's that for?

"Gloria doesn't deserve to see my art."

As she leaves the room, I realize how happy I am that she's coming with me. If she wasn't here I'd never do it alone.

I take a deep breath, letting the feeling fizz inside of me until I move into the kitchen. I toss the empty donut box in the garbage and what's left of the cookies into the cabinet. Lola leaves through the side door just as Gloria opens the front. I'm living with Marla and Tyler in *Fight Club*.

Gloria calls "Hello!" then walks into the kitchen, carrying a heavy grocery bag. She places it on the kitchen table, then her pocketbook, and then she slips off her coat. She's wearing jeans and a blue shirt, its sleeves hiked to her elbows in a 'ready to dig in' kind of way. She glances around the room, searching for Lola as if she'll find her peeking out from the cabinets.

Finally it's: "Hi sweetie. Feeling okay?"

I tell her I'm better.

"Good. Where's Mom?"

"Sleeping."

She produces a pot from the bag, walks it over to the stove. "Lentils."

I wait for her to mention nursing homes. She uncovers the pot, makes sure everything's in there, then covers it again. There's no reason for Gloria to do this, unless she's listening to see if Lola is here too. Suddenly, I don't trust her. Partly because of PineGlen, but mostly because she's made it obvious that she doesn't want Lola around. Wishing everyone could be nicer to each other, I say, "Lola's not here."

"Okay." She unzips her pocketbook. "Here's the pamphlet." She holds it out.

I'm afraid that if I touch it, Mom will teleport into a nursing room.

Gloria folds it open, then flattens it on the table like it's a map to the Lost Ark. An older woman wearing a cable knit sweater walks along a stone path, which is surrounded by flowers. Next to her a nurse in maroon scrubs holds her arm, leading her to whatever lies ahead. (Obviously death.) The photo's Granny Graveyard subtext is so obvious that my skin prickles. On the top of the page is the slogan *Your Comfort is Paramount*, written in a loopy, golden script, as if by the hand of St. Peter himself.

I count to twenty, hoping Gloria considers that a fair amount of staring time. She examines it, still open, on the table. "A friend of mine's mother stays there." I imagine Greg and Sarah there, watching reruns of *Family Feud* as they complain about their hemorrhoids.

Gloria grabs my shoulders so we're facing each other. "'Right' isn't always easy, honey." She squeezes my shoulders, highlighting her point. "You'll feel worse when something happens to her here." She waits, and maybe it's the photo, but I think of Mom being locked in my bathroom, the chicken cutlet on the coffee burner—or worse, her not being able to climb into bed—and this intense fear grips me, and Gloria's warnings become visible in a white flash, like some sort of psychic transference. I almost push her hands, but luckily she lets go, and I see a smaller, yet closer future: I'm losing her. My heart hiccups like the chains of a swing when you've hit height capacity. My eyes glass over, ready to cry.

Gloria lets go and steps away from me. She's serious about this.

"Thanks." I have no idea why I'm thanking her. "Back by ten."

"Okay. Let's see your mom first. I want her to see us together."

I follow Gloria into the bedroom. When she opens the door, Mom is facing the window, snoring. "Let her sleep. I'm cheating anyway, I just wanted to see her."

"Well, there she is. Being taken care of."

"PineGlen. It's a nice place, Wes."

I glance at my wrist, as though I'm wearing a watch. "I'll be home by ten."

Gloria tells me she'll be here, but there's a sigh, or a catch of breathy hesitation, as she taps Pause between the last two words, Be and Here. It's a slight stress in her rhythm, her voice struggling to keep her tone steady, concealing the simple truth that her time here with us, with me, is ending. In movies, it's called the Final Draw scene. The fed-up partner, friend, spouse has finally decided at last (if only to move the plot) that it's not worth the effort. Those final awkward weeks where routine lugs the weight of loss, where neither wants to admit it's over, finally stop.

Of course, I try to ignore the inevitable. I keep walking toward the door, hoping that if I can only move fast enough, the meaning will never reach me.

CHAPTER 20

I pop from the side door of the house and I'm flung headlong into easy distractions. The weather has changed since this morning. March clouds, wispy and thin, crowd the runner of sky between the pitched roofs. The air is cooler. I smell smoldering wood, a spark from the EL. The evening is light and buzzy. Outside, it's easy to shake off the breakup queasiness of Gloria.

Maybe I'm overreacting? Gloria had a gazillion reasons not to help today, but she did. She even cooked lentils! When I get home we'll have a serious conversation, but not the one she expects. Instead of senior living and routines, I'll explain to her how happy Mom is to be home, the truth about our financial situation. I'm sure she'll have counter arguments for all my explanations, but if that happens I'll show her undeniable proof of Mom's happiness. I'll sit her on the plastic covers of the couch, and show her my movie, *The Worst Possible Thing*. Gloria will see how Mom's personality changes when we're filming. How much she loves Lola. Gloria is a caring person. She'll understand. I was too rattled by finding the lease to understand Gloria's warnings the way I should've. I read the moment wrong. If anything, she was probably just nervous about seeing Lola again. It's my fault. I should've had Lola come into the kitchen and talk to her before I went to work. After I find the truth about my father, I'll apologize. They need to be friendly. If Mom is going to stay at home, then we all have to work together.

I fetch Lola from the yard, relieved that she's still there, and we walk the block to the Cutlass. Lola grazes her fingers along the hood until she shoots up her hands, as though she's about to be run over and screams "Help!" startling a row of pigeons that were eyeing us from the phone lines. She runs her hand along the top of the car as if it's a chariot, a flying carpet. Convinced that the Cutlass is part of our reality, Lola slides in next to me. She breaks into her best Morrissey and sings, "Take me out tonight. Where there's music and there's people."

"That's a good song."

"The best." She rocks in the bucket seat. "Pilot chairs! Sexy." She peeks over to check the back like she's scanning for an intruder. "Never know," she says, then she clicks the seatbelt and laughs, as excited as if we're strapping into the Cyclone. "So glad you didn't get leather."

"It's my mom's car."

"Figures. It's a very sensible choice."

"Actually, she hates it. She wanted an Acura Legend for the heated seats. She thought it'd help with her hemorrhoids." I realize that this is the most unsexy thing you can say while driving with your girlfriend. I tap the steering wheel. "She digs foreign cars."

Now that I'm behind the wheel, it feels too light out to go hunt down my father. This afternoon I was convinced I'd unraveled the big family mystery, but now it's hard to know if Mom was telling the truth, or talking about an episode of *General Hospital*. Sure, I'd found the lease, but I doubt my father still lives there. And if he does, who's to say he wants to see me? But I do want to look. At least, that's what I'm telling myself. And besides, I am a little worried Lola's not enthusiastic about the filming, no matter how much she says she loves my mom. I truly believe she does, but we need a break, a night on the town. Well, Queens.

I say, "Where should we go?"

Lola shrugs.

"Okay. We'll just drive, then."

We turn onto Liberty Avenue and I turn right, away from 134th street, and toward City Line. We pass the cemetery and I roll down the window. The air rushing past makes a shushing sound. Lola finds an oldies station. She says, "Let's find something snazzy, Daddy-O." She hits scan until we hear jazz, the reception fuzzy, as though we're tuning in a broadcast from fifty years ago. The saxophone, which might be Sonny Rollins, is out in front of the recording, and by the way the drummer is keeping time with a Caribbean feel, I think it's "St. Thomas," but I'm not sure. Lola rests her head back, closes her eyes. I remember that I'm twenty-six, too young never to be out like this. Suddenly, with the song and the forward motion of the Cutlass, I could be one of Kerouac's mad ones. I say, "Hungry?"

"Always."

I ask her what she wants.

"The only food that matters."

"Sounds good." I turn down 76th Street, around 101st and into the McDonald's parking lot, toward the arrows to the drive-thru.

Lola grabs my arm, "Inside."

I cut the wheel, almost hitting an orange Mustang, and coast into a spot, a bit crooked but cool, as though I'm too hip to worry about parking straight. We step out of the car and walk through the lot, our arms looped inside each other, together, always together, just how we'd walk to the park in high school.

Walking inside, I remember my favorite part from *Catcher in the Rye*, when Holden talks about the museum always staying the same. How the only difference is you. I think he meant it's a hideaway, a place filled with the quiet comfort of predictability that makes you feel safe, content. And so, too, here. The benches are the same. The brick-colored ceramic tile is the same. The counter and popcorn ceiling are the same. The statue of Ronald in his bright-yellow outfit and red shoes, smiling like he's waited a decade-plus for me to visit, is the same. Sure, it's sad to realize that I'm different, but I'm also twelve again.

Lola rushes up to the counter and orders two cheeseburger Happy Meals. The cashier rings us up; his long hair is trapped in a net, which is trapped under his blue visor. As I pay, Lola rushes down the aisle towards the window seat facing the street. She places the tray between us and tells me to pick one.

I take the closest box, take out the fries, and then grab a napkin to keep them off the table. When I look up, Lola is already eating her cheeseburger. She says, "This is so good." The fries are greasy and salty and warm.

The last time I ate at McDonald's, I was twelve. Then Mom had told me that she'd read in the newspaper that Ronny Boy was buying up all these worm farms. I asked her why, and she whispered, "Filler. For the burgers." I knew we weren't actually eating patties made of nightcrawlers, but I couldn't convince Mom otherwise. It became a big huge thing between us. I was even forbidden to go to birthday parties. So I missed the toys. The colorful boxes. I'd see a clown and long for a Big Mac. I was perpetually taunted by the burger wrappers that littered the parks. One time I told my mom her ban was McBullshit. (She slapped me, of course.) Being barred from McDonald's was traumatic. I made a list of the other places, quickly reasoning why they were all inferior. Burger King felt like an infidelity. Nathan's meant a subway ride. Roy Rogers wasn't in my neighborhood. White Castle had bulletproof glass. And who the hell even was Arthur Treacher? There were exceptions. Pizza and Chinese were fine, I decided, for obvious reasons. And diners in Queens were a cultural artifact. But I'd sworn off all the other fast food places.

Now, I lift the cheeseburger out of the box and unwrap it. I close my eyes and inhale. I say, "A Royale with Cheese," in my best Samuel L. Jackson voice. WORM FARM flashes neon in my brain. I take a bite. It's perfect. Tack another note onto Mom's lie-board. If worms be thy food of love, chew on.

She says, "You like it?"

"It's amazing. First time in forever. Man, this is good."

She gulps down some soda. "I brought you some earlier!"

"I had fries. In my room."

"Yeah but not the burgers?"

I don't have the heart to tell her Mom's conspiracy. "It's...I'll have to tell you about that later."

Lola balls her wrapper and flicks it on the tray. She says, "You're forgetting the best part." She reaches into the box. It's a Snoopy figure dressed in a Mountie uniform. She rips open the plastic with her teeth and places it on the table, then stares at it like she's Indiana Jones gazing on the idol. "Now you."

I reach into the box. It's another Snoopy in a pilot-cap and goggles, seated on his doghouse. She says, "Red Baron Snoopy is my fav," and I place it in front of her.

She leans across the table and kisses me, our lips greasy. "Thanks, Charlie Brown."

"I'm really not Charlie Brown."

"What's the matter with Charlie? I get so tired of that male roar. You're quiet. Soft. No...moody."

I'd call myself depressed and sulking, but I say, "Uh, thanks I guess?"

"You're welly-welcome. Only I'm choosing the Christmas tree." She sticks the toys into her bag. "Have you thought about the film contest?"

"Not really. I don't think I'll win."

"We're doing something completely different."

A quick scroll of Mom's closet, her horse story, sitting like King Lear in the yard. Then there's the pain of her confessions. "I don't think I have the skill to even edit it all." I sip soda, trying to verbalize my recorded images into feelings. I can't, so I just streak my fingers across the wet halo of cup sweat.

Lola sticks a fry into her mouth. "Just send it. You have a month or so to try to get it together, you know?"

I say, "I guess," feeling as though I've already lost everything anyway.

"That's my Charlie Brown."

"Please stop calling me that."

For a while, we sit there, watching the cars pull in and out of the lot. I imagine an older, heavier version of my father, walking, hunched and beetle-like, toward the McDonald's after a long day of shoddy bets, with only enough change to buy a small coffee. If he would've came here, then I definitely would've seen him. Then it hits me. Mom's worm-farm excuse was to avoid a chance meeting. Did she meet him here? Did they *plan* to meet here? This is the only McDonald's around. I glance around the room as if I'm going to catch him sitting in one of the booths, hidden by one of the faux ferns tucked in the corner. What were they doing? Was she giving him money? Did he beg to come home? Did they eat and then go back to his apartment for...the thing no son wants to imagine their parents doing? As though reading my mind, Lola says, "Think your dad's there?"

I toss my wrappers in the box. "I hope so, I guess."

"I haven't seen my mom in years," she says, "I'd be freaking out."

"I thought you lived with your mom?"

She unfastens the lid and pops ice-cubes into her mouth. "Yeah. Kind of. She doesn't speak to me, though."

Why does everyone feel compelled to lie to me? Am I that much of a jerk? "What the hell kind of bullshit is this?"

She laughs. "Chill! I named my cat 'Mom.'"

"What?"

"Yeah. She stares at me with that same disappointed look." She crunches the ice, watching a van pull into the lot, its wheels chirping.

Maybe she'll finally reveal more about her past. "What about your real mom?"

She scoops ice onto the tray. She pokes it with her finger, leaving a streak of water. "We should go."

She slides off the seat and paces up the aisle in such a hurry that she left her toys on the table. I grab them and follow her outside. It's getting dark, made darker by the clouds. It smells like rain. She sits in the back seat.

"Hey, you forgot these." I set the toys on the passenger seat and slide behind the wheel. "Are you okay?"

She flops down sideways on the back seat. "Good to go."

"You should put your seatbelt on."

"It's fine."

I turn on the radio. It's Art Blakely's "Are you Real?" which feels too cheery, so I hit Scan, but then switch it off. I pull around the block back onto Liberty with no issues. But on the drive over to his place, as I pass through one light after the next with no comment from Lucy and the Peanuts Gallery, I'm freaking out. Scoping out his house is one thing. But what if he's actually there? I'm unprepared. Maybe he won't be. Maybe too much time has passed. Maybe I'll be okay.

No.

I stop at the light. Maybe I should abort this mission. I'll go to Forest Park. We'll ride the carousel, watch kids play basketball. She might perk up again.

But then the car behind me beeps and I drive to 134th.

The block is a row of houses, just like mine except behind them is the Van Wyck Expressway and in front is Atlantic Avenue. As we drive I notice a line of pigeons perched on the phone lines. I check for a dangling sneaker. There isn't one, and I read that as a sign that he doesn't live there anymore. For a moment, I almost want to keep going, but we're here now. Of course, it wouldn't be Queens if I found quick parking, so it takes a few loops until I land a spot on the corner of 95th Avenue and 134th.

So here we are. A desperate son and his suddenly-mute girlfriend. I shut the car. "We're here. It's down the block."

She pops up and starts humming the *Mission Impossible* theme song, which isn't very helpful to my nerves. At least she seems back to normal. "We should've brought disguises." She's still wearing her eighties gear, plus a white sweatband that she apparently strapped on her head while lying prone in the backseat. She couldn't be more noticeable if she tried.

I say, "Next time." I grab the camera and get out of the car. I hear the traffic, like a giant exhalation of breath, hushing along the expressway. Lola swings open her door, then bumps it shut with her ass. "Let's go."

We cross 95th and walk along his block, on the opposite side of the street. The houses all have brick or metal-post fences, bars on the windows and doors. Cars pass along Atlantic Avenue, swerving away and cutting each other off. The block smells like automobile exhaust and laundry detergent. Lola tugs my sleeve. "There, 94-21."

I stop. "That's weird."

My father's house is the same buttery yellow as my mother's. The same pitched roof. The only difference is that here there's a birdbath on the manicured lawn. The windows have red metal bars that match the metal fence. The house looks too cared for, worried about, to be lodging a degenerate. Maybe he's moved. Still, inside or not, I've never felt his absence more than seeing his house. We stare at it, mesmerized by the similarities.

I say, "Like *The Twilight Zone*."

"Yeah. An alternate version of you is living in there," Lola says. "And me too, but this one's normal." She pokes me, checking which version of me she's standing with. I'm not even sure. "Well, it is the address..."

"Yeah, I guess."

"Well, dicks to donuts, if your Mom picked the house, that's the one." She's right. We study the facade. "Do you think she knew Mrs. Kerouac?"

I picture Jack locked away in his room next door, hunched over his Underwood, clicking keys, pumped on amphetamine as his mother folds his laundry, cooks his meals. How she watched her son disappear into the city for a weekend of binge drinking. How she fetched him aspirin for his bouts of phlebitis, and then after all of that, she stepped onto her stoop to complain with my mom about grocery prices. It's ridiculous. Again, she probably heard that bit of Queens history and worked it into her delusions. "Honestly, I think she's confused."

"The air was soft, the stars so fine, the promise of every cobbled alley so great, that I thought I was in a dream."

I turn, surprised by her poetry. "You wrote that?"

"That's *On the Road*. I have a first edition. I filched it from the hospital library. I used to hit the bakery below his house in Ozone Park, just to be in the same building where he lived. I always wanted to ask you to come with me. But...graduation. So. We know how that went."

I don't really know how it went, or how it's going or how it'll go. I thought taking Lola with me to see the house would solve my problems. But now I couldn't feel more confused about things if I tried. I'm afraid she'll clam up if I bring up her past again. All I can say is: "We're here now."

Lola bumps my shoulder. "We sure are."

We stare at the house as though Jack will wave from the window, which seems more likely than that we'll see my father. It's silly. Like I'd find him waiting here for me. Wrongs made right, connections found, as though this were a neat movie ending edited into a series of cut-scenes: Greg and Sarah, wearing their bathing suits, watching the footage of me struggling to free Mom from the bathroom. Then a long shot of me staring at the house. A quiet movie of quiet loss. *The Worst Possible Thing*. It's not dark enough outside for the lights inside to be on, so I'm not sure yet that he (or whoever) is home. Lola says "What are we doing?"

"I don't know."

She snaps her headband. "Maybe I can pretend I'm selling raffle tickets."

"You don't have any tickets."

"Details, details."

Then a light switches on in the right-front window.

Lola steps to the side and points with her chin. "Look, he's there."

She grabs the camera from me and walks to the front of the Regal, then crouches down at the end of the bumper on an angle toward the house and says, "I'll film it." A guy steps out onto the stoop. He's wearing jeans and a blue jacket, the shiny cheap material. He opens the gate. He watches the sidewalk as he walks towards his trash can, his head down, so it's hard for me to tell if it's him or not, though I'm comparing his image to a fifteen-year old photo.

Before I realize what I'm doing, I cross the street towards the house. I try to slow my legs, but I'm speeding up. He tosses the bag in, closes the lid. He walks into the front yard. I say, "Excuse me."

He lets the gate shut, locking himself inside his yard, which feels appropriate. He's wearing glasses with metal frames. His face is puffy; deep wrinkle lines run from his nostrils to his mouth. Smoking wrinkles. His hair is dyed red and thinning, combed to the side to conceal his bald spot in that Gene Hackman kind of way. He watches me with a suspicious look. Makes sense. His house is gated like Troy. He says, "Something on your mind?"

A second passes where maybe it's nerves, but I want to pretend it's not him. But then he smiles, his lip slightly curling more on the left side of his face than the right, and it's exactly how he'd look after winning a race, and I know that this slick bastard is my father. When the weight of this hits, I'm gripped with this spinning feeling. How he never bothered to see us. How my mother *did* sign that lease. How, essentially, my whole childhood was a lie. Trying to stop my tailspin, I take a deep breath. "I'm looking for my dog? He's a brown terrier. Named Potchky."

"Good name for a dog."

That's the dog that ate Jack's original draft of *On the Road*. "My girl's idea."

He glances down the block and I catch a square of stubble on his jawline, below his ear. The same spot I miss, as though shaving hitches are hereditary. Standing this close, there is a resemblance to my picture. He says, "Does he got a license?"

I say, "She doesn't," wanting to correct him.

He clenches the bars. "Dogs get kidnapped."

A dented-up Chevy speeds down the block; he watches as though he'd see Potchky's sad face blurring past.

When I was seven Dad had brought home a puppy named Bowie as penance after he'd spent the night drinking, gambling, whatever. Before Bowie, there'd been Flipper the goldfish, who died tits-up from overfeeding. (Hey, I was a kid.) And we'd had a cat named Fluffster who spit and hissed and clawed; we'd kept him locked in the bathroom, the toilet-seat up as a water bowl, a litterbox in the bathtub, until we all got skeeved out from stepping on grit every time we showered and Fluffster slashing our legs from behind the toilet bowl when we did our business, at which point Dad gave him away. But we'd all loved Bowie. Then during a thunderstorm, he bolted out the door as Mom rushed in with the groceries. My father searched for

Bowie for hours. I remember him coming back soaked. It was the only time I heard him apologize. So when he says, "I'm sorry, buddy. I love dogs. I hope he's okay," I get a positive match on him that even denial can't compete against.

I say, "Thanks," and we wait, silent as the strangers we are.

Watching him now, I want to be angry, like I was just a few minutes ago. But he's here. It's pathetic how fast we give up our confrontations, our dignity, for people who are so undeserving. In the movies, kids appear on doorsteps and confess their lineage, and they're taken in, if only begrudgingly. Maybe if he realizes it's me, we can film that scene, or at least he'll let me call him once in a while. I'm not defending his choices, but the one thing I've learned from *The Worst Possible Thing* is that memory shifts. The truth blurs, or is completely forgotten.

See how fast I make excuses for this man?

Still, Mom's story has to be at least a little skewed, right? She's vilified him for half of my life, and it's hard not to let that poison bleed into my thinking. Maybe she told him I didn't want to see him. Maybe he was ashamed. Anyway, the only sure thing is that he's standing in front of me. "I'll give you my number. In case you find him."

He squints. Does he recognize me? But the moment passes and he shrugs. "Why not?" Just as all of this emotion bubbles up and I want to reveal my identity, his front door opens and a woman steps onto the stoop.

She's wearing black sweat-shorts and a t-shirt with a cartoon rainbow. Her black hair is short, sprayed back. She's holding a cordless phone. At first, another wife or girlfriend seems impossible. He gambled and drank. Who would take that on? Does she know that she's standing on my mother's old stoop? Mom never met anyone else. Why would he have better luck?

"Is everything okay?" she asks, with a heavy Staten Island accent.

He turns, "It's fine, honey. Lost dog."

There it is. Honey. I feel sick.

"Awe, how long has he been gone?"

The stunt double mom is talking to me. I fight the urge to run. "A few hours. Anyway, thanks." My pocket vibrates. I press my hand against my cell. I drift from the gate and he says, "What if I find him?" but I move across the street, dizzy and sad, leaving Lola's parallel universe behind me.

I say, "It's fine. Thanks."

Dad, because that's who it is, says, "Well, you know where to find me."

I expected him to be drunk, wearing a stained t-shirt with a stretched collar and unmatched socks, his bloated feet squished into a pair of cracked-leather slippers. I wanted a degenerate gambler. I wanted him to be filled with guilt. I wanted him to regret the years he's missed with his son. But he's fine. He is probably married to that hag. On Sundays, they eat breakfast in diners after going to First Reformed. They see movies. They take walks. They are together. They are happy without me.

When I walk past Lola, she pops up and follows me towards the Cutlass. She says, "What are we doing?" We stop at the corner. The light changes and we cross the street. I pray for a guy juiced up on Thunderbird to blow the intersection and whack me into another hemisphere. "Did you tell him?"

"Of course not."

She touches my arm and I turn. "How would he know?"

"I'm his son."

"Right. Who he hasn't seen in fifteen years."

Wrong. Who he ignored. I say, "It doesn't matter." I open the car door. She opens her door. Sits next to me. I put the key in the ignition. "He seems happy."

Lola says, "You can't tell that by talking for five minutes."

"He used her to sign the lease and then forgot her." I start the car and put it in Drive. She tells me to wait, so I put it back into Park.

"It's hard with addicts." She watches a woman in flannel pajama bottoms walk a poodle. "You get caught in your addiction. Then, after a while, maybe you're okay. You want the people you know to be the same. Like before. But it's different. You lied and stole and cheated everyone so badly." The lady hurries past our car. "So they're not gonna be the same."

"You weren't in a car accident, were you?"

She grabs the keys out of the ignition.

I look at her like she just slapped me. "Hey, what'dja do that for?"

She pauses for a big moment, then says: "I have to tell you something. About the hospital."

Now I stare straight ahead. What did I expect?

She tries to hand me the camera. "Here. Interview me."

I grip the steering-wheel and twist. "Can we do it later?"

She says, "Wait." We listen to the subway pass. "Okay, now it's later. Interview."

"First, let's go check on Mom." I just want to escape.

"Now. Please. Before I lose my nerve."

Here we go. I take the camera, hit Power, and zoom the lens out, giving her space. The angle's bad, so the shot records a bit papery, thin. Also, I can't keep my hand steady, so I have to prop the camera on my knee. She looks toward the windshield as though we're driving. Her profile is sharp, matching the serious look on her face. She takes a deep breath, like when she falls into her Joan character. She asks me if I'm ready. Ready for what? I tell her I'm recording, at least.

She says, "I didn't go to graduation because I almost killed someone."

Now there's a sentence. "Come again?"

"Listen. I was at the park. By the bay. I took all these pills. Then smoked weed. Then 'shrooms. I was at the farthest end of the park, staring out at the diamond reflection of the water, this tiny fishing boat close to shore. So I was just sitting on the base of the pillar of the bridge when I saw a little girl. I thought she'd fallen off a boat. I mean, now I know she'd be dead. But I was stoned out of my gourd. So I stripped naked and swam until my feet didn't touch. I'm a good swimmer. But seaweed or a plastic bag or something got wrapped around my ankles. I freaked out. I thought long fingers were pulling me down. I started screaming, and this old guy fishing pulled next to me on his boat. He yanked me out of the water and wrapped a towel around me. But the girl was waving at me. I believed, truly believed, she needed to be saved. I tried to show him. He told me I was hallucinating. But I tried to grab the wheel. We struggled. I pushed him into the water. He hit his head, falling in, but I didn't even realize it, I was that messed up. I jumped back in myself, and swam to the pillar. It was only like ten more yards. The pillar was too high to climb. I held onto the edge. The little girl peeked down at me. Telling me to climb. To play with her, save her. I had no strength."

She runs her hand along the dashboard as if she has to convince herself that she's in the car. I've wanted to hear this, but I wish she would've hit Pause until things were a little less topsy-turvy for me. Heck, even until twenty minutes from now, back at home. But she's upset, so I squeeze her arm, letting her know she's okay, to keep going. "How did you get out?"

"So this police boat idled up beside me. They got me, then they fished the old guy out of the water. He said I tried to kill him. He was wearing a fucking life vest, and he said I tried to kill him! No one was going to believe me. Not at that point. The cops said I was unstable. I was transferred into a mental ward for observation. I was there for sixteen months. Then another hospital for three years. My mother's doing. I'd only been seventeen when this happened. Still a minor. So when I was in the psych ward she'd taken power of attorney over me. No judge in the world was going to deny her with a story like mine. Anyway, I could've left the hospital in seven days, if it wasn't for that. We'd always fought, you know? But she wanted no part of me." She runs her fingers along the teeth of the car keys. "So then, when I finally got out, I lived with my aunt. Going to meetings. I was so horrified that I never did drugs again. Then my aunt died, and I came back here. But my mom still wouldn't talk to me! She'd had to sell our house to pay the lawyers because that old fucker had pressed charges. I told her I'd get a job. Give her my SSI checks. She wanted nothing from me. Said her daughter died at sea. Asshole. So I rented rooms. Even slept in shelters. I have a place now, but it's a crappy basement apartment. Fucking boiler in it. God, I hate it so much."

I stare at my dashboard, trying to make sense of this all. "So the aunt is true? The hospital is true, but you lied about the reason?"

Lola says, "I didn't lie. I was afraid to tell you."

"But you're okay now. Right?"

"Yeah. I'm fine now. I'm fine, I'm fine, I'm fine! I mean, you see me all the time! I'm clean! You know it. Don't you believe it?" She's crying. She wipes her face.

I do know, but I wish she would've just told me outright. I can't say this.

She goes on: "I'm only telling this story to make you feel better."

"I can tell," I say, feeling anything but better.

"You should try to speak to your dad again."

I only realize now that I've stopped recording. Outside the sky has that pinkish color: the streets, the edges of the houses, seem sharp, as though traced with a highlighter. If I didn't feel paralyzed I'd roll down the window, let some air into the car, this life.

She says, "I love you. Your mom. I paid my debt. I haven't touched drugs in eons. That's why I wanted to find you. You were always nice. When we were eating lunch you complained about your parents. But you were forgiving, too."

"Why didn't you ever call?"

"At the hospital, I'd stand in front of the phone. Trying to get the nerve. I was afraid you'd forget me. Have a girlfriend. Then I came home. Our whole neighborhood had changed, but people were acting like I was still the same. Even my mom."

We watch the lady walk her poodle back down the block. That's all I can muster by way of response.

She goes on: "But I knew that you were the same and that we were friends and we wanted more. And now with our parents...I mean, we've got this in common, too."

I don't understand her comparison. Her mom had her committed. My father decided not to see me. I imagine her in the hospital, staring at the phone. Then coming back to Queens and calling video stores, hiding in yards, as she tried to find me.

I say, "I'm sorry."

"About what?"

I watch a kid ride past on a bike. "My film. Dad hunting. Joan. Anyway, we should..."

She looks at me, bleary-eyed, like she's waiting for the other shoe to drop. "We should what?"

I feel a pang. Pity? Love? "I dunno. Go on a normal date or something."

She laughs, wipes her eyes again. "We went to McDonald's!"

I say, "Right. But, like, you've had enough problems. Taking on mine."

Lola says, "It's okay. I feel like, we're...you know." She shrugs. "We're like a family." She leans over and puts the key back in the ignition, then grabs my hand and squeezes. Three short pulses. Three long pulses. Three short pulses: S.O.S.

I crank the Cutlass. "Some family."

CHAPTER 21

We step into the kitchen and find Gloria sitting in a chair, pulled away from the table, with an ice pack pressed against her nose. An arrow of dried blood stains her shirt. She lifts her chin towards the light, either displaying the damage, or refusing to look at me.

On the table there's a violin case. I think of gangster movies, and Tommy guns packed away in instrument cases. Unless Gloria plays the violin? Or found it? Or wants me to play it for her? I shut the lights, trying to ease her discomfort, but then we're in the dark. I switch them on again, hoping for a better reality, and this guy appears next to her. I flinch, and then say hello, but he just watches me like a mute goon, silent and threatening.

I say, "Where did you come from?"

He points to Gloria, says, "From her."

"What?"

She says, "This is Julian," her voice nasal from the pressure of the pack against her nose. "I called him."

I feel this ache in my chest. "You're dating a guy named Julian?"

He says, "I'm her son."

The ache shifts into a stabbing pain. She has a son? I scroll through Gloria's time here, trying to remember if she had ever mentioned him. She did tell me she was divorced. Her first month or so, I seem to remember her saying the name 'Julian,' but for some reason I thought he was her nephew. Maybe I was too busy pretending she was related to me. Now he's standing in my kitchen. At last I say, "Of course you are."

He's a few years younger than me, dressed in a black overcoat and slacks. The top button of his dress shirt is undone. His black tie is loosened, the knot askew. He extends his hand. When I shake it he squeezes. I realize that he is one of those confident, aggressive hand shakers, a type of person who I hate, so I wriggle free and say, "I'm Wes."

He stands next to his mother's chair and rubs her shoulders: a real son, against all enemies, foreign or domestic.

"So..." I have to say something, right? "You play the violin?"

"If you consider Julliard just playing."

"Julian from Julliard. Lucky."

He snorts. "I think you mean: Practice."

In the living room Lola sits with Mom, watching *Jeopardy*. The contestant says, "Who is Douglas Adams?"

Mom answers, "I don't know, who is he?"

Juilliard glances at the floor, an all-teeth smile. I want to pummel him into a silty pile of regret for laughing.

Here's where I should ask Gloria what happened, or explain that I found my father, but I'm too occupied with this other man in my house, this dickweed, and I can't. Gloria takes the ice pack off her nose. "Can I have water?"

Before I can get to the sink, Juilliard cuts me off and grabs *Best Mom Ever* from the drainboard. He fills the mug, and gazes into it as though my faucet is infested with cooties, then hands it to her. She takes a sip, then Juilliard takes it from her and places it on the table. Next to the pamphlet.

Juilliard says, "It was a bit milky. Mom, you should bring your own water."

I say, "We have air in our pipes. Should've let it run a bit. But you wouldn't know about air. You're a string man."

"No. I'm not a plumber."

I'm an only child, but for a second I feel the twinge of sibling jealousy. Or jealousy of people who have siblings, I should say. If he was my brother, I could totally dropkick him right now. "My water is wet."

Gloria says, "Please. I have a headache."

Finally, I say, "Gloria, are you okay?"

"My nose is bleeding!"

Juilliard translates: "That means 'no.'"

Gloria tells him to sit. Without arguing, he walks around the table and falls back into the chair, its legs sliding into the wall with a thud. He tugs his violin towards him like I'd steal it.

In the other room, Mom says, "I don't know, what *is* World War II?"

Lola says something I can't hear.

Mom says, "Why doesn't he answer any of the questions? He's so rude!"

Gloria pulls the ice pack away from her face. "What happened to you?"

"I could ask the same thing. Besides, I didn't know you had a son."

Mom says, "But who *is* the man from LaMancha?"

Gloria says, "You didn't get fired or anything?"

At this point, being fired would be the easiest option. "Of course not." Again, here's where I should ask what happened. Still, I'd rather ask about Julian from

Julliard. It's not the same as Dad cashing his old family for a new one, but Gloria cashing me in for a son feels similar, at least. Unless she already told me—which, granted, is a possibility.

Mom says, "What *is* St. Augustine's *Confessions*?"

Gloria places the ice pack onto the table. "Don't you want to know?"

Not really. "Okay."

Gloria points into the other room. "I went to bring her the soup. She asked me where her husband was hiding. She yelled about finding Joan to help her. She knocked the soup off the tray. I was afraid she'd burn herself. And I went over to check and she hit me in the nose with a glass! Why did she have one in her room?"

I remember seeing Lola sitting in her room, guzzling glasses of soda. But I say, "I'm not sure."

Juilliard sucks his teeth. "You're not sure of much."

"I'm sure you're a horsefucker!"

Gloria hammers the ice pack on the table. "Stop!" She stares at me, a disappointed stare that zips me hard.

Julian from Julliard snorts. "Sorry."

Gloria waits for me to apologize, but I don't answer. She says, "Tell me the truth, okay? Where were you?"

Mom says, "Who *is* Abe Lincoln?"

I say, "Working?"

"No you weren't. I called Video Planet. Look, if you wanted to have a night with Lola, you could have just said it. You should be on dates! I want you to go out! Have fun. But you can't do that and keep your Mom home. It's not fair to her."

Too many things have happened. The truth is I do want to go on dates, especially after our talk in the car. I want to take Lola to movies, walk through parks, eat

Happy Meals, but I will sacrifice all of it if it means dumping my mother in a home.

Gloria wants an answer. I can tell her about finding my father, but I'm not risking coming off even more pathetic than I already seem in front of Julian. Anyway, there's no defense against her being hurt, so I stare at the *Best Mom Ever* mug and wait for the moment to pass. It does. She stands and Juilliard clasps her arm exactly how I've led my mother around for the last few years, as though Gloria's an invalid, fragile, incapable of walking herself. Unlike his mother, my mother is all of those things. Worse, Gloria will remember that kindness tonight as they drive home, or in her living room watching shows from a television that Gloria doesn't mistake for a real-life conversation. To quote the benevolent words of Saint Augustine: I am squarely fucked. Julian or not, even I know it is time to grovel.

"I'm really sorry. Please. Never again"

"I can't do this." She touches the pamphlet. "This is where she should be."

The kitchen light buzzes, an electrical pulse, a dying heart. I say "So you're quitting cause Mom hit you?"

She squints at me, as though I'm a small child. I shift uncomfortably until Gloria says, "She's hit me lots of times. It's about the next stage of care." I think of the word "hospice" but that's not what she means. "I'll help. Call me. But I can't continue to do this."

I tell her I understand. The words drizzle from my mouth. The same way I would've told my father.

Gloria smiles. "Good. It's a nice place."

Mom says, "What *is* Shangri-la?"

Lola marches into the kitchen and opens the fridge. She takes out the orange juice. "Don't worry, I'll use a glass. I have manners. I'm refined! Educated! Pearls and ivory and sugar and spice." She fetches a glass and pours juice, moving the carton in a tight spiral, as though she's mixing a cocktail. "What's in the case?"

I think of *Seven*, and Gwyneth Paltrow's severed head. At this point I wish it was mine.

Juilliard says "A violin."

Lola drinks, swallowing loudly, letting juice drizzle down the sides of her mouth, razzing Gloria. She says, "Well, I play a mean skin-flute." She starts laughing but the rest of us stand there, awkwardly silent. This isn't really the final impression I wanted for them to have, but then again, Gloria is ditching us, so who cares.

Lola says, "Get it?"

Gloria says "Think about what I said. It's for the best."

Her son walks toward the living room. But she pulls his coat and they walk out the side, avoiding Mom. I don't think I could feel more sad if I tried. We're over. The final act. What the movies call the "All is Lost" moment.

Lola sips juice, then burps. "She didn't even say she liked my outfit." She places the glass in the sink, as though this was a normal day. I wait for her to read the gravity of the moment and ask if I'm okay, or help me form a plan. Instead, she says, "What'cha wanna do?" as though we're deciding between playing Zelda or Mario Bros.

How about this: I wanna evaporate.

Mom says, "What's a vowel?" *Wheel* is on now.

I press my wrist against my forehead. "Can you put Mom to bed?"

"Sure. After the show. Then I'll snuggle in beside you."

"Sounds good," I say, though I want to be alone.

I walk into my room. The blankets are still on the floor. I move to the VCR. I press Power, then turn on the television. Leaning against the cabinet is another 4x8 painting of Mom. Mom is painted from the neck up; she's smiling and has a flower in her hair. The background is raw-meat red, with darker streaks above her head. I know that picture. I took that picture after a small party to celebrate her job promotion for bank manager. It was one of the few times I can remember that she was truly happy. Still, the painting captures the far-off gaze, a stare that only comes with illness.

"What am I going to do with you, Mom?" No answer, of course. "You were right. I should've left Dad alone. If I'd just stayed home, nothing would've changed." The only sound in the room is the low static of the TV. I move the painting against the bed, facing the television. I say, "Comfortable?" Silence. "You must be tired, too."

For no real reason, I fast-forward, hoping to gain some insight, comfort. I hit Play. The footage blinks on. Greg and Sarah are in the back seat of a car, and it takes me a second to realize they're leaving JFK. The sky is pinkish so it's hard to tell if it's early morning or sunset. The taxi loops the on-ramp for the Belt Parkway then stops, the camera recording a line of taillights, which means it's late afternoon.

I say, "My friends are home."

Greg zooms in on Sarah. She's wearing sunglasses that cover half her face and a wide-brimmed hat, pink and too big for the backseat of a taxi.

He says, "So around the world and back again." Sarah glances out the window. "Happy?" She covers her mouth, concealing a smile. The traffic picks up and the cab gets onto the Van Wyck. I lean forward to hit Rewind, but I realize they're driving home. I'll see where they live. Maybe their ride will reveal why they left the videotape in front of the store. The cabbie asks where they went. Greg says, "Paradise." He asks if Greg means Paradise Island in the Bahamas. Sarah says, "No. We mean paradise," and they all laugh.

The taxi takes the Liberty Avenue exit, then turns left onto 101st. My chest squeezes like a belt is tied around my lungs. I refuse to believe where their ride is leading them until they turn onto 134th. "Mom, see where they're going?" I say, rolling onto my knees and leaning close. I'm sweating, so I take off my hoodie, leaving me in just my t-shirt. They're quiet now, Greg filming the street that only an hour ago I had visited. They pass 97th. I call for Lola, but only a gaspy whisper escapes. They pass the phone-pole on the corner where I parked. I feel shaky. I mush the blankets around me, a nest. Greg says, "This is it, on the right." He pays the driver thirty bucks, and they step out of the cab. Sarah opens the gate next to my father's house. It's white with pink borders. I hear a "How are you?" and the camera turns. My father is coming out of his gate, tugging his trash can to the curb. Greg says, "Smile, you're on candid camera." Dad laughs, "You'll break the lens." Sarah hugs him. She actually fucking hugs him! I'm so jealous I could kill someone. She says, "Come over with Ingrid! Watch our vacation!" Greg laughs. "Yeah, let us bore you to death!" Dad says. "Okay. But not tonight. Some other time," which we all know means never. Dad says, "I got your mail." I slap the screen. I say, "Peaches to everyone but your fucking son, huh, you douche?" Greg turns the lens, facing Atlantic. A truck lays on its horn as it speeds past. "Ah, back to reality."

The screen goes black. I say to her portrait, "Sorry you had to see that, Mom."

I wait for more. But that's all the footage. I hit Stop. I pick up the camera, eject the tape. I crawl forward, plug the three-pronged cable into the machine connecting my camera to the VCR. I rewind my footage, counting to three, then stop. I say, "Here's reality. Here's my fucking movie." I stick my footage of Mom into the adjoining slot in the dubbing VCR. "Here's *The Worst Possible Thing*." I hit Play. Greg and Sarah on the beach. I hit Stop, then Record and splice in Mom staring into her bowl of cereal as though she could see her reflection. I hit Stop on the camera. Rewind the footage. Greg walking the beach. I hit Stop. Record on the camera. Mom's twitching eye. I hit Stop, Record, Stop, Record until I can't tell which reality I'm viewing, which one is playing. Here's Mom stumbling down the hallway. No, it's Sarah shashsaying from the pool. Mom asks where her husband went. Greg asks if she wants a daiquiri. Mom says her fake coffee is too strong. Play. Stop. Record. Record. Play. Stop. A scale. A riff. A song. Here, a dusty wind rustles Mom's hair. A tropical breeze rustles Sarah's. Here are Mom's coats. Stop. Play. Record. Greg is eating a steak. Mom pushing her lentils away. Mom in bed, holding Lola's hand. Sarah holding Greg's hand as they traverse the rocks of the tidal pool. A towel draped on a beach chair. A row of dusty coats wrapped in cellophane. A black space in the film, a marker, where I should've filmed Gloria, whose absence already feels total. A close-up of Sarah. A close-up of Mom's portrait, her eyes haloed in thick red and purple and black. I wanted fiction, then reality played as fiction, now I have reality dubbed over reality, a mixtape of fiction, strangely connected to me. I hit Stop. A sailboat sits on a flat opal sea. Mom lost in the kitchen. I hit Play. Mom asks where her husband ran off to. I fast-forward, a stream of time, interrupted.

Sarah sits in her cabana. I feel nothing. I fast-forward. I see the curve of the exit ramp as the taxi merges onto the parkway. My home, removed. My mother's home, removed. My father's home, removed from us.

"I hope everyone likes my movie, *The Worst Possible Thing*."

No. *Play, Rewind*.

Then I hit Stop. Right before the sad parts.

CHAPTER 22

For once, Dom isn't exaggerating or paranoid. He's right. This is bad.

Placed outside the front of Video Planet are racks filled with bootleg DVDs. Movies that haven't been released on video yet: *Scream 3*, *The Beach*, *Boiler Room*, and other movies that are still in theaters such as *High Fidelity*, *Mission to Mars*, *My Dog Skip*. A crowd gathers in front of the racks jam-packed with DVDs and boxes spilling over with videotapes. The crowd is all elbows and body blocks, as though they're edging up for some midnight special, some doorbuster deal. Across from the herd of customers, Vic sits in front of a fold-out table, blocking customers who simply want to go inside and rent a video instead of buying a DVD. Placed on the table is a metal box stuffed with cash next to an empty tape case for his cigarette ashes. Vic is wearing his standard black shirt and maroon pants. He also has a black baseball cap slung low, its brim resting on the frames of his glasses. He has a box of popcorn and an unopened Manhattan Special. I squeeze through the crowd and hide behind a rack.

This morning, I left Mom with Lola. I wrote a schedule for her meds, and just to be safe, a list of reminders, such as no candy or coffee or backyard. Lola kissed my forehead and said, "I'm her sister. I know what to do." She told me that she had activities planned.

She'd bought coloring books and watercolors. A babydoll. She knows the basics of Mom Care. I felt bad even asking, like I was being a selfish jerk, putting my problems on her again. I'd even considered calling out from Video Planet, but I figured Dom would keep bothering me to work. Besides, I thought the quiet of Video Planet would be an opportunity to figure out how I'll care for Mom by myself.

So the last thing I want to do now is stand in front of the store as Vic sells bootlegs and I wait for the police to raid us like it's an episode of *Cops*. Vic smiles, tells customers, "That's a good one," for movies I'm guessing he hasn't seen. (Unless the directors stuck cartoon animals in *Rules of Engagement*.) He's a better salesman than Dom, who bullies the poor customer into renting the movies *he* likes, or even me, who stays mute and fetches whatever horrible film they choose. I wish that Dom would have cared a little more about Video Planet. He wouldn't have had to narc on Royal. We would've put them out of business the old-fashioned, dare I say, the American way: we would've earned it.

Vic shakes a woman's hand. He tells her to check back tomorrow for whatever bootleg she needs. Everything is murky and disorienting. What I do know is Video Planet will end as quietly as a dumpster fire.

Vic spots me and waves. As I push through the crowd, he says, "Hey, let the kid through." Two guys wearing leather jackets argue over a DVD. It's sad that it took something this illegal to make Video Planet's fortune. Vic says, "Whoever had it first, buy it. I'll get another tomorrow. Come back." They both thank him.

I turn and Tina Hart gives this half-wave and scoots between the racks, trying to flirt her way to a discount. To Vic I say, "When did you start doing this?"

"Your first vacation day, I think." He shrugs, watching the customers dig through the boxes. "Whenever we talked to your friend."

"Rich? He's just a customer."

Still watching the crowd, Vic says, "Right. That's it."

I'm not sure why, maybe it's his inability to look at me, but I realize that he might've given me those days off because he knew I'd try to change his mind, or tell Dom. This flutter of mistrust swirls inside my chest. "Shouldn't we do this inside?"

He sours his face. "Nah. It's a nice day. People buy more when stuff is outside." He's right about that. "Besides, I can't take looking at Dom's mopey face."

He's right about that too. "What about the cops?"

"They're out catching criminals." He holds out his arms. "We're selling entertainment." He points at the store. "You're smarter than that banana-head ever was, kid. You're goin' places."

Yeah. The clink. He's selling the videos eight bucks each, three for ten. Customers are bringing over columns of videos higher than the ones Dom leaves for me on the counter every morning when I open the store. With each sale, Vic pats me on the back. The sun and the crowd is making my stomach sour.

My phone buzzes. A text from Lola: *A-OK*. I stick it back in my pocket. When I look up I spot Rich, his chin raised as he skims the cases.

I say, "Be right back." I hustle towards the door, head down, trying to avoid Rich. Video Planet feels cooler, darker. Movie banners hang from the ceiling like stalactites. *The Hurricane*, the re-release of *Fantasia*, of course.

Dom stands and leans over, his elbows bracing against the counter, as though he's getting an enema. In a way, he is.

I say, "Fix it up more, huh?"

"New suit on a dead guy."

He's still wearing his Mets shirt. I wish he'd taken it off. My team has enough hexes. Dom pinches his lips until I'm standing in front of him; he belches, deep and froggy, all booze. I say, "Are you okay?"

"Guess." He goes head-down on the counter and swishes his forehead from side-to-side. "I'm fucked."

I wait for him to raise his head. He doesn't. "How long has this been going on?"

He mumbles he's fucked again and again. I see why Vic decided to set up his fresco market instead of dealing with Dom's melodrama, even if Dom's right and Vic's wrong. Whatever money Vic is making from his special bootlegs, none of it's going to Video Planet. The customers are buying from Vic, not renting from Dom.

I say, "You want a coffee?"

"Sure. Extra cyanide." He lifts his head, glances around the store, places it on the counter. "What happened yesterday? Gladys called."

I walk around the counter and sit in his chair. I think of her being led by her son, her real son. My father, Lola's confession. "Gloria."

Dom never listens on a good day, forget being drunk and depressed. "Can't believe this. I never did nothing to nobody."

"You called the cops! They raided his store!"

"Can't a guy love movies?" Dom lifts his head, resting his chin on the counter. Watching him, I suddenly want to record this moment. "I run a legit business." Except for the bootlegs. "Grade-A Certified. Gold Standard. Grandma's Best."

"Highest quality."

"Right. With great power comes great responsibility. I could've been a contender! Use the force, Luke!"

Listening to Dom spew movie quotes is depressing, even by my standards. I thought circling back to Video Planet would help me forget about everything else. That for a few hours, I'd be alone. But Dom is drunk, watching his store close one bootleg at a time. So on top of everything, I'm feeling bad for him, too. I shouldn't, but if anything, I understand how hope deflates faster than you can patch the holes.

Still I'm hopeful. "Any rentals?"

"Nope. And get out of my chair." He hobbles to it and flops down. "Worst of this." I brace myself for a tearful tirade about his mom. "I miss Vicki."

"You mean your gun?"

"No, I mean Vicki." He shakes his head. "That squeaky fucker. Greasing her parts." Trying to distract his psychotic doldrums, I grab *Jurassic Park*, still resting on the VCR, and stick it into the machine. I hit Play and Jeff Goldblum is pontificating about condors. Dom tells me to shut it off, but then twists toward the television for a better view. He leans against the back of the chair and shuts his eyes. I lower the volume, hoping he dozes off. My phone buzzes. *Mom's sleeping*. I dial Gloria. It rings and rings. I flip my phone closed.

I hear, "What you know, what you say?" Rich is striding up the aisle, holding a tape, most likely *Platoon*. He stops midway and raises his arms like he's going to embrace me. He's wearing stonewashed jeans, deck shoes, and a leather jacket zipped halfway up. His shirt is only a nest of peppered chest hair. "How's it going, guy?"

Here's a list of words that I hate to be called: chief, boss, guy, pal, buddy, friend. I say, "It's going," which is as accurate as I'll own up to.

"Three deuces, right?" He does that pointy thing. "Hey, he remembers."

I shush him and step aside so he'll see Dom snoring away.

"He's sick? I know all about that."

I bet you do. I tap *Platoon*. "It's late."

"That's what she said," he laughs, a loud barky cough thing. He slips his sneaker off and peels two dollars from the insole. The money's damp with sweat, but these dirty bills are the only legit money this store will make today. "Keep the change." Behind us, Dom snores, shudders, curses, and snores again. "Holy baalow-ly, he's zonked!"

I hit *Sale*, and when the drawer opens, it's empty.

I slide the money back, hoping Rich'll leave. His tongue juts between his teeth. "My idea's making you big loot, huh?"

I shut the drawer and glance over my shoulder.

Rich repeats himself. I nod, trying to get him out of here. He says it again.

Dom lifts his head. "What idea is that, buddy?"

Rich says, "All them extra doughnuts."

Dom pushes off the chair and timbers forward, catching himself on the counter. Here's where I should tell Dom to ignore him. That he watches war movies until he's wonky enough to pass his SSI test. But I feel cold and bloodless.

Dom says, "How would you know what to do with my store?"

Rich says, "Take it easy. I just told him that I wished you had new movies." We stand there. "Watch the newest of the new, new movies at home."

Dom tilts toward me. "What is he talking about?"

I tell him I don't know.

Rich says, "Sure he does. I asked him for a new release. He said it wouldn't be out yet. I told him I saw it being sold on the street."

I ebb towards the counter door to escape. "I told him we don't do that."

Rich says, "Right. But now you do! My idea!"

I say, "It didn't happen like that."

Rich says, "Sure did."

Dom slicks his hair. "Get out."

I say, "Me?"

"No. I got to talk to you. I mean this shirtless, pit smelling, bottom-feeding, raggamuffin wannabe gangster garbage. Him!"

Rich zips up his coat, covering his chest. "Can't toss me. I was in Vietnam!"

Dom says, "Yeah, well this is Queens, so get out."

"Royal was better. The king of videos. This place sucks horse dicks."

Dom pounds his fist against the counter. "Eat it!"

"The king!" Rich walks toward the door, slapping cases off the racks. The boxes flick into the air, then slide across the balding carpet. "You'll be sorry."

Dom yells, "Everybody bleeds."

Now is a good time to slip away, if one were so inclined. I drift through the door and between the rack and the wall, where he can't see me. He calls my name, but I keep rabbit-still. He says, louder, "Where's the traitor?"

I step around the rack and into the aisle. "Dom, that guy's nuts. It didn't happen like that."

I edge farther from the counter. I should quit. It doesn't matter if I stay now. Dom doesn't have the money to pay me. With Vic selling bootleg DVDs outside, the cops are a second away from raiding this place. I lift one of the boxes off the ground: *Independence Day*. I place it on the racks. I haven't left yet, but I already feel this sappy sentimentality for the place.

I lie, "I came in to let you know Gloria quit, Dom. I have to be off for a while. Stay home, you know?" I place the box on the rack. "For my mom."

Dom hobbles around the counter. He squares off in front of me. "How much did he give you?"

"Who?"

"Vic, you savant!" He crosses his arms.

"You're crazy." I walk backwards. "It's not like that."

"No? That's why you didn't say nothing on the stoop? Acting like you don't know shit from granola."

"It's Shinola, Dom."

"You know who you are? That pencilneck wormy guy from *Aliens*."

"Paul Reiser? Sure. When you were napping, I impregnated you with an alien."

"You ain't good enough to impregnate me." The windshield wiper lady walks into the store. Dom points at her: "Get out." She hurries onto the sidewalk. "I can't believe you'd do this!"

"Rich is crazy! He keeps money in his sneakers!"

"My mother's dying words were, 'Give him a job.'"

I stare up at the ceiling and exhale, long and slow. "C'mon. Her *last* words?"

Here Dom realizes he's gone a bridge too far. He bites his lip, stifling a laugh. Another psycho moodswing and now we're both laughing.

Once I'm convinced he's truly calm, I walk over to the counter, next to him. "I'd never sell you out. I love this place." But I never felt it so deeply until I saw it in its death throes. I glance at the low ceilings, the counter, absorbing Video Planet's beautiful ruins. "I mean it." Am I saying it for him, or myself? No it's for me, all me.

Dom leans against the counter, his knees bent, his eyes closed. He's weighing out the situation, but it looks as though he's soiling his pants. "Fucking guy."

"I'm sorry. Okay?" Dom is a crazy bastard, but he's been my boss for years; I owe him this, at least. "Mistakes were made."

He moves closer and hugs me. It's a cocktail of beer, cigarettes and B.O. "Video Planet loves you too."

"Thanks."

"And I'm sure you could impregnate me, if you wanted."

I thank him again.

He straightens, points. "But that doesn't make all this better."

I pick up a box and place it on the rack, a sign of solidarity.

He crosses his arms. "You still owe me. We're a perfect pair, together in this mess. Like peanut butter and jelly. Cookies and milk. Porn and pancakes." He scratches his chin, a conspiring smile on his sweaty, defeated face. "You're gonna help me?"

I'll agree to just about anything to get him away from me, if only for a few minutes. I say, "With the store? Of course."

Technically I'm his boss now, but he tells me to get to work.

I pick up the box. Michael Douglas's head is sharding off into a plume of jigsaw puzzle pieces, a curtain of black behind him. *The Game.*

CHAPTER 23

As an apology to Dom, I decided to stay after Video Planet closed and help him clean. When Vic saw me scooping the garbage into the metal dustpan, he'd told me to let Dom handle it, and then walked to his Civic with the sacred cashbox of DVD money tucked under his arm. But I stuck around, folding up the foldout table and herding the racks into the store. It took us over an hour to clean, then another hour to convince Dom to drink enough coffee to sober up for his drive home. Then he wanted me to buy him scratch-offs. Then he wanted me to buy him *Newsday*. Then he wanted pickles. After all of this cleaning and convincing and fetching, I returned home after midnight to, thankfully, a dark and quiet house.

After all that, I overslept. So now as I swerve into the kitchen, blurry-eyed and exhausted, the afternoon is well underway. I give a slow winding yawn as a way of a greeting, which then sets off a chain-reaction yawn from Lola, and then Mom.

It's a comfort to see Mom and Lola sitting at the table. Lola has painted Mom's fingernails bright green. She's wearing lipstick that is the color of a Corvette in an eighties teen movie. Mom's hair is held in place by clips, their tortoiseshell grips poking out. Lola's hair is shaved, so she fastened a hair clip around her thumb. Another clip is latched onto the shoulder of her Radiohead t-shirt. They have this sleepover friends vibe about them. (Not that I would know. My mother never allowed me to have a sleepover, blaming work. I couldn't go to my friends' sleepovers in case their parents were perverts. The Pervert Rule was also applied to camps, youth sports, religious instruction, and movies with parent chaperones, especially dads. Hooray for childhood!)

I take a mug from the drainboard and pour a cup of coffee. They're playing cards, kind of. The deck is split between them. Lola is studying her cards, her nose close, while Mom has the cards face up on the table. She's eating another sleeve of Oreos. Lola says, "Got any fives?"

Mom bites her cookie. "Five what?"

Lola presses her cards to her chest and looks at Mom's cards on the table. She says, "You don't have any, Sis. Say, 'Go fish.'"

Mom says, "I hate fish."

Lola takes a card from the deck.

"You're a dealer?" Mom puts her cards down. "Flush."

I say, "Mom, I don't think that's the game you're playing."

"I'm not playing anything."

"Right." I open the fridge. Except for the two leftover meals from Gloria and a bottle of flat Pepsi, it's empty. I don't even have milk for the coffee. Gloria is really forcing my hand. Lola tells Mom to ask if she has any jacks, but Mom stuffs another cookie into her mouth. Lola takes the Jack of Spades from her hand and places it onto the table, helping her win. If they're going to play cards (sort of), I'll go to the store. I'll stick to the basics: bread, peanut butter, crackers and cans of tomato soup. The Oreos she likes so much. In other words, bomb-shelter food. I say, "How is she?"

Lola shrugs, "Terrible."

Mom sniffs the cookie and tosses it over her shoulder as if it were a rotted macintosh. I didn't expect Mom to be scrawling astrophysics on a napkin, but I'm still disappointed that she's already having a bad day. Unless something happened while I was working and missed it. "Why? Last night? Is it her eyes again?"

"She's lost three hands."

"I mean, apart from that."

She snaps. "She's okay! I made her toast and gave her juice! She is eating cookies now. While you were in your third dream, I played the *Grease* soundtrack and did her makeup. Looks good, right?"

"Snazzy."

Lola sings, "Beauty school dropout. No graduation day." I sit next to Lola. She rests her head on my shoulder and Mom smiles, happy her son and sister are getting along. Lola says, "How's worky work?"

I say, "Fine," choking on the word. I'm so disgusted by it all. "Finey fine."

Lola says, "Got any kings?"

"I don't know any kings. Oh wait, Chesterfield King." Mom runs her finger around the cookie wrapper. Lola leans over, examines her hand and takes one off the deck. Playing cards this way would make me crazy, yet she doesn't seem to mind. Watching her, I realize Lola's found the mother that I've lost. She never yells at her. She doesn't get frustrated by Mom's confusion. She cares about her. Lola wants to be here, with her, with me. If only Gloria would've seen this side of her...

Mom pats her robe. "Where's my money? How am I even betting?" She glances around, truly lost. "I want to play blackjack. But watch my husband don't overbet! He does that."

I say, "It's okay. Don't worry about it."

Mom says, "Well I do. I like to eat, you know?"

"Then eat your cookies, Mom."

Mom says, "Eat shit and die."

"Can't you talk nice to me?"

Mom says, "I didn't say anything."

Lola notices the upset look on my face. She nudges my shoulder. "Me and Sis are gonna have a movie night. I bought pretzels and root beer. We're gonna watch *The Wizard of Oz*." Lola places her cards down.

"Sounds fun."

She takes a card from the deck. "Remember the contest? I looked again, and you should totally do it. It says that anyone can enter. That it's open"

"Lola, how would I--"

"You just send in a film." She whispers, "We have a good one." She heaps the cards into a pile. Mom says she had a good hand.

"It's kind of rough, don't you think?"

"I just think if you're trying for school, now's it. You don't have a lot of time left to submit. Besides, you don't want to be some slick sellout movie director. We're making art. Think about it." Lola puts the cards away. "Okay. Me and Sis have coloring to do."

Mom pushes the roll of cookies off the table. When they hit the ground she giggles as though she's a toddler.

I say, "It's just not a good time."

"Everyone says that. If I felt that way I'd still be hiding in your bush. News flash: It's never a good time. Submit, and then worry when it happens."

Mom says, "Look at this hotel!" When I turn, she's looking at the ShadyPines Glen brochure. I reach for it, but Mom pulls her hand back. Lola says "Psych!" and they laugh.

Mom says, "They have a nice lobby. Can I go there?" She drops it onto the table and stares at the picture of the woman leading the patient (or resident, or whatever they're called) along the path. "We can stay a night or two. Me and Sis."

Lola says, "Sounds great."

"We can't stay there." Mom asks why, and I want to tell her that's where mothers go to die, but I say, "We can't afford it," which is also true.

Mom says, "Fucking tightwad."

I try to slide the brochure away from her, and she presses her palm on the paper and stops me. I'm keeping her with me because that's what she really wants, and now she's pushing for a home because she thinks it's a casino. I smile out of pure frustration and say, "I'm not cheap."

Lola says, "He did buy me a Happy Meal, Sis."

Mom says, "Yeah sure. I'm tired of this hotel. It needs a revamp."

No kidding. This time, she lets me slide the pamphlet free. I close it and flip it, revealing the number to call. Lola says to Mom, "Let's go. He's being a crankypants." She walks around the table and touches Mom's shoulder. Mom actually stands. "Think about school." Lola leads her by the elbow into her room. The door closes.

I've already realized my application can only have two outcomes: get rejected and feel worthless, or get accepted and feel helpless. If I had a choice, a Greg-and-Sarah choice, I'd apply. At this moment, rejection feels better than being helpless. I look into my empty mug, trying to decipher my future. The grounds look like a middle-finger. I take the brochure so Mom won't find it again and walk down the hall. Taped onto Mom's door is a sign that says *SISSIES ONLY! DON'T EVEN*

KNOCK! in red crayon. The words are bordered by purple skulls, gold machetes, and strangely enough, silver hearts.

I continue into my room and sit on the bed, next to the camera.

I open the brochure. They have a picture of one of the bedrooms. There is a television mounted on a gold-colored wall, a small table. There is a library and a living room that have "elegance and Victorian decor." There is a "Main Street" within the complex that has a movie theater. There's laundry and housekeeping services. This place must cost a fortune. Why would Gloria even suggest it? Then again, maybe they are all like this. I mean they're not prisoners. They're just confused, sad, lonely, old people. I trace my fingers along the phone number, written in gold. I do my best Kurt Russell and say, "You know what ol' Jack Burton always says in a time like this? Fuck it."

I dial the number. I wait for an automated director but a woman picks up the phone. She says, "ShadyGlen Pines, how may I help you?"

"Hi. I'm...uh...Jack Russell," I say, then pause. Maybe I should gone with Kurt Burton. "I'm calling about my mom."

"Okay, Mr...Russell. Is she a resident?"

"No!" I take a deep breath. "No. I'm calling for information about sticking her there. I mean, moving her out. In. Yeah. Can you help me?"

"Sure, I'll transfer you to Ms. Pine. One moment."

Before I can ask her if Ms. Pine's first name is Shady, I hear Muzak, which I think is "La Vie en Rose." A strange panic grips me. I'm just about to hang up when I'm switched over and a woman introduces herself as

Ms. Pine. If this place was cheap, I'd be waiting longer. I say, "Hello. I'm calling about lodging for my mom?"

"Okay. I'll gladly help you. Your mother's name?"

I want to lie, but say, "Camilla."

"Lovely name. Does Camilla have insurance?"

I say, "Yes. BlueCross."

She types something. "Any supplemental?"

I say, "She has dementia."

There's a quiet pause that might be rehearsed, unless she's trying to figure out if I'm a pranker, or wonky, or both. She says, "It's difficult. I know. But many of our residents have various health distractions."

Balls to buttermilk do I hate reflective listening. "Distractions?"

Ms. Pine says, "Yes. Distractions from living their most comfortable lives. But we have well trained staff and one of the safest and cleanest care homes in the five boroughs." There's another rehearsed pause. In the next room Lola tells my mother that her picture is beautiful, and I feel this tug in my chest, as though Ms. Pine is going to signal a SWAT team to confiscate her. Ms. Pine clears her throat. "Hello? So it's better to discuss this in person, but I'd like to get an overview about her?"

"Sure."

"Her age?"

"Sixty-five."

I wait for her to tell me how young my mother is to be so sick that she already needs a home. She's typing, a fast ticking. It must be missing from her sales script. "So we talked about insurance. Does she have any assets?"

"What do you mean?"

"You know. Bank accounts. 401(k)s, things like that."

"She has a bank account, but it's been mostly depleted. I've taken care of her. How much is it?"

More typing. "It depends. We first have to calculate all of her insurance and assets. The payment amount varies, but our care is about twelve thousand dollars."

My chest flutters. Does she mean a year? Maybe I should at least take a look. Mom did like the brochure. I feel this twist of both guilt for even considering this, and excitement that the film school contest might now be a real possibility. In the next room, Mom tells Lola she loves her picture, and I snap back to reality. No. It can't happen now. If it *is* that cheap I can keep it as an option, when she gets too bad. "That's for a year? I mean, that's really affordable. I'd have to think it over and see what Mom wants. When I can't take care of her anymore, I mean."

Ms. Pine clears her throat. "I'm sorry for the confusion. That's a month."

I try to say something, but the weight of the number sits on my chest.

She goes on, oblivious. "Of course, this doesn't include the additional services. Laundry. Activities and trips. This is a rough number that we can work out. Also, they're given an allowance."

"Allowance? Like they do chores?"

Ms. Pine laughs: humorless, greedy. "No. The residents do partake in activities which help them in practical ways, but usually we move money from their account and let them use it to buy things. Feel independent."

I say, "So you pay them the money they gave you, so they can then pay you?"

"Exactly. Also, it's always their money. If they transfer or move on—"

I say, "You mean die, right?"

There's another pause. "If the resident moves on, all assets are transferred to the dependent on the contract. Does that make sense?"

I really want to tell this lady to blow me, but I say, "We're shit broke."

"I'm sorry."

"*I'm* sorry. What does insurance cover?"

"It varies. Most often, the insurance covers half of the monthly payment, and then the rest is left to the assets."

"You mean, I pay?"

"No. Her assets. As we discussed. Her bank account is signed to ShadyPines, where the funds are placed in a non-interest earning account. The remaining balance after insurance is charged monthly. Unless you'd prefer to pay the balance privately. Which is an option. We have various payment plans. There's also a sliding scale."

Sure. I'll slide right into a lava pit. I say, "I'm just confused why I'd have to sign over her assets to you. Anyway, she would run out of assets in three months." A lie. It's actually two months. Also, I cashed out most of her 401(k) to pay the mortgage. "That's all her assets. Maybe she can sell bootleg DVDs out of her room."

"Excuse me?"

"Nevermind."

"Well, people have assets. You'd be surprised what a bit of digging you'd find. If you come in, we can discuss it."

"Wait. You mean assets like our house?"

There's a long pause, this time very unrehearsed. "Yes."

I hang up. "Fucking vultures."

I let the brochure fall onto my lap. So much for golden retreats and film school.

For some reason, it reminds me of when I was ten and all of my friends were going to Six Flags Great Adventure. The commercials had all these kids zigzagging through the theme park, happy and wild. The commercial cuts to the Buccaneer Pirate Ship and the Lightning Loop, the first roller coaster to hang upside down. The coily-looking Viper. On Mondays, kids would come to school wearing Six Flags shirts or hats. Joe Sclafani wore his wristband for two weeks straight, before the paper finally disintegrated from showering. But Mom always said we couldn't go. First, we couldn't afford it. Then I brought home a few Coca-Cola cans with coupons printed on the back. So then Mom changed her excuse, saying she was afraid to drive from Queens to New Jersey. And of course I wasn't allowed to go with my friends (the Pervert Rule). Instead we went to Coney Island, which reeked like rotted fish. The rides were rickety. The boardwalk was sleazy. Broken glass, beer caps, and Coney Island whitefish on the beach. Mostly, It reminded me of OTB and my father's lies. And...well, it wasn't a Great Adventure.

That's what ShadyPines Glen feels like. The Coney Island of nursing homes. Gloria has to know this. ShadyPines Glen was *her* escape plan, not mine. If I didn't call, then that was on me. And if I did call, she figured she could leave, free of blame. I flick the brochure onto the carpet. I'm tired of being manipulated. I thought we were friends, but she's just a nurse, a bloodsuck like Ms. Pine.

I pick up the camera and place it on my lap like a thousand possibilities.

The weight of it on my thighs helps me shake off Gloria's plan and evil Ms. Pine. I think about possible shots. I'd love to sneak into the room and film them coloring. I try to decide on Mom's lines—hectic and wide, or fine and deliberate. What color would she choose? Cerise, Fuzzy Wuzzy, Orchid, Periwinkle, Bittersweet? I frame the shot over her shoulder, her hair frizzy and gray, a contrast to the vivid color on her page.

I take the camera and walk toward her room, but there's a knock at the front door. I move down the hall, hoping Ms. Pine actually didn't send a SWAT team.

When I open it, Dom is standing on the stoop. He's dressed in all black and smells like a shot of Crown Royal and Paco Rabaan. I'm not sure what he was doing after he left Video Planet last night, but he must not have slept. I thumb the power button on the camera, but I'm not making a horror movie. Before I ask him what he's doing he says, "Leave the camera. Take the cannoli."

"What are you talking about? I thought you were at the store today."

He sneers. "Vic's at the store today. I'm just stopping by."

"How did you drive in your condition?"

"If you can't drive sober, drive slooooow." He watches a woman walk past holding grocery bags. He salutes her. "I have to talk to you."

"Can't this just wait?" I want to call Gloria and explain that we can't afford ShadyPine Glen. I need to do it now, before I lose my nerve. Maybe she'll come back and help.

Dom says, "Forget it. See you when I see you." He knocks into the railing as he sways down the steps. He's going to t-bone a bus full of nuns.

I need to stay home, but the last thing I need is death guilt. Lola is coloring with Mom. They're together, safe. I'll drop this maniac off at home and then buy some groceries. Pretend I know how to cook like Gloria.

"Dom. Let me take you home, at least." Behind me I can hear Lola asking if my mother is finished using the yellow. "We have to hurry. I have to make a phone call"

Dom says, barely audible, slurring, "We'll be quick as video clerks whose store is slowly being drilled into the ground."

He misses the gate latch, then taps the top of the fence as though that's what he had planned the whole time. Trying again, he swings open the gate and smiles, impressed with himself. He tosses his head back and gawks at the sky, his mouth open, his face glistening with sweat.

"I'll get it, Dom."

"You're clever."

"Sure. Fine. Let's just go."

CHAPTER 24

We're sitting in my Cutlass, across the street from Dom's place. The roof's brown shingles spill over the brickface. Beside the door are a pair of concrete planters, flowerless and cracked. A single wind chime hangs above the door, surrounded by wires that once held other chimes, but are now crooked and flailing. It looks as defeated as Dom does. He says, "There's my commode."

"I think you mean abode."

"That's what I said."

Dom picks his ear and smears his haul down my dashboard, a rubber cement sheen that makes me question my driving him, being sucked into another one of his perfect catastrophes. He'll vanish soon enough, then I'll fly through the supermarket and hopefully get back in time to film my mother coloring. Lately, I've been in the mood for animal crackers, the good ones with the circus printed on the little box. I imagine my mother picking them out with shaky fingers. It'll be great footage.

I also want to see how Lola and Mom do without me. She's easier to manage at night, as long as she sticks to her routine. It's caring for Mom during the daytime, when she's buzzing and awake, that's the real test. If Gloria doesn't come back I might have to ask Lola to watch her from time to time. I feel bad about it, but I'm not sure what else I can do...

Dom intrudes: "You never been inside, have you?"

"It isn't high on my list."

He guzzles from one of the three airplane bottles he brought along for the ride. "My adobe ain't good enough for you?" He elbows my ribs. "C'mon, be a pal." He puckers his lip like a five-year old.

I shut the car. I'll stop in for ten minutes and leave. "Fine. Let's go."

Dom chugs the rest of the bottle, drizzling vodka down the corners of his mouth. He exhales, fogging the windshield, and it feels as though we're lime wedges trapped inside a glass of vodka. He drops the bottles into the footwell and swings open the door. "Let's make like two bananas and beat it."

We cross the street and stand in front of the caged storm door. The windows are thin, almost like eyeholes, like he's living inside the bell of a Spartan helmet. Dom jiggles his key into the lock. He opens the cage, then uses the same key for the front door.

He winks. "See? Key fits as tight as a girl's panties."

God he's a jerk. "Wow. You opened your door. Congrats."

"You're a real thrill-joy, you know that?"

"You mean kill-joy."

This time, Dom just raises an eyebrow, a whaddaya-want-from-me look before he staggers inside.

I follow him into the living room. His couch is a white-leathered sectional monstrosity. Crumpled against the armrest is a pillow and a blanket. There's a matching loveseat. A coffee table with racing forms. A television sits on a stand, bordered by Formica end-tables. The set hisses with static. Next to the TV is a bookcase filled with videos. He sways toward the couch and plops down, then tosses the blanket onto the floor.

I point toward the bookcase. "I didn't know you had these."

"They were my mom's."

I skim through her collection, a movie-lover habit of mine. There's *Casablanca* and *Dr. Zhivago*. *Lawrence of Arabia* and *King Kong*. A slew of Humphrey Bogart and a lot of Errol Fylnn. He has *The Man Who Shot Liberty Valance*, *Psycho*, *Some Like it Hot* and *Cat on a Hot Tin Roof*. *Twelve Angry Men* and *The Maltese Falcon*. Staring at her videos is like staring at her ghost. This feeling of sadness overwhelms me. "I'm going to go."

Dom says, "Nah, hang out. You can give me a lift to the wine store."

"Sure, I love driving you around."

He snuggles into the cushion. "I shouldn't have to ask. After the DVD thing."

Of course Dom thinks he's completely blameless. "That was that maniac Vic's fault. Not mine." Still, I think of the crowd looming in front of Video Planet, flicking through pirated DVDs. Maybe it is on me, somehow. I love guilt, so I embrace it.

"Details, details. C'mon, hang around."

"Alright. Just a sec." I flip open my phone and text Lola: *Mom coloring?* The response comes quickly: *She really wants to play blackjack.* I answer: *OK. Hoping that I can still film her.* Then I plop down on the leather chair next to him. "You've been sleeping there?"

"Nope." He lifts the remote off the table. He presses Play. There is a click and I expect to see Greg, or even Mom, but it's Dorothy running along the dirt road, glancing back as Toto trails behind her. "So I can watch my favorite movie."

"I thought it was *Predator*."

"That's my favorite video. *Wizard of Oz* is my favorite movie."

"I've never seen you watch it at the store."

He says, "Before this video bullshit, Wizard only came on around Thanksgiving. It was special. I'd make my bed on the couch. Mom would burn Jiffy Pop an inch away from its life and we'd watch it. Together. At first, I only had a black-and-white television. So I didn't know what I was missing. Then we got a Zenith, a big hunk of furniture. With the wood casing."

"We had one of those! In the basement." I don't tell him my father hocked it for horse money.

"First time Dorothy opened the door. All that green and gold." He nods. "You get it."

"I did the same thing with my mother. But instead of Jiffy Pop, it was Wise potato chips and onion dip mix poured into sour cream. What a stomachache that was!"

"I bet."

"Still, I ate it every time." I smile. Tonight, Mom is gonna be watching *Oz* with Lola.

He exhales a deep, boozy breath. "I put my life into buying Video Planet. Mom took loans to buy the inventory. She missed the store's legacy."

"Legacy? The store is dying."

"I just wanted her to be proud. She loved going to video stores. She'd say they were like bookstores, but better, cause you could yell." He laughs, a quick snort that could easily turn into a sob. "I thought if I opened one she wouldn't be so disappointed in me. I let her down. Big time."

On the screen, Professor Marvel tells Dorothy how Auntie Ann is placing her hand over her heart. How she falls onto her bed. How his crystal has gone dark.

Dom's shelves of movies feel like a memorial to his mom. The only evidence of their lives together. Maybe we're both hoarding memories. But instead of watching one of my mother's movies, I get to watch a movie of my mother. I can play her image, listen to her stories, and then rewind them repeatedly, until it feels as though she is still with me. But I should've been filming her sooner. I missed so much; so much is unsalvageable. This pang of regret suffocates me. So I can understand Dom's feelings of failure. If anything, I'm all for failure.

Dom mutters, "I really let her down."

I look over and his eyes are glistening, maybe more than a normal drunk's. Is he crying? "That's not true, Dom. She loved Video Planet. She was always smiling, watching *Upstairs, Downstairs*. Teasing you. She was proud of you!"

"You think?"

I nod. "Definitely."

My phone buzzes, and I remember I'd forgotten to wait for a response. A stab of panic. Lola's response: *Where's her money?* Disappointed, I text: *Bag*. They're playing fake casino games, and Mom is searching for her Monopoly money. Lola texts back: *Found it. So she can play blackjack? Really?* I text back: *Let her*. She texts: *Sure?* I text, *Yup*. I should leave, but Lola will let me know if Mom is being difficult, right? They're okay.

I look over and Dom is full-on weeping now, trying to pinch the tears from his eyes with thumb and forefinger, and failing. "Sorry." Dom coughs a sob. "I like talking about Mom."

This is the most sincere, dare I say, sympathetic, I have ever seen him. A horrible thought flashes: he owns a firearm. I can't leave him home alone, not this drunk and this depressed. "Where is your gun, anyway?"

"Vicki? He wants five hundred dollars." He's gone from sad to mad. "Can you believe that?"

"Who? Vic?" I should've known. Can't something be simple. "What happened? Really."

"The truth of the fact?"

The possibility of Dom telling the truth, possibly for the first time since I've known him, is an opportunity I can't refuse. "Both. All together now."

He shrugs, as if that answers everything.

I think of Lola, managing alone. The last thing I need is for Mom to lock herself in the bathroom again, while I'm trying to dig through this. "Quick. Tell me or I'm leaving."

He reaches into his pocket and unholsters one of the other shot bottles. "OK, if you're gonna be a jerk about it. I was buying Vic's bootlegs."

Now I remember the last few months. Dom's mystery seller. Of course it was Vic. "Were you paying?"

"Sure. I just. Owed. One day I followed Vic to Royal. He had bags of bootlegs. Tapes he should've been selling me. Better stuff, newer stuff. He was trying to sink my business by selling to my competition."

"Why would he keep selling you more tapes if you hadn't paid for the stock you already had?"

"I needed the cash from the new releases! To make that debt good! That's how we make the most money, right? 'Cause he wasn't selling them to me, I couldn't pay him back! So I figured, make a call. Royal goes away. If he wasn't gonna sell me the new stuff, I could make sure *he* couldn't do it, either! Then my business picks up. Do him a favor by paying the money down. Everybody wins."

On the screen Dorothy grips the mattress, her world spinning.

Dom says, "I just thought he'd be desperate and we'd work a deal. I didn't think he'd take over. Sell DVDs out front. Steal Vicki away from me."

I'm not sure, but after saying his plan aloud, maybe he finally realizes it was a mistake. He watches the TV, refusing to look at me, yet shifting his eyes to see if I'm still watching him. God, I'm an idiot.

Finally I speak: "You knew Royal was his store all along, didn't you?"

"It was a misunderstanding."

"Tell me the fucking truth! You owe me that."

"Owe you? You made him sell DVDs outside."

I hold up my hand, so he doesn't switch the subject. "Okay. You were talking about how you let your mother down. If she were here, sitting next to you right now, what would she say about your plan? Calling the police, on *that* guy? Be honest."

Dom wipes his face, then he mumbles, "I knew it was his place."

Of course Dom's truth is full of lies. To have Royal raided is horrible, although doing it to save your own store is almost understandable. But to do it because you thought you'd be turning the tables on a guy like Vic, in some cockeyed power reversal way, is pretty insane, even for Dom. It also means Vic will never stop until he drains Dom into oblivion. Then he'll call the police to raid the store. Probably with me working there. As the silent partner. Vic will disappear. Dom will deny everything and then disappear. With my luck, I'll be arrested.

Still, the worst part of this whole mess is how Dom knew all along that he cheated Vic, and he still let me work. He didn't think about my well-being, or that I was helping my mother. He didn't care. If anything, he took advantage of me because I was desperate. That's what these kinds of people do: Dom, Vic, my stupid father. They take from you until you're either useless to them, or you're in such a horrible situation, you're useless to yourself.

I'm done with this. "I quit."

Dom sighs. "Please, finish the week?"

I'd quit now, if things weren't so messy with Mom's care. I need time to work things out. I say, "Okay. But you deserve less, Dominick."

He says, "I know."

On the screen Dorothy opens the door and steps into all that green and gold.

CHAPTER 25

Our house is empty.

The Wizard of Oz is playing on the television. Glinda giving final instructions to Dorothy. I move into the kitchen. Plates are stacked in the drainboard. Cards, mid-hand, are placed neatly on the table.

"Mom?" I move down the hall and open her door.

The bed is still made. Mom's coloring book is open, a yellow rainbow. The closet is open. There are clothes strewn on the floor. "Lola?" I wait, listening as Dorothy clicks her heels together. There's no place like home? Yeah, right.

Then: Why would she take her out? Last time it took both of us and twenty minutes to get into the yard. How did she do it so fast? Then I realize: Mom was extra good for her sister Joan.

I look out the window facing the yard; it's quiet, dark. Still, if they're sitting off to the side, away from the window, I might not see them, but they have to be there. I don't have Gloria. I obviously overestimated Lola's ability to watch Mom. That leaves ShadyPines and I'm not doing that. I'll finish the week for Dom. We have enough money in savings until I find a better job. I'll just explain to Lola that they have to stay inside from now on. I say, "We'll be good," not really believing it, so I downgrade my hope to, "One thing at a time."

I walk out of Mom's room and move into my room and squat in front of the television. I want to hold my movie, hoping it will make me feel less nervous, more grounded and able to think about what I should do next. I press Eject. Then again. I open the VCR door and peek inside the tray. Everything is here but my movie. My movie is always in the VCR. Why is it missing? Maybe Lola took it with them for comfort? That sounds crazy, but not any crazier than them not being here. Where could they be? I flip my phone cover.

It's Lola. *Playing blackjack.*

I stare at the words trying to piece together the symbols and their meaning.

Then it sinks in.

What would possess Lola to take her to a casino, a real, actual house of betting? My phone buzzes. Again, it's Lola. *This was a bad idea.*

My stomach twists with panic. I wait for Lola to explain. My phone buzzes. Lola has texted a sad face.

I dial her and it just rings. I know she's getting it.

My phone buzzes. *Casino.* My phone buzzes. *Her idea.*

I yell at the phone. Then I text her my scream: *WHAT?*

She answers, *Find us.*

Then I'm stuck on the Belt Parkway, rolling towards the casino.

The traffic is at a standstill, with infinite rows of red lights. The only movement comes from the planes overhead. I cut into the service lane and move past the line of traffic, praying a cop isn't waiting for jerks like me. Mom babbles about casinos all the time. Lola has seen me pretend we were sitting in a lobby or on a deck or in a suite. Why the hell would Lola bring her there?

And where is my movie? And Mom can't go to the clink. She's sick. I cut across three lanes of honking traffic, swerving onto the exit ramp. I pull into the gate, pay five bucks for parking, and pull into the spot closest to the casino.

The building is tan with red spires, a Taj Mahal knockoff. Cars park in front of a small booth and valets; guys my age take the keys from couples, also my age, to their cars. Across from the casino is the track, the stands casting a shadow across the parking lot. I haven't been here since I was a kid.

Being here, the same nervous tension brought on by lying to my mother for my father grips me. My desperate hope that he'd win. That we'd have money for luxury items, like groceries. I remember helping my father forage for discarded tickets in the lot as he hoped to profit off of someone's mistake, when the only mistake was my father spending his weekend spending his entire paycheck on horses. A gust of wind kicks up. I smell the salt and jet fuel and I feel disappointed that Greg and Sarah are stuck in Queens with Lola, Mom, my father, all of us, smelling the same polluted air. There's no escaping this place. The best we can hope for is a distraction, something we can replay to remember the happy moments—one tropical vacation, say, and a lifetime rewinding back to it to escape the horrible present.

Play, Rewind.

It's too painful to think about, but I try to listen to my own meandering advice and concentrate on my present horrible moment. It isn't easy, especially standing here, directly in front of the track, the past in brick-and-mortar form, physical evidence of all of our family's problems.

I move into the casino, its doors parting only to swallow me whole.

Inside reeks of cigarette smoke. The casino has orange carpets with swirly patterns. The ceilings are red marble and have recess lighting. The sound of ringing bells plays counterpoint to the pulsing electronic music. I move past slot machines and tables. I move past the steakhouse and the large room for horse bets. I move past an older guy seated in a mobile cart, a change bucket placed in its basket as he feeds quarters into a Joker Poker machine. A group of people who look like work friends gather around a blackjack table cheering a youngish guy with red hair and a brown sweater as he asks for another card. There are rows of slot machines depicting alluring mermaids, fairies, rainbows and unicorns, all promising magical, favorable outcomes. I see serious dealers and friendly cocktail waitresses. Pit bosses and slot managers. Couples playing together and singles playing alone. I see everyone but my mother. I check my phone. There aren't any new messages.

I text, *Where R U?*

I stop dead in the middle of the gambling room, as if being still will make her respond faster. This is an endless maze of slots, beeping and buzzing, ringing and dinging, and people, laughing and cheering and smoking. I'm Jennifer Connely in *Labyrinth*, but instead of looking for a crying baby, I'm searching for a confused mother and her dead sister. I move along the aisle until I'm at the rear of the casino.

Once I'm finally out of the sea of slots, I walk along the perimeter searching for a security guard, or sign. I only find ATMs and bathrooms. By the time I find them, Mom will already be tossed in the clink. Again, I remind myself that they can't do that. She's sick.

A cocktail waitress wearing a red dress with tassels walks towards me. Her hair is red. I wonder if they make them match their dresses with their hair. What a stupid thought. On her tray sit impossibly blue margaritas.

I say, "Can you help me?"

She smiles. "Sure I'll get you a drink. Let me run these over first."

"I'm not thirsty," I say, as though people buy alcohol at a casino out of thirst. "I'm looking for my mother. She's here." I point towards the slots. "Somewhere."

She puckers her lips into a frown. "We'll say her name over the intercom. The older ones get lost more than you think."

I say, "She's not lost. I just can't find her."

A crowd of voices cheer. She says, "Isn't that lost?"

"Well she's always lost. Even when we know where to find her." She arches her eyebrow, waiting for a punchline. I realize how mean I sounded. "I'm only saying she's, well, out of sorts."

"She's sick?"

"Right, sick. Maybe security, then?"

She nods. "Between those two potted palms. See?" She squeezes my wrist. "Hope it's nothing serious."

"Isn't it always serious?"

I move along the hallway, passing an exhibition hall and another row of ATMs until I get to the palms. I think of my birthday, me and my mother walking the length of the casino as we tried to guess which of the slots had that winning magic. It was one of the few times I can honestly say she had a lot of fun. She'd startle with each winner's buzzer. She'd giggle when getting her spritzers. There was so much joy in her gambling, compared to my father who entered the OTB or track seething and desperate—angry, or eager, anything but enjoying the gambling experience; it was like he was expunging some searing pain. His addiction, I guess. Another slot rings and people cheer, conjuring memories of Mom being dressed in white, so proud of treating her son. I picture her, my real mom. Healthy Mom. Her hair is really brushed. Her clothes are really well-matched. Her brain is really her own. Her memories are really her own. Another slot rings, bringing me back to this horrible moment, and this sadness rips through me. All I want to do is find her.

I roll onto my toes and peek over the machines. A couple of guys wearing identical tan suits shuffle by me, complaining about the hands they were dealt. I move towards the perimeter of the room and follow the red bar in the center of the carpet, as though I'm a horse hustling around the track.

The waitress from before passes me and points toward the far end of the casino. I nod and keep moving. The room feels endless. I walk past a bar encased in frosted glass, a goldfish engraved on its door. There's another, smaller, hallway, one that is clearly for personnel, that leads to a guard standing in front of a podium, placed in front of a set of double-doors. He watches me. I feel this flutter of guilty panic. I don't want to explain to him how I let this happen. I don't want to be judged by someone who has no idea how hard these years have been for us. I'm not ready to deal with this.

I move away from the entrance and squeeze behind the palm, where he can't see me from where he's seated. Behind the palm the wall feels warmer, safer. I run my finger along the trunk. The bark feels scratchy. The fronds are paler than the ones Greg filmed, and I'm disappointed. I'll hide here for a few minutes until I'm ready to keep searching. A couple walks past. An older man wearing a blue suit. A woman stops in front of me and digs through her purple pocketbook. She nods and then turns down the closet aisle of slot machines. How can we all be in this casino, but I can't find the two people I need? I run my fingers along the palm leaf and listen for them, then think of the footage, hoping it will ease my anxiety. Now that I know that Sarah and Greg know my father, I can't reach that place. My vacation is officially over. I won't be going back. Feeling even more desperate, I say, "Where are you?" aloud as if that'll conjure them in front of me, as if that'll help. But, strangely it does: my phone buzzes. I flip the lid. It's Lola. *ICU. BJ.*

Blowjob? Wait. I snort at my stupidity. Of course. She's playing blackjack. I step away from the plant and scan the casino floor until I see an older woman dressed in a pink robe. Her hair is brushed straight back, held in place by a pink banana clip. Without thinking, I think, "What crazy woman would gamble like that?" Then I realize it's Mom.

Mom is standing in the center of the half-moon shaped blackjack table. Lola is standing next to her, wearing my mother's purple sweater, the bottom hanging in big folds around her legs. Huddled around the blackjack table is a man wearing a cowboy hat. He has a thick white mustache, bushy eyebrows and a bolo tie. He's pointing at the table, his face pinched and angry.

A woman wearing a black t-shirt and a lot of gold chains leans over to pick up what I'm guessing are her chips off of the table. Mom slaps at her hand, but misses. The woman pokes Mom's arm and Lola swings around in front and blocks Mom, protecting her. The woman rushes away, but the cowboy rolls onto his toes and waves, fetching security. Lola clasps Mom's hand, trying to lead her from the table. Mom wriggles her hand free. Forgetting what has just happened, Mom picks up red chips off of the table and presses them to her chest. She sticks a chip in her pocket, as though she's hiding Oreos in our kitchen. Lola peels another chip from Mom's grasp and drops them onto the table. I watch them feeling both heartbroken and amazed.

Lola mouths "Help." The dealer points to three men dressed in black suits.

As I walk towards the table, one of the guards blocks my path. His black hair is shaved military-style. A walkie-talkie is clipped to his belt, a thin wire running up to a speaker in his ear. His name tag says *Clutch*, a great name for an eighties action hero.

I say, "That's my mom."

He crosses his arms. "I'm sorry, but we can't let you through."

"Let him through!" Lola yells.

But Clutch just says, "She's in some trouble."

Isn't that a bit obvious? "Please, let me just talk to her."

He turns to look at the other guards. An older guard is picking yellow papers off the table. Mom leans forward and rips them out of his hands.

"Please! I can calm her down!"

Mom yells: "Joan! Help!"

"Come on," I tell Clutch. "The last thing you guys want is a news story about wrestling an old lady, right?"

He bites his lip, mulling it over.

"Please. She has dementia."

He moves aside. Mom leans over the table picking up her Monopoly money and stuffing it into her robe. She's shiny with sweat; she stinks of the perfume she used to wear to work, which must've gone stale from lack of use. Lola probably sprayed it on her.

Mom looks at me and says, "This dealer is stealing from me!"

She's angry, but there's confusion in her voice too. This is her worst combination of emotions. I'm afraid if I take the money from her, she'll become even more volatile. I say, "He's helping."

"I said he's stealing!" She shuffles through her wad of fake money, counting, then again. She might be double checking the amount, unless she forgot she just counted. "Where's the manager?"

"I don't know," which is true.

Mom says, "Find him! I'm complaining."

She crinkles the Monopoly money in her fist, the green and yellow papers sticking out from between her fingers. Can't the guards see that she's sick? We need to get out of here. The faster the better.

I take a breath. Try a different approach. "Wow, I can't believe how much you won! Congrats!"

Mom says, "I won?"

I kiss her cheek. "You sure did! Right, Joan?"

Lola hugs her. "You hit the big time, Sis!"

Mom smiles, and for a fleeting moment I wish I had my camera. "Let's go home and count your winnings."

"I won?" She gives me a teal-colored twenty. "For you." I take it and tell her we're going home. She says, "I can't. Not when I'm on a lucky streak!"

I say, "Mom. That's why we should stop when we're ahead!" As though we've ever been ahead.

Mom says, "Up your nose with a rubber hose! I'm playing slots!"

The security guard says he'll take over.

I say, "Look, we'll get her out of here."

Mom says, "Get out of my way. I'm lucky. L-U-C-KEEEEEY."

Lola says, "Let me try." She puts her arm around Mom. "Sis, I want to freshen up. We'll come right back." When Lola tries to take the money, Mom yanks it back and smacks her hand. Lola's face prickles. She looks devastated.

I exhale, shake my head, completely exasperated.

To me, Lola says: "I'm sorry."

"What did you expect would happen?" I've never been this mad. At her, or maybe ever. "Card games in the kitchen, coloring, musicals...all fine! Taking her to a casino. Not so much, right?"

She frowns, confused. "You said it was okay."

"When? When did I say it was okay? In what universe would I ever agree to something like this?"

She says, "Yes you did." She reaches into her pocket and flips open her phone. She points to *Blackjack*, then my *OK*. "See?"

"I meant at home, Lola! I meant at home!"

"I didn't realize, Wes! I just wanted her to be happy."

A guard scoops fake money off the table. Mom says, "Don't steal my money. It's mine." She rips it out of his hand.

He steps back, squaring off, and tells her to relax. I turn toward the guard. "Look. I'll take her home, okay!"

He touches the microphone in his ear. "Not possible."

"Why not? She's obviously sick!"

"She was grabbing chips! She might have stolen some. She assaulted the guards trying to help."

Lola tells me he's lying. I say, "Assault? She's a frail old woman!"

The security guard standing behind us tells me that they're taking her to the holding room, and I have to wait in the lobby. I stare at the Monopoly money scattered on the table. First, all I wanted were animal crackers, then all I wanted was to dump Dom at home. Now, all I want is my mother not to be arrested. Why are things always the hardest when you need them to be the quietest?

I say, "You can't take her. She's sick."

"Yeah? If she is so sick, why is she in here?"

I stare at my sneakers, unable to meet his stare. "Mistakes were made."

Mom stuffs a chip into her pocket. Clutch says, "See? She's stealing." He grips underneath her arm and the two other guards circle in front of us. To me, he says: "Look, I'm sorry."

Lola tries to push between them. An older guard who just appeared nudges her with his forearm. Lola stumbles over my foot and flops onto the carpet. She yells, "You fucking asshole!"

Mom looks back as they shuffle her away. "I hit big! They're cashing me out!"

I stare at Lola sitting on the floor, her nose ring shining from the overhead light, her forehead glistening with sweat. She has been around sick people, first at the hospital as a patient, and then helping her aunt. How does she not understand that taking my mother to a casino was the worst thing she could've done?

"I'm sorry," she says from the floor.

I shake my head in disgust.

"Look, we can talk about this later," she says. "Can you help me up, at least?"

Reluctantly I offer my hand.

"Let's just follow them," she says.

We hustle after them until we see the guards standing on either side of her, gripping her by her arms. The bottom of her robe trails behind them, a frayed and pink bustle. We follow them back to the palms, but this time we walk up to the podium. The guard, a thin man with brown eyeglasses, holds up his veiny hand.

His name tag reads Chesnutt. He says, "You have to wait here."

I say, "I'm her son."

Lola says, "And I'm her sis..." She catches a dirty look I'm giving her. "...I'm something."

An asterisk of halogen light catches in the guard's glasses. "After we question her."

I fight the urge to wrestle past him and rescue her.

Lola pleads, "Can't we just check on her?"

"It can't happen."

I remember the time I was caught shoplifting baseball cards at Modell's. The manager, this sweaty balding guy named Kent Riggly, called my mother into his office and told her he was calling the police. She said, "I'll settle this now," and smacked me in the face so hard it echoed off the walls. Kent flinched like he was next. As I waited for my cheek to stop tingling, she dug into her purse and tossed a wad of money onto his desk. Then she hauled me up by the wrist and said, "No one arrests my son," and we left.

I say, "She has dementia. Look at how she's dressed! She was playing with Monopoly money! What's there to question?"

He picks at a long fingernail. "She was also pocketing chips."

"Look, you'll never see us here again."

He points toward a line of hardback plastic chairs. "Go sit there."

I say, "Where there?"

Lola says, "Where, over there, by the chair, chair?"

He says, "God, you're both obnoxious."

I nod and sit on the chair closest to the door.

Lola shifts into the seat next to me, missing the clue that I need space. She says, "We were watching the part in *The Wizard of Oz* with the Emerald City and your mom thought it was a casino." A guard walks past. "She said she needed to go there. She started throwing things. I got scared." She waits, but I don't say anything. "She was convinced the Wizard told her to go to the casino. I couldn't settle her. I didn't know what to do. So I texted you. I know it was wrong but I was desperate. I wanted to prove that I could watch her. Like if you wanted to go to film school. That we're a family and we all help each other out, you know?"

"Family? Film school? Lola, you brought her to a casino."

She scratches her finger against the plastic seat. "I had a good reason."

"There isn't a good reason! You know that! You're with her all the time!"

"She was crying! She was confused and scared! I didn't know what to do, Wes! I called a taxi to cheer her up! I thought we'd do a lap and go home."

"You could've just...walked from my room to the kitchen, and she would've thought it was a different place."

She squeezes my arm. "I forgot about the fake money. I'm sorry."

The guard watches us, listening. I whisper. "Did you take my movie?"

She wipes her nose. "I made a copy and submitted it. To the contest."

"You fucking what?"

"Wes...I watched it. I liked it! It's wonky and sad. You have a chance."

I sit straight in my chair. "How? Gloria is gone. Video Planet is over. Mom is going to jail. Besides, everything is ruined. All I have is *The Worst Possible Thing*, and now I don't even have that."

Lola says, "No. You have the original." Then lower, "And me."

Lola picks at the armrest. What she did was wrong. Very wrong. I can't forgive her, not yet. I'm too angry. Maybe after I get my mother back.

If this was a movie, I'd have that big reveal. I'd tell her how much I love her. That one day we'll go on a tropical vacation, a real one. Her art will be in shows. I'll make movies. Mom will be there too, a family, exactly how she wants, and all our failures and misery will be dubbed over, never seen or even thought of again. But my head feels as though it's filled with a cloud of smoke puffed from one of the casino's hopefuls. And because this isn't a movie and in real life things just move forward, quietly unresolved, I say, "You should go home."

"Why would I do that?"

"If Mom says anything even slightly coherent she's going to name you."

"I've been in jail. Hospitals. I'm not leaving my sister."

"She's not your sister, Lola! And you need to let me handle this."

She slaps the armrest and Chestnutt gazes at us. "That's what you want?"

I shrug. "You want to get in trouble?"

"Maybe I'm not Gloria, but I'd take a golf shoe to the face for your mom. You too."

"Okay." I wait for her to leave. She doesn't. "I want my video back."

"You'll get it." Then she starts to cry, which isn't what I wanted at all. Before I can apologize, she rushes down the hallway, wiping her face. She turns the corner fast. I hear a loud bang and the palm timbers onto the rug. Silver beads from inside the flowerpot spill along the red carpet. Lola steps where I can see her and points to the palm. She says, "That's us," and disappears. I wait for her to come back. She doesn't.

A bit later, I feel a nudge and I'm startled awake.

I'm still seated by the security door. A phone rings and Chestnutt answers. He nods as he mumbles, then hangs up the phone. "You can see her before she leaves." He walks towards the metal door. I pop up as though I'm going to talk to one of her doctors about medications or tests. He scans his card and opens the metal door.

I step inside. The door leads me into another long hallway.

As I walk through the innards of the casino, all the posh of the gaming floor has vanished. The room has cinderblock walls and a concrete floor. The air feels stuffy and smells like dust. This hallway is way too serious for what my mother did. She doesn't understand that she stole, or was playing with fake money. Also, she's in her sixties, and she's going to fucking jail? She can't even dress herself without help. I imagine her slumped over, dressed in her robe, seated on a wooden bench. She'll act out. They'll restrain her. She's going to get hurt. It'll be my fault.

This panic sinks into my chest. The thought of her being in prison is terrifying, yet feels less scary than how

I'll explain to her where she is going. Should I lie and pretend that she is going to her suite? I can't imagine that she would even mistake prison for a suite. I have to tell her something. Maybe, for once, I'll try the truth.

We turn another corner and there's a slight incline. I follow the hallway right, then left. The hall feels claustrophobic. In front of the only door is another security guard. He's bald and has a pudgy broad face. His tag reads *Chef*. He opens the door and holds it for me, as though he's a bellhop, and follows me inside.

It's a green room with a matching green rug. Mom is seated and sleeping in a metal chair; her wrist is handcuffed to a loop in the center of the table. Uncuff me.

I turn and say, "Is that really necessary?"

"We were going to release her, but she punched a guard. Then while we were restraining her we found more chips. We notified the police."

"Really? Look at her."

Chef says, "I'm sorry. It's protocol."

Mom's head is tucked into her chest. Her robe lapels are covering her face. She's wearing a yellow t-shirt underneath. At least Lola didn't let her go in her house dress. The light shines above her, forming a white halo around her, like the interrogation scene from *Clockers*.

This acidy feeling drops into my stomach. I say, "Can I take her home? She has dementia. This just seems excessive."

He watches my mother. "The police will understand. They probably won't take her to jail, since she's old. She'll probably be placed in a hospital." He reaches to pat my shoulder, but doubts the moment, and pulls his hand back. "Maybe it's best?"

I say, "There's no one I can talk to?"

"I'm the guy." We listen to her snoring. "Stay here, if you want." He opens the door. "It'll be a bit," he says, then disappears.

I move around the table. I slide the metal chair, its legs scraping against the floor, away from the table and sit across from her. Mom snorts and her whole body shakes. Her eyes flutter, as she sleeps. She's dreaming. I'm not sure if I should wake her. My phone buzzes. I dig into my pocket. It's a text from Lola. *She okay?* I place my phone on the table. I say, "Mom. What are we doing here?" and she opens her eyes, smiles, then closes them again, as though we shared a quiet moment in her dream.

When I was fourteen, I'd pretend to get ready for school, then go hide in the basement until my mother went to work. Then I'd play Nintendo until around 2:30 and then grab a slice of pizza. I'd hang out at the pizzeria until 3:30 when it was time to come home. If the school called, I'd just tell them I was home sick. I'd snatch the attendance letters out of the mailbox. I was careful to only drink from the same glass or eat and drink things that couldn't be measured, a snack-size bag of chips, a can of soda, say. I called it my Sneaky Mouse Phase. I had a good run until one day I was hiding in the basement and Mom didn't go to work. I was afraid she'd lug the laundry to the washer, so I hid behind the bar in the basement. For a while, I counted spiderwebs and noticed how the syrupy stains of spilled alcohol left shapes on the pressed-wood shelf underneath the bar; I imagined them into a bear, a car, a dragon with spines. After three hours of listening to her footsteps above me I cracked. I was hungry, thirsty. I had to pee really bad. Mostly, I was bored. I hated to admit it but school was better than being trapped behind a bar. Unable to take my solitary confinement, I went upstairs and said, "Mom I cut class. I'm sorry."

I thought she'd take a ladle to my head. She asked me why. At first, I was going to tell her about how boring school was, but instead, I started crying and my reasons had to do with missing my father, my inability to understand rain cycles or math volumes. How I was cornered in the bathroom and forced to hand over my lunch money. My lack of friends. How even the equally unpopular girls failed to notice me (this was way before Lola). She sat me at the kitchen table and we drank Sanka and ate powdered donuts. Sitting there, I felt better. I remember she kissed me on the forehead and told me, "An honest life is a quiet life." She wasted her whole life waiting for a man who loved his trifectas more than us. A woman who was humiliated by her husband only to waste away with one of the most humiliating diseases a person could get. She should've taken her own advice. Still, back then, it helped. I never cut another day after that.

There's a knock and I startle. Chef peeks his head in and says, "They should be here in ten minutes or so."

"Okay."

He watches me. "I hope it works out."

I say, "Thanks. Me too," as though I'm applying for a job.

Chef shuts the door slowly, trying not to wake her.

I watch her sleep. The only sounds in the room are the buzz of the lights. The heat humming from a dust fuzzy vent above our heads feels dry, stale. Every so often, I hear footsteps walking to the door, then a short muffled conversation. Each time, I tense up, waiting for them to shuffle into the room and take her away. When they don't, my body goes slack with relief, but it only makes the next set of footsteps outside of the door feel scarier.

I say, "Mom, hey. Can we talk?"

She doesn't stir, or hear me.

Watching her, I notice how frail she looks in this holding room, flung headlong into normal, everyday life. It's hard to see her fragility when she is sitting in her bed, or eating cookies in her kitchen. When she's inside of a place that she knows, or at least finds familiar. Watching her now, I realize that our home was a place of distractions. A place that gave me a misguided sense of security. When taking care of her was too exhausting or painful, I'd hide in my room. I'd go to work. I'd let Gloria handle it. But being here, stripped of all safeguards, I see how impossibly dangerous it is for her to navigate a normal, healthy landscape. This time I can't unscrew the bathroom doorknob, or stick her wet clothes into my hamper. I can't pretend that this never happened. This mistake is bigger than us. And I can't even pause it, let alone rewind.

I say, "Mom."

She slouches further down in her chair.

"Please, let's just talk. Like we used to. Please, if only for a few minutes. It'll be our secret. Talk. Just us. Please, talk. Please, don't leave."

Of course she opens her eyes just as Chef, two EMTs, and three cops enter the room to steal her away from me. Of course I've failed her yet again. Still, that's not the worst part. And the worst part isn't how, in twenty minutes, she'll be cuffed inside the carriage of an ambulance, whisked off to a psych ward, or jail. No, the worst part is that I was here for her, that I'm always here for her. That she saw me waiting with her, and she won't remember any of it. That is the worst part.

CHAPTER 26

I follow Mom's gurney out of the casino and watch as they load her into the ambulance. The driver says they're going to take her to Jamaica Hospital for a psych evaluation and, if all goes well, I can pick her up in seventy-two hours.

When I gather the strength to go home it's after two in the morning. I park and walk the block. A train passes and it's enough light for me to spot Lola seated on my stoop. She's wearing a sweatshirt, no jacket, though it's cold enough that your breath puffs frost. I open the fence, the hinges creaking, and walk up the steps. I lean against the rail. Her cheeks are chafed. Snot leaks from her nose. She's been crying.

I say, "Why didn't you just go inside?"

She reaches into the front of her hoodie and slides out the tape.

"You're freezing."

She says, "Where's Sis?" but maybe catches the look on my face and switches to "I mean...your mom."

I sit, and she places the tape on my lap. I say, "The police took her to Jamaica Hospital."

With everything that's happened, I forgot that Gloria worked at Jamaica Hospital. Tomorrow, I'll call and see if she can get her out earlier. It's a long shot but I have to try. "Here." I slide off my jacket and place it over her shoulders.

A train passes. Lola says, "I can't watch her again. Alone. I'm terrified that she'll get hurt. I thought it would be like my aunt. She's not the same."

I can't even do it anymore myself. "I understand."

"I'm sorry, Wes. Don't be angry."

I'm still mad. A little. But caring about Mom is completely different than caring for Mom. "I'm sorry. It was a lot to ask of you."

"Think she's okay?"

I imagine Mom confused, floating on sedatives, handcuffed to the bedrail. This time not to record the intricacies of her brainwaves, but because she's been arrested, charged with a lack of understanding. "She'll be there for seventy-two hours. She's impaired. We'll get her back."

"Then what?"

I try to think of my options but they're impossible to know. "Let's go in."

"Tell me first."

I stand, unable to look at her. "I don't know." I watch another train pass. I count the cars, nine total, all of them empty. "Gloria wants her in a home. She's not helping me anymore. I can't take care of her. That leaves one horrible option."

She stands, her face glows from the streetlamp. "It's not bad, you know. The hospital." She slips off the jacket and hands it back to me. I never asked her how she felt. I only wanted to know why she was there. Embarrassed, I face the church. The shadow of the cross stretches along its tiled roof. I say, "What was it like?"

She picks rust from the railing. "You know when there's a blizzard, but instead of digging out your car, or trudging through snow drifts, you do nothing." She flicks the rust. "Instead of that storm whirling around you, you're home, still in your flannels, watching the blizzard on the news. You're not in any part of it. You're just watching the storm's hazards. Tuning in from afar. That's the hospital. See?"

I hate the snow, so I totally understand. "Then why were you against it?"

She shrugs. "I was never against it. I wanted whatever you wanted."

I put my arm around her and she leans into me. "It's not safe for her. Here."

I glance at the house, yellow and looming. I know it's the right decision, but I feel scared and awful even considering it. Unable to think past the moment, what that would truly mean, I unlock the door.

The house feels off, as though I've walked onto a set of my living room. It can only be my home if my mother is here with us. Otherwise, it's just a house. On the screen, Dorothy's standing in front of the balloon hugging her friends, crying as she says her goodbyes. I shut the television off. We move into my bedroom. She plops down on the bed. Without saying a word, I stick my movie into the VCR. It's no longer called *The Worst Possible Thing* anymore. I've decided to call it *Play, Rewind*.

Look, it's our movie premiere.

I hit Play and sit. Lola slides next to me. The screen blinks on and Greg is walking towards the hammock, the first shot of his home movie. I say, "I know how this one ends." I press Fast-Forward, speeding past Greg on the hammock, the beach, until I see Mom seated at the kitchen table. She is staring into her coffee. A white band rolls down the screen and it's Sarah sitting on the rocks near the tide-pool. I fast-forward to Mom talking about the horse and the duck. This time, instead of getting angry, I laugh at how excited she is. I understand it's because she's talking about my father, a man she obviously still loves. Mom says she only likes farm animals and Lola bursts into a squeaky laugh. She covers her mouth, embarrassed, like when you're so sad at a funeral that you laugh at anything even though you know it's wrong. But you're with family, so it's mostly okay.

I say, "You think she really did that?"

Lola says, "Nope. I *know* she really did that," and this time I believe it.

She rolls up onto her knees. "I want to see the part when she's in the yard. When you pull the crates over, she smiles. You're totally her son there."

"You think so?"

"I'll show you." Lola fast-forwards past Sarah and Greg seated in the cabana until the screen flashes and Mom is in the yard. She hits Stop. Lola points. "There, see it?" The camera dips, probably when I was fixing the crate, but just catches Mom smiling at Lola. Her eyes look focused. My mother must like Lola, as Lola, if only briefly. "She's totally kidding."

I rewind it and hit Play. This time I swear she sees me. For a few seconds, we're closer than we've been in a long time. I say, "You're right."

Again I rewind. Hit Play again. We notice how the wind blows through the line of bushes. The sparrow that shoots past her head and almost hits her. The sunspot catching the kitchen window. The curl of Mom's lip. Her pilled robe. It becomes a contest of who can notice more. As we watch, we talk about funny or silly things that she did or that happened, like losing the cookie roll. Her blinky eye. Asking for waiters. Lola tells me how she got every eighties song wrong. I tell Lola about the time Mom locked herself in the bathroom and sang Bette Milder. Even if they weren't funny at the time, now they're hilarious simply because it's the past. We rewind to those places we loved or missed or remembered best. The footage aggregates memory. Cut and splice. Pause, Rewind. A jumble, a mishmash, a mixtape. I stop the footage just before Greg and Sarah consume the screen. If it weren't for Lola I never would've filmed Mom. Mom is with us. To prove that she's here, we take turns rewinding and pressing Play. Each time we watch Mom who is watching us.

CHAPTER 27

Restless, I went to Video Planet an hour early. The store was locked, the windows dark, even the parking-lot was empty. I stood outside watching the same but different 747s spew the same but different exhaust, the same but different traffic, even the same deflated condom pasted on the pavement.

Play, Rewind.

I unlock Video Planet and charge down the aisle toward the security keypad with the usual vigor, only to realize that the alarm isn't ringing. Dom didn't bother to set the code. I switch the light on and stare at his mother's chair. It feels disrespectful to sit on it, after everything he told me at his place, so I lean against the counter. The boxes face out on the racks. The popcorn machine is filled and glowing. The carpet is vacuumed. The store smells like a lemon-scented nightmare. I'd give anything for a dead mouse right about now.

I pick up the phone and dial Gloria, hoping Julliard doesn't answer the phone. It rings three times before she answers. "Hi Gloria. How's it going?"

"Wes! How are you?"

The question seems impossible. I think of all the lies and half-truths I could tell as a way to ease into this, the most difficult conversation I'll ever have, but it's easier to just tell her. If I lie, I'm no better than Dom. I say, "Mom is in the hospital."

A woman dressed in a green flowered dress and black hat stops in front of the store. She has long blond hair that hangs in knots so thick that I notice them from the counter. She peers in, shifts left, right, then walks towards the diner. I yank my attention back to the impossible conversation. "She's in Jamaica Hospital." Here's where I want to avoid words like 'casino' or 'arrested,' or above all, 'Lola.' I say, "I was wondering if you could help."

"What is she there for?"

"Observation."

"Why are they observing her?" A male voice, Julian, asks her something. She shushes him. "I'll do what I can. I just need to know the situation."

"She had an episode. So she was taken to the hospital." That's a good enough Cliff Notes version, if there ever was one. "I need you to—"

Gloria says, "Episode. You mean a seizure?"

I mean an episode as in Lola took Mom to a casino to play blackjack with funny money until she was whisked away by security.

I say, "No nothing like that."

"Did she fall?"

Juilliard asks if she's playing charades. He obviously knows it's me on the phone because he switches on and cranks up the radio. It's all violins. I'm no classical-head but I think it's Chopin, the go-to composer in films when they want to show depth of character or a poignancy moment. In *Silence of the Lambs,* Lecter was listening to a Gould-y improvisation on Bach. In *Alien*, Tom Skerritt (Dallas) was listening to Mozart. I'm stalling. The music lowers as Gloria walks into another room. "Sorry, the radio is broken," she says, covering for her real son.

There's a pause and everything that has happened swells up inside of me. So when Gloria says, "Wes, can you just tell me? Whatever it is, I'll understand," this click happens inside my chest, and it all spills out. Dom's insane business plan. The fate of Video Planet. The lease. How my father is living in Queens. The casino. The vacation footage. *Play, Rewind.* How much I love Lola. How I'm jealous of Julliard and I'd pretend she was *my* mother instead. How I miss her so much and I wish she'd visit.

I'm crying and it feels as though I'm trapped, but Gloria tells me sweet things that I'm embarrassed to hear. I'm so disoriented with grief, I flinch when I realize that I'm standing in the video store. From crying my head pulses, as though it had a heart of its own. I rub it and wince. I say, "That's what happened."

Gloria breathes into the phone. "Holy baaloley."

The lady out front is back. She stops in front of the glass and points at her wrist, as though I'm wasting her precious time. I throw my hands up in a 'What do you want?' kind of way. She gives me the finger and walks towards Tubby's.

To Gloria I say, "So I hoped you could help Mom. Get her early, since you worked there?"

"Not if she's on psych eval." She coughs. "Then what?"

"What do you mean?"

There's a long pause. She says, "Let me call my friend."

"At the hospital?"

"At ShadyPine Glen."

"I spoke to Ms. Pine. I can't afford it."

"Not her. Janice. She's my friend. She's in charge of the whole facility. Mom has insurance and social security. She'll be safe. You can visit. Lola too."

I take a deep hard breath. "I'll have to sell the house."

Gloria says, "Maybe not," but I hear in her voice that I will have to sell the house. I can tell she's afraid it'll scare me off. It kind of does.

I stare at the passing traffic. I can't take care of her. Lola really can't take care of her. Gloria won't take care of her. If Mom can't live in our house, then I don't think I want to live there either. There's the promise I made to her, but I think if my mother could see all of the sacrifices I've made, the weight of caring for her, she'd forgive me. If only I can forgive myself. I run my finger along the counter. I say, "Okay."

"Okay then," she says, her voice sounding ten years younger. "I'll set it up. We'll transfer her from Jamaica to ShadyPine Glen. Usually there is a wait. But like I said, I know the director. We've been friends since high school."

I say, "Will you come?"

"Of course. I'll help you fill out the papers."

"No, I mean. Will you visit Mom with me?"

"Anytime you want, Wes. It's a nice place, you'll see."

I feel overwhelmed. I don't want to cry again, so I tell her that I'll call her later. I hang up and wipe my face. My choices are completely horrible to me, but that doesn't make them completely horrible choices.

I say, "It'll be okay," if only because I need to hear it.

A cold breeze blows into the store. I look up and it's that lady. She's walking up the aisle. As she gets closer, she—well, he—says, "You got *Tootsie*?"

"I think so," I burst out laughing.

As though I don't know who it is, Dom covers his mouth with his stringy blond hair. "What about *Mrs. Doubtfire*?" He hitches his dress, revealing curls of hair on his leg. "What about *The Birdcage*?" He pushes his purple handbag onto his shoulder. "Is your boss here?"

"Dom?" I chuckle. "No, Dom might be in later."

"No, not that handsome fellow," Dom says. "The ugly, squeaky prick."

"He's not in yet."

Dom reaches up and pulls his hair off. "Ta-da!" He pats my shoulder. "I'm some kind of sexy, right?"

"Why the hell are you dressed like that?"

Dom flops the wig back onto his head. "My disguise? This is Plan B."

It's hard to be mad at your boss, even if it's Dom, when he's dressed in a schmatta, one my mother would wear, one his mother did wear. Besides, despite all his double-dealing and lies, he is the one losing his video store.

He pats my hand. My friend, Dom. He points to the chair. "A little help?"

I lift his mother's chair over the counter. He grabs it, winded by the effort. He places it onto the floor and nods, mumbles something, as though touching the chair has summoned the ghost of his mother. I say, "You're leaving?"

"Well. There's only one way out. But are we brave enough?"

I wait. Finally I say, "What?"

He tugs the collar of his schmatta and sticks his hand inside his stuffed bra—yes, he stuffed his bra. He shimmies a card in a purple envelope free, and places it on the counter. He says, "Look when I'm gone, okay?"

"Where are you going?"

He pats the back of the chair. "Better not to say. Give your sexy girl a hug." I do, and he smells of perfume. Completely in character.

He hobbles down the aisle, dragging his mother's chair behind him, breathing heavily until he turns to face me. He says, "You're a good kid." I wave goodbye. "Be seeing you," and just like Eastwood in *Unforgiven* Dom rides off into the unknown. I really hope I see him again, but if not, this is how I want to remember him: dressed in a wig and dragging his mother's chair. What a Dom way to go.

I lift the card.

It's the size of a Thank You card. I rip it open and wiggle it out of the envelope. On the front is a photo of a tropical beach. There's a sunset low on the horizon centered between two palm trees, tilted to form a heart; I think of Lola. Above the palms are the words *Welcome to Paradise* in white script.

Maybe he gave me a check to give to Vic?

I'm afraid to open it. But I do, of course.

It's a blue FBI warning sticker, the one that's pasted onto the videotapes that we rent. I read the label, the phone number, looking for a hidden clue, a sign. On the blank side of the card is a note from Dom, written in boxy letters: *Be a rat, not a mouse* then below it, *Call then leave*, and then below that, *Your welcome*.

I stare at the words until I pick up the salmon-colored receiver, the one with the *Be Kind, Rewind* stickers pasted along the handle, the one I'm going to carry out of this joyfully horrible place, right after I make the last phone call Video Planet will ever see.

But then I think of Dom calling on Vic's store, simply because he was either unable or unwilling to pay. Then all of the nice things Vic did for me—raises, movies and popcorn--and I can't bring myself to be part of hurting Vic for a second time. I place the receiver back on the cradle and glance at boxes, the racks, the blinking lights in the front windows, the posters flat and crisp along the wall. It's perfect, exactly how I imagined a video store should be.

I flip through the files. I wiggle my membership card free, number 1100, and stick it in my back pocket. I want to walk the aisles, but Vic can appear at any minute. Besides, I'm only a video clerk for the next few minutes. It feels really fucking good. But quitting, leaving this all behind, feels even better.

CHAPTER 28

For the last two days I've been waiting for this moment, only to realize that picking up your mother from the P-ward at Jamaica Hospital is its own circle of hell.

I'm seated in a large room painted sea-green. The rows of plastic hardback chairs are the color of a tangerine. The armrests are bolted together. The seats are scarred by keys, a can-can line of graffiti tags and a phone number advertising a sloppy blowjob. There are vending machines filled with sweet or salty snacks, and another machine filled with sodas. Perched on a platform is an old television playing the local news. Every third story someone is killed or mugged or robbed. Then the weather. Then sports. Like the DMV, time doesn't exist. I've been counting time by recycled news stories. I've watched the same house fire three times now. The Mets lost in Spring training, then again, then again.

Play, Rewind.

Instead of snitching on Video Planet, I locked the store, and went home. I left a message on Dom's phone and told him that I quit. That I never called the FBI. That we're still friends, but none of this is my problem. Not anymore. He never called me back. Vic never called me either, but he was never the legit owner anyway, so I guess he ended up being happy with whatever losses he took from Dom.

Anyway, I have bigger problems. I have to drive Mom to ShadyPines by noon. I got here at six, thinking the earlier the better. If the doctors are waiting for her to sign her release form, they'll be waiting forever. Our last hospital visits, the guard would hand me a pass and I'd head to her room, pack her stuff, and sign the forms myself. But since she's on the P-ward, she'll be brought to me. Sitting here, all I think about is the meds she isn't packing, the clothes she'll forget.

I walk to the counter along the far wall. The check-in nurse is hiding behind a thick sheet of bulletproof glass with holes augered out so she'll hear you beg to be let inside like the gatekeeper droid from *Return of the Jedi*.

She's around my age, with tight cornrows that have purple beads fastened onto the ends. The purple matches her scrubs and the stone in her nostril. Her name tag reads *Candi* and I wonder if it's short for Candice. She is typing, the keys clicking, her face dyed yellow from the screen. She says, "Please sit and wait, sir. We'll call your name when it's your turn."

"I have to take my mom to another hospital after this."

She glances up at me. "What? Care here ain't good enough?" Before I can apologize, she smiles, says, "It's a joke. Things take time around here."

I feel the desperate, sick eyes watching me: a guy with his chin buried into his chest because his spine is brittled from scoliosis. A dad with his arm around his son, the kid's hand bandaged with a checked dishrag. A woman with an ice pack pressed against her nose, a triangle of blood spread across her t-shirt. I think about name-dropping Gloria, but it's a big hospital and I'll just come off as annoying. Instead, I say, "So this is the place to pick up patients?"

She smacks the spacebar with her thumb. "Mm-hmm."

I wait and it feels as though I'm missing points for my license. "Can you at least...check her status or something?"

"Alright. You win. What's her name?"

"Camilla."

"Is she famous?"

"No."

"Then she goes by a last name too, right?" I tell her. More typing. "She's been released. On her way." She touches a purple bead.

I thank her just as the metal doors open. Mom is sitting in a wheelchair. She's wearing her robe. Behind her is a nurse with pink hair. Attached to her stethoscope is a toy monkey. On her lapel is a white button with *Cancer Sucks* written in the same color as her hair. She says, "Here we go, last stop!"

I wave at Mom. She smiles, but there's no recognition. I could be the mailman. The nurse hands me her papers. "She's a handful, this one."

I'm sure they earned their money, but I say, "She's not so bad, once you know her." Always the protective son.

The nurse rolls her forward, ignoring me, yet relieved Mom is now my problem. The nurse locks the wheels.

We have to hurry to make it to ShadyPines. I grab Mom's purse and hang it on my shoulder, then reach for her hands. I tug and she stands, wobbles, then steadies herself. I say, "Let's go."

Mom says, "Wait." The lady with the ice pack lowers her head for a better view. "Where's my husband?"

I say, "I'm your son. I'm here. I'll help."

"Where's Joan?"

"We're going to see her."

Mom sucks her teeth. "I want to see her now."

"That's where we're going."

I clench her arm and navigate her to the glass doors, which open with a shush, and out onto the street. The air smells like budding trees mixed with the exhaust fumes from the traffic speeding along the Van Wyck. Slowly, oh so slowly, we walk along the sidewalk and into the lot. I stop her in front of the Cutlass.

She says, "Who's car is this?"

"It's your car, Mom."

"I'd never buy a car this color."

"Okay it's mine."

"Why'd you buy a car this color? It's awful."

"Right."

I unlock her door. She's probably safer in the backseat, but back there I have her suitcases, her bedroom television, VCR with *The Wizard of Oz* still in the machine. Her robe pockets are heavy. I say, "Wait a minute."

I reach into her pocket and she slaps my hand, says, "That stuff is mine."

"You'll get it back."

"Yeah, sure."

I dig into her pocket. She has an unopened cup of chocolate ice cream, a spork, three toothbrushes (still in their wrappers), crumbled pieces of a brownie, a stack of tiny cups the nurses use for pills, and a book of matches. She drifts away from me. I say, "Wait, please." Her other pocket has shriveled peas, an empty cup of vanilla ice cream, and unopened Tylenol packets. "Why is this stuff in your robe?"

She stares at me, says, "In. My. Robe…"

I move my hand around her pocket and pull out a picture. It's the one of me and my father. It's easier to imagine it's a supernatural moment: the picture is a sign that he wants to reconnect with his son. Most likely, Lola gave her the photo, hoping it would calm her down. I stick the picture into my coat. "Well, let me put the stuff in your pocket."

"I don't want that garbage," she says.

Five minutes of being with her, and I'm already exhausted. I drop all of the stuff onto the cement.

She says: "Don't be a litter thug."

I sigh. "Bug, Mom."

She looks up. "I'm allergic to bees."

"No you're not."

"Hurry, you asshole. Get me in the car."

I hold her arm as she slides into the seat. I shut the door. She presses her nose against the glass and watches me as though the car is moving. She looks childish, sad, and tired. A plastic bag is caught on a spiral of chainlink fence. It puffs and flutters, breathing and alive, struggling to free itself. Mom knocks on the glass. I move along the side of the car, open the driver side door and get inside. The car still reeks of Dom's cologne, another ghost. I start the car, pay the five dollars, and head into traffic. "How was the hospital?"

She shakes her head. "I wasn't in the hospital."

"Right."

"We're going home?"

The question hurts so much that my gums tingle. I don't want to lie, but the truth is impossible for her to understand. I barely understand it myself. I cross lanes for no real reason, other than trying to escape this conversation. I can speak in the language of overused movie expressions such as: "It's for the best," or "I'm worried about your safety." Sadly, it is real life. Sadly, it's just silence, traffic, and lies. She asks again. I wring my hands against the steering wheel. "We'll be there soon."

Mom unzips her pocketbook. "What about my husband?"

I jam on the brakes as a Lexus—always a Lexus—cuts in front of me. "What about him?"

"I want to see him."

"You want to see your husband?"

"Of course I do."

She tugs on the seatbelt. This will be her last chance to ever see him. I don't want to do it, but who am I to deny a sick mother's request? "Okay, then."

I cut over to the exit. I turn right onto 95th, then left onto 134th. The whole trip takes less than six minutes. I pull in front of the fire hydrant, across the street from his house. "Here you go."

Mom is completely oblivious that we're parked in front of her husband's house. Sitting in the car, I feel like it's her last meal before I dump her in ShadyPines. It would've never occurred to me to bring her here on my own, but now that we're here, it feels necessary. I say, "Do you recognize this place?"

"What place?"

I shut the car. "The yellow house, Mom."

"That's more like a honeycomb."

I touch the key, then wait. I'll push a bit more. "It's your husband's house. Remember? The milk factory and Jack Kerouac's mother?"

She frowns, trying hard to make a connection. Maybe she did make that Jack stuff up? Still, if she understands that her husband lives there, I'm lugging her to his door.

I add: "You told Joan all about it?"

She glances over her shoulder, searching for her sister, or her memories.

She says, "The blowout?"

I laugh. "Right, Mom. You helped him rent this house."

"Rent. This. House."

"After he left," I say. A man passes the car, a loaf of Italian bread tucked under his arm. "I think you hoped he'd stop gambling and come home. So you signed his lease. He never came back, though." I wait, wanting her to remember.

Mom says, "Are you sure? I just talked to him."

She doesn't understand. Maybe it's better that she remains clueless. I say, "Okay. Let's get out of here," just as my father's door opens.

He's there.

He walks down the steps and scoops up the newspaper. He's wearing navy-colored sweat-shorts and a purple t-shirt, a cigarette dangling from his lips. "There's your husband." I must've yelled because he looks over to the car.

"Who? That old man?"

"You're old too, Mom."

She snorts. "I'm thirty-seven."

"Nevermind." He walks into the house.

Desperate for her to make the connection, I reach into my pocket and show her the photo. I say, "Look, that's him."

"Who? Who's him? Who?"

It's like riding around with an owl. I say, "Your husband."

She takes the picture. "That's my husband?"

"Yes."

"Who's that little boy?"

She never remembers me. I say, "That's little Wes. Your son."

"You mean to tell me that I have a son?"

I nod. "Yes. It's me."

"Oh that's so nice. No one ever told me!" She kisses my hand, truly surprised, and it cheers me up. "And that's my husband."

She watches the photo, fusing the two faces together. We're going to be late for ShadyPines. I start the car to leave, but my father, again, steps outside. Now he's wearing a jacket, the leather faded white on the shoulders and elbow sleeves. He puffs on his cigarette. "Look. The same guy in the photo."

She leans closer to the window, clouding the glass. "You know who that is?"

Excited, thinking she recognizes him, I lurch forward and my chest hits the steering-wheel. "No, tell me."

"Tony Ottomenelli."

"Who is fuck is that?"

She taps my arm for cursing. "The butcher. He only had six fingers? We called him Thumbs?"

"Mom, I have no clue what you're talking about."

"I think he died before you were born."

I laugh, then say, "Yet there he is."

"I wonder why he's not working."

My father takes a long drag of his cigarette, his pointer and thumb pinched, his other fingers extended flipper-like. He flicks the nub into his front yard in the exact way he'd flick it at the track. I'm nine again, being dragged around, not because I'm his son. I'm just an easy excuse to leave the house.

Mom says, "I'm hungry."

I say, "Me too. I guess we should go."

I glance over my shoulder, checking that the street is clear and I can pull the car away from this place. When I turn forward, my father is standing in front of my window. He taps on the glass and I roll it down.

He says, "Hey, help you?"

Mom says, "Look, it's that old man. Take a number. I'm next."

He leans into the window. His breath smells like orange juice. I pretend to smell vodka too, so that this guy isn't my father, just a drunk old bastard, and I can simply pull away from him, the way he did to us. But it's not that easy. After everything, I still want him to care about us. "You know me."

He watches my mother, his face expressionless, but I see he recognizes her. Good thing poker isn't his game. His bluffing face is garbage. "I don't think so."

His response stings a bit. I shift in my seat. "Sure. Potchky, remember?"

He says, "That's right. Find the dog?"

I grip the steering wheel. "No. But you know how dogs just run out of the house." He glances down the street, a guilty tell. "Run away, say, to...I don't know, Florida. And never come back."

He takes a long drag of his cigarette. "Maybe the dog wasn't happy. Maybe he got kicked out. Then maybe he realized it was for the best."

Mom says, "Slice those cutlets thinner."

I say, "Or maybe the dog had no sense of responsibility."

He flicks his cigarette into the street. He exhales the smoke through his nose, a steady stream. "So no dog, then."

I say, "Nope. But it's okay. I found something else." I twist the wheel, the leather crunching. "I found your wife."

I wait for him to say something. He doesn't.

"So how's it going, Dad? By the way, your wife has dementia. I'm taking her to ShadyPines Glen. This is your last chance to talk to her," though I really mean me. "Well. Here she is. Not as snazzy as your new wife."

"Girlfriend. She's my girlfriend."

Mom says, "You got boneless pork chops?"

I tell Mom to stop, then I say, "Until you run away again, right?"

"It's a little more complicated than that." He glances down the block. We watch a brown Seville speed past us. "Look. I should've." He steps into the center of the street, distancing himself from us. Again. He says, "Always liked dogs."

I say, "Me too. So much in common."

Mom says, "A third of a pound of roast beef, sliced thin."

He says, "What?"

"See the fun you've been missing?"

"Hey. If you need help finding your dog, I'm in." He unzips his jacket. "Looking for anything else, can't help you. I'm sorry. It's just, you know?"

"No," I say, "I really don't."

He gnaws his lip, negotiating the odds. We're two players searching for each other's weakness, trying to block our gambling tells. I say, "Tell Greg I said hello."

He frowns, confused. "How do you know them?"

I say, "We went on vacation together." Then just to make Greg's life a bit harder too, I say, "They lent me their vacation video. The tropical vacation, you know? They told me where I can find you."

Before he answers, I pull the Cutlass into the street, leaving my father behind, watching us. What can I say? I waited for him to find me, only for me to find him, only to realize he doesn't want to be found. It hurts, even now, the ache of knowing a parent simply doesn't want to be bothered. It's that simple, it's that complicated. Still, the saddest part of this is how my mother has only moved forward as much as her mind would allow, only to hit Rewind and start the whole horrible process of regret and loneliness again. To prove me right, my father disappears from my rearview mirror, just as my mother checks over her shoulder and finds the street empty.

CHAPTER 29

The living room of ShadyPines Glen has red carpets with gold trim. The curtains hang thick and heavy, cinched with gold ropes with large tassely heads. The lamps have taupe-colored shades, casting a warm glow. There are portraits of famous donors dressed in peacock-colored dresses and wide-brimmed hats holding calico cats. The couches are velvety red. The coffee tables are dark wood, the kind where you need fancy coasters as buffers for your drinks. Instead of the rooms reeking like body odor and sanitizer, the hallway smells of flowers and furniture polish.

We're seated on the couch waiting for our meeting with Gloria's friend Janice Tinsel. Yes, that's her real name. I forgot that there's an interview. This will be as seamless as dysentery in an opera house. I should've taken her home and had Lola fix her hair, or dip her into a vat of perfume to hide the hospital smell, though technically, this is a kind of hospital. I take in the poshness, the gold and red. I'm gripped with overwhelming shame, as though we don't deserve to even sit on this couch. Or maybe that's just residual hurt from being dumped by such a scuzzy bastard of a father. I say, "This is a nice place," trying to shake the feeling.

Mom rummages through her bag. "What casino is this?"

A woman dressed in a pink jumpsuit walks past us. She's holding a coloring book. A nurse with blond hair and a kind face leads her by the hand, as though ShadyGlen hired an army of Glorias. I say, "It's a new one."

She folds her robe over her legs. "Looks expensive."

"You have no idea."

In the next room, music is playing. I think it's Bing Crosby. Mom taps her foot, says, "Did you ever meet my husband?"

Oh yeah. This interview will be blissful. "No. Never have."

I close my eyes, hoping that when I open them, Mom will be a bit more focused. I feel someone in front of me. I see a pair of purple shoes. I look up. A woman wearing a black suit extends her hand. She has high cheekbones and her skin is that deep brown that you get from either a tanning booth or a frying basket.

She says, "Wes? I'm Janice Tinsel."

I stand while shaking her hand, a bit awkward. "Nice to meet you. This is my mother. Camilla." I touch my mother's arm, her cue to stand, but she leans back into the chair. "Mom. I think we have to walk with Mrs. Tinsel."

She says, "Janice. Please. It's fine, we can stay here. Gloria faxed over all your insurance information and her medical records."

Two minutes and we're already talking about the cost. "Is that enough?"

"If we need any additional medical records we can contact her doctor."

"I mean financially, sorry."

She says, "I don't have the numbers in front of me," with a look on her face that says she has them memorized. I wait, hoping she'll tell me, but she is tightlipped and tan-y, tilting her head in that reflective listening pose.

She says, "Gloria spoke very highly of you."

"We're very close," which feels truer than it sounded. I'd asked Gloria to meet us here. She'd said she had a doctor's appointment. It sounded like an excuse, but I'm hoping she was telling the truth. Besides, she called Mrs. Tinsel. What a tale that must've been.

She sits down next to Mom and I regret standing. I wish she'd have a little distance. To Mom she says, "How are you?"

Mom digs through her bag. "I guess my room isn't ready yet."

"You want to be here?"

Mom says, "Sure. Just look at the lobby!" She pulls out a wad of yellow Monopoly bills. "This'll cover it."

I lurch forward to swipe them, but Janice takes the money. "That's plenty." She does that dramatic pause that anyone remotely attached to the medical field gives, but then she actually counts the fake bills. "Yup! Perfect."

Mom says, "I knew it was enough. I'm good with money, you know."

I say, "She worked in a bank."

Mom says, "Get a loan today! Rates are low."

Janice smiles. "I'll think about it."

A man wearing striped pajamas and a blue suit jacket walks past, his slippers shuffling along the carpet.

Janice says, "We do have a room ready. Usually it takes a few weeks, but you have a connection." She winks, then as though she's a magician, pulls a sheet of paper from behind her back. "Here is the balance per month after insurance and your mother's social security.

The payments are made quarterly. It allows the family to plan their payments."

I guess it's time to talk about money now. Does she want me to agree in the lobby? I watch Mom glance around the hall, a smile on her face, clearly impressed. Mrs. Tinsel waves at a patient or resident or whatever they're called, displaying how happy the patients, or whatever, are to be slowly depleted of their benefits and the savings that they've worked so hard for in jobs they hated, just to pass it over to care facilities that bleed you as fast as they can sop up your blood. Hooray for capitalism. I say, "May I see it?"

Janice says, "Yes. How silly of me."

Mom says, "Always read the fine print. I worked in a bank."

I say, "Okay, Mom," hoping she'll stop talking.

I take the paper. It's six hundred dollars more than Mom's mortgage payments. The first payment is due at the end of two months. Or maybe I just read it wrong? I stare at the number as though it's a hieroglyph. I'll never be able to afford ShadyGlen. I'm right. People like us don't belong here.

Janice must see the worry in my face. She says, "I know it's a bit overwhelming. We have payment plans. We can negotiate with your mother's insurance. Also, we're going to give you a fifteen-percent discount, which I haven't updated on your paper, but will give you once we go to my office."

I shrug confused about why we're getting a discount.

She says, "Gloria claimed you as family."

"She did?"

Janice winks and says, "You are her nephew, right?"

There's this hiccup of disappointment, wishing she would've designated me her son, which even I know is a ridiculous reason to be upset. But I'm also grateful. I try to do the math in my head. The fifteen percent will help, sure, but it's still impossible. I don't even have a job. I stare at the velvet couches, the tables. The guilt of placing her in a home hurts less than seeing a nice home and not being able to place her here. I know what I have to do. I want to ignore it for as long as possible. I say, "Do I have to decide right this second?"

She says, "Of course not. Look around. Take your time."

I have to make this decision. Today. I thought I'd have more time to think about it, which is ridiculous. I look down at the paper, the price, unsure what to say or do. Before I can even try to answer, Mom says, "Wait. Want to hear a joke?"

Janice nods. Here we go.

Mom says, "What's the best part of Easter?"

Of all the things to fucking remember. Mrs. Tinsel waits.

Mom says, "The eggs!"

Janice laughs. Thank God for small mercies.

Mom says, "Always leave them laughing."

"Right," I say. "Can we walk around?"

She says, "Sure. Lunch is in the rec room. Before you leave, let me know when you'd like to start her stay."

Mom says, "See, this is a casino."

Janice squeezes my arm, and then walks the hallway, nodding at patients.

I should leave, not stand around while I make my big decision, but Lola is meeting us here. She says she's lived in these places. She'll know right away if it's a keeper. I'll text her and tell her: *Go home. We'll talk it over tonight.*

I lift Mom off the chair. Mom pulls free. "I want to play the slots."

"We can't."

She shuffles down the hall, her left shoulder grazing along the wall. I follow behind her in case she falls. I call her name. Without answering, she enters the next room along the hallway. It's a dining room. There are round tables made of cherrywood. Placed on each is a carnation in a vase. There are older people sitting around a few of the tables, with tiny cups of coffee, plates of food. A few are talking, but most are concentrating on the food in front of them. A woman with a green sweatshirt rocks slowly, as a nurse in maroon scrubs takes the lid off her tray. Two men wearing Yankees hats talk and nod at each other. I try to read some unhappiness in their faces, a reason why, against all common sense, I should take her home. They look a bit tired and hungry, but seem okay.

I guide her to an empty table near the window.

Outside there is a prayer garden. There is a statue of Mary. Newly budding tulips encircle her feet like small children. There are maple trees and hedges. I'm ashamed of my dirt lawn and milkcrate chairs. The way we've lived for so long. It's too much, so I watch people shuffle in front of the metal serving trays. They each have a nurse who scoops food onto their plates. No family.

I sit next to Mom and another nurse wearing maroon-colored scrubs gives us plates of food. It's beef stew with egg noodles and dinner rolls. I know it's paranoid, but I feel like they slip medications into the food. I push the tray away.

Mom picks up a noodle with her fingers and stuffs it into her mouth. I say, "Here." I rip the fork out of its plastic and stick it flagpole-style into her stew.

Mom says, "Thanks."

"Least I could do."

"Got that right."

I want to leave, so of course she actually finds the cognitive stamina to take the fork, scoop food and stick it into her mouth. I say, "It's good?"

"Delicious," she says, spraying flecks of beef onto the red striped tablecloth.

"This much money, it should be fucking ambrosia and nectar of the gods."

Mom says, "Relax, I'm buying."

Mounted to the cream-colored wall is a large television. *Singing in the Rain*. She seems relaxed. I had imagined her cursing me, clawing the nurses as she tried to escape. She sways from side to side as she watches Gene Kelly on rollerskates swirl around lamp posts with a grace that seems ethereal. She forks more stew. I say, "What did the hospital feed you?"

"What hospital?"

"Forget it."

We sit there, Mom scooping stew into her mouth, and me wishing I had worked a real job, one that paid better, had insurance, sick time, vacation days. I'm crushed by every decision I've ever made. Going along with things when I should've thought of long-term consequences. It's not just me. Lola and her swim. Dom and his bootlegs. My father and his sure bets. I remember this one weekend we were rummaging through discarded race tickets. He had a tip and bet all of his money on the seventh race. The horse's name was Lucky Day. But the horse wasn't lucky at all. We spent the rest of the day in the parking lot checking discarded tickets on the off chance that someone tossed a winner. With each losing ticket, he'd get angrier. That morning, the phone company had pulled the plug. Two days before that, he'd written a check to ConEd that he said had so much rubber in it that it'd bounce over the Empire State Building. It was a hot day and I'd dressed in jeans and a sweatshirt, instead of a t-shirt like Mom suggested. I was tired. I longed for my slice of pizza. I had a bunch of losers in my hand and when I turned he was sitting on the pavement, flicking tickets like baseball cards. I said, "Dad we always lose. Why do this?" He looked up, a sunstar caught in his glasses. "Cause every day is a new chance to win." If I could teleport through time to that moment, I'd tell him that with enough losses, the wins don't matter. Then again, if I was going to Marty McFly into the past, I'd rather use the chance to warn myself.

A man wearing a red jacket stands next to my mother. On his head sits a navy hat with lots of pins. He's holding a plate of food. He pulls out the chair next to my mother. He says, "Excuse me, my dear, is this seat taken?"

Mom turns. "Sorry, I'm spoken for."

He touches his hat and bows a little. "I meant no offense. Good day to you."

Great. Now I'm trapped inside an episode of *Upstairs, Downstairs*.

"Hey guys." I turn and Lola is marching toward us with a Happy Meal in each hand, a book bag slung on her shoulder. She has three stickers on her chest that all read *Guest*. She places the food on the table and sits. Then she says, "How's it going, Sis?" and opens the box and places the cheeseburger in front of my mother like it's the idol from *Raiders of the Lost Ark*. "Wait until you see the prizes!"

Mom says, "Joan, isn't this casino great?"

Lola smiles at me, as though that's a sign.

"Wait." Lola opens her Happy Meal and places the toy in front of me. Snoopy in his pilot hat, seated on top of his doghouse. "Now we both have one." She leans over and pecks me on the cheek. I tell her thanks. "Nothing's too good for my man. This is some place." She unwraps her burger and takes a bite.

I tell Lola the price and she nods. I read the disappointment in her face. "We'll just keep her."

I say, "We can't just keep her."

"I know."

I curl the pamphlet, hiding its glossy cover. It hurts to look at. "I always pictured a home looking like a prison. Concrete walls, rotting food, abusive orderlies. This is nicer than most of the casinos Mom loves. And our house."

Lola bites a fry. "There's one way," she says.

I look around at the dining room, the people, then Mom scooping noodles with a look of quiet satisfaction. Then I say the unthinkable, the smoldering truth I've been trying to stifle since we were in the casino, the truth I've told myself because it was always far away, a remote possibility, a possible truth, but now having no other choice, I finally say it aloud: "Sell the house?"

Lola folds the wrapper. "I mean, get a full-time job."

"I'll need that, too."

"I got an interview at McDonald's tomorrow. I'll chip in for Sis."

I imagine endless Happy Meals in my future. "Great."

Lola nods. "Ain't it? So, like, what are we going to do?"

Okay. It truly hurts to consider, but what if I did sell the house? With the inflated housing prices in Queens, I'd find myself a place and I'd still have enough to pay for ShadyPines for the next twenty years. Our yellow house is the only place I've ever known, but the thought of walking through our yellow kitchen where I filmed her eating cookies with Lola, or stepping into her empty bedroom where Gloria filed her nails, or rummaging through the closet where she keeps her coats, feels like a sadness that I'd never be able to recover from.

I say, "I'll sell the house."

"Are you sure?"

I realize I am. "We can get a place. You know, together."

She jolts forward with excitement. "I'd like that. But I have to bring Mother."

"You're talking about your cat, right?"

"I mean, she's just like a mom. Cranky, demanding. Judgemental. You'll have to earn her love."

Mom sniffs her fork and places it onto the tray. "Let's play cards."

I say, "So you want to stay?"

Mom stares up at the ceiling. She says, "I'll leave when I win."

"So you're staying, then? This is a really nice place, Mom."

Lola picks up her backpack. "Wait. I have a housewarming gift."

She unzips her bag and slips out an 8x10 canvas. She flips it around and it's a painting of Mom sitting at the kitchen table with a roll of Oreos and the *Best Mom Ever* mug in front of her. Beams of sunlight fall around her. Mom is smiling; her eyes have a life, an awareness that I haven't seen in years. She's happy, content, and this is how I imagine she feels. Lola says, "This is the best one yet. "

"Yeah. I really like it."

Mom glances around the room. "Expensive casino."

I say, "Yeah. But I've taken care of it. You'll be here for a bit, so..."

"Will you be here?"

I exhale slowly, the weight and meaning of this decision hitting me in the stomach. I say, "I work. But I'll see you every day."

Mom says, "What about Joan?"

Lola says, "Of course, Sis. Every damn day!"

Mom grabs my hand. Her hand feels small, fragile, nothing like my mother's touch. "You're a good boy paying for this hotel." She kisses my wrist. "My good boy."

Mom's acceptance is so rare I take it as forgiveness. Maybe, all these years, that's all I ever wanted, needed. I say, "So you want to stay?"

"Of course! We just got here!"

"You're right. We did."

Then she wiggles her hand free, and though it hurts, I let go.

I'm standing in front of my father's house.

I imagine Greg and Sarah and my father together, watching me from his living room window. For a second, I wish I had my camera to film it, but the moment passes. Maybe it's better to cut some scenes. His gate is locked and it feels intentional, letting me know he's serious about his decision.

I slip a copy of *Play, Rewind* out of my jacket.

On the label there is a yellow square of paper with the word, "Watch." I wiggle the video between the bars. The tape lands with a satisfying slap. Soon our house will be sold and there won't be a fossilized lease or even a phone number that will lead him to me. Not that he ever wants to see us again. Still, he should witness the state in which he left his family. I say, "Well, that's it," and give the house the middle-finger.

Before I cross the street, my phone rings. I'm sure it's Janice Tinsel, already tired of my mother, so I hit the button and say hello.

A woman's voice says, "Is this Wes?"

"Is she okay?"

"Who?"

I realize that she's not from ShadyPines Glen. I say, "Sorry. Is this a realtor?"

"No. I'm Jeane Riley, from the MFSNY school."

I'm walking so fast that I'm winded. I stop and traffic whizzes past me. I'm standing in the middle of the street.

I dodge a white van and hustle back onto the sidewalk.

I search for someplace quiet, but it's all storefronts. I stick my finger in my free ear. She says something that I can't hear, and now I'm walking until I'm opposite my father's house again. I crouch, hoping that being closer to the sidewalk translates into quieter. It doesn't.

I say, "Sorry. I didn't hear you."

"Is this a good time to talk?"

"Sure."

"Okay. We viewed your entry and the film was...well, different. And very...well, emotionally engaging. We'd like to meet and discuss it. Is next Tuesday good?"

I can't form words. I think I've said yes.

"Good. I'll send you the interview information via the email you gave. I look forward to meeting you." She thanks me for some reason, and I think I thank her, too.

Then she hangs up.

My legs feel shaky, so I flop back onto the curb.

I flip my phone open and check incoming calls to make sure I didn't make this up. She called. This is happening. Still it feels fake, like a videotaped beach. But then I see a man navigate his schnauzer, who is definitely not Potchky, around me. I hear the shift-horn from the milk factory buzzing until the tinny speakers crackle. An "A" train clacks past, and finally I'll be on it, oh yes, finally on and finally off to that place, finally and finally, a chance for that place where I finally want to be. Play.

Acknowledgments

First, thank you Gerald Brennan for all of your advice and dedication. You're an amazing person and this has been such an amazing experience. I'm so happy to be part of the Tortoise Books family. To Alena Graedon for unending support--for advocating and believing in me even when I didn't. To Alex Gilvarry for your guidance, feedback and friendship. To Mihaela Moscaliuc, Michael Waters, Scott Cheshire, Katherine Dykstra and Benjamin Nugent. For my fellow writers and friends: Allison Long, Michael Qualiano, Jenna Puglisi, Corrine Cavallo, Damian Lubbock and so many others who have read versions of this novel. Thank you. To my closest friend John Howard, who has read my writing for years--you're like a brother to me. To Frank Lomonaco, who is a brother to me. Most of all to my wife Marianne, who has read, my daughter Ana, who will read, and my son John, who hopefully can read, this novel one day. Lastly, for my mother. I hope you find the peace you deserve.

About the Author

John Vurro's debut novel *Play, Rewind* was shortlisted for the *Masters Review* Novel Excerpt Contest, and was also a finalist in *Craft's* First Chapter Contest. His story "Turnkey" was chosen for *Carve's* One to Watch feature in their 2015 summer issue. His story "Carmine's War" won *Harpur Palate's* 2013 John Gardner Award. His fiction has been published in *The Literary Review*, *Eclipse, Glint,* and elsewhere; his poems have been published in *The Examined Life, Sugar House Review, Action,* and *Spectacle*; his essay "Guardians" was published in *The Sun*. He lives in New Jersey. Find him on Instagram @johnvurrowriter.

About Tortoise Books

Slow and steady wins in the end, even in publishing. Tortoise Books is dedicated to finding and promoting quality authors who haven't yet found a niche in the marketplace—writers producing memorable and engaging works that will stand the test of time.

Learn more at www.tortoisebooks.com or follow us on BlueSky @tortoisebooks.bsky.social.